24.95
B T
3-1-80

 **W9-CBD-069**

NO LONGER THE PROPERTY OF
BALDWIN PUBLIC LIBRARY

NO
DEFENSE

✦ ALSO BY KATE WILHELM

Defense for the Devil (1999)

Malice Prepense (1996)

A Flush of Shadows (1995)

The Best Defense (1994)

Justice for Some (1993)

Seven Kinds of Death (1992)

Naming the Flowers (1992)

And the Angels Sing (1992)

Death Qualified (1991)

State of Grace (1991)

Sweet, Sweet Poison (1990)

Cambrio Bay (1990)

Children of the Wind (1989)

Smart House (1989)

The Dark Door (1988)

Crazy Time (1988)

The Hamlet Trap (1987)

The Hills Are Dancing
(with Richard Wilhelm)
(1986)

Huysman's Pets (1986)

Welcome, Chaos (1983)

Oh, Susannah! (1982)

A Sense of Shadow (1981)

Listen, Listen (1981)

Better than One
(with Damon Knight) (1980)

Juniper Time (1979)

*Somerset Dreams and Other
Fictions* (1978)

Fault Lines (1977)

*Where Late the Sweet Birds
Sang* (1976)

The Clewiston Test (1976)

The Infinity Box (1975)

City of Cain (1974)

Margaret and I (1971)

Abyss (1971)

Year of the Cloud (with
Theodore L. Thomas) (1970)

Let the Fire Fall (1969)

*The Downstairs Room and
Other Speculative Fiction*
(1968)

The Killer Thing (1967)

The Nevermore Affair (1966)

The Clone (with Theodore L.
Thomas) (1965)

The Mile-Long Spaceship
(1963)

More Bitter than Death (1963)

KATE
 WILHELM

NO
DEFENSE

 ST. MARTIN'S MINOTAUR ☎ NEW YORK

BALDWIN PUBLIC LIBRARY

NO DEFENSE. Copyright © 2000 by Kate Wilhelm. All rights reserved. Printed in the United States of America. No part of this book may be used or reproduced in any manner whatsoever without written permission except in the case of brief quotations embodied in critical articles or reviews. For information, address St. Martin's Press, 175 Fifth Avenue, New York, N.Y. 10010.

Edited by Gordon Van Gelder

ISBN 0-312-20953-3

First Edition: January 2000

10 9 8 7 6 5 4 3 2 1

◈ PART ONE

LARA

1

The rising sun is veiled with desert haze, rose-red streaks extending north and south against a royal blue that only gradually turns mauve. A high cirrus cloud glows brilliantly pink for a short time, vanishes; the haze dances a morning ritual, rising and falling, then it vanishes also, and finally there is only the sun, not visible as a thing in itself, but rather as if the sky, haze, clouds are being rent apart to reveal an intolerable brilliance. Sunlight flares on snow-topped mountains, the Wallowas, Blue Mountains, Steens, and closer, on the Strawberry Mountains; it is cast back by the obsidian on Glass Butte, windows placed by giants untaught in human architecture. It shines on dawn-still needles of juniper trees, on motionless sage and bitter grasses, and casts preternaturally elongated shadows as black as openings into the abyss.

On the southern flank of Lookout Mountain, sunlight, like an Aztec signal on a shard of a mirror, is blindingly bright, but no human is on Lookout Mountain to be blinded that early in the morning. It falls on a hand that is shades darker than the ground on which it has come to rest, is reflected for an instant in three fingernails; the little finger and the thumb are in shadow. The rest of the man's body lies hidden beneath the wreckage of a van. Only the hand and part of the lower arm are exposed.

Two coyotes lift their heads simultaneously as if joined to each other, sniffing the air, sniffing the scent of gasoline, of motor oil, of raw metal. The scent of man, of blood, of death. The scent comes from above them, on the side of the steep, rocky mountain with scant undergrowth. They hesitate, but the smell of gasoline is too strong. They turn and trot away together.

The sunbeams light up the redwood deck of the Jessup house, the grill, chairs, and tables that gleam as if covered with ice. Sunlight races across the deck to enter the living room through wide windows where the drapes were left open the night before. A lamp pales and casts no light of its own, overwhelmed by sunlight. Light falls on the red-blond hair of a woman; her hair is curly and short. Although her face is sunburned, with a scattering of freckles, it has the delicacy and the sculpted beauty of Michelangelo's *Pietà*. Fine hairs on her arm gleam like gold. She stirs and turns away from the glare. In sleep she looks younger than her years; she is thirty-three. Stirring, she uncovers her feet, and she moves again, still sleeping, to adjust a gold and green throw that is too short to be used as a blanket. Now the sunlight falls on her eyelids, and she moves restlessly, as if unwilling to leave a dream.

Then abruptly she is awake, so suddenly that she can't move for a moment, as if her mind and body are obeying different signals.

For Lara Jessup, awakening is the beginning of a nightmare.

She jumped up and rubbed her eyes; then, barefooted, she hurried to the study door and looked inside. She looked into the guest room next to the study; Vinny's bed was neat and untouched. She ran now, down the stairs to the lower level of the house, to look inside the garage, just to be certain, but she knew. Vinny had not come home last night.

She raced through the house, looked inside every room, looked in her son, Nathan's, room, where he was sound asleep; then she ran to the kitchen phone and hit the automatic dialer for Manny Truewater.

She knew she was incoherent, but she couldn't control her voice or her words, and dimly, as if he were underwater speaking to her, she heard Manny telling her to put on coffee, he would be there as soon as possible.

"I should have stopped him," she said to Manny Truewater fifteen minutes later. "I could have stopped him, or gone with him. Something!"

"Lara! Sit down. What happened? Where was he heading?"

Manny was from the Warm Springs tribe, short and thick, thick in the chest, with a broad face, black hair cut short, his skin the color of old mahogany. In his fifties, ten or twelve years younger than Vinny, he was Vinny's best friend.

She sat down hard on one of the kitchen chairs, and he placed coffee in front of her. Her hands were shaking too hard to lift the cup, although she had been so steady minutes earlier that she had felt almost somnolent.

"We had fish out on the deck. With the Cornings. And Vinny remembered that he had told Judge McReady that he would give him some documents. He said he would take them over, and he left."

"When did he leave?"

"Nearly ten. They left, the Cornings, and he got the papers together, and then he left. I wanted him to mail them or wait until this morning, or something. I should have driven over with him."

"Okay. You go get dressed, and I'll call the sheriff and get him to send a car out. Vinny might be sleeping on the mountain, maybe ran out of gas and didn't want to walk home in the dark. Take it easy, Lara. Just get dressed now."

"You know how he's been these past months. . . . I didn't want him to go. I was afraid. . . . He said it was a perfect golden day. Yesterday."

"Lara! Go get some clothes on. I'll talk to the sheriff."

She stood up, as obedient as a child, stilled by the harshness that had entered his voice. For a moment his gaze met hers, and she saw the same fear that had seized her. "It's my fault," she said in a low voice. "I could have stopped him."

She turned and left the kitchen. She didn't remember putting on her robe, but she was wearing one, huddled inside it, freezing, her feet like ice on the bare hardwood floor.

At first they said it had been an accident: Vinny's van had rolled over the side of the mountain; he had lost control on that bad curve just before the driveway to the Lynch house.

"Lara, they'll have to investigate," Manny told her. "You understand that, don't you? They'll want to ask you some questions. You don't have to talk to them now, today, if you're not up to it."

"I have to go to the hospital," she said vaguely. "I'm on today."

"Lara, pull yourself together. Listen to me. I'll call Norm and tell him what happened. You don't have to go anywhere. The sheriff will want to know what happened last night, who was here, what Vinny said he had to do. That's all you have to tell him, just what you told me. That's all he'll be interested in. Can you do that now, or would you rather wait a day or two?"

"I have to call Alene and Roger. . . ." They were Vinny's adult children, both of them older than she was.

The nightmare persisted, a waking nightmare; first she was here, then there, with no recollection of moving. Sitting on the couch with Manny, then in her bedroom lying down, in the kitchen trying to drink some of the broth that Manny's wife had placed before her, gazing at Norm Oglespeak, her boss at the hospital, where she was a nurse. She had seen many people in shock and could deal with them gently and effectively; she did not recognize shock in herself.

Then the sheriff suggested suicide. Alene and Roger were both there, red-eyed and grieving; Nathan, her twelve-year-old son, was red-eyed and silent. Manny was with them. The sheriff said maybe Nathan could go out on the deck so they could talk, and without a word Nathan left. He had said almost nothing since Manny told him about Vinny's death.

"Mrs. Jessup," the sheriff started after Nathan had gone out, "was Vinny disturbed about anything? Upset?"

She shook her head. A lie. She found it too difficult to say any of the things racing through her head without letup. *What a beautiful sight you are! Rising like a water nymph, shaking off diamonds. This is one of those rare and wonderful perfect golden days. You should have a special place in your head to store such days so that you can open the door and walk back into them later. You've given me so many perfect golden days. I am very grateful.*

"Was he worried about his checkup? Norm tells me he was overdue to check in at the hospital."

You know what I fell in love with? Your hands. You get to know the hands that tend you in a hospital. Hard and efficient, or careless and even indifferent, some so soft and fluttery they seem to take twice as long to do what needs doing as they should, but your hands were soft and gentle and swift. You hands knew this old body didn't want much handling, and they got the job done as fast as possible without hurting. Your hands never hurt me.

"When you've had cancer," she said in a very low voice, "you're always concerned about the next checkup. It's impossible not to be concerned."

"But no more than usual?"

She shook her head.

"What's this all about?" Roger demanded then.

He was sitting on one side of Lara on the couch; Alene was on her other side, as if Lara needed protection. They had not started out on friendly terms; their hostility to her, to their father's unseemly marriage to a woman younger than his own children, had been open and vocal. Then Vinny had taken them out somewhere, and when they all arrived home that night, Alene had held Lara and wept. Lara never had learned what he said to them.

"Well, Roger," the sheriff said, "it's this note that turned up. Here's a photocopy; we'll have to keep the original for a while."

He handed a sheet of paper to Roger, who read it and turned very pale. "It's a lie!"

Alene reached across Lara and took the paper from him, then she and Lara read the typewritten words together.

I'm sorry about this. But it's best this way. Forgive me, Lara. Manny knows what to do with the practice. It was unsigned.

Lara looked up to find the sheriff regarding her with an unblinking gaze; he looked cold and hard. She had met him, Sylvester Gouin, going on sixty, going to fat, but he had been genial and smiling before. The town children called him Silly Gooey.

"It's a lie," she said. "It's a fake." Her voice was a hoarse whisper.

Manny yanked the note from Alene's hand and read it, then tossed it down on the coffee table. "Where'd you get that?"

"In his shirt pocket. They found it when they peeled off his clothes. Mrs. Jessup, is there a typewriter in the house?"

"No. A computer and printer. In his study."

He stood up and motioned to a deputy leaning against the doorframe. "Maybe we can have a look."

Afterward they padlocked the study. "You folks have a bit of trouble?" the sheriff asked at the door of the guest room. Inside, a few folders and loose papers were on a bedside table.

"No," Lara said. "Vinny had the flu back in the winter, and he had a persistent cough. He wanted a room where he wouldn't disturb me."

They padlocked the guest-room door also. She wished Vinny had taken him out for a talk, that he had taken them all out for a talk, the whole town, all the old men who looked at her like that, all of them speculating on the May and December marriage, wondering what a "girl like her" was doing with an old man like him. She had heard a whisper, had been meant to hear it: "A girl like her, she's out for money. What else?" *Honey, they're so jealous, they see you and jerk off before they even get home to their wives. And know what? I don't blame them.*

Then, nightmarelike, the sheriff was gone and she was sitting with Alene, Roger, and Manny. Roger was furious.

"That note's a fake, and even that dimwit should see through it!"

"Maybe he does, maybe not," Manny said. "McReady says Vinny never showed up that night. McReady, his wife, and her folks waited up for him until nearly eleven, then they went on to bed. No papers turned up in the wreckage on the mountain. So the question is, What happened to them? And another question is, What was in them? They're going to do an autopsy. All we can do is sit tight and wait it out. After the funeral, some of us will go over all of Vinny's files. The sheriff will get a court order to allow a court-appointed attorney to oversee the whole thing, and try to spot those missing papers, just in case Vinny changed his mind and went back to the office or put them in his files here."

Manny was executor of the estate, and now he said that Vinny had given him instructions about what to do if the hospital decided to keep him awhile. "You know, when he went in years ago, it was four months before he got back home. He knew that could happen again. So I have instructions." Vinny had known that many of his clients would refuse to have a Native American attorney, although he and Manny had worked together many times in the past. Manny would get in touch with those people whose legal business had anything to do with Indian affairs, he said that day, and Robert Sheffield would get in touch with the rest of the clients and offer his services. "It's all going to take time," he said soberly. "And the insurance isn't going to come through until the case is settled one way or the other. Lara, how are you fixed for money? Your joint accounts and your safe-deposit box will both be frozen pending the outcome of the investigation."

She moistened her lips. "When I started working, he said I should have my own account."

Lara, that's your money. I went broke years back, but we're not broke now. Keep it for Nathan's education. You don't suppose Curtis is likely to help out with that, do you? His eyes had been knowing. Curtis begrudged every penny he had to pay in support for his son. *Let's talk just a bit about money. I could say "if anything happens to me," but I won't. No euphemisms. When I die, you'll get the insurance. That's what I got it for, to take care of my wife if the day came that I couldn't do it myself. It's yours, or will be. Just wanted you to know that.* But his wife had died first, and then he had fallen in love with gentle, capable hands. *I nearly let it lapse, but I kept thinking of the nurse with the magic hands, and I kept up my premiums. If you'd said no,*

I would have chucked it and spent the money on booze or video poker, or down in Vegas.

She was blinking back tears again.

The next time the sheriff came back, he had several other men with him; he was grimmer than ever, and he had a court order to search the house.

"We got the autopsy report," Sheriff Gouin said curtly. "Vinny died of a gunshot wound in the head."

Lara and Alene huddled on the couch while the sheriff and his detectives searched; Roger stayed with the officers. When they were done, he told Lara about it. "They were looking for weapons, guns and ammunition, and drugs," he said. "The autopsy turned up narcotics—codeine—in his system. And they took the tape from the answering machine."

Lara groaned. Late the night before, Curtis had called and left an ugly message. "Pick up the phone, damn you! I know you're there. Now that old moneybags fart is gone, get your ass back here where you belong."

They released Vinny's body, and the funeral was scheduled. Roger's wife and Alene's husband arrived with their children. Alene wept when Lara said Vinny should be buried next to his first wife. They had been married a long time; their children and their grandchildren should come first. Then even that was done with, and a stillness settled over Lara and her house.

Sometimes during the night she imagined she could hear the creak of a wheelchair, an old-fashioned chair, not a modern motorized one. She could imagine Marilyn, Vinny's first wife, wheeling herself through the silent house, looking for something, always looking for something.

Marilyn never was really alive after Lewis vanished. A nervous breakdown, prescription drugs that turned her into a zom-

bie, then the strokes started. It was never her house. I doubt she ever really saw it or knew where she was. It's your choice, Lara. If you want to move to a different house, we will.

It had never bothered her. She knew that Marilyn couldn't have gone up and down the different levels, that the house held no ghosts, no memories of a creaking wheelchair, but now and then she strained to identify what she imagined she heard.

In a few days school would be over for the year, and Nathan would go to Portland to stay with his father for a month, and for the first time in her life, she would be alone. Alone in a town where the residents whispered about her and stared openly at her, where rumors about Vinny's death circulated and became more and more vicious. Alone in a house where she would hear the wheelchair creaking and groaning.

She yearned for the door to open into one of the perfect golden days, but behind every door there was only more of the nightmare.

Over and over, as if acting under an irresistible compulsion, she relived that last day and night. They had come home in the Corning van, Nathan and Tod Corning sunburned and ripe with fish smells and mud, and very happy. They grilled fish on the deck, and then as they were all clearing dishes, carrying utensils back inside the house, Vinny uttered a soft curse. "I forgot something," he said. "Excuse me a minute." She heard him on the telephone, heard his call to Harris McReady, heard him say, "I'll bring them over at ten. I don't want to come in; just meet me at ten down by the road."

"Tonight! For heaven's sake, let it go until morning. You're too tired now." He *was* too tired; everything he did exhausted him. She was nearly shrill in her protest.

"Can't let it go. They plan to be out of here first thing in the morning. It won't take long. Don't fret."

The Cornings had looked embarrassed, perhaps sensing an argument; everyone seemed to expect to see them arguing, even their friends. Lara didn't press the point then. Later, after the Corning family was gone, she brought it up again.

"You can put things off only so long before time runs out on you," Vinny said. "I've put this off long enough, more than long enough. Take a bath—use some of that nice bath oil, the lemony kind—relax, and go on to bed. You're sunburned. Be sure to put some lotion on your nose and cheeks, or you'll peel. A nurse with a peeling nose is the last thing a patient needs to see."

Then he touched her cheek gently and smiled at her. "Ah, Lara. Lara. Don't wait up for me. I have a few things to do in the study when I get back."

"Vinny—"

"Hush, now. Go take your bath." He picked up his briefcase and walked down the steps to the lower-level garage, and she went to the deck and watched him back out of the drive, then turn toward Lookout Road.

Without thought, without volition, without wanting to do it, she followed minutes later. At first all she could think was that something was terribly wrong, something fearful, big, important. Not just his health; she knew he was ill again. Something else, something worse than that, and nothing could be worse than that.

Then her fear of the road took precedence. She had been up Lookout Mountain only one other time, and that had been on a sunny afternoon. The road was hardly wide enough for two cars, and it climbed the mountain in switchbacks, perilously close to the precipice one second, skirting the basalt cliff the next. The road was red lava rock that looked black in her headlights, like dried blood.

Suddenly she was seized with a rush of shame. This was what Curtis had done to her, followed her, always checking up on her. He called her supervisor at the hospital to make sure she was on duty; he tailed after her to the library, even to the grocery store a time or two. And she was doing the same thing, tailing her husband. . . . And now she could not even be certain he had come up here. She had seen no car lights, no house lights, just the bloodred road and the blackness of the chasm on one side and the black cliff on the other.

There was no place to turn around; she had to keep driving, up higher and higher, knowing she had missed the Lynch driveway, uncertain where there was another one. Everything was too black, featureless.

Finally she saw two reflectors that indicated a driveway, and she drove onto it cautiously; then, clenching the steering wheel hard, she backed out, made her turn, and started retracing the tortuous track, this time on the outside of the road all the way. Minutes later, edging around a switchback, she saw headlights sweep across the chasm below, and she realized a car was coming up the mountain. The lights vanished. Another curve, then suddenly there was the narrow turnout, the lookout where they had stopped before when they went all the way up, with Vinny driving that day.

The turnout was no more than a widening of the road, with no guardrails, no boulders to mark the edge. She pulled onto it parallel to the road, afraid to head in, too uncertain where her wheels would be, and then she turned off the headlights and rested her forehead on the steering wheel to wait for the oncoming car to reach this point and pass. Of course there would be other cars on the road; people lived on the mountain; they drove up and down all the time. She was shaking.

When the approaching car drew near, she ducked down out of sight. She knew people talked about her and Vinny, and this, discovering her out on the mountain spying on him . . . No one would ask her about it, but there would be talk, and eventually

someone would mention it ever so casually to Vinny. She drew
in a deep breath when the blackness was complete again and the
other car noise was no longer audible, then she continued to
drive on down the mountain.

Now, lying in bed in a house at once too quiet and unquiet
with the imagined sounds of a wheelchair that she found herself
straining to hear, she faced again the awareness that if she had
not been so ashamed, so cowardly that night, she would have
waited at the turnoff; Vinny would have seen her there and
stopped, and she would have followed him home to talk.

She had not told anyone. At first she had not thought of telling, then she had been too ashamed, and finally, not having told,
she had been afraid to tell.

On Saturday she took Nathan to Bend, fifteen miles down the
highway, to put him on the express bus to Portland. He had not
wanted to go this year.

"Mom, you aren't going to sell the house or move or anything, are you?" He was watching the highway, as if looking for
the bus, but really to avoid her gaze. He had been avoiding her
gaze ever since Vinny's death. They had their meals together,
but they didn't talk. They sat before the television together and
watched films or the news, or something, but they didn't talk
then, either. And he avoided looking at her.

He was as tall as she was, with her coloring, freckled fair skin
sunburned most of the summer, the same red-blond hair, but he
was going to be a large man, like his father. She desperately
missed the little boy she had been able to hug and rock and play
silly games with, the boy she could always talk things over with.
She wanted to put her arms around him there at the bus station,
but he had drawn himself into a place she couldn't enter; he was
avoiding her, and there was an unnatural stillness like an aura
about him that she couldn't penetrate. Her few attempts to rees-

tablish something of their past closeness had been met with a blank look and an unresponsiveness that she had found forbidding.

"I can't sell anything," she said then in answer to his question. "But I wouldn't do anything like that before we talked it over. You know that. Call as soon as you get there," she added. "And I'll call you and let you know when to expect me next month."

She would drive over and pick him up after his visit with Curtis. He would come home with a lot more stuff than he was taking; Curtis was certain that buying him things was a good substitute for all the things he couldn't give his son—trust, faith in him, love. . . . Nathan would have a good time, she told herself firmly; Curtis had planned a trip back to Indiana to visit Nathan's grandparents. Nathan had been excited about the airplane ride. And he needed to get away, to break through the wall of silence he had erected.

"Hey," she added, "this time drop me a postcard or something on the road." Pleading? Probably, she thought, but couldn't help herself.

"Sure," he said. But likely he would not do it. Somehow when he was with Curtis, it seemed that even though she had provided stamps, there were never mailboxes anywhere around, or time to stop. . . .

Then the bus arrived and he boarded. She stood watching the bus until it was out of sight on Highway 97. When she finally turned toward her car in the parking lot, she saw Wynona Truewater waving at her.

"Lara, glad I caught you. I called and told your machine you're invited to dinner with Manny and me. Our place. But this is better. I've got to be in town most of the day, so let us pick you up, and one of us will take you back home later on. Deal?"

Wynona was nearly six feet tall; her hair was in a heavy braid down her back, and she was dressed in jeans and a plaid shirt, the only clothes most people ever saw her wear. A social worker from the Warm Springs Reservation, she spent a lot of time in Bend and in Salt Creek, probably even more time out on the desert, making her rounds.

"Thanks," Lara said, aware that others in the parking lot had overheard, no doubt half believing that Wynona was on the job, with Lara as a new client. "I can drive over. That's too much trouble for you."

"No trouble, and the fact is, you'd never find our place by yourself. Five-thirty or six, around then. I've got to run."

Lara admitted that she would have had trouble finding their house, set back against a rocky mountain and reached by a series of winding dirt and rock roads. She had been here before, but with Vinny driving, she had not paid a lot of attention to the many twists and turns. The first time she had come out here, she had commented on the lack of decent roads as soon as they were away from the highway and the entrance to the plush Warm Springs resort that brought in tourist dollars. Vinny had laughed. "When they want roads, they'll put them in."

The reservation had been set aside, he said that day, and members of five different tribes had been herded together and marched to it. Plains Indians, river Indians, forest Indians—all the same to the government in those days. But here at Warm Springs, they had made the most of it and for a long time were considered among the richest of the Native American reservations in the Northwest, because of the resort. Now that other tribes had added casinos, that no longer was true, but here they ran their own affairs to suit themselves. Some of them liked to live close together—spitting distance, he had said with a grin— and others, like Manny and Wynona, preferred privacy.

He had turned on the reservation radio station that played

drums and chants day and night, and for a time they had listened quietly to the rhythmic sounds that at first seemed repetitious but gradually became distinguishable as separate and variable, hypnotic. Then he had said meditatively, "When Manny passed the bar exam and came home, I offered him a real partnership, and he turned me down. Nothing legal, nothing binding; he had been a token Native American all through school, and he was done with that. But I think the real reason was that he knew better than I did that a partnership back then would have damaged both of us." He added bitterly, "And it would have."

Manny was slowing down at last as the house came into view. He stopped for Wynona and Lara to get out, and he parked around back. The house was modern, sprawling and handsome, with a lot of glowing cedar and silvery juniper-wood paneling and flooring, and a lot of bright rugs, heavy pottery planters with lush plants, and pictures of their children everywhere. . . .

Through dinner Manny and Wynona did most of the talking, mostly about their three children, now going to college, working summer jobs here and there.

Afterward they sat outside on a stone-paved deck and watched the reflected sunset in the eastern sky. "Out here," Vinny had said, "twilight is deceptive; the sun dips behind the mountains, but the clouds let you know it's still on the job, and we get a light show every day, almost." The clouds took on rainbow hues, deep reds, cerise, gold, luminous green, against a mauve background.

Then Lara said she should be going, before it got too late, and Manny went to bring his Land Rover around the house. She thanked Wynona, and to her surprise the tall woman embraced her and kissed her cheek.

A few minutes later, driving slowly, not wanting to stir up too much dust, Manny said, "Lara, now's a good chance to talk to you. A week before he died, Vinny left a box with me with instructions to give it to you if anything happened to him. He didn't say what he meant by *anything,* and I thought he meant during his next checkup. That was the day he gave me instructions about his client list. We're through with that business now, and tonight when we get to your place, I'll haul the box out and take it in."

"What's in it?"

"I don't know. He didn't tell me. But he was very precise in his instructions. He knew they would go all over the files and your house, too. I was to wait until they were finished with all that and then deliver the box. I suspect that this evening, knowing you'd be gone, that Nathan's out of the way, they went over your house again."

A shudder raced through her. People searching her house? "I don't understand! What are you telling me?"

He negotiated a sharp turn, then said soberly, "Vinny had a lot of friends out here, but he had enemies, too. You can't be a country lawyer and not make enemies. He knew all about that. He said he didn't want that box to fall into anyone's hands but yours. And he said they'd never trust important papers to an Injun, so they won't suspect he would, either."

"Who, Manny? Who are you talking about?"

He kept his gaze on the road; they had reached Highway 97, and he picked up speed.

"You mean Harris McReady, don't you?" she whispered. "The papers he said he had to deliver to McReady. Are they in that box? Then what was he carrying that night?"

"I don't know. Go over the stuff, and on Monday I'll come around and we can talk," he said.

"What am I supposed to do with the box, the papers?"

"I don't know," he said. "Vinny seemed to think you'd know what to do with them."

But late that night, sleepless, alone in a house that had developed new and strange noises day after day, she could not think of what she was supposed to do with the material. She had scanned it; there was too much to read through in less than a week, even two weeks. Many files were about Vinny's son Lewis, who had vanished years before. There were files on Marilyn, his first wife, her illness and death. But most of the material seemed to be about Harris McReady, a complete dossier, starting with his college days—newspaper articles, clippings from a service, speeches, decisions he had made that had been reprinted in legal journals. . . .

One of the last items she had read was a photocopy of an op-ed column that stated that Judge McReady was certain to be the nominee in the coming year for the United States Supreme Court and, if nominated, would be a shoo-in.

PART TWO

THE JUDGE

2

Frank Holloway strolled into his office at ten that morning, in no particular hurry, with nothing much on his mind, certainly no pressing business at the law firm. Look over his mail, tell his secretary, Patsy Meares, what to do with it—he grinned at the thought of the expression that would appear on her face if he really told her what to do with it—see if the other senior partner, Sam Bixby, needed baiting, then beat it back home, get a little weeding done. That was his game plan for the day. If anyone had dared ask, he would have admitted readily that the only reason he showed up at all was that he had promised himself to keep walking at least a mile a day, and it was almost exactly a mile round-trip from his house to his office.

Patsy's office door was open; she was keeping an eye out for him, he understood, and he scowled. When Patsy decided to corner him as soon as he arrived, she more often than not was the bearer of news he didn't want to receive. He greeted her and was not at all surprised when she got up from her desk and followed him into his office. Patsy was probably the only person in that firm whom he could not intimidate with a glance.

Patsy was plump, with what he thought of as a monobosom, no waistline at all, and coal-black hair that she touched up with the regularity of sunrise. Her eyes were black, and that morning they were shining with excitement and there was a flush on her cheeks; she looked as if she had won the lottery, or gotten engaged.

"So what is it?" he said in a growly tone as he headed toward his desk, which was a beautiful and comforting sight—satin smooth and absolutely clean, without a paper or even a paper clip in view.

"Two calls," Patsy said, not quite breathlessly. "Mr. Donald Fleishman from New York."

"Who the hell is Donald Fleishman?"

"Your editor from Grenadier Press."

He stopped moving, then turned to stare at her. She was beaming.

"He called at nine our time," she said, "and I told him you would be tied up until ten or ten-thirty. And he said he would be out to lunch then, but he'd call back around two-thirty, New York time. Eleven-thirty here."

Patsy knew him too well for him to pretend not to be stunned. "Good Christ!" he said, then went on to sit at his desk. "Good Christ! I never even heard of Donald Fleishman."

"You're going to be published, a famous writer! Be on talk shows, Oprah, sign books in stores, Barnes and Noble, go on a book tour—"

"Patsy, knock it off. We don't know what he wants. Eleven-thirty? Let's wait a bit to celebrate. What's the other call? You said two."

"Yes. Mrs. Lara Jessup. She called late yesterday and said she would take a chance and drive over from Salt Creek or someplace, that she has to see you, and if you can't see her today, she'll plan to stay over until tomorrow or even the next day. I told her you might be free between ten and noon, but I couldn't guarantee it."

He shrugged. Fleishman? He had sent his book on the art of cross-examination to Grenadier Press because they had done some scholarly books concerning the law, but he had not sent it to anyone in particular, just to the Editor. Fleishman. Donald Fleishman. Maybe his editor.

"She said you knew her late husband, Vinny Jessup," Patsy continued, "and that she met you back in March at a bar meeting here in Eugene."

He recalled her then; a pretty young thing was all that came to mind. A trophy wife. But he had known Vinny for many years, never as a close friend, but as an admired and respected attorney from east of the mountains. "Okay," he said then. "If she turns up before eleven or so, give me a buzz. I have a few things here to take care of. . . ."

Patsy, he knew, was undeceived. He would wait for Fleishman's call and try to look busy while he waited. Patsy had already sorted his mail and taken care of routine matters, so there really was very little for him to do, beyond okaying what she had done. She didn't need him to show up at all, but she pretended she did, and he went along amiably enough most of the time. When the Jessup woman arrived, he would send her around to one of the younger attorneys, and that would be that. He was little more than a gatekeeper these days; new clients showed up, and he directed them to hungry young attorneys. Not a bad way to ease out of the business, but he remembered very clearly how it had been when he was a young and hungry lawyer and no one had been there to send anything but bills in his direction.

Of course, if anyone brought in a criminal case, he would direct that person to his daughter, Barbara; his prestigious firm was no longer interested in dealing with overtly criminal cases.

Patsy returned to her own office, and he thought she could have taken care of Lara Jessup with the same dispatch she had shown with the other matters. He imagined that Lara Jessup was in a dispute with Vinny's adult children over a will or property, something of that sort, but now, trying to decide which of the young attorneys to send her to, he recalled the last time he had seen Vinny. Frank had gone to one of the bar association luncheons that he generally avoided, this time drawn to it out of curiosity about Harris McReady, the wonder boy who was aiming for the Supreme Court. McReady had been the guest speaker that day, and the reception that followed his talk had been abuzz with speculation about him.

Frank had been chatting with several other attorneys when he saw Vinny approaching the group with his young wife. Behind him, Frank heard one of the men saying, "By this time next year he'll be on the Court." And Vinny, close enough to hear also, had muttered in a low voice, "Over my dead body!"

Frank was surprised at the sharpness of the memory; Vinny had meant it, had meant something. His face had gone almost savage with hatred for a moment; then his expression had changed and, smiling at Frank, he had introduced Lara. And today Vinny was dead, an accident of some sort, Lara was a pretty young widow, and McReady was a step or two closer to his goal. So it went.

It was nearly eleven when Patsy buzzed to say that Mrs. Jessup had arrived, and she, Patsy, was sending one of the maintenance men down to help her carry a box, and should they come straight in with it?

Frank glanced at his watch again and said bring them on in, box and all. He was annoyed with himself, as eager as a pup awaiting his master; if looking at a watch could impose wear and tear on it, his would be fraying at the edges by now. Another half hour, an hour . . . He stood up to greet Lara Jessup when there was a tap at the door.

She was even younger than he remembered, and she looked like a child who had not yet quite recovered from one of the scourges of childhood, with deeply shadowed eyes and a weariness that seemed to be weighing her down, making her shoulders droop, her steps heavy and deliberate. The maintenance man wheeled in a dolly with a big file-storage box on it.

"On the desk," Frank said, and watched him heave it up. It looked very heavy. Patsy and the man left.

"Mrs. Jessup," Frank said then, "I was so sorry to hear about Vinny's death. It's a terrible loss to everyone. Please, sit here." Her hand was cold when he shook it and then held it as he led her to the visitor's chair at his desk. He sat in a matching chair close to hers. "What can I do for you?"

"That's what I came to find out," she said. "I don't know what anyone can do." Her voice was surprisingly steady. "When we were in town last March, Vinny and I, at a lunch meeting, Vinny said he particularly wanted me to meet you. He said there were maybe three men in that room that he'd trust to hold his coat, and you were one. He said if I ever needed help, advice, you'd be his first choice for me to ask. So I came to you."

Frank nodded without comment, and she continued. "The night he died," she said, her voice shaky now, "he was on his way to take some papers to Judge McReady, and they said he lost control of his car and ran off a cliff road. A simple accident." She swallowed hard. "Then they said he died of a gunshot wound in the head, that he shot himself and the car just rolled over the cliff. They found a note that they say is a suicide note. I brought you a copy. But he wouldn't have done that, not that way. And the papers were gone and haven't turned up anywhere. Judge McReady said Vinny never showed up that night."

Bare bones without a shred of meat on them, Frank thought,

as she talked about that day, that night, what followed, but he didn't ask a thing yet, even though questions were lining up like soldiers, surging forward. He waited.

She told him about the instructions Vinny had left concerning his law practice, how the three attorneys had gone through every file, the dispensation of the active cases, the search of her house. "Then, last Saturday, Manny gave me that box." She repeated the instructions Vinny had given him about it.

"I read what I could of it," she said. "Saturday night, all day Sunday, most of Monday. Most of it is too legalistic for me to follow, too technical. Late Monday Manny came by and I asked him to take the box and do what he thought best, but he wouldn't. He said if Vinny had wanted him to have it, he would have said so. He said—" She had to stop to swallow hard again, and this time Frank stood up and went to the coffee table across the room to pour her a glass of water. He handed it to her, and while she drank it, he buzzed Patsy.

"We could use some coffee in here," he said. By then Lara was ready to continue.

"He said Vinny told him that I was the only one he wanted to have that box, that I would know what to do with the stuff in it. But I didn't. I don't. All day yesterday I kept trying to decide, and then I remembered you, that he wanted me to meet you, that he trusted you, and I called."

Frank was eyeing the big file box speculatively. "What's in it?"

"A lot of files from years ago. His son was accused of a double murder, and he ran away, or just vanished, before the trial. Vinny and his wife lost their ranch, and then she became ill and was an invalid for years until she finally died. It's all in there."

Patsy tapped lightly on the door, and Frank called for her to come on in. She put the coffee service on the low table across the room and left silently.

"Let's sit over there," Frank said. He waited until Lara was seated in one of the comfortable chairs with coffee in place before he asked what else was in the box.

"Most of it is material he gathered for years and years about Harris McReady. He had an obsessional hatred of him. I never suspected. . . . He had services send him clippings, his speeches, everything. . . ."

"Why?"

"He believed McReady killed his son Lewis, or had him killed or knew who killed him, something like that, and that he was responsible for the illness and death of his first wife." She picked up her cup, then put it down without tasting the coffee. "I believe McReady killed Vinny, that he got the papers Vinny had," she said in a rush. "Maybe he had found something to prove what he believed and was going to confront him with proof. So McReady killed him and tried to make it look like suicide."

Cursing inwardly, Frank regarded her without expression. She looked terrified, fully aware of what she was saying, what it meant. He sipped his coffee, and she lifted her cup again and this time actually drank from it.

"Mrs. Jessup," he said, "that is a very serious accusation, as you know. Have you said anything like that to anyone else?"

"No."

"Good. Have you told anyone else that you had that box in your possession?"

She shook her head. "Manny knows, of course, and probably his wife does, too. That's all."

"All right. The only advice I can give you right now is to go home, sit tight, and be patient. And don't breathe a word about this visit, that box, or your suspicions to anyone. No one at all. I'll go through those files, and afterward we can talk again; at that time maybe I'll have something concrete for you. Is that acceptable?"

She nodded. "I've been so worried about those files, about having them when I thought other people were looking for them. Knowing they're here, safe . . . Thank you, Mr. Holloway. I'll have to tell Manny something. He was afraid for me to have them at home."

"Vinny trusted him enough to hand that stuff over to him," Frank said slowly, trying to recall if he had ever heard of Manny Truewater. Nothing came to mind. "Do you have the same trust in him?"

"Absolutely."

"Then tell him what you've done, but no one else. And give my secretary your home address and a phone number where I can get you after I've looked everything over. I'll be in touch as soon as I can, but it will take time."

They both stood up, and he added kindly, "Mrs. Jessup, try to get some sleep. We'll do something about all this." He escorted her out to Patsy's office and left her there. "Patsy, when you're free, come by for a minute, will you?"

Then, back in his own office, he eyed the box again, and this time he hefted it. He could manhandle it into the safe alone, but it was a heavy son of a bitch, he thought. It must be packed to the brim. Patsy knocked on the door and entered.

"I think for now we keep Mrs. Jessup under wraps," Frank said. "Not a word." She looked a bit indignant—she never talked about his clients—but he was taking no chances. Although it was fun to wave the red flag under Sam Bixby's nose now and then, he was too fond of his old partner to want to cause him any real harm, and the mention of Harris McReady's name in connection with anything unsavory was possible cause for a coronary. "Two things," he said. "They'll keep until after lunch. Try to find Bailey and tell him to give me a call later on today. I don't want him to come here, just call. And see if we have anything about an attorney named Manny Truewater." Bailey was Bailey Novell, the only private investigator he had any use for, and even if Vinny Jessup had trusted Manny Truewater all the way, Frank always liked to know who was sitting at the table when the cards got shuffled.

"I'll get on them right now," Patsy said, and he understood that she was not going to leave the office until after Fleishman called back.

And neither was he, he admitted to himself after Patsy hurried out. He opened his wall safe, as big as a closet, with very little in it at the moment, although it could hold a full-grown man. At one time he had hidden a man in there, in fact. But he didn't put the box inside just yet. It was twelve o'clock, his call might not come for another hour, two hours. He doubted it would come after two—five, New York time. He got out his pocket knife, cut the tape on the box, lifted the cover, and groaned. It was packed so tightly that to get anything out would be a chore in itself. Were the files organized in any particular way? Just randomly packed in? Even sorting them would be a major task. With a sigh he began to work out some of the file folders.

At one-fifteen Patsy buzzed him: Mr. Fleishman was on the line. To his chagrin he found that his hand was sweating when he picked up the phone.

"Holloway," he said.

"Mr. Holloway! Don Fleishman here. I'm glad I caught you. I have to tell you we love your book here! All of us who've read it, we love it. It's wonderful! Mr. Holloway, I want to send you a contract right away, five thousand advance, half on signing, half on pub."

"Five thousand—"

"I might be able to get it up to six thousand, maybe even six five. I can try. It's a natural for us right now. There's so much interest in the criminal justice system, in criminal lawyers and real-life crimes and cases. Memoirs. You don't have an agent, do you?" He laughed. "Hah, that's a joke! You're a lawyer; you can read your own contract. What we'll do is send you the contract, and meanwhile I'll be going over the manuscript again and make some notes on a few revisions."

"Revisions?"

"Not much, Mr. Holloway—Frank. But it's standard, just a few changes, additions more than anything. You're too modest. The details of the cases are riveting, but you've left yourself out too much. There won't be much to do. Hardly anything. Do you ever get to New York?"

"Rarely."

"And be thinking about the title, will you? It's a good title, but something with a little more—not zing exactly, but a little more suggestive of the contents, of the life-and-death dramas you write about. Anyway, that's minor. Our sales team will get their heads together and make some suggestions, and you be thinking along those lines. When the contract arrives, if there's anything in it that you find puzzling, don't hesitate to call. But it's a very standard contract and I don't think you'll have any problem with it. I wanted to get in touch with you personally and not hit you with a letter that might not express my enthusiasm fully. And as soon as we have the contract settled, our publicist will get in touch for some bio, some personal stuff about *you*. As I said, you're too modest."

"The book isn't about me, Mr. Fleishman," Frank said.

"Please, it's Don. Call me Don. We'll be working together on this project. . . ."

When Frank hung up a few minutes later, he felt in a daze; then he began to chuckle. Six thousand five hundred dollars! He knew that lawyers who turned to publishing came from the bottom of the barrel, a ragtag bunch who couldn't make a dime as ambulance chasers, even. But sixty five hundred! He had been prepared to pay them to publish the damn book. Grinning, he called Barbara and left a message on her machine, an invitation to dinner at the Chanterelle. There had been a time when he would have added the name of the fashionable restaurant to alert her to put on some real clothes, but he didn't care what she wore anymore. So his daughter was a little bit eccentric, so what? He added the name of the restaurant this time just to pique her curiosity, to alert her that a celebration was in order.

Patsy returned, she said with the dope on Truewater, but really to find out what Fleishman had said, and he told her.

"We did it, by God!" he said. She had done the index, ready to add as soon as they had real page numbers.

"Can I tell anyone about this?"

"You bet! Yell it from the street corners!"

Then, ever practical, Patsy glanced at the box crammed with papers. "What you need is a couple more of those surplus-file boxes. I'll bring some in from supplies before I start yelling on street corners. Are you going out for lunch?"

He had not given lunch a thought and shook his head. "I think I'll work awhile and let the adrenaline subside. I feel like a little kid with his first bike."

"I'll have the deli send in something," she said at the door. "Bailey will give you a call around three. Here first, then the house if you've left already."

Frank was still grinning when he started to read the files he had taken from the box; his smile faded, was replaced by a frown as he quickly skimmed through page after page, not reading closely now, but getting the gist of the story about Lewis Jessup, who had been accused of a double homicide, and whose prosecutor had been Harris McReady.

3

On Friday that week, two days after the celebratory dinner with her father, Barbara was explaining to two boys and their parents that no, she couldn't get them off scot-free; no one else could, either.

"Look," she said patiently, "you did it, and you were caught. There are witnesses. You even told the police that you did it. You can't decide now that maybe you were somewhere else that night." They had burned down a Porta Potti at a construction site. A little beer, a little grass, a dare, boredom, whatever the reason, now they had to take their lumps, and the parents were determined not to let that happen, although both boys seemed prepared to do community service, pay damages out of their own pocket, every penalty the court was likely to impose.

Mrs. Lawton, one of the mothers, stood up, her mouth a tight, hard line without lips at the moment. "I think we're through here," she said. "We're wasting time. You can send us your bill."

Barbara nodded and stood up also. She had explained that if they tried to weasel out of it now, their sentence would be tougher than if they stuck to their confessions, expressed remorse, and agreed to pay the price. She knew they could find another attorney who would go along—no problem there—but the kids would still pay and the price would be upped considerably. She walked out with them through the hallway to the reception room, where she was surprised to see her father chatting with Maria Velasquez, her secretary and receptionist and all-around aide and comfort.

She nodded to Frank, escorted the group to the door, and wished them luck. One of the boys looked embarrassed; they were both sixteen, too young to be labeled criminals for a very childish prank.

Then she turned to Frank. "What's up?"

"Wondered if you have a few minutes," he said. "I was going to call, but I was out walking and just dropped in instead."

"Sure. Maria, knock off anytime. I'll close up when I leave." It was four-thirty, and if she couldn't determine office hours in her own office, what good was it? "Come on in, Dad, and I'll give you a slug of supermarket wine."

He winced, but followed her back to her own office and sat down on her couch. He liked her office; it looked busy, with papers on the desk, a plant that needed watering, some coffee cups on the ornate table. It looked busy, but he well knew that her cases these days were mostly nickel-and-dime stuff, minor-league stuff, and apparently she had sent the last bunch away empty-handed. He didn't ask about them or their problem.

She poured wine, a fairly respectable pinot noir from one of the Oregon vineyards. "Client gave it to me," she said cheerfully, "and it isn't going to keep past about six or seven this evening. He drank most of it, so what the hell, we'll kill the rest."

He waited until she sat down and put her feet on the coffee table. If that table had been a priceless heirloom, she would use it for a footrest, he knew; he didn't even raise a disapproving eyebrow.

"Let me guess," she said then. "Your editor called to say it's all a mistake, he was talking about two other books. Or he wants to call it *Naked at the Bar*, or he suggested it needs a little lurid sex, a few car chases, a dozen shoot-outs. Maybe an explosion or two."

He grimaced. "All of the above, but we'll talk about them later. Right now, a situation has come up. What do you know about Harris McReady?"

Regarding him, she sobered instantly. After a moment she said, "Damn all. Our own homegrown wunderkind, headed for stardom in the Court. Way conservative. Why?"

He told her about Lara Jessup's visit, then he said, "I had Bailey rustle up a quick reading of Vinny's death, just a skim off the top, and it stinks. No one believes in the suicide note; apparently there weren't any prints on the gun; and the papers he said he was delivering vanished. It stinks. McReady says he was at his wife's folks' house all night, and they vouch for that. Her folks are Thomas and Anna Lynch." He added, "That's supposed to be Loomis County, but it's really Lynch County; Thomas owns most of the land, and probably all the local government."

Barbara sipped her wine, not asking a single question yet any more than he had interrupted Lara to ask questions.

Frank went on. "The autopsy revealed death by a gunshot wound to the head, point-blank range. And it also revealed that his cancer had come back in spades. Bone cancer. He went through hell with it six or seven years ago, and it came back and probably would have done him in within a few months. He had a lot of codeine in his system."

For a moment they were both silent, then Frank said, "Okay, some history. In 1981 Lewis Jessup was indicted for the murder of two kids who had been hiking in the wilderness area around Sisters. Lewis was nineteen. Bail was high, a million, and Vinny scraped together one hundred thousand and got his boy out awaiting trial. Vinny constructed a damn fine brief. He was a good lawyer and did a good job, but he was too smart to try to defend his son in court. He hired Lester DeFeo for that."

Barbara raised her eyebrows at the name, and he nodded. In his eighties by now, DeFeo had been one of the best criminal lawyers in the country for more than forty years.

"It's all in the box, their correspondence, discovery, everything. They would have gotten him off, I have no doubt, but a few weeks before the trial, Lewis vanished. Depending on whose side you believe, he skipped or was killed and buried out in the desert. Anyway, Vinny and his wife lost their ranch, which had been in her family for three generations, and they moved to the town of Salt Creek. She had a nervous breakdown, and never really recovered, and then a series of strokes. . . . So, the string that ties it all to McReady. He was named prosecutor. The ranch was forfeited, Lynch bought it, and within the year McReady married his daughter, Bethany Lynch."

He stopped talking and picked up his wine; Barbara stood up and walked across the office to her desk, not to do anything, but because she had to move.

"I haven't had time to read much beyond the history part," Frank said. "Apparently Vinny had it in his head that McReady was directly responsible for all his troubles, and he began to assemble a complete file on him. For what purpose, I don't know. I saw Vinny back in March," he said reflectively, and told her about the incident. "He hated McReady with the kind of raw hatred you don't often see displayed."

"Obsessional," she said in a low voice. "Irrational?"

"Maybe."

"If Jessup had uncovered something damaging about Mc-Ready, he never would have taken the original papers to hand over, not if he was obsessional," she said, returning to the coffee table to pick up the wine bottle. She emptied it into their glasses. "If there are any such documents, they might be in the box. If he was killed for those papers, whoever did it knows the originals exist."

Frank nodded, appreciative of the fact that she was leaping instantly over the same hurdles he had considered.

She raised her glass in a mock salute. "I think we have a situation."

They talked about it, even argued a little about it, but in the end they agreed that the best course now was to have Bailey send someone around to move the box, to bring it to Barbara's office and stash it in her safe.

"You can hole up in here and read the material whenever it's convenient," she said. "And I can get to it when I'm not chasing around trying to keep dumb-ass kids out of jail."

"It could turn pretty messy," Frank commented. "Or there could be absolutely nothing to it, and all I'll have to do is reassure Lara Jessup and tell her to get on with her life."

Barbara nodded. "McReady's smart," she said. "Was Jessup smart?"

"Yes. He was a good lawyer, a fine man, and plenty smart. And he was dying and had to have known it. He could have put a bullet in his own head, someone came along and found him, went through the briefcase he was carrying, and found something worth keeping. He wasn't robbed, except for the papers, apparently. But the papers could have been more than enough. That someone could have given the car a shove over the cliff."

"And that someone wiped prints off the gun, just to muddy the waters," she said skeptically. "Right. Dad, if there is something, do you really want to go after McReady?"

He regarded her for a moment, then stood up. "Problem is that Jessup was savvy as well as smart, as McReady is. From what little I saw of Lara Jessup, I'd say she's pretty smart, too, but she's bone ignorant, and way out of her depth. Even if the locals call it suicide, in spite of no fingerprints on the gun and a suicide note that smells to heaven, there's an insurance company in the picture, too. And a big policy. We didn't talk about it, and

I haven't seen the policy, but I knew Jessup a bit, and I'd put down money that it has a double-indemnity clause that won't pay zilch on a death by suicide and won't pay a cent more than that to the beneficiary if that person also happened to be the killer. I think that if the locals can't get away with calling it suicide, and they go for murder, that young lady is in for a hell of a lot of trouble."

"Could be that Jessup had some pretty rough enemies out there," Barbara said. "She might be way down on the list of possible suspects."

"Well, we sure as hell don't know much at this point," he said. He glanced around the office, at the coffee table with cups and saucers and now wine glasses. "You going to do anything about this stuff now?"

"Nope. In the morning."

"Why don't you drive me home and let me rustle something out of the freezer and throw together some dinner for us."

"You're on," she said. She knew very well that it gave him nearly as much pleasure to cook for her as it did for her to eat his food. Without a qualm she closed blinds, turned off her computer, turned off lights, set her security system, and they went out to her car, which had been collecting heat for the past hour or so and was oven-hot. Every day that she drove to her office, she intended to go out and move the car when the sun drifted into the western sky. Every day she forgot. They opened windows, and she began to drive. She suspected that Frank had timed his unexpected visit precisely, knowing to the minute when the discussion would wind down, and exactly when it would be a good time to ask her over for dinner. She appreciated that he hadn't asked if she was busy, had a date, or anything like that.

In January, at the sliding glass door in his kitchen, watching snow fall, with her back to him, she had said quietly, "John showed up yesterday. We had a talk, and he's moving out." Actually, it had not been much of a talk, more like a subdued yelling match. At least no one had called the cops.

"Want to talk about it?"

"No. What I intend to do in the coming year is build up a law practice. I think it will keep me busy." And she had kept busy, training Maria Velasquez, checking in four days a week at Martin's restaurant, handling clients from the office, and weekends hiking, climbing mountains, walking. . . . Busy, busy, busy, she mocked herself. Physically she probably had never been in better shape, but recently she had started to wonder which one of them had been hurt more, she or John Mureau, although last January there had been no doubt in her mind.

Driving now, she said, "I love these long summer days, don't you?" She turned onto his street, where everything that knew how to flower seemed to be in bloom. Eugene had started to bloom by March first, and the bouquet was just now reaching its peak, changing day by day subtly, sneaking in a new red bush here, a new yellow something there. . . .

Then, in his house, stroking one of the cats, Thing One or Thing Two, identical twins that were fast becoming monsters, as Frank washed peas from the garden, she said, "You know there are maybe a dozen little problems with that situation you brought up. If McReady is smart, would he have staged a suicide that is blatantly fake? If he was just the prosecutor of the case against Lewis Jessup, he had nothing really to do with the preliminary investigation, and he never got around to the prosecution if the boy skipped bail. He probably was handed a bad case and had to make the best of it—not his fault. Usually you wait until the prosecutor plays foul in court before you set your sights on him. If Jessup really had evidence against him, would McReady have agreed to meet him alone at night like that to demonstrate it?" She paused and sniffed garlic and rosemary in the air. Her stomach growled.

Frank made a noncommittal sound and continued preparing dinner.

"Or if Lara Jessup isn't quite as innocent as you seem to think, she could have found her dead husband and tried to make his suicide look like murder in order to collect the insurance."

She stood up to pour herself a glass of wine and have a bit of cheese; her stomach was embarrassingly loud in its mumbling and groaning. "Or," she continued, "a secret stalker or an angry client, a defeated adversary, a scorned lover, a nut on the loose, a jealous admirer of Lara's . . . In any of the above, McReady is out of it. And the question of whether we want to tangle with him is moot."

Frank stopped mincing herbs and garlic and regarded her. "Or it could be that someone who *is* clever and savvy set the scene to make it appear that someone who is inept and not savvy tried to cover up a murder."

Ah, Barbara thought when he resumed his chore at the counter, she had an answer to her question: he did want to go after McReady. She sipped chardonnay and said under her breath, "Here's to a worthy opponent."

Holding the knife poised over the cutting board, Frank looked at her and said, "Bobby, this could erupt into a real media circus, you understand. It could become very, very nasty. I think we'd better agree that McReady's name isn't to come into play unless and until we have something hard and quite definitive to offer up."

4

At five Saturday evening Barbara put down the paper she had been reading. She sighed loud enough to be heard.

Across the office sitting on her couch, Frank glanced up from his own document. "That bad?"

"How can one man be so overwhelmingly boring all the time? You'd think something human would sneak in just to spite him."

Frank grinned and returned to his own reading.

She surveyed stacks of papers gloomily. One pile of stuff they had both finished, the smallest of them all. A large stack Frank had worked through, another small one of papers she had read that he had not yet touched. And the biggest by far was the stack neither of them had looked at yet. She stretched. Enough for one day; her eyes were glazing over. Although she had hoped they would get through it all by the end of the day Sunday, she now doubted that they could. So on into Monday, maybe even Tuesday.

Frank finished his paper and sighed as melodramatically as she had done. "The damn man's an enigma. Let's knock off. Want some dinner?"

"Can't. Why don't you come home with me, actually. A pool party. Lane Hornsby in concert, even."

He looked at her in disbelief. "I'd rather eat cat food."

Together they put the material back into her safe. Then they walked out into the bright sunlight. It was pleasantly warm; the sun felt good after the air-conditioned office all day.

They walked without talking for several blocks, then he said, "There's something nagging at me. I don't see any point in having you read every damn decision the man made. Cut-and-dried, programmed stuff. I'll put aside whatever I think might be of interest for you. Deal?"

"Deal," she said gratefully. There wasn't any point in any of this, as far as she could see. In all those papers, neither of them had come up with a thing interesting about McReady, much less incriminating.

They were drawing closer to the bicycle path along the river, where they would separate, Frank to walk on to his house, she to go on to her apartment complex.

Frank walked slower, and when they reached the river, flashing like silver in sunlight, he stopped. "You know what happens when you read a collection of stories by one person, one writer. Even if it's someone you like very much, after about the third or fourth story in a row, you find yourself spotting mannerisms, bits of technique that are repeated, characters who get redrawn a bit differently but are the same people, phrases that show up over and over, little things that you never notice if the stories are spaced out over time. You begin to see the writer at work. That's what bothers me about McReady. I can't find him in anything of his I've read so far. And that's uncanny."

"Maybe he's all facade; there's no one there to find."

Frank nodded. "Maybe. Well, I'll see you in the morning sometime."

She was hot by the time she entered her apartment. There were four groups of buildings in the complex, each with twelve apartments and a small swimming pool; she had come to know most of the people in her own unit, and most of them would be at the poolside party. She surveyed packages of salmon burgers from her freezer, her contribution, and doubted that they were the right thing for a party like this. They were too expensive, for one thing. She should have bought hamburger; it was potluck, and many of the others would have spent the afternoon preparing a casserole or salad. . . . The hell with it, she thought. Her hamburgers were always too salty or not salty enough, too dry, stringy, tasteless, and the salmon burgers came already seasoned and shaped, ready to be popped onto a grill. They would do.

Leaving the burgers on the counter to thaw, she changed into her swimsuit and went down for a quick dip, just to cool off; she wasn't a serious swimmer. She waved to Shelley McGinnis and Bill Spassero, playing in the pool like a pair of golden dolphins. A few children were there, and she didn't linger long.

They ate by seven-thirty, and everyone declared all the food delicious, and for the most part it was, although Tilly Maryhill couldn't make potato salad worth a darn and she always brought it. Then promptly at eight-thirty someone beat on a pan with a metal spoon and silence fell over the laughing, talking group. Lane Hornsby strode out from his first-floor apartment, splendid in white satin with sequins and gold trim.

By day he was a bespectacled, slightly stooped, shy CPA with a prestigious firm downtown. On weekends and for special occasions he became Elvis. Perfecting a new act for a contest coming up in Portland over the Fourth of July, he used this party as his dress rehearsal. He was a good Elvis, twitching his hips, thrusting his pelvis, strumming his guitar, flicking a wayward strand of hair back now and again.

People drifted in from other apartment units for the show, which management had said had to be over by ten, no later.

Lane was a super performer, and since most of the people in his audience had never seen the real Elvis, they all thought he was perfect. He received a thunderous ovation when he finally bowed and walked back into his apartment.

People began to drift away; Shelley and Bill walked toward her apartment at the far end of the unit, hand in hand, both wearing white shorts and white T-shirts, both with gleaming blond hair, a perfect match. Abruptly Barbara stood up and said good night in a general way and went up to her own apartment, where she stood at the kitchen window and gazed at the diminishing party below.

Harry Teasdale and Joan Edding, always furtive, in their sixties, so afraid someone would reveal that they were married; they were afraid of the marriage penalty to their Social Security income and pensions. Tilly and Mae, lesbian lovers, who by day were so prim and proper that they might have been mistaken for missionaries; in their fifties now, they had grown so used to hiding, they found it impossible to come out. Janet and Mike Spencer, she a topless dancer and he a history teacher in one of the local schools. No one knew what Gary Neumann did. His wife, if she was his wife, was a librarian. And Lane Hornsby, so shy that he had become terrified one day when by chance he bumped into Barbara at the corner of their building, and he had blurted out that he wasn't there on purpose, that he wasn't looking for her or anything. And by night, Elvis. Even Shelley and Bill, Barbara thought, were hidden behind perfect and false facades. Shelley looked like a homecoming queen, and he like a campus jock, but they were both independently wealthy, working their butts off for peanuts. He was with the public defender's office, and poor Shelley was struggling for acceptance with clients who regarded her as a pretty little Barbie doll. Frank called her the golden-haired pink fairy. Barbara knew to the penny how much Shelley earned for her efforts; she paid her meager salary.

She realized she was thinking of what her father had said

about McReady; Frank couldn't find him in his written decisions or in his speeches. Hiding. Masked. But someone was behind the mask, she thought then. There was always another self behind the mask.

Then she realized that for the first time, she had come across something interesting about Harris McReady: he had been wearing a mask for at least seventeen years.

She turned from the window, frowning. Nearly everyone at the party tonight had confided in her, some with little confidences, some with bigger secrets. She had not sought them out, had not gone looking for their secret selves, and wouldn't have done such a thing if she had thought of it. People confided in her, asked for advice often, and not just for legal advice, and that was her role, she thought mockingly. Spinster, confessor aunt to the world.

Then suddenly it hit her. She thought of it as an emotional tsunami that swept over her and dissolved all thought, all reason, and in passing left her raw, emotionally flayed and despairing. Nothing as simple as nostalgia for what might have been; nostalgia was a bittersweet ache, not a searing pain. Not as simple as pure grief; she had suffered grief at her mother's death, and later again at her lover's death in the river, and had come to terms with grief, the words never spoken, actions never taken, all the unfinished business, the regrets, the guilt. . . . Grief, finally, was endurable. But the storm surge was not. The last time it happened or the time before, one time, she had promised herself that it would spend its energy, it would weaken eventually. Never again would she be caught unaware and vulnerable, defenseless. Empty promise.

Dully she picked up her keys, put a ten-dollar bill and some change in her pocket, and left the apartment to walk. One time she had walked so long that at three in the morning, she had been miles from home without a cent to call a cab.

Sunday evening, after another day of reading endlessly boring speeches and decisions, Barbara and Frank sat on his back porch.

"If you were on a panel to consider him for the Court, what would your opinion be?" she asked.

Frank shrugged. "Can't find anything concrete against him. Conservative, but who isn't these days? Not a deep thinker, but he has a knack for telling his audience what they want to hear, what they expect to hear. It's as if he set his sights on the Court at puberty, and made damn sure ever since that nothing happened that could bar his way. The problem is that if you vote no, you're expected to have something to back it up. I wouldn't have diddly." He eyed her shrewdly. "What about you?"

"I'd vote no," she said. "And I wouldn't need anything to back it up. I'd want to see what's behind that neat and tidy public image he's built so carefully." For several minutes neither spoke, then she asked, "What are you going to tell Lara Jessup?"

"I don't know," Frank said. "I'll wrap up the reading in the morning. It won't take long." Then he said, "I knew a fellow once, a long time ago, before your time even, who talked to Jesus and got answers. No one would have guessed from observing him, from working alongside him or going fishing with him. His wife suspected that it was deeper than he let on, not enough to frighten her, just to make her uneasy. Then one day Jesus told him to take his shotgun and blast her and their two kids to kingdom come. And he did. He got the chair. Point is, no one suspected he was mad, and after the fact no one believed it."

"You think Vinny Jessup was that far gone on the subject of McReady?"

"Don't know. It keeps coming back to the boy, Lewis Jessup. Why did Vinny blame McReady if he was only the prosecutor, who never even prosecuted him? Why not the sheriff or one of the investigators?"

She mulled it over. "Jessup lost his son, his wife, his ranch. He went broke and then lost his health. But damn the man, if he had something real, why didn't he tell someone or write a letter, a detailed account, to go into that stupid box?"

Frank stood up. "Don't know that, either. I'm going to make dinner."

She continued to sit there, angry with Jessup, who had presented them with a gigantic four-dimensional jigsaw puzzle, spread out over space and a period of seventeen years, who seemed to have thought that Frank, or someone else, could put the pieces together to form a coherent picture. And then, to make it just a little tougher, he had left out an unknown number of pieces.

A blue jay began to screech, and a golden coon cat strolled out from behind a rosebush, not sheepish at all, merely disdainful; it passed the birdbath as if unaware of the two robins splashing. The second cat appeared from another bush, and they both joined her on the porch and proceeded to clean themselves meticulously.

The jay sounded as if it were laughing at them.

Soon Barbara stood up and walked inside the house. Frank was basting something in the oven; it smelled spicy, and good.

"Well," she said, "if there's nothing on McReady, and if the cops over in Loomis County settle on murder, the May/December marriage, a pretty widow, big insurance policy . . . I'd say they won't bother to look far and wide for a likely suspect. You intend to tell her that?"

Frank scowled and did not bother to answer.

Tuesday afternoon when Barbara escorted a client from her office, she was not surprised to see Frank already in the reception room, telling Maria a long, involved story, apparently. He wrapped it up as she bade her client good-bye and told her not to worry and the usual somewhat inane things she usually said to dismiss a nonproblem. Then she shrugged at Frank, and said, "Anytime you're ready."

He was ready. He followed her into her office, where they were expecting Lara Jessup at about three. It was two-thirty. He had told Lara she might as well collect the material, that he had found nothing in it for her to be concerned about. And he had given her Barbara's office address. They had repacked the material into three boxes, manageable now without outside help.

At ten minutes before three Maria buzzed Barbara; there was a call for Mr. Holloway. Mrs. Jessup was on the line.

Frank picked up the phone. "Holloway—"

"Mr. Holloway, someone's following me. All the way across the mountains, and off the highway into a mall. All the way. I'm scared."

 5

"Lara Jessup," Frank said to Barbara. "She's being followed."

"Keep her on the line, find out what you can. Right back." She ran from the office, down the hall to the reception room, and said to Maria, "Get Bailey. Track him down and give us a call when you locate him, and give Shelley a ring. I want her."

Then, back in the office, thinking hard, she listened to Frank quiz Lara Jessup for a few seconds.

"Have they made any overt threat of any kind, crowded your car, anything like that?" He shook his head at Barbara.

"Introduce me," she said. "Let me talk to her."

"I'm going to turn you over to my colleague, Barbara," Frank said. "She'll tell you what to do. Okay?" After another moment he handed the phone to Barbara.

"Mrs. Jessup, exactly where are you?"

"In a fast-food place, in the restroom. It's a big mall off Highway 126 in Springfield."

"Can the people following you see you there?"

"No. I think they're waiting in a car outside."

"Good. What you should do is buy a take-out drink, and then go back to your car. Are you familiar with the streets there, and over here?" Lara said not really, and Barbara gave her precise instructions about driving to Franklin Boulevard, where to turn to find the Fifth Street Public Market.

As she listened to Lara repeat her instructions, Shelley entered the office and stood by the desk looking bewildered.

"Okay," Barbara said then. "Park at the market and go on inside, don't rush, and don't pay any attention to the people following you. Don't look for them. It would be good if they don't know you're onto them. In the market make your way to the lower level and find Tilly's Flowers and Gifts Shop. It's not hard to find. Either Tilly or another woman, Mae, will be there. Pretend to know them, and don't be surprised if they pretend they know you. They might offer you a cup of tea or something, as if you were an old friend. Then you just wait with them until someone comes to collect you. She'll be young, pretty, with big blond hair, and she'll address you by name and ask if you're ready to go. After that, just do what she says."

When Barbara hung up, Shelley's eyes were wide with excitement. She sometimes grumbled that she had not become a criminal lawyer in order to resolve neighborhood disputes over fences or late payments of debts, but those were the only kind of cases that had come her way so far.

Barbara gave her a sketchy synopsis of the affair, and then said, "They must still be after the papers. If they'd wanted to do her harm, this isn't the way to go about it." She turned toward Frank, who was frowning and troubled by this new development. "I think we keep those boxes right where they are for the time being." He nodded.

"If Bailey calls in the next half hour," she said, "I'll sic him on those guys and see if he can find out who they are. If he doesn't call, I'll try to get a peek at them, get their license number, and have him follow up later. Meanwhile, Shelley, you meet her in Tillie's shop, then drive around a little in her car; don't rush anything. If I'm the one trying to get a make on them, I'll need a little time. And don't look for them. Eventually go to the west end of Skinner Butte Park. Leave the car and take a stroll along the river, then head for your apartment. It isn't likely that anyone would try to follow you on foot; they'll probably wait near the car. We'll send someone to get her car later. If someone does tag along, just take a stroll, use your cell phone to call here or my apartment, and we'll think of something else."

It would take Lara at least half an hour to get from Springfield to the market, another few minutes in Tilly's shop, drive around a little, and then head for the park. By then, Barbara hoped, Bailey would be on hand. If not, they'd go without him. She called Tilly's shop to tell her, or Mae, that an out-of-town guest would drop in and hang out to wait for Shelley, if that was okay. "She's recently bereaved, lost her husband, and is feeling pretty low," she added, and listened for a moment. When she hung up, she said, "They'll try to cheer her up."

When it was time to start, she drove Shelley's car, since she and Frank had both walked to the office that day. "I'll hang out in the Electric Station parking lot and watch for you," she said.

She let Shelley out half a block from the Fifth Street Market—
yuppie heaven, where she fit right in.

Barbara felt too conspicuous sitting in Shelley's bright red
MG, with red leather seats, and tinted windows, and a Pooh Bear
dangling from the rearview mirror. Minutes dragged, the car got
overheated in the sunlight, and she was starting to think there
had been a snag, something had gone wrong, when she spotted
Shelley in the passenger seat of a passing car. Shelley glanced her
way, but made no sign of recognition, and Barbara pulled over
to the driveway to move out into the traffic. Three, four cars
came after Lara Jessup's Toyota, and then, to her relief, she saw
Bailey's old Dodge. His nod was almost imperceptible; she let
out a sigh of relief, and when she joined the traffic, she went
straight back to her office to collect Frank, and then drive to the
apartment complex.

Nearly an hour later, in Barbara's apartment, Lara was explaining how she had come to spot her followers.

"I saw the car yesterday in Bend. I came out of a health-food
store and put things in my car, and I noticed that this man started
his engine. I didn't pay much attention, but then I went to a
different store and when I got back, I saw that the car was still
there, and two men were in it looking at a map. The reason I
noticed that time was because they had turned off the engine,
and cars are ovens out in the sun over there." She shook her
head. "I drove home, and the other car went up Highway 97 in
the same direction. Today, driving through Sisters, I saw it again,
and I remembered that I had seen it in the lot at McCauley's
Cafe, in Salt Creek, when I passed there."

She looked from Barbara to Frank, back to Barbara, and said
slowly, "The car is dark green, shiny and clean, but there's a dull
patch on the hood, as if a dent was rubbed out and not refinished
right, not waxed, something like that, just a dull patch. Other-

wise, I never would have noticed that it was the same car, but I did notice. It's as if I became sensitized to it, and could pick it out from a dozen other cars with no problem at all, and it was always there behind me, sometimes three or four cars back, sometimes closer."

She sounded both defiant and defensive, as if she felt she would be disbelieved, questioned. No one raised a single objection, and she continued.

"I tried to convince myself that it was a coincidence, but I don't think it was. There are a few places where slower drivers can pull over and let faster ones pass; I did that two or three times, and almost everyone behind me did pass, but that car didn't. Then I decided to pull off the road at the mall in Springfield, just to see if they would, too. And they did. Mr. Holloway told me not to mention that I had seen him, and I didn't want to lead anyone to him, so I called."

Barbara studied Lara as she talked, and made many notes to herself to follow up on later. Why so defensive? Why the defiance? Frank had said she was pretty, but that wasn't exactly right. Shelley was pretty, with a Valley girl prettiness that made people smile in appreciation. Lara had a beauty that was deeper than that, a classic beauty of features finely chiseled, with clean lines, high cheekbones, very fine blue-almost-violet eyes, the kind of face that appeared on heirloom cameos. With her red-blond hair curling around her face, she might have been the model for a Greek statue of Athena, or more likely Aphrodite.

One of the questions Barbara knew she would have to ask eventually was why a young woman of such beauty had married a man more than twice her age.

When Lara stopped speaking, Frank said, "You did exactly the right thing, and you showed great presence of mind. Good going."

"I agree completely," Barbara said. She glanced at her watch, nearly five. "Mrs. Jessup, we have a lot of things we have to talk over. And it's getting late. Can you stay over for the night? I don't like the idea of your driving home after dark."

Lara said doubtfully, "I guess I can find a motel room this late. But I didn't come prepared to spend the night."

"You can have my couch," Barbara said, "and I have an extra toothbrush and stuff, and a nightshirt. That's no problem. Will anyone get concerned if you don't return tonight, and don't call?"

"No. I didn't mention to anyone that I was leaving. No one's going to miss me."

"Okay. We have to wait here for a detective to call and tell us what's happened to those two guys, and someone has to go get your car, so we'll have to wait to hand over keys."

"If a man picks up my car, they'll think I'm having an affair or something," Lara said quickly, defensive again.

"I should get it," Shelley said. "They already saw me and probably won't think much of it if I turn up again."

"Not alone," Frank said.

"Right, not alone," Barbara agreed. "Do you have a date?"

Shelley shrugged. "Just Bill. We're going to dinner. I'm supposed to let him know when I'm free."

Poor Bill, Barbara thought. He might have a long wait. She stood up. "Well, I'll see what I can find to nibble on while we're waiting for Bailey to check in."

Shelley got up, too. "If you'll excuse me, I'll give Bill a call and tell him it's off for tonight. Be right back." She hurried from the apartment.

Barbara was rummaging in her kitchen cabinets when Shelley returned carrying a tray.

"I had this stuff around," Shelley said, almost apologetically, and Frank snorted in laughter. She knew as well as he did that Barbara would eventually come up with some rat cheese and possibly some stale soda crackers. Shelley, on the other hand, had brought Brie, pâté, even a tin of smoked clams, and an assortment of breads and crackers.

Barbara grinned at the goodies, and they all began to help themselves. Bailey called at six-thirty.

"They set up shop in the High Street Cafe, on the sidewalk where they can keep an eye on the street," Bailey said. "They know by now that it's the only street out of the park, so they'll watch for her car. I'm staying with them, and Alan's keeping an eye on the car, just in case they bring in someone else."

"Okay. Can you get word to Alan to come over here to pick up Shelley? They'll get the car together. And, Bailey, I don't want strangers to tag along back over here."

He made a rude sound. "Jeez, Barbara, give me a break. Alan will be there in five minutes. He's on his bike. I'll stay with your guys until they light somewhere."

"All set," Barbara said after she hung up. "Shelley, five minutes. I'll drive you and Alan to the barricade at the west side of the park, and you bring the car back here."

Alan Macagno on his bike was a familiar sight around Eugene; he could go anywhere, and did, without anyone even noticing him, any more than anyone noticed the street food vendors. He and Shelley would do fine. Later that night they walked to Martin's and ate his special shrimp gumbo; afterward Shelley volunteered to drive Frank home, and he accepted gratefully.

Then, finally, Barbara and Lara were alone in her apartment, and Barbara asked if it was too late to talk. It wasn't.

They had already told Lara that they had not found a thing in Vinny's box that appeared incriminating, but they wanted to hold the material and have another go at it. Now Barbara said, "Is there a possibility that Manny Truewater removed anything?"

"No. Absolutely not. I don't suppose anyone does the blood-

brother ritual any longer—you know, the pocket knife and mix-
ing of blood—but Manny and Vinny were blood brothers in
every other way."

Unsatisfied but unwilling to press it until she had met Manny
Truewater, Barbara said, "Lara, we're pretty puzzled, as you
know. It could help if you can recall every single time Vinny
mentioned Harris McReady in any way."

Lara was sitting on the couch, Barbara in her good chair, both
of them with coffee cups in their hands. Lara put hers down on
the end table and leaned back. She looked exhausted, and for a
moment Barbara regretted starting a conversation. She decided
to cut it short.

"I've gone over it so many times, it starts to sound phony in
my head," Lara said. "All those years, five years together, and
he never mentioned the name, not once, until March. And even
then I didn't know why he wanted to come over to Eugene for
the lunch and speech. He just said it was something he should
do now and then, to keep his hand in." She looked down at her
own hands and said in a faint voice, "I knew he was ill; I think
I had known it for weeks, but he denied it. Then he asked if I
wanted to drive over; it was unusual because he liked to do the
driving."

She looked at Barbara with a pained expression, as if her
memory was a recurring ache that had not yet started to heal. "I
was so out of place," she said softly. "There were a few other
women, wives, professional women, politicians, I think, city ad-
ministrators or lawyers. . . . I don't know who they all were, but
I didn't belong. I was bored and intimidated." Then, to Barbara's
surprise, she asked, "Did your father ever say you couldn't do
something, not for any reason, just that you weren't capable or
smart enough, or just couldn't do it?"

Barbara shook her head. "I don't think so. He always seemed
to assume I could do whatever I set out to do." In fact, she could

recall times when she had felt as if he had stranded her out on a sandbar in shark-infested waters, expecting her to swim to shore without a complaint.

"All my life," Lara said, looking past Barbara, as if watching a movie on the wall, "first my parents and my brothers, then Curtis, seemed to drill it into my head that I couldn't do things. There, at that reception that day, suddenly I felt as if my father was watching my every move, my mother watching to see that I didn't commit some sort of social blunder, those other women, and many of the men, watching to make sure I behaved properly. Isn't that ridiculous! I thought I had put all that behind me, but you carry such a load of garbage from childhood, all your life, maybe."

Barbara didn't try to nudge her back to the subject of Harris McReady. That would come, but perhaps not until another day. Neither did she signal bedtime. Right now it appeared that Lara wanted to talk, needed to talk, and for now Barbara was content to sit back and listen to her rambling, nearly free-association monologue. She had learned that often a client told her much more this way than she could have found out in a long series of questions and answers.

It was one-thirty when Lara yawned widely, then sat straight up on the couch in dismay. "My God, I've gone on and on. I'm sorry. You must be exhausted."

Barbara was, but she lied and said, "Not as much as you are, I imagine. Let's call it a day. I'll get some sheets and a pillow. Do you want a glass of milk or something?"

Later, after settling Lara on the couch, Barbara made a few notes and thought about the life that had been revealed. Strict parents, religionists who knew exactly what was right and proper and didn't trust their daughter to know anything about either. Brothers who mocked her for her freckles, for her inability to do things they could do, things forbidden to her to try. A husband who had been insanely jealous. And finally Vinny, who had fallen in love with her capable hands, not her beautiful face and body, just her hands; the rest had come later. And she had fallen in love with him, probably not at first, but in time. He had been the first man, the first male in her life, who had recognized a strong, capable woman in her, and he had set out to teach her the truth about herself. But, as she said, all that childhood garbage doesn't go away; it might hide out, but it was still there, ready to reassert itself at the first opportunity, like the chicken-pox virus coming back in the form of excruciating shingles.

She put down her notebook and turned off the light, thinking about the most astonishing revelation of all. Lara did not know how beautiful she was.

Her parents had drilled into her the belief that beauty was a trick of the devil to lure the unwary into sin. To avoid sin, deny beauty. Then fundamentalist Christian schools. No dates until she was seventeen. Then Curtis had come along, offering freedom, a way out, a life not in her parents' house. They married, and six years later his jealousy separated them.

But would his jealousy alone have been enough to drive her away? Barbara doubted it; her upbringing would have made divorce a major trespass, if not a mortal sin. Lara had endured his rages, his tirades, and his spying for the sake of their son. It was when Curtis started calling his son numskull, dummy, stupid that she had recognized a pattern, a reiterative past: her own. She knew she had to leave. She had stayed for her son's sake; she left to save him. Yet even now the burden of her own early years weighed her down: she still couldn't see her own beauty, and she doubted her own competency.

In spite of herself, Barbara could not help thinking how a prosecutor would also use Lara's beauty as a weapon. Lovely young woman, much older man doomed by cancer, insurance.

She could almost hear a summation: Look at her, still lovely, still young, and think of the victim, old and dying. Ask yourselves, was that a real marriage? Could it have been a real marriage? What was in it for her, so young and beautiful? And the only answer is the insurance he carried.

 6

"All right," Barbara said the next morning at her dining table with Lara. They were both having toast, orange juice, and coffee. Barbara had offered either toast or bran flakes; she was out of eggs, she had found to her surprise. "So Vinny didn't refer to Harris McReady after that March speech. When was the next time you saw McReady or Vinny mentioned him?"

"In May, the Sunday before ... Mr. and Mrs. Lynch were having a reception to celebrate their wedding anniversary. I was surprised when Vinny said we should pay our respects, because he had made no secret of his dislike of Mr. Lynch and we'd been invited to other parties and things up there, but we never went. We drove up at around two. There was a crowd milling about on a terrace and in the gardens. McReady and his wife were there. Vinny took me to meet them and the Lynches. But that was all, just to introduce me. We moved on and didn't talk with them, not really. This time I knew several other guests, and it wasn't so bad. After about an hour, Vinny found me talking to Risa Oglespeak and a couple of other people and asked if I'd had enough, and we left."

"Did he say anything about McReady?"

"Not then. We drove up the mountain to the fire lookout and spent a little time looking at the landscape. He said he hadn't been up there in years, and then he said the land didn't change. They could put in houses and streets, but out there nothing changed, not really. Then he said neither did most of the people. Thomas and Anna Lynch were still what they had always been, McReady and Babe—everyone calls her Babe, I think—anyway, they were still the same, a little older, but as unchanged as the land itself in spite of the cosmetics." She looked at her toast, which she had hardly touched. "He sounded sad, distant and sad. That's all he said, and then he began to tease me about my fear of heights. He said I'd been very brave all the way up, but maybe I should keep my eyes closed going down again." She moved her toast away and finished her coffee, her gaze remote and unfocused. "He stopped for just a minute at the turnout where he . . . He didn't even turn off the motor. And he said, 'Isn't that pretty.' I felt as if I was on a diving board above a mile of empty space. Then he drove on home."

Barbara was struggling to keep her frustration from surfacing. "Okay, you and Vinny weren't together constantly that day, I take it. Did he have a private talk with McReady?"

"I don't know. We both mingled with other guests; I just don't know where all he was, or who he might have talked to. I didn't see him and McReady talking, except when he introduced me." Her eyes narrowed, and she said slowly, "He might have, though. Just before he asked if I was ready to leave, I saw him coming out of the house. It's a huge mansion, apparently with a lot of different entrances. Anyway, he came out from one side, and maybe a second later McReady came out from a different door. They could have been together inside."

"Did they meet after that day?"

"There was one more meeting. A luncheon given by a local

judge, and this time I didn't go. Vinny said I'd hate it. Just politics and bad food, that's all it would amount to. That was on Saturday. McReady and his wife stayed with her parents all that week, and he seemed to have had meetings and speaking engagements all the time. Anyway, Vinny went on Saturday."

"Lara, they must have talked about the papers, about delivering them to McReady. When could that talk have taken place?"

Lara shook her head. "I don't know. Maybe on the telephone, not in person. I just don't know."

"Weren't you curious about Vinny's interest in McReady? Didn't you ask him anything about it?"

"I didn't realize he was interested in McReady, not really, except as someone who was politicking for a position on the Supreme Court. Until March, McReady was simply a name, one that I wouldn't have recognized out of context. Vinny never spoke about him. Barbara, you have to realize that I was really frightened about Vinny's health, and McReady was not on my mind. I knew Vinny was worried, upset, but I thought he was afraid, too, just as much as I was. In January when he was supposed to get his regular checkup, he had the flu, a bad case that lingered. Then he put off going, until in May I spoke to our doctor, Norm Oglespeak, and asked him to urge Vinny to go to Portland for the tests. Every other time, twice a year, he had been okay, the cancer still in remission, but I was afraid this time. Finally he told me he had made his appointment for May thirteenth, and I could go ahead and get a hotel reservation, and plan for Nathan to stay with friends. The tests always took several days. I was so relieved, and tried to convince myself that he had just been weakened by the flu, and he was coming out of it at last. But underneath, I was afraid. So McReady was nothing to me."

"All right," Barbara said. "I understand. Tell me about the last Sunday, what you did all that day, how Vinny acted."

"He and Ty Corning had been wanting to take our boys fishing, and Vinny said that Sunday would be perfect. Ty has a small boat, and the boys—Tod Corning and my son, Nathan—are in school together, best friends. They were excited about it. We went to Prineville, the reservoir down there, and spent all day. In the afternoon everyone except Vinny went swimming. He said the water was still too cold, and probably it was, but everyone else swam, and we ate all the food we had brought, and then, since the boys had caught a lot of fish, we decided to go to our house and grill them out on the deck. Vinny sat on a blanket most of the day, watching everyone, smiling. He was very fond of Nathan, and Nathan adored him. . . . Vinny said that it was a perfect golden day, and how rare such days are." She stopped talking and looked at her hands, the way she had done before. Then she continued to tell about the rest of the day.

Her voice became flat, and she gazed past Barbara at nothing. "That night I couldn't stop him. He said he had put off something long enough, too long, that you put things off too long and time runs out. He took his briefcase and left."

"Did he ever talk about Lewis, his trouble?"

"A little. He told me about it, that there had been two murders and Lewis had been arrested, but that he was innocent, and Vinny and another lawyer knew he would not be convicted. He believed that Lewis had been killed. Then they lost the ranch and his wife had a breakdown. He never went into great detail about any of it; it was too painful for him. I thought he had been working to put it out of mind, to start his life over with me, and not dwell on the past, that he had said all he intended to say, and I never asked him any questions about it. I really didn't want to think about it because it had been so ugly and, I thought, over and done with. I didn't talk much about my past life, and he didn't talk about his. We were starting fresh."

For a time neither spoke. Barbara was thinking that Frank had said he'd see them at the office around nine, and Bailey probably would call in at the office. And then what? She had no answer.

Lara broke the silence. "You and your father must have talked about all this. What's going to happen? What should I do?"

"I don't know yet," Barbara said. Then more decisively she said, "Lara, they aren't likely to let this drag out too long, not with an insurance company pushing, and even a faint suspicion of McReady floating around. They could say it was a suicide that someone tried to make look like a murder, or they could say it was murder and a clumsy effort to make it look like a suicide. Either decision could be very bad for you. Why would anyone but a beneficiary want it to look like murder if it wasn't? And there's nothing to implicate McReady at this time. He sticks to his story that he was with his wife and her parents all evening, they back him up, and that's that. I doubt anyone would seriously question Thomas Lynch's word out there. How likely is it that a stranger happened along and committed a murder? Even if he had bitter enemies, how could anyone have anticipated his movements that night? I'm very much afraid they'll come after you. You have to be prepared for such an eventuality, and hope it doesn't happen."

Lara had turned pale with her words, but she was not truly surprised, Barbara understood. She was not stupid.

"Prepared how?" Lara asked.

"Emotionally prepared. There's not a lot you can do except wait. Are you back at work yet?"

"No. Norm, Dr. Oglespeak, said I should take some time off, rest. . . . Right after the Fourth of July, Nathan will be back home. We'll have to sell the house, but I can't do anything until this is settled."

"Want a house guest?" Barbara asked, coming to a decision swiftly. She wanted to meet Manny Truewater and find out more about Lewis Jessup and the double homicide of which he was accused. More about Vinny and his first wife, her death, their ranch.

"Would you?" Lara said eagerly. "I'd be relieved. It's a big house and with no one else in it, it's a little . . ." She spread her hands. "I don't know, just that it's strange being so alone, knowing others have gotten in to search."

Barbara stood up. "You've got a guest. Let's head for the office; there are some things I have to attend to." Her mind was racing; there were matters hanging that Shelley could take care of; she would have to tell Maria how to handle a few things, find out if Bailey knew someone in Bend who could be trusted to put in new locks for Lara. . . . Shelley could fill in for her at Martin's. . . .

Frank was not happy with Barbara's decision to go home with Lara, but in the end he had to admit that they needed more information than they were likely to get from the material in Vinny's box.

"I'll use my middle name," she said. "Barbara Lee. Maybe I can use a few southernisms to make it sound authentic, y'all."

Frank scowled. "Don't. Okay, so you'll go over in her car, and on Saturday Bailey will meet you, have a look around, and drive you home. Right?"

They had agreed that for now no one should know that Lara was talking to criminal lawyers, no license plate should point to Barbara or Frank.

Bailey had said with a shrug that no one would trace a license plate to him, no way. The two men following Lara were holed up in a motel off Highway 126, probably taking turns watching the highway for her car. They were private detectives who worked for the Callagher group in Portland. And no one was likely to find out more than that about them or who had hired them or why. Bailey was philosophical about them, just two guys doing their job, and not doing it all that well.

Barbara was relieved; she had been afraid they were sheriff's detectives, and that would have meant they were focusing too much attention on Lara. She did not mention this to Lara.

At noon they were on the highway, heading east. As they left the outskirts of Springfield, Lara said in a tight voice, "They're back there. Dark green car with a smudge on the hood. Two men."

"Well, ignore them. I've always loved this drive over the mountains. And this time of year is maybe the best, when everything's still so green and fresh."

The highway was busy; tourists were out, trucks, the usual maniacal drivers who felt obliged to pass everything that moved in front of them. Lara was a good driver, but Barbara noticed that she kept her gaze on the road and apparently never once looked at the mountainside falling away from them as they climbed up to the pass.

Then, leaving the village of Sisters, heading for the northern route that bypassed Bend, Barbara said, "I think that for the time being you probably shouldn't say anything on your phone that you don't want broadcast. If private detectives are on the job, they've had plenty of time during your absence to put a tap in place."

Lara made a choked sound, and her hands tightened on the steering wheel.

The landscape had changed from a lush, sometimes impenetrable understory of ferns and vine maples, brambles, and huckleberries crowded together beneath towering dark fir trees to an open ponderosa pine forest, with tree trunks that glowed red in the afternoon sunlight, and pale ground sparsely dotted with gray sagebrush and juniper trees. The air was hotter and drier; Barbara could already feel the drying effect of the high desert on her lips, her cheeks.

They reached the plateau and turned north on Highway 97, and soon Salt Creek came into view. A town of twelve hundred, with a courthouse, a couple of supermarkets, video store, gas station or two, some restaurants, the usual gift shops, and not a lot more.

"If there's a telephone at the supermarket," Barbara said, "maybe we can stop, and I'll browse for lotion and you could give Manny Truewater a call, see when we can get together."

"They're slowing down, too," Lara said in a low voice. She pulled into the supermarket lot and parked. The green car was three car lengths behind; it pulled into a gas station.

When they got out of the car, Lara pointed ahead. "That's the turnoff for the house, over that bridge. Across the street, that's McCauley's Cafe, where they started from before."

"Is that the only road up to your place?"

"Yes. About a mile in, the road forks; one part goes to the house, the other goes past the Lynch house, on up to the fire tower."

And past the place where Vinny's car had gone over the side of the mountain, Barbara thought. She patted Lara's arm and said, "I won't be long." She went into the store, and Lara went to a telephone near the entrance. When they were back in the car going up the road to Lara's house, the other car did not follow them.

The road they were on was a narrow black county road with no markings, just a curving road that started to climb into the pine forest almost instantly.

"Manny said he'll drop in when he leaves his office, around five," Lara said.

"He knows who I am?"

"Yes. I told him."

After a few minutes Lara said, "That's Lookout Mountain Road off to the left."

The road was crushed red lava rock, and narrower than the one they were on. It twisted out of sight immediately. Their road went past a few driveways, past a few houses, and then Lara said, "My house."

The house was built to conform to the shape of the mountain, rising like stair steps up the rocky incline, with the garage at the lowest level. The building was clad in wood the dun color of the surrounding land, the trim the same color as the pine needles, the roof red clay tiles. There was a deck over the garage. Lara turned onto the driveway and then into a garage with an automatic door opener.

Before they got out of the car, she said, "Barbara, maybe I was being silly, schoolgirl silly, but I put some hairs here and there so I could tell if anyone had gotten in while I was gone."

"Good for you," Barbara said. "Let's get my gear from the trunk, and you lead the way."

They went up a few steps to enter a spacious foyer with a high ceiling, with several wide stairs on one side to a living room and dining room, and ahead a narrow flight of stairs going up to a hallway. "I'll show you around and then take you to your room," Lara said, looking at the foyer with a searching intensity. A low table held a basket of thunder eggs, some of them cut and polished, most of them not. A clay planter contained a large philodendron. Lara started up the stairs to the living room. This section of the house was all open, one room leading to the next and the separation of areas achieved by the different patterns of the rugs and curtains and drapes. There were many windows, and so much light made the rooms appear more spacious than they actually were. In the dining room Lara stopped at a hutch and opened a drawer, then nodded to Barbara. Someone else had opened it, too. She stopped at a magazine rack in the living room, then examined the cushions on a rattan sofa, and each time she nodded. The deck continued around the back of the house; the living room, dining room, and kitchen all opened onto it.

"I might as well just take you to your room," Lara said in a faint voice. "You can explore as much as you want."

They retraced their steps, then went up to the narrow hallway, where Lara pointed out Vinny's study and the guest room next to it. Up more steps to Nathan's room and Lara's bedroom, up a few more steps to several more bedrooms.

Barbara's windows afforded a spectacular view of the desert, distant mountains, closer mesas, and even a few houses on the edge of Salt Creek. But, she thought uneasily, this house had altogether too many easy ways in and out, too many big windows that could be opened by anyone determined to get in, too many patio doors that offered no resistance. Tomorrow they would have additional security put in, new locks, bolts, whatever it took to make it more difficult to enter.

"I'll be down in the kitchen," Lara said. "Some iced tea would be good after that drive. Take your time."

When Barbara went down, Lara was finishing making sandwiches. "Tuna on toast," she said. "I'm so used to eating all my bread toasted, I automatically do it. As soon as it's opened, it starts drying out, so I keep it in the freezer."

"Fine with me," Barbara said. "You want to call that company we talked about, you remember, about new locks?"

Lara nodded, and using the phone on the wall next to a patio door, she called the security company.

"Is that the phone Vinny used that night?" Barbara asked when she hung up. Lara said it was. Outside the patio door on the deck was a large table and some heavy chairs. The grill was out of sight. Moving in and out with dishes and things, Lara and the Cornings could have heard every word he spoke on this phone.

"Let's sit out there," Barbara said, and they went out to the chairs that were built not to blow away in a high wind. Barbara closed the patio door after them.

"Tell me something about Vinny's kids, Roger and Alene," she said when they were settled with sandwiches and iced tea.

"They're both pretty special," Lara said. "Alene's a film editor down in San Francisco, and Roger manages a huge wildlife refuge in southern California. Roger always had planned to stay around and run the ranch, but after they lost it, there wasn't much here for him to do. Vinny said he practically drove him away. He said out here there are ranchers, lawyers, doctors, merchants, and Indian chiefs, and everyone else worked for one or another of them. He couldn't stand to see Roger working as a ranch hand, a common wrangler, he said, and told him to get out. Alene was still in college, and he told her to go back and finish her education. He bought this big house because they were still with him, and then he realized that he and Marilyn didn't need such a big place, but he liked it. Alene and Roger were both miserable with guilt for a long time; they felt they had abandoned him and their mother, but he made them get on with their lives."

Lara talked on and Barbara listened intently. She, too, wondered what Vinny had said to them to make them accept Lara, but Lara was obviously not the one to tell her.

They were still talking when they heard a car enter the driveway. Lara stood up and went to the front railing of the deck and called, "We're up here."

In a moment Manny Truewater appeared on the outside steps. Barbara had stood up and moved to the deck railing, and Lara brought Manny over to introduce her, as Barbara Lee.

Before he could comment on the name, while shaking his hand, Barbara said in a low voice, "She was followed to Eugene and back, and I suspect that there could be a bug in the house as well as her phone. We're just admiring the view."

Without missing a beat, Manny Truewater said, "Ms. Lee, it would give me and my wife great pleasure if you and Lara joined us for dinner this evening. You think this view is good, wait until you see the desert from my house."

He would do, she thought. "I'd like that very much."

"Good. I'll drive you over. It's a little hard to find, and getting out again after dark is harder."

"I'll get my purse," Barbara said. And her laptop, she added silently. She didn't want any stranger rummaging in her hard drive. If they planned to stay until after dark, that meant Manny and she would have time to talk, and it meant that he was ready to talk. If he planned to drive them there and back, it could mean he didn't want Lara out on the desert after dark. And, she thought, that sounded like good advice, even if unspoken.

 7

Barbara suspected that Manny Truewater's driving was not always as idiosyncratic as it appeared that afternoon as he drove her and Lara to his house on the Warm Springs Reservation. On U.S. Highway 97, a good, modern road, arrow-straight for the most part, sometimes four lanes, then two, or three with a passing lane, he dawdled, even pulling over to point

out a sight now and then. The road was the main north-south
route through Oregon east of the Cascade Mountains, and it was
heavily traveled; at that time of day it was especially heavily
traveled, but he seemed not to notice. Cars lined up behind them,
then sped past when there were lanes to do so.

Where the land was irrigated, it was fertile and lush, with
wheat fields, pastures with cattle grazing, sheep and goats, gardens, shade trees. Where there was no irrigation, it was high
desert: pale, sun-bleached earth, clumps of sage, scattered grasses
that looked wiry and tough, and rocks. "See that line of cotton-
woods," Manny said at one of the stops on the side of the road.
"Water seepage. A spring. Two, three miles past it there's an
outcropping of jasper, picture jasper, agate, some rough opal.
Good rock hunting."

He was watching cars whiz by, and a faint smile appeared on
his dark face and vanished as the green car with a smudge on the
hood went past. It probably would go up the road and the driver
would pull over and wait for them, as he had done twice already,
no doubt cursing the cat-and-mouse game Manny was playing.

Soon after that Manny turned off the highway onto a dirt
road, and, strangely, now he picked up speed. Barbara glanced
behind them and saw a great cloud of dust billowing up, hiding
everything back there. If Manny noticed it, he gave no indica-
tion. He slowed to a crawl when a ranch house came into sight,
with several boys playing softball in front. He waved; they
waved back. Then, when it was well behind them, he picked up
speed again. And so he drove, fast, slow, turning now and then
from a bad road to one that was worse, and always keeping an
eye on the rearview mirror.

"They gave it up," he said at last. "Or maybe their gas line
got fouled, or something." There was no trace of laughter in his
voice. "Most of the reservation roads won't show on your
maps," he said to Barbara. "Even Vinny got lost back here once."

"I wonder if those guys in the green car will find their way out," Barbara said.

"Eventually, especially if they stop and ask for directions," Manny said, still not laughing.

She was delighted with the airy, spacious house they finally reached, and with the stillness. Not another building was visible, no people, no traffic, not a sound louder than the sighing of wind through sagebrush and whispering juniper needles. Wynona came out to greet them; if she was dismayed or even surprised by two unexpected guests, she did not betray it by a flicker. She held both of Lara's hands for a moment, then shook hands with Barbara when Manny introduced her, and ushered everyone inside. Next to this statuesque woman, Lara appeared doll-like, and Barbara, who rarely felt dwarfed by another woman, felt as if magically she had shrunken. Wynona was not merely tall, her shoulders were broad, her hands and feet were very large; she was not an ounce overweight, just very large.

"You'll want something cold to drink, I imagine," Wynona said, walking into the kitchen. "Cider. Or would you like a Coke instead?"

They had cider, and then Manny said, "We'll be in the study. Call if you want any help." He motioned to Barbara and Lara, and they followed him to another bright room, outfitted as an office. Several rattan chairs with brilliant red and yellow cushions were arranged before more wide windows.

"Have you gone over all the material in the box?" Manny asked.

"Most of it. I didn't read through all the judicial decisions, but enough to get the drift. Dad is doing a much more thorough job with them."

"Lara told me the sort of things she came across, and, Ms. Holloway, I have to tell you I don't know why Vinny collected all that material or what his intentions were for it."

"You'd better call me Barbara. We don't want anyone to know yet that Lara has consulted criminal lawyers. For the present, I'm Barbara Lee."

He nodded, and she said, "Did Vinny give you a hint of what he meant for Lara to do with the box?"

"He said she would know, and obviously she did. She came to you and your father." He looked at her appraisingly. "I know about you, the cases you've handled these past few years, and I've known about your father for a long time. Others around here will know, too, as soon as the name comes up."

"I'm afraid so," she said. "Do you know why he didn't just give you the box and let you take care of the contents?"

Manny hesitated for a moment, then said no.

Lara had been standing near a window, gazing out. She moved toward the door. "I'll see if I can help Wynona."

Neither Manny nor Barbara objected, and as soon as she left, Manny said, "I think he wanted to make certain that the material would end up in the hands of someone who would know how to make use of it. I'm in too close, and I might not be considered objective enough."

Slowly she said, "I read Vinny's brief concerning Lewis, and his correspondence with DeFeo, but it might be helpful if you could give me your take on it. Maybe you know something he left out, or lost. . . . We, Dad and I, are both groping for what his intention was in all that stuff, and nothing has worked for us so far."

He nodded. "We'll need the map." He opened a closet door to bring out a large county map, which he unrolled on his desk. Barbara blinked rapidly; for a moment she had seen John Mureau at their table, opening a big map, bending over it. Pointing, Manny said, "This is Garnet Falls. Over spring break every year a lot of kids come to camp and hike. Susan Cullen and Will Emory came over to spend a week. She was seventeen, he was nineteen. They were in his VW van. All weekend the crowd of kids partied, but on Monday Susan and Will headed out to hike up Three Fingered Jack to a high meadow. For a school project in photography, he was going to do a study of the meadow from the time the snow melted until late fall. It would have been a good project. They took the van up this road, and parked here at the trailhead on Monday, and started up the mountain."

He moved his finger. "This was Vinny and Marilyn's family ranch. That same week Lewis was home from OSU; he was going into forestry. And he had a project, to study a burn up on Three Fingered Jack mountain. It had burned a few years before, and he planned to document how the forest recovered without human intervention."

He traced a road, then a forest service road up the mountain. "He went in over here and parked by daybreak and started up the mountain." The distance on the map did not appear very far from where he had parked to where the two kids had left their van. As if he had read her mind, Manny said, "On foot, half a day. We'd had heavy snowfall that year, and March came in with a lot of rain and warm weather, a lot of snowmelt going on. There are half a dozen creeks coming off the mountain at that time of year, chasms, cliffs, waterfalls, and in sheltered places still a lot of snow. Anyway, he went up. And right about here, there was a landslide. It was still unstable, and when he tried to get around it, a new slide came down and he hurt his hand. He saw that he wouldn't be able to go farther, so he turned around and headed back out."

He pointed to another spot on the map. "He had reached here when he heard someone whistling, and he stopped to warn them about the slide. Susan and Will were on their way to the meadow, and he was on his way down, but the trails crossed here and they all met and talked for a few minutes. The girl said they'd been whistling to warn off bears. He thought that was pretty funny."

Manny paused, considering the map. "Lewis's hand was bothering him more and more, and he began to suspect that he had broken some bones. By the time he reached his truck, he was nearly passing out. He made tea and took aspirin, and finally started for home. Got there around six and went straight to the upstairs bathroom and took a long, soaking bath. A little later when Marilyn saw his hand, she had Roger take him in to the doctor, Norm Oglespeak. Two broken fingers and a lot of cuts and abrasions."

In her mind's eye Barbara had seen it as he talked; she knew how rough that country was, how wild the mountains were, how dangerous and slow the going could get.

"Okay," Manny said. "Back at the trailhead here, a ranger saw the van early in the day, and he checked the box to see if anyone had signed in. They had, and he went on his way. You know about signing in at the trailheads?"

She nodded. You were supposed to sign in—how many in your party, where you were heading, when you expected to come out.

"Later, nearly dark, when he passed by again, the van was gone, and he checked, but they hadn't signed out. He didn't think much of it. Lots of folks forget to sign in or out, and the van was gone. So he assumed they had taken off as planned."

Manny continued to study the map, then put his finger on it once more. "Here, half a mile off the county road, the van turned up on Friday, mostly hidden in heavy brambles. A few kids out hiking spotted it and reported it to the sheriff's office when they got out of the woods, and by Saturday a search was started. They concentrated on the lower mountain for days," Manny said, drawing away from the map. "Lewis hadn't told anyone he'd seen the kids; he was in pain, broken fingers, a hospital visit, a cast, some dope to help him sleep; he just didn't think of them. He went back to school before a search was started. A couple of weeks later he heard about them and realized they must have been the couple he had come across, and he got in touch with the sheriff. If he'd kept quiet, he wouldn't have been involved; maybe they never would have been found." He shrugged.

"Anyway, there had been more rain, more snowmelt, but now the search began again up around the meadow, and the trail leading to it. And they found the bodies here, off the trail, about a quarter of a mile from the trailhead. That's a deep ravine; the trail skirts it for a distance. They had been down there for nearly three weeks by then, and it was hard to tell much about cause of death, or anything else. Animals had got to them."

Frowning, Barbara said, "What convinced Vinny that he and DeFeo could get him off?"

"Pictures in the cameras," Manny said, "for one thing. Lewis had taken a lot of pictures of the landslide. A burn, heavy snow, no ground cover, comes a thaw and the mountain begins to shift, if not immediately, eventually. And the Emory boy had pictures of the meadow in his camera. A good camera, waterproof case, the film was recoverable. The point is, the kids hadn't had time to get to the meadow and back down yet when Lewis saw them. Lewis took his pictures by noon, and the Emory boy's pictures were taken at about three. Anyone could read the shadows and tell what time it was. By four Lewis was nearly back to the truck and by four-thirty he was heading out of the woods on his way home. Although going down would have been faster than going up, it would have been nearly five by the time the boy and the girl got down to the van, or close to it. So that's the first thing.

"Next, the hand injury. Norm Oglespeak would have testified that his hand had been crushed by falling rocks, before noon probably, according to the amount of swelling. And there wasn't another mark on him, just the hand. They couldn't have it both ways. If the boys fought, there should have been signs of a fight on Lewis; if he killed the Emory boy with a club or something, he shouldn't have broken his fingers and scraped the skin off the top of his hand doing it.

"So that's where it stood, at a dead end. School got out and Lewis came home for the summer. The Cullen family was bringing pressure for an arrest. They're the Cullen Forest Products family, lots of money, lots of influence, lots of friends. On July sixth, the sheriff arrested Lewis."

Manny motioned toward the gaudy rattan chairs, and they sat down. "By December Vinny was pretty upbeat," he said. "He had rounded up some witnesses who saw Lewis heading home that day around five. The trial was scheduled for early January. Then, on the twentieth of December Lewis disappeared. He hadn't gone back to school that fall. He was out on bail, under court order not to leave the county, and he spent his time working on the ranch. That afternoon he went out to check the deicers in the water troughs. It can get bitter cold out here in the winter; you've got to keep the water thawed for the cattle, and someone has to go check it every day. He didn't get back by dark, so Roger and Vinny went out looking for him. You don't want to leave anyone out overnight with the temperature dropping down around zero. There was no sign of him or the truck, and they had to head back and try again in daylight. The truck turned up the next day in Bend. And a week later word from the district attorney's office was that there had been a report that Lewis had been spotted in Portland. Two detectives went to collar him, but they said he slipped away again. A few weeks later they said they had confirmed a report that he had been seen in San Francisco, but the detectives didn't find him that time, either. There was another sighting reported in the spring, and after that nothing."

"You said the district attorney's office. Was it from the D.A., or his assistant, McReady?"

"It was Harris McReady's case," Manny said. "Everything was coming out of his office."

Sunlight was starting to enter the study through one of the tall, wide windows. Manny got up to adjust a blind and stood there before the light, a thick, nearly squat man without features.

"Did you find out where McReady was that week in December?" Barbara asked in a low voice.

"Here in town until the twenty-first, when he took off for Spokane, where his parents lived. Specifically, on the twentieth, he was in and out of his office all day, and left around three to go do a little shopping, and then home, an apartment in Bend."

"Anyone with him?"

"No. Just a routine day for him. He was seen shopping, then at dinner, going home after dinner, getting his car filled at the gas station. . . ."

"What about Vinny and Marilyn? Did they go to Portland or down to San Francisco looking for Lewis?"

"No. We spent a month searching the desert for a new grave, searching ravines and gorges and rock piles. As for Marilyn . . . On Christmas Eve she took off on her own, on foot, looking for him. Roger caught up with her and dragged her home. It was snowing, ten degrees. She said she could hear Lewis crying, that she had to find him. She got out again the day after Christmas, and one more time, and then Vinny called in Norm Oglespeak; they sedated her and kept her drugged for a few weeks. But when they eased up, it was the same thing; she could hear her son calling her, crying. She was in a hospital in Portland for a few months, and when she got home, she was different."

His voice was toneless when he continued. "She would sit by the window all day, listening, hardly saying a word, just listening. When she did talk, it was to Lewis. And she cried. Sat by the window listening to him or talking to him, crying. We all thought moving into Salt Creek would help her. It didn't. She went to the hospital and came home to a strange house, and she believed she was being held prisoner there, that it was an institution of some sort. Then, a year later, she had a stroke; she never walked again and she had severe aphasia."

"During that period, did Vinny ever say he blamed Harris McReady personally?"

Manny regarded her soberly, then nodded. "He said he was going to kill him. That was right after Thomas Lynch got possession of the ranch, and McReady was going out with Babe. Vinny said he had to kill him, that it would end only when McReady was dead. That's when he got the big insurance policy, to protect Marilyn. Wynona took him in hand. She made him face the fact that he still had two good kids, and if he did something like that, he would kill them, too. She said Marilyn needed him. That he would be in prison all his life and Marilyn would die in an institution. I don't know what all she said to him, but she brought him around. I don't think he ever mentioned McReady's name to either of us after that night."

Barbara felt a surge of pity for Vinny, his dead wife, his children, mixed with frustration that all of the past was simply a dead end. "Did he have anything concrete, anything real to link McReady to Lewis's disappearance or his arrest?"

"Concrete? No. If he'd found something, he would have torn down the state pressing his case. That's why he said he had to kill him, because he found nothing concrete. But he knew."

"And you? Did you believe that, too?"

"Yes. Then and now. Nothing's changed."

"Why, Manny? There's nothing in those papers to indicate that he was anything more than a prosecutor. Why?"

Manny left the window and went back to the map. He moved with a fluidity that was unexpected, like a cat. "The case looked good on the map," he said as she joined him. "Distances aren't too far, hike a few miles, meet, drive the van down. But there's not a man in the county who knows that area who would go along with it. Vinny and DeFeo planned to haul the jury, judge, prosecutor, the whole crew out there to demonstrate the fact. Make them all hike those few miles. See, the point is, the sheriff, man named Elvin Flemer, he knew that. And the district attorney, Pete Tolman, he knew that, too. But McReady was from Spokane, he'd been here only a few months, and he didn't know that, at least not at first. See here, where the van was found? It stopped there because that line just beyond it is a deep gorge, not very wide, but deep. You'd have to hike six miles to get around it and connect with the forest service road, or else climb down one side and up the other, and you'd need both hands to do that. Lewis didn't have the couple of hours it would have taken, and he didn't have the use of both hands."

After a moment Barbara said, "But the district attorney's office took the case to the grand jury. Why?"

Manny began to roll up the map. "I don't know. Flemer's dead now, died a few years ago, but Tolman's living over at Burns. He didn't run for office again after that case; he retired to his place out on the desert."

"What did Vinny think? Why do you think they went ahead with it?"

Slowly he said, "There was a lot of pressure being brought to arrest someone and convict him. And McReady was a real hotshot, even in those days. He sniffed out the power base from the first day he got here, and he cozied up to it like a snake on a sunny rock. We both thought McReady talked Tolman into letting him have Lewis, let him prove something, and whatever his reasons were, Tolman went along."

"And did it become clear to him that he was going to lose? Is that what you're implying?"

"I'm not implying anything, Barbara. He knew he was going to lose."

She shook her head impatiently and went to the window to gaze out at the desert. "It's not enough. God, it's not nearly enough! You win some, lose some. Everyone knows that. One case doesn't make or break an attorney. Vinny accused him of murdering his son to keep from losing a case. It just won't hold water."

Manny put the map back in the closet. "Sometimes one case does exactly that, make or break a man. This case, by never reaching trial, made McReady. Lynch got the old Jessup ranch, McReady got the Lynch daughter and the position and influence that were part of the package, and he was on his way."

Lara came to the door then to say dinner would be ready in five minutes.

"One more question," Barbara said. "Is there a chance that Vinny found something real, something damning along the way?"

Manny shrugged. "I don't know. But someone out there seems to believe he did. Keep that in mind. Now, let's go eat dinner."

 8

They had a rich and satisfying casserole with venison and many vegetables for dinner; afterward they watched a spectacular sunset that made the rocks look on fire, made the sage glow, and turned the pale desert floor to gold. Barbara found herself thinking how John Mureau had described the desert. He said it was geologists' heaven, where nothing was hidden, every cataclysm left its footprints to be read by anyone with eyes. The most beautiful landscape on earth.

No one talked much, but before they began to gather themselves up for the ride back to Lara's house, Wynona said, "The desert has many faces, depending on who is looking at it. For some, it's a barren wasteland; for others, a fairyland. Some people come out here and recognize home; often for the first time in their lives, they feel they've reached home. There's a belief that wherever your Ancestors took shape from the sticks and stones that formed them, that's home. Ancestors from the coast leave their mark, Ancestors from the mountains, from the desert, they all leave their mark on the genes. When you come home, the genes rejoice."

Barbara thought her Ancestors had dwelled in misty, forested mountains.

"Nathan's Ancestors were from the desert," Lara said after a moment. "The minute he arrived here, he changed; he doesn't want to leave, ever."

Wynona nodded, as if to say she knew that.

Soon after dark Manny brought the Land Rover around and drove Barbara and Lara back to Salt Creek. He entered the house with them and checked each room, and then said that when the security people were done the next day, to give him a call at his office, and he would take Barbara out sightseeing.

The following day when Lara said with a shudder that she did not want to go with them up Lookout Mountain, Barbara thought at least part of the reason had nothing to do with her fear of heights. Lara seemed to accept that Barbara and Manny wanted to talk further in private.

But the fear of heights would have been sufficient reason, she

realized a little later as they drove up the red lava road higher
and higher.

When Manny pulled over at the widened spot, she felt a clutch
of fear in her own stomach. "This is where he went off," Manny
said as he opened his door and got out.

She followed, but stayed well back from the edge. Below,
great volcanic rocks jutted out from the mountainside; there was
little growth on the steep slope.

Manny pointed to the mountain behind them. "That's a
volcano shoulder; the original road came almost all the way
out here, then they did some blasting and took the road in
closer, but left this place as a turnout, passing lane, something
like that."

It was an arc, about fifty feet long, and little more than one
car width across.

"Where did his car go over?" she asked.

He pointed toward a section to the left of where he had pulled
off. Barbara frowned and looked at the road, then at the place
he had indicated. "He must have been on his way down."

"That's how I figure it," Manny said.

"Or," she said, studying the turnoff, "he could have stopped
and turned here and was heading that way when he parked. If
that's how it happened."

Manny shrugged.

"It would have taken some fancy maneuvering," she said. "At
night, no markings on the road, no barrier . . ." She remembered
what Lara had told her; Vinny had not been up Lookout Mountain in years before the day he took her up; he would not have
been that familiar with the road, and he couldn't have seen where
his wheels were that night.

"Kids do it all the time. Come up here and park."

"Here? With all that empty land down there?"

"It's pretty at night. Watch the lights go off down there, come on in the sky. It's pretty."

She shuddered and he smiled. They got in the Land Rover again, and Manny pulled back onto the lava road and rounded the next curve. There was a little stretch of relatively straight road ahead, and a driveway.

"The Lynch property," he said. To her surprise, he turned in there, drove a short distance, and stopped in a white gravel parking area large enough for half a dozen cars, although no other car was there. At the other side she could see broad stone steps going up.

"Their driveway winds around awhile before it reaches the house," Manny said. "Close to a mile. The stairs go up to the gardens."

"Ah," Barbara said then. "He told McReady he'd meet him down by the road. He meant here?"

"McReady said they waited for him up at the house," Manny said. His voice was as toneless as a robot's, his face as impassive as a carving. He backed out of the parking space, turned and drove out to the road, then continued upward. The road was terrifying in its narrowness and in the way it ended at the side, without shoulders, without a guardrail, and many blind curves, sharp and steep. There were half a dozen or more driveways, leading to invisible houses perched on a dormant volcano in a deep woods.

"Do people live here year-round?"

"Some do. The Lynches have the ranch over by the Strawberry Mountains and come up here when it starts getting too hot down there. Others come out from Portland or Salem, spend a few weeks, most of the summer."

They reached the summit, where the fire tower looked like a bird's nest perched on top of a hundred-foot-tall wooden structure with narrow steps zigzagging up its sides. It looked very vulnerable, as if a strong wind might topple it. There was a parking area and a railed lookout. They got out and stood at the rail, and Manny told her what she was seeing in the Lilliputian world below.

"Bachelor Butte at the far right, then China Hat, past it Glass Butte, and then look straight north to the Strawberry Mountains. In the shadow of the mountains, this side, the Lynch ranch, and what used to be Marilyn and Vinny's ranch. Good ranches. Good water, good graze, protected from the northeast winds by the mountains, more rainfall than most parts out here."

After gazing at the landscape for several minutes, Manny said in his expressionless voice, "Now you can understand why we couldn't find Lewis's body."

From here the desert looked nearly featureless, with the occasional butte, a rimrock ridge here or there all that broke the monotony. Everything human had vanished; the desert had reclaimed the land, swallowed buildings, roads—everything built by mankind. Vinny had told Lara the land didn't change, and from here his meaning became very clear. The desert had taken back its own.

Turning away from the vast empty expanse, Barbara looked at Manny and asked, "Are they going to try to make the suicide stick?"

"It depends on who ends up as primary investigators. You've run into a political situation here. As soon as you cross the bridge out of town, you're in the county, the sheriff's domain. He has two deputies, and none of the three could find their shoelaces without help. The sheriff will do whatever Lynch wants. But the state could get involved; they took the car away, and there are special investigators stationed in Bend with jurisdiction anywhere in the state. If it drags on too long, they might get involved. And eventually they might come for Lara. Or the sheriff could beat them to it, if Lynch doesn't want the state to start asking questions. If that happens, if you're the lead attorney, I would like to assist you. My office can be your office, my secretary your secretary. Whatever I have will be at your disposal."

"No one's asked for a formal statement yet. Why not?"

"It's still in the sheriff's hands, and he must have orders to find the papers," he said. "If Vinny had papers that night, they weren't originals, as you know. And as they know. If they can't locate them one way, they may try another. Eventually they'll have to do something. When they decide to move, they'll ask for a statement."

"When that happens, I will advise her to say nothing unless you're there."

He nodded.

They started back down, and Barbara remembered what Lara had said; Vinny had told her to close her eyes going down. Coming up, they had hugged the rocky mountain; going down they skirted the abyss, at times so close, she could no longer see the road on her side.

Then they were on the blacktop road again, and soon they drew near the Jessup house. "Company," Manny said as he slowed to turn into the driveway. "Robert Sheffield's Jeep."

Lara opened the door for them and waved toward the house vaguely. "I think Robert's really looking for you, Manny. He just got here."

They followed her to the bright living room, where a young man jumped to his feet at their entrance. He was very tall, over six feet, and very thin, as if he hadn't had enough to eat in all his life. Like the young Lincoln, all angles and bones, big hands and feet. His hair was a little too long, dark brown and straight, his eyes chocolate brown, features instantly forgettable, but his long, gaunt frame was not. Lara introduced him, and there was an awkward pause, during which Barbara remembered what she had heard about him. Thirty, a new attorney in town, he and Manny had jointly inherited Vinny's stranded clients. He looked too unsure of himself, too hesitant to make much of an impression.

"Manny, I called your office and Nadia said I'd find you here," he said, still hesitant, wary of Barbara. "I'd like just a word with you and Lara, and I'll be on my way."

"Barbara can hear anything you have to say," Lara said quickly. "I have no secrets from her."

He looked doubtful, but Manny nodded and sat down solidly on one of the comfortable chairs. "Been showing Barbara around a bit," he said. "So what's up?"

Sheffield still looked uncertain, and Lara sat down on the couch and motioned Barbara to a chair. With a touch of impatience, Lara said, "Robert, whatever it is, just tell us. Sit down."

He sat down uneasily. "It's just a rumor I've heard around," he said. "Probably nothing to it. You know how rumors get around in a place like Salt Creek. Anyway, I wanted to tell you and Manny." He was eyeing Barbara again. She returned his gaze placidly and did not say a word.

"So, tell me," Lara said.

He shifted his lanky frame as if the chair did not fit well, and that was exactly right; no chair in the room would have been a good fit. "Well, what I heard is that the sheriff is saying maybe Vinny shot himself up there that night. Maybe you knew something was wrong and went up after him and found him, and you made it look like a possible murder, to save his kids the burden of his suicide. Not to defraud the insurance company or anything like that, but just to keep it cleaner for the kids' sake."

Lara gasped and shook her head. Before she could speak, Manny said, "You know that's not true."

Robert Sheffield blushed and ducked his head. "I know that," he mumbled. "But I thought you should know what they're considering."

"What else?" Lara demanded. "They didn't stop there, did they?"

"They think that there weren't any papers or anything else that he wanted to hand over to Judge McReady, that he said that just as an excuse to get out, and go up where he could look at the desert at night before he died. If there had been any documents, copies would have turned up, or you would have found them and turned them over. They're saying that if you, a trained nurse, found him, you would have known he was dead, that he couldn't be helped, and you just lost your head and did what you thought you had to do."

Lara jumped up and ran from the room, her face colorless. Robert was on his feet as swiftly as she, and was nearly as colorless as he watched her run out. Manny watched them both impassively, and Barbara didn't move.

After a moment Barbara asked, "Does that mean they would label it a suicide and close the case, be done with it?"

Robert turned a blank gaze toward her, as if he had forgotten her. "Something like that," he said. "They would accept an Alford plea. She would agree not to press for an insurance settlement, agree to take her son and leave the area. . . ." He took a breath and started to walk toward the stairs to the foyer. "I thought she should know what they're saying," he said, almost as if to himself. "Manny, you're going to stick with her, aren't you? As her attorney?"

Manny nodded.

"Good. She needs someone. . . ." He hurried down the stairs, then stopped and turned once more. "Manny, if she knows anything about documents, what they are, where they are, for God's sake, tell her to turn them over and be done with this." He hurried across the foyer and out the door.

"Well," Barbara said. "Well, well."

 9

"There are several possible scenarios," Barbara said on Saturday night to Frank. "None of them involves McReady directly. He had an alibi. One, Lewis got spooked and ran. Two, whoever killed those two kids also killed Lewis and drove the truck to Bend later that night. Three, someone was hired to do the same thing. Four, a stranger passed by and didn't like the way he combed his hair, and bingo! Five"—she paused and regarded Frank with a speculative gaze—"Lynch and his crew did the work, in collusion with McReady." She shrugged. "Or he fell down a rabbit hole."

"The point is," Frank said brusquely, "at this late date, any one of those possibilities is as likely as any other, and you're not going to prove a damn thing about that. Vinny Jessup had seventeen years to work it out and there's nothing in any of the papers I've read to indicate that he ever did."

She agreed. "So, we're left with other possibilities. Vinny never had anything real to show McReady, about the death of his son or anything else. Or he had documents and they vanished into thin air. Or Manny swiped them. Or Lara did. Or he had something, and it's still in that box." She added softly, "But,

Dad, someone thinks there are papers somewhere, and the opening gambit has been played. The Alford." An Alford plea meant that Lara would not have to admit to guilt, but she would have to admit that her guilt could be proven. It was the most tempting plea the state had to offer.

"If there's anything in that box, it's written in invisible ink between the lines," Frank said.

They were on his back porch with the evening settling in around them, a dusky, dim twilight shadowing the garden, the air still and heavy. A slow-moving front had come ashore, according to the weather reports, and rain would cross the Coast Range later, and start in the valley during the night and continue into the following day. Some years it didn't rain from May until October, or it might rain day after day in June; some years the rain hit the day after school got out, Barbara remembered from her childhood, and it had seemed that in those years there had not been enough summer to get tired of it. Now, after only a few days out on the desert, she would welcome a misty rain.

"What about the Cornings?" Frank asked after a minute or two of silence.

"Vinny handled a problem for them a few years ago; they were indebted to him, and they were friends. Besides, they went home and were seen by neighbors unloading their van, unhitching the boat, things like that. Impossible for them to have gotten back up to the mountain by ten or even eleven."

Frank gazed out over the garden unhappily. Lara or McReady; he groaned. "If Lara had anything of interest to anyone on earth, at this point I'd advise her to hand it over, call it a suicide, and get out of this mess. She's young, pretty, and skilled; she'd make out all right."

Gravely Barbara said, "Well, you're the writer in the family; maybe you could come up with some documents for her to hand over, enough to get them off her back."

Frank didn't snarl at her; he never snarled at her, but he gave her a very mean look.

If it weren't for her overnight bag and laptop, she would walk home, Barbara thought then. She loved the walk at dusk, when the trees gradually became black, the shadows purple, and the river turned into a silver secretive waterway that held mysteries. But she had asked Bailey to drop her at Frank's house, and she had burdens to carry home. She stood up and stretched.

"Get a lift?" she asked.

"Whenever you're ready."

Frank took her home and waited in the car until she was inside and, she suspected, until he saw her lights come on upstairs. He would have seen her all the way to the door if she had allowed him. Upstairs, in her apartment, she opened windows, turned on a window fan, and made a pot of coffee. It was nearly ten and she would be up for hours keystroking in notes on Lewis, Manny Truewater, Salt Creek. . . .

At ten-thirty her door buzzer sounded. Frowning, she went down the stairs to the ground-level entrance and peered out the peephole. A man was standing outside on the stoop, his back to her, his head lowered.

"John," she whispered.

For a long time neither of them moved; then he started to leave, and she opened the door.

Silently she moved aside for him to enter. It seemed that everything was happening in a dreamlike manner, their movements in slow motion, their silence, searching gazes. Dreamlike: climbing the stairs with him close behind her, entering her own apartment, standing apart, careful not to touch each other. His scarred face was taut; she could see the blood pounding in the veins in his temples. She felt light-headed, as if her blood pressure had plummeted.

"I had to see you," he said at last. "Oh, Christ—"

She turned her back and shut her eyes hard. "John, don't do this. I'm still who I was then. Nothing's changed. The same choices, the same decisions, the same hurt. We don't need that again."

He put a hand on her shoulder, his other hand on her arm, and very gently pulled her around to face him. "Look at me, Barbara. Please. You're the best thing that ever happened in my life, and I blew it. You can't know how ashamed I am. How sorry I am." He touched her cheek. "Look at me. If you tell me to go away, that you don't care, that you despise me, that you don't want me in your life, I'll leave."

She opened her eyes. "We'll kill each other," she whispered. "No one can hurt either of us the way we can hurt each other."

"I know," he said. "I know."

They made love, frenzied, out of control, savage even, and she slept, or fainted, or passed into a deathlike state, or something. When she opened her eyes, he was propped up on his elbow watching her.

"I remember the first time you did that," he said softly. He touched her cheek. "And the first time you cried."

They made love again, slowly this time, tenderly rediscovering each other's body, her body rediscovering the feel of his hands on her, his mouth on her; her hands rediscovering his scars, his ribs, the twin hard muscles that formed a valley for his spine. . . .

They dozed, locked in an embrace. Her arm was numbed by the weight of his body, and she shifted; later he pulled his hand from under her, and they slept. Once she stirred, smelling rain, and thought that she should get up and close windows, but he was asleep and she didn't move, then drifted back into sleep.

The next time she came awake, it was to smell the rose verbena soap she liked and, more strongly, coffee. She got up and put on a housecoat, then went to the kitchen barefoot, to see him standing at the window over the sink, gazing out. It would be just like before, she thought suddenly with a bleakness that made her want to weep.

As if sensing her presence, he turned and smiled. His hair was still wet from the shower and he had not shaved. His eyes were luminous, his smile infectious. "Sit down and I'll bring you coffee."

She sat at the table and watched him pour the coffee, watched him bring his cup and hers and seat himself across from her.

"Why did you come back? Nothing's changed. I'm still who I was; I do what I've always done."

"Something's changed. We both know the kind of power we have over each other."

She sipped her coffee, then said, "Something else changed, too. I didn't know before that I could put you in a position where you had to choose between me and your children. I didn't fully understand what that meant. Now I do."

He nodded. "If you were a cardiologist, you wouldn't talk about every bypass, every heart murmur, every valve job, and I wouldn't expect you to. And neither would I question any procedure you might use. God knows I wouldn't ask you to abandon a patient in midstream, lay down the scalpel, and walk out. I was out of line and I know it. I'm sorry. You have a professional life, and so do I. No questions, no comments. And I'd never again ask you to shoulder the responsibility for my kids. That's my job."

She watched her hands holding her coffee cup, both of them, as if the cup were in danger of slipping away. "It didn't work before," she said. "We tried, I tried, and it didn't work."

"Not like before. I don't want a housekeeper and cook. I want you. I have to go up to Canada—come with me. Spend a week in the mountains up there; let's talk about it."

"I can't," she said. She thought of all the past months, the weekends hiking, all the books she had read, the weekdays spent watching the clock spin out the minutes in slow motion, all the free weeks. Weeks alone. She shook her head. "I can't leave right now."

"All right. But hear me out. In March the Arizona School of Mining asked me to fill in for a professor who dropped dead. I did, and now they've offered me a tenured professorship. My old alma mater wants me back. I said yes. Barbara, we could be together, not like before, but in our own house, as big as you want, as big as I want, your own offices, your own professional life. Two professionals working two professions. No questions, no comments. I would still do consulting, poke around holes in the ground; you would still have a practice. But when we're not wrapped up in things, when we're done with work, we would be home together. It would be different."

She stood up and walked to the window. It was raining, not a serious rain, but steady.

"I don't expect you to decide right now," John said, coming to her side. "But, God, Barbara, if ever two people needed to be together, we're them."

"I need some time," she said faintly. "How long are you staying here in town? Where are you staying?"

"I have to leave almost instantly," he said. "I'm supposed to be at a noon meeting tomorrow. I detoured to see you."

Detoured from Arizona to Oregon? She closed her eyes and shook her head. "So you've had a chance to work it all out? Solve all the problems?"

"No. All I could think of was seeing you. I hoped you'd be free so we could camp out and work things out together in the woods. All I could think of was seeing you," he said huskily.

They made love again, and afterward showered together; then Barbara drove him to his motel and stayed until he packed up his few things and got into his camper van and left. Then she sat in her own car and watched the rain making erratic tracks on her windshield. It was strange, she thought, that she couldn't track a single drop all the way down the glass; the drops ran crazily this way and that, merged, and were lost.

It was still raining when Barbara entered her office later that Sunday. Frank was there, rereading some of the files from Vinny's box.

"If there's anything, I sure as hell can't find it," he said, disgruntled. Looking up at her then, he stopped. There were times when he felt he had been caught up in a time vortex, past, present, future all intermingled in a way that made him doubt his eyes, or even his sanity. She looked so much like her mother at times, and then in a flashing instant he saw her as a child—approaching a baby elephant in a petting zoo, with a look of wonder, reverence, awe, and determination. At those times she seemed to have glimpsed something he couldn't see, the universe had opened a window for her to peer through, had revealed something he could only dimly comprehend. Then she became the wily, supersmart attorney possessed of an intuitive grasp of reality that was fearsome. He didn't understand how the turn of her head, a fleeting expression, a shrug, the way she sometimes shook her head in impatience, how any of that could have been passed on to her in her genes, but they were all expressions inherited from her mother, and now, avoiding his gaze, dreamy-eyed in an unsettling way, with a soft smile that was reminiscent of the awkward adolescent she had been, she looked strange and unknowable.

She sat at her desk and regarded him for a moment. "John came by last night," she said.

He tried to keep his face neutral, tried hard not to reveal his disappointment, his rage that had not diminished over the past months, but he knew she was aware of his feelings. He didn't say a word.

"He wants us to try again," she said softly. "On a different basis. No playing housekeeper or cook in my future. Just two people who are willing to try again."

She waited for him to respond, and when he didn't, she said, "Dad, you told me that once you sent Mother and me away until a trial was over, done with. And I recall another time when suddenly we left town. It happens. For my safety, for hers, you knew we had to leave. He knew the same thing, he had to get out for the safety of his children. I put him in that position, and he did what he had to do."

It hadn't been the same, Frank wanted to say. John had had choices, and he made a bad one. He could have left his kids with their mother back East, where they were safe; he didn't have to bring them here, where they weren't. He held his tongue. He stood up and looked at the piles of papers he had been sorting through. "I've had enough of all this for now," he said. "I'll be going."

He turned away from the look she gave him, pleading, beseeching, whatever it was, and started for the door. There he stopped and looked back at her. "If they indict Lara Jessup, are you still going to take her on? You realize you'll be spending a lot of time east of the mountains?"

She nodded. "I know. I already told John I'll be tied up for the next few months."

He left and she remained at her desk, unmoving, for a long time. He hadn't invited her to dinner, she thought distantly. He thought she would slight Lara Jessup, not give her the time it would take to prepare a case. He had not accepted John's decision to leave and still thought of it as abandonment. He didn't trust her, Barbara, to keep her head. . . . She clenched her hands and felt tension settling in her shoulders, remembering Frank's unease when John first appeared on the scene, his unspoken warning about him then, how gradual his acceptance had been when she and John first got together, how guarded he had been. What had he seen then? What was he seeing now? She shook her head angrily. She couldn't live her life according to her father's prescription of what was best for her, his ideas of propriety, of honor. When she realized how angry she had become, she stood up and walked back and forth a few times in the office, then went out to the reception room and back, walking faster and faster, as if her feet were trying to keep up with her thoughts.

Inside her office once more, she regarded the various piles of documents, papers, clippings, and she knew she couldn't concentrate on any of that material right now. Harris McReady was a power-hungry bore, but that was not a crime. Lara Jessup would be indicted for murder, and no one—not Barbara, not her father, no one—could do a lot for her. She wished she had never heard of Lara Jessup.

10

How strange, Lara thought that Sunday morning, out here they ring bells when it rains. Then she bolted upright in bed and reached for the phone.

"Lara? Are you awake? It's Stephanie. We have an emergency, a bus and a truck tangled up on McKenzie Pass. They're bringing in a load of hurt kids. Can you come in?"

"Ten minutes," Lara said. Stephanie Calder was the night nurse on weekends at the hospital in Bend. Lara dressed swiftly, poured a glass of orange juice, and took it with her to drink on the way. It was ten minutes before seven.

All day three doctors and five nurses worked on seventeen injured teenage kids who had been on their way to a church camp. During the day someone put coffee in Lara's hand and she drank it, and later someone else gave her a sandwich and she ate it; she assisted in the operating room for three surgeries and helped set two broken legs.

Then someone took her arm and said, "Sit down awhile." It was Risa Oglespeak, who had been on the phone most of the day contacting parents, making arrangements for two medical evacuations to specialists in Portland. Risa was seventy-something and she looked ancient, drawn and pale, her hands shaking with spastic movements, but her voice was firm and brooked no argument. Lara sank down into a chair in the lounge; exhaustion hit her like an avalanche.

"Things are under control," Risa said, "and I'm dragging Norm out of here for a meal and a break. You need a break, too."

"Mrs. Jessup, I wonder if I could have a few words with you?" someone else said from the doorway.

Lara looked around, startled to see Sheriff Gouin standing in the doorway with another man at his shoulder. They entered the lounge. Norm Oglespeak was close behind them, still in his operating-room greens, now splattered with blood.

"No, you can't," Norm said.

"I just have a few questions, and while she's right here, seems it might be a good time to get at them."

"Sylvester, don't be a bigger jackass than God intended for you," Norm snapped. "Anything you have to ask can wait until tomorrow. That girl's been on her feet for twelve hours. We're going to take her home with us, feed her some supper, and send her off to bed."

The sheriff's mouth tightened, but before he could say anything, Risa said, "If you have even a trace of a brain, you'd better use it and get out of here before Norm puts you to work emptying bedpans."

The sheriff looked from her to Norm, then he turned to Lara and said stiffly, "I want to see you in the morning. Ten, your place." He walked out. The other man followed.

"Idiot," Risa said. "Norm, get out of those clothes and let's go home. Lara, we'll drive you to the house with us. Later on, Norm will bring you back and you can get your car, when he checks on those kids."

Lara felt almost as if she should salute, but she was too tired. While they waited for Norm to change his clothes, Risa outlined the schedule she had made up for the coming week. Lara was due the next day at noon, if she managed to get rid of that idiot sheriff by then, and for the rest of the week she would be on the early shift, starting at six in the morning. Risa didn't ask if that was acceptable, but stated it as a fact; no one ever argued with Risa, and Lara didn't now. The hospital held forty beds, seldom all in use at once, but now they were, and the staff would all work long hours for the next few days.

Norm drove and no one spoke until they reached their sprawling house on the mountain. Norm left the car in the driveway, and they entered by a side door, where he yelled, "Martha! We're here. Three of us."

Lara realized belatedly that they hadn't planned on her coming with them, that it had been an impromptu invitation that she should have refused, but she had been too tired.

"Damn shame you don't drink," Norm said, leading the way to the living room. "Because if three souls ever needed a drink, they're us, and the time is now. Risa?"

"God, yes! Bourbon, straight, and water."

"See?" Norm said, grinning. He went to a side table and poured two large drinks, and handed one to his wife. He was a tall, rangy man with long, bony fingers that looked clumsy until he was with a patient, holding a scalpel, applying a bandage, delivering a baby, feeling for a pulse. He did it all, he sometimes said, a bad habit, a carryover from the days when he and Risa had been the only staff the hospital had. It was his hospital; everyone knew that. He ran it like a little fiefdom, but now the HMOs were crowding him, making demands, requiring more damn paperwork than a government agency, he complained. It was generally thought that he would retire soon, that he could not stand so much interference. He poured water into a glass, looked at it suspiciously, and stalked out with the pitcher. Soon he returned with fresh water. "That damn woman wouldn't change the water from one month to the next if her life depended on it."

He handed a glass of water to Lara, then held up his whiskey in a toast. "To the workers of the world. Us. Cheers. Martha said we can eat in ten minutes."

In the past when Lara had come to this house with Vinny, she had never felt comfortable, and she suspected that neither had Norm or Risa. They and Vinny had been contemporaries, she an outsider, an underage outsider, and Norm still thought of her as a girl, but the atmosphere tonight was different, as if they accepted her in a way they hadn't been able to before.

"You're a good nurse," Norm said suddenly. "Good in the operating room. You did a good day's work today."

"Thanks," she said, surprised. He had never complimented her before, but seemed to have taken for granted that she could do the work he had hired her to do.

"I'm going to wash up," Norm said. "You know where the powder room is down the hall? Risa, want to come along with me?"

Lara understood that they wanted a few minutes in private. They all walked into a wide hallway together; Norm and Risa started up the stairs, and she kept going straight through to the powder room, wishing again that she had turned down their invitation, wishing she were home with some cheese and bread. She was too tired to make conversation, too tired to respond to anything others said.

Martha had placed dinner on the dining room table: bowls of vegetables, a large bowl of salad greens, sliced tomatoes, and a lamb roast that Norm sliced and served. All three of them were hungry and didn't talk as they ate dinner.

Then, sipping coffee, Norm said, "Lara, the sheriff's been asking questions about you in town and at the hospital. I told him he couldn't see your personnel file, but he got a court order that let him do it. And they went through your locker. I couldn't stop them."

When she started to speak, he held up his hand. "Wait, there's more. One of my patients passed on a rumor that they're going before the grand jury in July and ask for an indictment. If they ask for it, it's a done deed, you understand."

"For what? I haven't done anything."

"I don't know for what. Obstruction of justice? Tampering with an official investigation? Withholding evidence of wrong-doing? Maybe even for murder."

She reached for her coffee, but her hand was shaking too much to pick up the cup; she put both hands in her lap.

"Lara," Risa said then, "the point is, you need a lawyer. Not just Manny. They've been gunning for him for a long time; he's like waving a red flag in the bullring."

"She's right," Norm said. "Silly Gooey ordered me not to mention a word to you." He pronounced *ordered* as if it were a dirty word. "After tonight he'll probably suspect that I've told you what little I know, and he could play hardball. You probably shouldn't see him until you've talked things over with Manny, and you definitely should not see him alone, or if you're beat. If you're not up to it tomorrow, tell him to chase his tail. The grand jury won't meet for a couple of weeks; you have a little time."

"What kind of questions was he asking?" Lara asked faintly. Her throat had constricted until she could hardly swallow; her voice was hoarse.

"Bullshit nonsense. Your relationship with Vinny, when you took separate bedrooms, if you fought, if you both knew his cancer had come back, if you were suspected of improper be-havior with patients." His blunt words and brusque manner softened, and he added, "Lara, I couldn't keep him out of the file or the locker, but I didn't have to tell him a damn thing. I didn't have anything to tell him." He looked at his watch, then drained his cup and set it down. "I have to go check on a couple of those kids in the ICU. Ready?"

They left Risa sitting at the table with a second cup of coffee. Probably she would smoke a cigarette or two now; everyone knew she did, but never in front of Norm.

At the hospital parking lot, Norm drove directly to his reserved space and they got out. "I'd say take the day off tomorrow, but I can't afford that luxury," he said. "I'll need you."

"I'll be here," she said. "And, Norm, thanks. Thanks a lot." He strode away and she turned to go to her own car farther down from the entrance. As she drew near it, two men stepped forward from the shadows, and one began taking flashbulb pictures of her automobile. The second man was the stranger who had been with the sheriff earlier.

"We won't be here more than a minute or two," he said politely.

She stood motionless for a moment, then walked to her car, unlocked the door, and got inside. The photographer was still taking pictures when she turned on the ignition, then her headlights, and started to back out. He moved to the driver's side and took several more pictures as she left the parking lot.

She drove in a daze, and when she was inside her own garage with the overhead door shut and locked, she started to shake. Then, moving fast through the empty house, she checked all her doors and windows, closed drapes, drew blinds, and finally sat at her kitchen table and pressed her hands hard against her eyes.

Improper behavior with patients. The words reverberated in her skull like a mantra. Curtis had done this—he had told them that. His insane jealousy, his accusations, his hatred had surfaced again. His words, his hateful, hurtful words were still in her head with as much power as on the day he had used them like a bludgeon: "You give them a little extra rub where it feels good, don't you? A little extra thrown in. Let them peek down your front at your titties. A little mercy fuck now and then."

Then, later, when she told him she was leaving: "You think I'll just sit back and moan and cry? You think I won't fight you all the way? Think again, sweetie. I'll get you. You'll pay for this. You'll pay, baby. I've been good to you, given you everything, and now you've got a fat cat on the string and I'm not good enough anymore. You'll see who ends up paying the price!"

The next morning Manny arrived before Sheriff Gouin. When she told him exactly what Norm had told her, his mouth tightened. "Let's hear what he has to say, and go on from there. I'll step in if he gets out of line."

Then the sheriff arrived, again accompanied by the unknown man.

"Detective Sergeant Poole," the sheriff said curtly.

To her surprise, it was Poole who seemed in charge now. He took a tape recorder from his briefcase and asked, "Do you mind if we tape the interview? It helps keep things straight."

Manny brought out a second tape recorder and set it on the coffee table. "If you do, I do," he said.

Sheriff Gouin frowned. "Now, Manny, don't get your back up. You know this is routine."

"So you won't mind if I tape also."

Poole shrugged. "Fine with me."

He spoke into the tape recorder, gave the date, who was present, the time of day it was, and then said, "Mrs. Jessup, we'd like a little background first. When did you first meet Vinny Jessup?"

Surprised again, she said, "Nearly seven years ago, when he was a patient in the hospital where I worked, in Portland."

"Were you married at the time?"

"Yes."

"At that time did you and Mr. Jessup form a friendship? A relationship?"

"No! He was extremely ill, undergoing chemotherapy, radiation treatments, and a bone marrow transplant. He was a gravely ill patient, that's all." In fact, she remembered, Margo Sealey, who was usually infallible in such matters, had pronounced him a loser. "The guy in four oh two is a goner," she had said matter-of-factly.

"Did you see him outside the hospital during that period?"

"No." She had hardly been aware of Vinny's discharge at that time; she had been preoccupied with finding a divorce lawyer, arranging payments of a lawyer's fee, preparing for a custody fight, facing scene after scene with Curtis. . . .

"When did you see him again after that?" Poole asked. He had a notebook that he referred to time and again, as if checking her answers against other information there.

"When he came back six months later for a checkup. He noticed that I didn't have my wedding ring on, and he asked me to go out for coffee with him."

"Were you still married?"

"I had filed for divorce by then."

Suddenly Manny spoke. He had been leaning back in a chair with a distant look on his face. "Maybe we could move on," he said blandly.

Poole gave him an equally bland look and asked, "When did you learn about Mr. Jessup's insurance policy?"

Lara felt her stomach tighten and the muscles in her face stiffen. "About three years ago, when I started to work at the hospital here."

"Why'd you go back to work?" the sheriff asked then. "Vinny had enough to support a wife."

Poole looked annoyed, as if he had planned his questions with a certain sequence in mind, and this threw him off track.

"I knew I would be responsible for my son's education," Lara said.

"You mean Vinny wouldn't spring for it? Was he tight with you?" Gouin asked before Poole could bring the questions back in line.

"Nathan's education was not Vinny's responsibility," Lara said. "That's all I mean."

Poole made a gesture to Gouin, and the sheriff subsided, frowning at Lara. "Did you read the insurance policy at that time, three years ago?" Poole asked.

"No, not then, not later. I never saw it."

"Did he explain it to you?"

"No. He said he had taken out insurance to protect his former wife if necessary, and he had kept it up. That's all I knew about it."

"Mrs. Jessup, what were your arrangements about your son's visits with his father?"

Lara was taken aback by the shift, and she had to think a second. "I'm the primary custodial parent. I agreed to drop off Nathan and pick him up every other weekend, and for alternate holidays, and during the summer vacation, when he spends a month with his father."

"What did you do in Portland after you left him with his father?"

Suddenly she felt her cheeks burn and she realized that Curtis had told them what he suspected.

"You think I don't know what you're up to?" he had snarled at her. "You ditch old moneybags for a weekend, dump the kid off on me, and shack up with someone, don't you?" He had followed her to a motel and waited for her return; she had been to a movie.

"Where's Nathan?"

"He's in bed, where he belongs. You expecting company at this hour? Who is he?"

"Get out of here! Does he have a sitter?" From the look on his face, she knew the answer. "If you ever leave Nathan alone again at night, I'll take you back to court."

"Mrs. Jessup, I asked what you did after you left your son."

Slowly she said, "I usually picked him up at school, and we drove up to Portland. I turned around and drove home most of the time. During the winter months, when the days are so short or the weather's bad, I sometimes stayed in Portland for the weekend and brought him home on Sunday."

"Did you stay with friends the times you remained up there for the weekend?"

She shook her head. She had no real friends in Portland. Making and keeping a friend had been impossible for years. "I stayed in a motel."

Poole turned the page in his notebook. "All right. Is that still your routine?"

"No. Nathan goes on the express bus and comes back the same way usually."

"Whose idea was that?"

"His, mine, all of us decided he was old enough to go alone. I went with him the first time, just to make sure it would be all right."

"Was it Mr. Jessup's idea?" Poole asked in the same bland, almost uninterested manner.

"No. Not specifically. We, the three of us, talked it over and made the decision." She paused, then added, "I call a-head and order a cab to meet the bus, and he takes a cab from Curtis's apartment back to the bus station. I meet him at this end."

"When did you start doing it that way?"

"Last winter. When Vinny became ill with the flu, I didn't want to be gone all weekend."

Poole nodded. "Please, for the record, tell us again about the night Mr. Jessup died. You had dinner on the deck with the Cornings, then what?"

She went through it again, exactly like before, almost as if reciting a lesson she had memorized.

"So you did the laundry without waiting for Mr. Jessup's clothes?"

"Yes. He hadn't gotten so muddy, not like the rest of us. I did laundry, took a bath, read awhile, and then fell asleep on the couch."

He nodded and closed his notebook. But Gouin was not finished. Roughly he asked, "When you knew Vinny didn't come home, why was your first thought to call a lawyer and not the police?"

She had no good answer. "I thought I needed a friend."

As soon as they were finished and left, she turned to Manny. "Who is that man? Poole?"

"He's with the state police. Special Investigations Department." He headed for the kitchen. "I'll call Barbara."

✧ 11

Waiting for Bailey to arrive that Monday afternoon, Barbara went to the reception room to make coffee. She had warned Bailey the day she had tacked up her shingle that she did not intend to keep a well-stocked bar the way Frank did; if he wanted anything to drink in her office, he would have to settle for coffee, tea, or water. Deadpan, he had asked, "Not even a six-pack tucked away in a file drawer?" A six-pack would be more in line with the kind of clients she had gotten those first few months, but no, not even that. She had relented only to the extent of a few cans of soda in the tiny fridge.

Maria Velasquez gave her a reproachful look when Barbara measured out the coffee, but Barbara had told her early on that she was to be a secretary, not a waitress. "I thought I could make coffee, do little things like that," Maria had said. "I would be happy to help out in little ways."

"I know, and now, today, you would be, but in a few months, a year from now, you might feel differently. My office, my rules." And now, six months later, Maria still gave her a hurt look over one of the little things, making coffee.

"When Bailey gets here, send him on back," Barbara said, and returned to her office to pace and think.

When he arrived, it sounded as if he were trying to kick down her door. She opened it to see him standing with a tray, the carafe, cups. . . .

"Maria said since I was headed this way, maybe I could save you a few steps," he said, then grinned. He was as disreputable as ever in appearance, ill-fitting clothes that were years out of date, not exactly unshaven, but rather as if his last shave had been quite a while ago, and his hair could stand a trim, but it always looked that way, and she couldn't understand how that could be. At least if she got a haircut, it showed for a time. He passed her and put the tray down on the table, and then slouched down on the couch. "I carry, don't pour," he said.

She poured, then seated herself in one of the comfortable chairs opposite him. "It's the Jessup case," she said. "I want us to move, but slowly." She told him what Manny had reported to her. "He'll make a copy of the tape and send it over, but he and I both think they're still trying to put a scare in her, soften her up. Telling the doctor about the grand jury, giving her two weeks before anything official happens—those are scare tactics, but apparently the state police are moving in. Meanwhile, there are some background things you can start on. Vinny Jessup's car, for openers. Where it was taken, how secure it has been since, what kind of investigation was made. You know the kind of thing."

"You realize there can be a problem working out of the Bend area. I don't have real contacts over there. A close community like that, they'll most likely clam up tighter than a chastity belt when I start asking anything."

"I know. You'll have to work through Manny. He must use people over there whom he trusts."

"What else?" he asked.

"The ex, Curtis Stroh, and the Oregon Hospital Science University where Lara worked in Portland—friends, coworkers, the whole scene. I want to know if anyone other than Curtis Stroh is talking about her, and what they're saying. And everything about him down to the color of his favorite socks, including his whereabouts the weekend Vinny Jessup died."

She went to her desk for a sheet of paper with Stroh's name and address and the address of the Portland hospital. "And Robert Sheffield," she said, handing Bailey the names. "Dig a little deeper. He looks at her with puppy-dog eyes, but is he a messenger boy, or acting out of the goodness of his heart? Did Vinny Jessup trust him with his client list, or tag him because there wasn't anyone else available?"

They talked a few more minutes, then as Bailey prepared to leave, she said, "I don't want to tip our hand until necessary. As long as they think Lara is relatively unprotected, they could come up with something useful as bait, but as soon as they know we're on the case, I think they'll play it rough and lowdown. In the next day or so, you should go over there and talk to Manny, see what kind of working arrangement you can come up with, and find out who else was staying up on the mountain the night Jessup died. Bailey, you report only to me, even if Manny is the second counsel."

Bailey regarded her for a moment. "You trust him? Is there any doubt?"

"I think I trust him," she said slowly, "but I'm not used to working with people I don't know. I want to play it in close for the time being."

"Gotcha," he said, and pulled himself upright. "Okeydokey. Off and running." His amble to the door belied his words; he paused and said, "Barbara, do yourself and your clients a favor. Let Maria make the coffee."

She glared at him as he grinned and saluted, then left. She considered whether there was anything else she could do now, and decided there wasn't, not until she received the tape from Manny. Reluctantly she returned to her desk and the stacks and stacks of documents Vinny Jessup had bequeathed to his widow, and on to her and Frank.

She had expected Frank to come by and pick up where he had left off; they were both determined to sift through everything one more time. There must be something, they had told each other grimly, or why had he left the stuff? But Frank had not put in an appearance, and she could only think that he was angry with her, that he needed time to cool off, not that he had washed his hands of this mess. She refused to let herself consider that possibility.

In his office eight blocks away, Frank was at his own desk, which was also covered with papers. His contract had arrived from Grenadier Press, and he regarded it with awe and disbelief. Five copies! What for? And incomprehensible. He knew full well what that was for, and he was determined to wrest the meaning from every damn clause before he signed a thing. The contract was twenty-two pages long, and he was still on page one. It had been written by a committee, whose members had all gone to the same classes in law school with the same instructor who not only believed the highest achievement of any attorney was to master totally obfuscatory language, but also that the attorney least likely to succeed was the one who could write a sentence in simple English that anyone could understand without a law degree.

But he had to admit he liked the way it started: "Agreement made as of this date . . . between Frank Holloway (Author) . . . and Grenadier Press (Publisher). . . ." They had zapped his title and called it *Untitled Work.*

He reread the beginning and pursed his lips when he realized that while he would grant them the right to publish the Work, it didn't say they had to publish it or even might publish it. They just would have the right to publish. . . .

"Calm down," he muttered under his breath. "It's in there somewhere." He continued to read, and presently he stood up and stalked to the door, out to Patsy's office and thrust a copy of the contract to her. "I want a Xerox made," he said, and stalked back toward his own office. He called over his shoulder, "And find me a highlighter."

An hour later he leaned back in his chair scowling. The Xerox copy he had been marking was a mess of yellow highlighted lines with very little space not lined. He needed help, he decided, and tried to think who would be good.

Wanda Doolittle's name came to mind. He had done some work for her in the past, and she wrote novels. She would know something. He called her.

After chatting a minute or two, he said diffidently, "Actually, what I'm looking for is a consultant, someone who knows how to read a book contract. Of course, we'll pay your fee."

She laughed. "Nonsense. Buy me some dinner and a drink, and we'll call it a deal. Who's the publisher? Maybe I have something about them lying about."

"Grenadier Press."

"Okay. Early dinner, sixish? And bring the contract along so we can eat it for dessert."

He regarded the contract he had made a mess of, then he shrugged. It would do. After a moment, more thoughtfully, he began to rummage in his desk, but he didn't have a Magic Marker. He went out to Patsy once more. "Magic Marker," he said. "Suppose you can round one up for me?"

She opened her desk drawer, took out a marker, and handed it to him silently. Just as silently, he took it and returned to his office, where he proceeded to obliterate his name on the contract.

Wanda had gained a little weight since their last meeting, and her hair was a little grayer, but her smile was as broad and infectious as he recalled. She was in her sixties. She had arrived at the Electric Station restaurant before him and already had a table on the front terrace.

"Frank, how are you? It's been ages. You don't change a hair. I think you must have a picture in the attic or something. I thought we could have our drinks out here and then go inside to eat. Okay?"

He suspected that she wanted to sit outside in order to smoke cigarettes. He kissed her cheek and they sat down; she already had a frosted gin and tonic.

"How are you doing?" he asked after the waitress took his order for wine.

"Not bad. They dumped the entire writing program in my lap a few years ago, so I'm busy, but I like it." She had been teaching at the university for twenty-five years or longer.

Once she had said in answer to his question about the literacy of her students that no, she wasn't teaching them commas and semicolons. She was teaching them how to hold their pencils. Now she talked a little about the program, and they were both laughing, and neither of them noticed that Barbara had come to a standstill in the parking lot across the street, staring at them.

Barbara began to walk fast toward the Fifth Street Public Market, where she intended to buy wine and coffee, maybe a good loaf of bread, and something to make a sandwich or two with. She had many more hours to put in on the Vinny Jessup files, trying to make sense of them.

And now, she thought, disgruntled, she might have to read all the truly boring judicial decisions McReady had written. Of course, she told herself, this was her case, not Frank's, and she shouldn't have counted on him to do the work she didn't want to do. It was good that he had a life beyond the office; it was time for him to have a life beyond what little work he still did and gardening and loafing. He wasn't too old to have dinner with a handsome woman, enjoy himself. She was happy for him, she told herself. Really happy for him, and he would have gotten around to mentioning his friend when he was ready. It wasn't as if he was keeping a secret or anything. She realized that she was muttering under her breath and stopped. But he might have mentioned it, she thought darkly.

Frank and Wanda had taken their time with dinner, putting off literary matters until the food was gone, but then Wanda said, "See how it goes? Grenadier was bought up by Arrowwood about seven or eight years ago. Nothing changed a great deal at that time; they just were not independent any longer. Okay, three years ago Arrowwood was gobbled up by C and M, the media people, into television, movies, CDs, comic books. You name it, they've got a piece of it. And this time there was a Friday night massacre. Big meeting called at the end of the day, and a bunch of senior editors got the ax. On Monday a flock of bright young fuzzy-cheeked MBAs took over, some of them out of Hollywood, some out of Saturday morning cartoons, some over from the comic book imprint. Your client happened to land one from Saturday morning cartoons. Tell him, sorry, but that's life in the fast lane. Think of the sleaziest talk show on the air; that's C and M for you, and they put Grenadier Press down in the same pit."

The waiter brought her cognac; she inhaled it and smiled. "Ah. It's a goddamn shame you gave up hard booze, Frank. But more for me." She tasted it and set her glass down.

"But they still publish books, don't they?"

"Sure. On their terms. That contract you showed me is a fine example. You did a pretty good job spotting some of the fish-hooks, but there are more, and what isn't in there is enough to fill a few more pages with gobbledygook."

He told her about the original offer of five thousand, and the suggestion that it might go up to sixty-five hundred; the contract said four thousand. One thousand when he signed the contract, a thousand when he completed revisions and the manuscript was accepted, and the remainder three months following publication.

"My friend isn't in it for the money, but still a verbal agreement ought to mean something."

She laughed. "The paper it's written on. Anyway, I know how your friend feels. He'd even pay them to publish his book. I see them all the time, starry-eyed neophytes desperate to get into print."

Embarrassed that he had been offered a contract that had seemed to his inexperienced eyes humiliating, he had invented a young friend to hide behind. He was glad now to have a shield.

"When you said book contract, I shoved a model contract into my bag for you," she said, rummaging in a large brocade bag. She drew out a big manila envelope and handed it to him. "Of course, a new writer won't be able to get a really good contract, but he shouldn't take this one the way it's written. For openers, they don't have to publish. Nowhere in there does it say they do. So they buy the book and they keep all the subsidiary rights to do with as they please—television, movies, CDs. Remember that clause about electronic rights? They want all rights to them, those in existence today, and whatever is invented in the future. My favorite phrase . . ." She scanned the page before her. "Ah, here it is, 'in perpetuity throughout the universe.' Isn't that lovely!" She laughed, then said, almost gently, "It's their property, there's no reversion-of-rights clause, and they can milk it forever if they want to. Nowhere does it mention royalties, that the four thousand is an advance against royalties. That means it's really in the category of a work for hire, the initial payment is all there is or will be. . . ." She continued and the more she talked, the glummer he became.

Finally, the cognac was gone, the espresso was finished, and they got up to leave the restaurant. "Thanks for the education," Frank said.

"Thank you for the dinner. Education is my business, remember? I enjoyed it."

He walked to her car with her, and then walked home. In his head he was already composing a letter to Mr. Donald ("Call me Don") Fleishman.

At midnight Barbara was pacing in her office.

She was going over the sequence of events of years before: In March two kids were killed. McReady was still the new kid on the block, sniffing out the power structure. In July Lewis Jessup was arrested and indicted. In July McReady was handed the case to prosecute. Trial date set for the following January. In September DeFeo was brought in. Sometime between then and December twentieth, McReady must have known he would lose the case. Then Lewis vanished. McReady, on the following day, went to Spokane to spend Christmas with his folks.

She nodded to herself. Until July there was no reason for Vinny Jessup to have paid any attention to McReady, just another young attorney putting in time in a hick town, waiting for something better to come along.

How had this young new attorney landed the case, which would have been fairly high-profile, involving the son of a prominent local attorney, the daughter of wealthy parents?

All the rest of that material, she thought then, the minute-by-minute tracking of McReady's career over the years, was gloss. Vinny must have known he could not sniff out anything through clippings, press reports, interviews, judicial decisions. Whatever he had believed about McReady had been set in concrete before he started that obsessive behavior.

Something happened between July and December twentieth that made Vinny suspect McReady of culpability, of murder possibly. But he had not found proof, or he would have acted on it. Maybe something that had appeared insignificant at the time, something that had seemed completely innocuous, that time and reflection had given meaning.

She needed to talk to people. Vinny Jessup's two adult children, who probably would be cooperative, and Lester DeFeo, the defense attorney Vinny had brought in, who was eighty or older and might not remember a thing about it. And, she thought grimly, she wanted to talk to the former district attorney who had handed the case over to his untried assistant, and he might not cooperate at all. Manny had said he had clammed up years ago.

And none of the Jessup history might have a thing to do with

Vinny Jessup's death, she reflected, just a waste of time, mis-
placed effort. But if they indicted Lara Jessup, history might
bring to light the only defense possible, she argued silently. If
there really were only two suspects and one was above reproach,
it didn't leave much.

 12

When Frank arrived at Barbara's office the next day, he
was grumpy and tired. He had struggled for hours with his letter
to Donald ("Call me Don") Fleishman, working at home on his
computer, reluctant to involve Patsy in a personal affair, he had
told himself more than once. He felt as if the text of his letter
had been imprinted on his brain. "Dear Mr. Fleishman: I have
had the opportunity to review the agreement you sent me, and
I regret to inform you that I find it unsatisfactory in many respects. . . . I have taken the liberty of submitting a model contract, which I respectfully request should be used as a basis for
future negotiations. . . . Please note that I have restored my
working title, in order to avoid any possible confusion, and also
I have restored the original offer of five thousand dollars
($5,000), as per our verbal agreement. . . ."

He had done that, too. He had typed out *The Art of Cross-
Examination,* and the amount of the verbal offer, then he had
cut out the lines with a razor blade, glued them onto the model
contract, and had taken the whole thing to Kinko's to get a

Xerox copy made. On his way to Barbara's office, he had
dropped the envelope in the mail.

Now he worried; perhaps he had been too abrupt, even rude.
Possibly he should have waited a day or two to think it over.
He really didn't expect to be treated like a star, a big-time writer,
a bestseller, anything like that. . . . He scowled. He had put it in
the mail to forestall such fainthearted second thoughts. It was
done.

Barbara was at her desk, in her court clothes. Years earlier he
had argued with her about proper clothing for court, and had
even won the argument, but only after informing her that certain
judges would rule against her clients to teach her a lesson. Some
of them, he had said, insisted on ties for men and skirts for
women, claiming they had to be able to tell the boys from the
girls, and there were precious few other clues these days.

"Morning," he said. "You coming or going?"

"Been and done."

"Win?"

"Sure."

He laughed. "Thought I might as well do some more reading."

"Before you start, let me tell you what I've been thinking,"
she said. He sat in one of her clients' chairs, and she told him
about Manny Truewater's call and the taping of a statement by
Lara, and then summarized her reasoning that whatever had happened between Vinny and McReady had been in the months
following the arrest of Lewis Jessup.

Neither of them commented on the fact that the other one
looked tired; he suspected he knew the reason for her sleepless-
ness, and it was not going to be a topic of conversation if he
could help it. He had not given her the opportunity to say much
about John's reappearance, where he was staying—no doubt at

her apartment—or for how long. He didn't want to know. And he had no intention of telling her about his struggle with the agreement with Grenadier Press, not until he had something he could show without embarrassment.

"I need to talk to Alene and Roger Jessup, and to the former D.A., Pete Tolman," Barbara said, winding down. "I called Alene, and she'll get back to me. And as soon as that's set up, I intend to drive over to Burns and corner Tolman. I'm afraid if I call first, he'll head for the hills or something."

"Tolman," he said thoughtfully. "He's eighty-one, eighty-two, something like that. He might not want to talk to you, and take off for the hills when you show your face." Then, cautiously he asked, "You going alone?"

"Yes, of course."

"Want some company?"

She laughed. "One old codger gabbing with another old codger, something like that?"

"Exactly like that."

"You're on." After a moment she said, "What do you have personally against McReady? You hinted that there's something."

"Personally, not a damn thing. You know how it is when you disagree politically with someone? You're primed to believe the worst. Like when Nixon was in and Watergate came along, it was almost as if I'd been waiting for it, no surprise at all. Well, with McReady, it's even more tenuous. You remember Brian Lowcroft? He was working up in Portland when McReady was the district attorney up there, making headlines with one win after another. Brian crossed swords with him several times, and generally lost to him. So you have to consider sore-loser syndrome could be at work, but Brian told me that McReady cooked evidence a couple of times. Never could prove a thing, but he believed it, probably still does. He's in Philadelphia these days." He shrugged. "Malicious gossip, hearsay, sour grapes, or the truth. Take your pick. I knew Brian pretty well, and I believed him."

Maria buzzed Barbara's phone then, and she picked up to speak with Alene Jessup Thorpe. When she hung up, she said with satisfaction, "That's great. She got in touch with Roger, and they'll both see me Sunday, all afternoon, as long as it takes. He'll fly up to San Francisco from Riverside or someplace down there, and she'll send her husband off with their two kids, so we'll have quiet and time to talk."

She picked up her phone again and asked Maria to get her a flight early Sunday morning, if possible, or Saturday, if necessary.

"So, let's plan our jaunt to Burns," she said. It would have to be an overnight trip. It was a five- or six-hour drive, too far to go, have a talk with Tolman, and then come back home. That was okay, she decided; maybe they could stay with Lara, have her invite Manny Truewater over, and let Frank meet him.

Frank had insisted on taking his Buick. "Air-conditioned," he had said brusquely when she offered to drive her car over. She had pointed out to him many times that in the valley air-conditioning was a meaningless expense since it was so seldom needed. But as soon as they drove through Bend, and the desert stretched out before them, she was grateful for the cool air circulating in the car. The road was an arrow pointing eastward, straight, smooth, without a dip or curve visible, and only the dun-colored desert on both sides sprinkled with a few clumps of dusty sage and a rare juniper tree. Every horizon was a jagged line of mesas, buttes, mountains; they were centered as if in a flat-bottomed bowl mile after mile. Now and then a dust devil rose in the distance, evidence of another vehicle on a distant dirt road.

Frank had driven across the mountains, where traffic had been heavy; they had switched places in Bend, where she had watched without comment as he set the cruise control at sixty-five, and now she drove so he could listen to Lara's taped interview.

He listened intently, then said, "Those are the lines of investigation they'll follow. Where she stayed, whom she met, if she had a fellow on the side. . . . I hope to God she can prove where she put in time those weekends. Her ex-husband must be a real sweetheart."

"Don't put the tape in the glove compartment," Barbara said. "It'll melt if we have to park in the sun."

He put it in her purse and watched the landscape flash by. Mile after mile, now and then with a crossroad that on the map had a name, but in reality was nothing more than a landmark to fill in some of the empty space.

Finally, at one o'clock the town of Burns rose in front of them like a mirage. A gas station, then a house or two, real streets, a supermarket, bank . . . An actual town. Frank had not been over this way in twenty years, and as far as he could tell, nothing had happened during all that time; nothing was changed.

"Parched," he said. "Let's head to a café for a sandwich and a cold drink, and directions." The bank thermometer registered ninety-seven degrees, and dry desert air or not, that was too damned hot, he thought, leaving the car.

The café was a few degrees cooler than the outside air, but it was dim, and two noisy ceiling fans kept the hot air in motion. It was like being inside a convection oven. They ate sandwiches and drank iced tea, and when Frank paid the tab, he asked the woman behind the counter how to find Pete Tolman.

"Old Pete? You want to see his partridge? You'd think no one ever saw one before, the way he goes on about it."

She was stocky and very suntanned, with thick gray hair in a ponytail. They were the only customers in the café.

"His partridge," Frank said without blinking an eye.

"Well, he lives over by the retirement village, not in it, but you go out that way, past the church, and turn left. His place is the third house after you turn."

"Where's the retirement village?" Frank asked, certain there had not been such a community the last time he had been in Burns.

"You can't miss it," the woman assured him. "Turn off Main at Third and go for four blocks, you'll see it. Keep on to the church, though, before you turn."

"Retirement village," he muttered, back in the car. "Good God."

The retirement village was a cluster of six or eight mobile homes, close together with a few trees in their midst. They looked like wagons waiting for an Indian attack. No one was in sight. Barbara drove past the turn to the village, and there was the church ahead, a small frame building that needed paint. Everything out here needed paint, she thought gloomily; no doubt the wind-driven sand scoured it off as fast as it was applied.

She made the next turn and they passed two small houses that also needed paint; she stopped at the third house. It was small, dingy, with an incongruous picket fence along the front of a lawnless expanse of pale rocky ground.

"I think we have arrived," she said.

"Just a second." He rummaged in the glove compartment and brought out a pair of binoculars, which he hung around his neck. Then he got out and opened the back door of the car and brought out his old straw hat that he used for gardening. She doubted that anyone except her had ever seen him in it.

When they turned toward the house, the door opened, and a tiny man stepped out onto the porch. At first Barbara thought he was a dwarf, but no, he was merely shrunken, wizened. "I grow old," she murmured. "I shall wear my trousers rolled." Frank made a grunting noise and walked up to the porch.

"Mr. Tolman? Frank Holloway, and my daughter, Barbara."

"Fred send you?" the little man asked. His voice was firm and deep, and his eyes were bright blue and sharp. He had little hair, wispy white strands that hung down to his neck; his skin was deep brown and tough-looking. Muscles and tendons in his neck, his arms and hands were like taut cables with brown leather coverings.

"Nope," Frank said. " 'Fraid not. We came on our own. Understand you spotted a partridge."

"Yep. Can't see her now, though. Too hot. She's holed up until the sun gets lower. Come on in." He moved aside for them to enter his house, then he closed the door. "Keeps the heat out," he said. The house was like an inferno, and it was filled with books on shelves, on tables, on the floor, a telescope on a stand, several pairs of binoculars on a coffee table, and photographs of birds on every wall.

"Come on to the kitchen," Tolman said. "I was just loading the Nikon for some more shots. You'll want something to drink."

They followed him from the cramped living room into the equally cramped kitchen, where a table was covered with a white cloth and several cameras.

Tolman went to an ancient refrigerator and brought out some bottled Genesis juice, organic natural juice from over in Eugene. "Alls I got left is apple and grape," he said, pouring out a glassful. "Pretty good stuff." He filled three glasses and handed them around, then motioned toward chairs at the table. "See, I spotted her three weeks ago tomorrow. Pretty little thing, with seven chicks. So I call Fred and he says the folks at OFO are pretty excited, and they've sent out two observers so far, and there's going to be a passel more of them if she survives long enough. So far, the coyotes haven't found her and her chicks." He drank some juice and set his glass down. "You can't see her until about five or six. She's canny, and keeps under cover until then. Best time's in the morning, though, right after dawn."

Barbara felt as if she had stumbled into the third act of a Beckett play, but apparently Frank was following the monologue without any trouble. She sipped her juice and let him take over, glad that he had come. Tolman ignored her and focused on Frank, possibly reassured by the binoculars and straw hat.

"I didn't realize partridges were that scarce," Frank said. "Used to be you couldn't walk to a river without seeing them."

"Used to be," Tolman agreed. "See, what happened is that they killed off the foxes, and they kept the coyotes in check, now the coyotes multiply like maggots in bad meat, and they'll eat anything and everything—cats, dogs, chickens, any bird they can catch. Come to town every evening looking for a cat or dog left out. But Miss Molly's doing all right. She's smart and she knows their ways, and so far it's her ball game."

He rambled on until Frank finally said, "Mr. Tolman, actually, I wondered if we could talk to you about something that happened a long time ago, seventeen years ago."

Tolman became very still, and his eyes narrowed. "What happened?"

"That's what we're trying to find out," Frank said. "You know that Vinny Jessup is dead?"

Tolman nodded. "I heard he killed himself."

"He didn't," Frank said.

"I heard that if he didn't, his pretty young wife did it."

"She didn't, either," Frank said. "I knew Vinny. He was a good man."

Tolman nodded again. "He was a good man. Wrongheaded sometimes, but a good man. What's your part in his death?"

"If his widow is accused of murdering him, we'll defend her."

"You've come to the wrong person. I haven't seen Vinny or heard anything about him since I moved out here, sixteen years ago. I can't help you."

"The way we see it," Frank said, as if Tolman had not spoken, "the widow is being measured for prison garb, a railroad job. Just another morsel for the coyotes to chew up for dinner. Vinny was on his way to have a face-off with Harris McReady and he never showed, according to McReady and the Lynch crew. He died instead, and now she's the prime suspect. Another fox is gone; the coyotes are multiplying over there, too."

Tolman stood up and walked to the sink, where he rinsed his glass and set it down on a drainer. He stood at the sink, gazing out the window. "You said seventeen years ago. What about seventeen years ago?"

"Lewis Jessup," Frank said quietly. "How did that case get as far as it did, with a trial date set and all? How did it end up in McReady's hands?"

For a time no one spoke, as Tolman continued to look out, as if the desert were changing in a fascinating way. At last, he turned to glance at Frank, then at Barbara. "You got some ID?"

They both got out drivers' licenses, and he looked at them, but not as if he needed confirmation, rather as if he was stalling for time to think. "I read about you," he said to Barbara. "And I've known about Holloway for many years. I'll tell you a story," he said after another silent struggle. "Off the record. I'll deny it if I have to, and I won't testify in any court. I washed my hands of all that bullshit a long time ago."

Frank nodded. "Deal."

Tolman went back to the sink, and he gazed out then as he spoke. "Elvin Flemer was the sheriff back then, a Lynch man. And he was under a lot of pressure to find the killer of those two kids, but he wasn't getting anywhere with it. We all thought it was one of the college kids did it, someone they picked up and drove up to the trailhead with them. Then one day Flemer came to me with McReady, and they said they had the killer and a case. Lewis Jessup. I knew they were both full of shit and told them so. McReady was new, green, and plenty ambitious. I needed him like a hole in the head, but he was hot to trot for Lewis. He wanted the case real bad. I told him to find something useful to do, and that same day, late, Thomas Lynch came by for a chat. Let McReady have it, he said. Let him end up with egg on his face, teach him a lesson in humility. He'd be good one day, he said, but he needed a hard lesson or two first."

Tolman's shoulders hunched; he picked up his glass and rinsed it again, set it down, then glanced at Frank. "Lynch ran the county those days, still does, I reckon. Anyway, in the end, he had his way. McReady got the case, took it to the grand jury, the whole thing. I knew there wasn't a case, and I sat on my hands. Guess I thought they'd get the boy off and then Vinny would sue the county, the sheriff, my office probably, for wrongful arrest, something like that. And that would have suited me fine. But Lewis vanished."

"What about that, when he disappeared? What happened?"

"Don't know," Tolman said after a moment. "And that's God's truth. I don't know. He had no cause to take off, that's all I know. But the day after he was missing, early in the morning that day, McReady took off for his folks' place up in Spokane, and the day before that he was in town all day, and all the evening, too. I checked," he said flatly.

For several seconds no one spoke. Then Frank asked in a low voice, "How bad did Lynch want that ranch?"

Tolman looked at him and shrugged. "Bad. Always wanted it. For years he talked like his daughter, Babe, and Roger Jessup would marry and the ranches would be joined, a dynasty, I reckon. But it didn't happen. Roger came home from school every year with new ideas about land management, about a model ranch that wouldn't leave the land like a war was fought on it, clean water, all kinds of things, but Thomas said that was his idealism, his boyhood talking, that he'd grow up. Then one day Roger brought a girlfriend home with him to meet the folks. So the dynasty was out."

"What about the calls claiming Lewis was in Portland, then down in San Francisco?"

Tolman shrugged. "That was all handled by McReady. He said he took the calls himself and acted on the information he got."

Barbara was suffocating with the heat that took away sweat before it could moisten her skin, dampen her clothes, offer some relief. Anger and impatience with this diminutive man were ready to erupt; that had been his office, McReady his assistant, but he was talking as if he had been powerless, as if none of it was any of his business. He wasn't going to give them a thing they didn't already know or suspect, and she wanted out of the airless house that was baking hot. She caught a warning look from Frank and held her tongue.

"You checked on McReady, but did you check on anyone else when Lewis vanished?" Frank asked softly. "What about the Lynch family?"

"I asked a few questions," Tolman said. "They didn't know a thing. Babe was home, her and the folks were all at home that night, all the next day, and they didn't see or hear a thing. Period. Then Lewis was spotted in Portland."

"Case closed," Frank said.

Tolman nodded. "Case closed." He left the sink and returned to the table, where he seated himself once more. "The point is, that's all history, not pretty, but done. Vinny couldn't find a connection he could make stick, and after all this time, you won't, either. Vinny, Roger, Truewater, and a bunch of trackers searched that whole damn county looking for a new grave, a new rock pile, anything to suggest a body had been hidden there. The ground was frozen; if there'd been any digging, or any rock hauling, anything to disturb it, they would have spotted it, and they didn't come up with a thing. Between them all, they knew every inch of that land, where to look, how to look, and they came up empty-handed."

"Searched the Lynch property, too?"

"Yep. Thomas rode out to see what they were up to, and Vinny pulled a gun on him and told him to his face he'd kill anyone tried to stop them. Thomas wanted to press charges, I told him to back off, and he did." He picked up a camera, put it down again. In a low voice he said, "Tell you the truth, if Marilyn hadn't got sick when she did, as bad as she did, he might have taken his gun over there and wiped out all the Lynches, and then McReady, too. He was primed to kill someone. I don't know what kind of willpower it took for him to hold his peace all those years, because he knew what they did to his boy. He knew."

"You said what *they* did to his boy. He believed Lynch was involved, not just McReady?"

Tolman gave Frank a long, measured look, then abruptly stood up. "Nothing happened in that county without Lynch's approval. Now, I've got things to do. Like I said, it's history, done with. Couldn't prove anything then, can't now. And it's not going to help Vinny's widow a damn bit, far's I can see."

They thanked him, and he walked out to the car with them.

"You might want to stop in Burns for something to drink," he said. "Folks don't realize how dry they can get out here. Dehydration can be a problem."

He looked as if all the moisture had long ago been wrung out of his system, except for his eyes, which were bright and keen. "Good luck," he said then. "You'll need it if they set their sights on the pretty young widow."

They stopped at a supermarket and bought bottled water, then settled in for the long drive back across the parched desert to Bend.

"Discouraging, isn't it?" Frank commented. "Just keep confirming the same story. How much confirmation does it take to make it true?"

"I don't know," she said, and turned off the cruise control. He didn't object. "A question, though. What's OFO stand for?"

Frank laughed. "Oregon Field Ornithologists. He's one of their ringleaders."

She didn't ask how he knew that; he knew things, that was enough. "Another question: If Vinny knew Lynch was equally to blame, or maybe even the prime mover, why did he just go after McReady? Why not Lynch as well?"

"Good question," Frank said. He pulled the straw hat over his eyes and leaned back against the headrest.

Another question, she thought then, but didn't voice this one. How had Roger and Babe Lynch reacted to the arranged marriage her father had counted on? That was a question for Roger, one that had to be asked gingerly.

Driving faster and faster on the nearly empty highway, she brooded again at how fruitless all this seemed. History, immutable, yielding nothing to help Lara Jessup now, what good was any of it? If it's all you've got, it's what you run with, she told herself, and wished she could find consolation in the sage words.

13

That night they sat on Lara's deck along with Lara and Manny Truewater. The temperature had plummeted to the low seventies and minute by minute it dropped another degree, then another. The cool air was a relief, but still too dry; Barbara felt as if her lips had been burned, her skin shriveled, and even her scalp itched. She was tired. Strange how both extreme heat and extreme cold could be so exhausting, she mused, content to let Frank and Manny discuss the politics of Loomis County. She didn't think the conversation would continue very long. Frank was even more tired than she was, and he showed it in a disconcerting way; his shoulders drooped, his face looked drawn. Her attention sharpened when Manny mentioned Pete Tolman's name.

"He chose not to run again, the story went, but in fact, Lynch had already picked McReady to take over. He kept the job for the next two years and then moved on up to Portland, and he's been moving up ever since. Carl Shinizer was the next shoo-in, and he's been in office ever since."

"What about the judge?" Frank asked.

"Herman Henkel." Manny turned toward Lara. "You must have met him around town a time or two. Short, fat, white hair, always with a new sunburn that looks painful. He hosted a lunch for McReady back in May, one that Vinny attended." He paused, then said in an expressionless tone, "I wouldn't call him crooked without hard proof, but neither would I want him to load my rifle if rabid mountain lions were attacking. He has a way of assessing guilt by the color of the defendant's skin, or gender."

"Any chance he would recuse himself?" Barbara asked.

"No. He's already let it be known that he was an admirer of Vinny's, and in no way partial to McReady. He held them in equal esteem."

"A change of venue?"

"No. This is Loomis County business, and he runs the court. He won't let it go."

For a time no one spoke, then Barbara said, "Lara, I know this is painful, but we have to discuss every aspect of the problem. The grand jury will convene on July sixth, and before then very likely the district attorney will make you an official offer." They already had explained the Alford plea to her. "You wouldn't have to stand trial. It will just end."

Lara made a low moaning sound, cleared her throat, then said, "I won't admit to anything I didn't do. If I went along with that, they'd wrap it up as a suicide, no one would be charged with murder. No one would pay for Vinny's death. McReady killed him. You all know it, and so do I. Would you be willing to let him just walk away from it? How many deaths can he just walk away from? And then sit on the Supreme Court! I'll kill him myself before I'll let that happen!" Her voice rose, became shrill.

"Take it easy," Barbara said. "And, Lara, don't ever say anything like that again. Not to anyone. Now, if they come up with an official offer of any sort, they'll work through Manny, and he'll tell you and give us a call. At that time, if it comes, we'll officially take over, but until then we'll keep in the background. Manny, where does Robert Sheffield fit in?"

"Robert's okay. He's been around for a couple of years, new

blood, new ideas. He's ready to blow his horn at the Jericho walls anytime and bring down the whole kingdom." He paused, then added, "And he has about as much influence as one of the reservation kids."

"But you want him."

"Yes."

Sheffield might feel indebted to Vinny for handing over many cases to him, Barbara thought; he might prove useful.

They let it go at that, and early the next morning Barbara drove Frank up the red lava road to the spot where Vinny had gone over the side, and then she turned the car around and headed for the highway, for the mountains, for home.

On Saturday night she had dinner in San Francisco with an old school friend, Fiona Wilkins. They sat at a window table in a restaurant on the Wharf with harbor seals yelping and barking an arm's length away. The window was closed, muting their cries, and it was just as well, or conversation would have been impossible, and Barbara suspected that the seals would have come right up to the table to share the largesse.

"You're getting another divorce?" she said to Fiona. "Good heavens! Give it up."

"But I always have a good cause," Fiona said complacently. "Don't ever marry a banker."

"Or a shoemaker or butcher or attorney..." Barbara laughed. "Seems that I recall just a couple of years ago when you were raving about the soon-to-be-ex."

"That was before the fact, dear. Well before the fact. He turned out to be as tight as shrink-wrap. Anyway, three isn't a record. Not these days."

Barbara had been her maid of honor the first time out; she remembered the wedding, a lavish affair that had cost Fiona's father and mother ten grand, she had announced proudly. Fiona was an executive with an accounting firm these days. Everything about her looked expensive.

"You see," Fiona explained, "you never know until you're married exactly what you've got. Take the first one, for example, what's his name—"

"Bob," Barbara said dryly.

"That's him. Bob. He was awfully sweet, right up until my salary topped his, and then he turned bitchy. Whine, whine, whine. I couldn't stand it. His supervisor hated him; the exec in charge of his department had it in for him; his secretary kept losing his mail, things like that. Poor baby. Then Daniel, what a hunk he was. And he knew it. He kept wanting to move somewhere else, always somewhere else, and he didn't like it that I wouldn't wear blinders and keep my eyes on him at all times. My shrink said that's a tactic they use, isolate you, cut you off from family and friends, make them be number one forever. So, out. Then Jerry, the banker. God, a banker can be a bore once the dotted line is signed. All he can talk about is money and how I don't know how to manage it."

They talked about old school friends, about Fiona's work, about the trip she was planning to Paris, about plays and books and movies, and altogether it was a pleasant, fun evening. In her hotel room afterward, Barbara was relaxed and ready for bed. She had said nothing about herself beyond yes, she was still keeping people from frying in the electric chair when she could, still in Oregon, and then it had been Fiona's turn again. She smiled; she had needed a night out like this.

And then she thought that it was not like that with John; he did not want to isolate her in any way. He just had a good job and wanted to share his life with her.

By the time she was in bed with the lights out, all the tension she had shed that evening had returned, and she had to admit to herself that it was not all caused by the problems of Lara Jessup. She had to think hard about John, his proposal, their needs, yet every time she tried to put her thoughts in order, her mind went numb, refused to deal with any of it, and she just felt tired.

Alene Jessup Thorpe lived in one of the nice Victorian houses on Russian Hill. Fourteen steps led up to the entrance, and the retaining wall out front had serious-looking cracks in it. Earthquake country; most houses showed signs of weathering a temblor. Barbara arrived at twelve, carrying her overnight bag, laptop, and purse. At five-thirty she had to get a cab and head out to the airport. Time enough, she thought, waiting for someone to respond to the bell and open the door.

Alene opened the door and admitted her. She was tall and solidly built, dressed in chinos and a silk shirt, sandals. Her hair was an unruly, coarse brown mop carelessly brushed back as if she had no time to spend on such nonessentials as style. Her eyes at first glance appeared black, but were just a very dark blue.

The entrance hall was carpeted with a blue Chinese runner with a gold and silver pattern; against one wall was a skateboard, and children's library books were scattered on a long, low table. A door to one side was open to a living room/parlor. Opposite it was a closed door.

"Thanks for giving me some time, Mrs. Thorpe," Barbara said.

"Please, this is California. No one has last names here. It's Alene, and you're Barbara. Okay?" She motioned, and started to walk down the hallway. "Roger flew in last night. He's waiting for us."

She led the way to a room down a few steps from the kitchen, with a bar and stools separating the two areas. The back wall had many uncurtained windows; sunlight flooded the space.

Handsome rattan furnishings seemed to be a repository for children's clothes and possessions. Alene gathered up a girl's sweater and more books, glanced around, and then put them on the bar.

"My brother Roger," she said as she made room for Barbara to sit down.

He was very much like her in appearance, the same coarse hair, same eyes, just on a larger scale. His handshake was firm without it turning into a contest.

"How much trouble is Lara in?" Roger asked bluntly as soon as they were all seated.

Barbara wouldn't have started like this. She would have sounded them out a bit first, tested the waters, but now she said, "She's in trouble. Real trouble."

"What can we do for her?" Roger asked.

Barbara decided she liked his straightforward way of getting right down to it, and she began to explain the various possibilities facing Lara, who had been stepmother to these two strong adults. She did not mention the box of files Vinny had left; she liked this pair and felt she could trust them, but still . . .

Neither spoke until she finished detailing the events to date.

"Does she know what the papers were? Does she have the originals?" Roger asked when she paused.

"No, on both counts. She has nothing to deal with."

"So it boils down to whatever Dad might have come across to ruin McReady, or do him damage at least," Alene said then. "It's a fuckup. He couldn't have found anything at this late date, and if he'd found something in the past, he would have used it."

Barbara nodded. "That's what it looks like from where I sit. I've been hearing about your brother's arrest, of course, but would you mind giving me your take on it? Maybe someone else missed something."

Another confirmation, she thought gloomily as they alternated talking about the past, the year Lewis had been accused of murder. How many confirmations does it take? she asked herself, repeating her father's words silently.

When they finally stopped talking, she asked, "Alene, Roger, is there a remote possibility that your brother was frightened of a trial, that he actually ran?"

Their denials, spoken in unison, were sharp and indisputable. "Wait a minute," Alene said; she jumped up and hurried from the room. Soon she returned with a photo album, which she paged through rapidly.

"Here, look at them. Roger, Lewis, and our father. Lewis was a Jessup through and through, and Jessups didn't scare and run, then or now."

They all looked alike, tall, broad-shouldered, all with the same unruly hair, the same expression of mild amusement and self-consciousness at posing. Lewis and Roger were nearly the same height; Lewis not as heavy yet, not finished, still a boy.

Barbara closed the album gently. "Did your father tell you about the insurance? That's going to be a driving point with the prosecution."

"Sure," Roger said. "Look, Barbara, he knew McReady was behind it, and he intended to kill him. There was a chance that he'd get killed doing it, so he took out the insurance to protect our mother. But Wynona Truewater talked him out of doing anything crazy. She told him that Mother would be in an institution where they'd tie her down in a bed, and she'd die there. He couldn't do it to her, so he lived with it. We all lived with it. I wanted to kill McReady, but I couldn't bring that kind of grief to my folks, either. See, we were all helpless, so we lived with it."

"Did you ever speak to Lara about the insurance?"

"No, of course not," Alene said. She looked at Roger as if questioning him, then went on. "At first, when Dad told us he was going to remarry, we were both pretty upset, especially when we realized how young she was, and how pretty. We thought what everyone up there still thinks—she was after his money, except there wasn't any real money. So it had to be the insurance. Then Dad took us both out to the cemetery one afternoon, and he talked about our mother, how it had been for years with her. He said that Lara was like a second chance at living for the next few years, that he had been dead, a walking corpse, that he knew he didn't have more than a few years before the cancer came back, and Lara had brought him comfort, love, joy. . . . We all cried that day, Barbara. He was so lonesome; he had been so good to our mother, and he had suffered so much." There were tears in her eyes. Abruptly she stood up and faced away.

"The years with Lara changed him back to the father he had been when we were kids, full of laughter and fun. He hadn't laughed for so long, I had forgotten how he had been once. She gave him that. I never even thought of the insurance again after I opened my eyes and saw them as they were, not as I expected them to be. He was happy again. She did that for him."

She walked to the kitchen. "I'm going to make us a sandwich and coffee."

Barbara turned toward Roger, who nodded.

"We talked about this last night," he said. "She's right about Lara. We'll do anything we can to help her."

"What about Lynch?" Barbara asked after a moment. "Did you and your father blame him as well as McReady?"

"He was on our list," Roger said quietly. "Ahead of McReady on my list, in fact." He began to talk passionately then about the differences of opinion about land management, about the old West and the new West butting heads, about the need to preserve the land, stop destroying the forests and water. . . . "It's feudalism, pure and simple," he said vehemently. "He considers himself lord of the county, with power granted him by a higher authority that can't be questioned, and no one below him better question his power. McReady wouldn't have moved without consulting him first, getting permission. . . ."

Alene brought a platter of sandwiches, went back for the coffee things, and then sat down. She made a helpless gesture, as if to say Barbara had started this with Roger, and there was nothing to be done except listen for a while.

"You do a favor for the lord, and in return you are given a land grant, the daughter in marriage, whatever deal you struck," Roger said bitterly.

"What about the daughter?" Barbara asked before he could go off on another rant. "Did Lynch try to arrange something between you and her?"

Roger looked startled, then shook his head. "She was older than me. We grew up together, rode together, hunted, everything. We'd get together and talk about improving our herds, about the coming roundup, where turkeys were gathering, things like that. She worked as hard on the Lynch ranch as I did on ours. She was a rancher, like me, and she still is, far as I know. We were buddies. There wasn't anything more than that."

"Don't be an idiot," Alene said sharply. "Babe was boy-crazy from the time she noticed that boys were different. And you were a holdout. She went off on a real tear when you brought Janice home the first time. Everyone knew she was hot for your bod."

He shook his head again. "She was after any male, not me in particular."

Alene shrugged. "Not the way I heard it, but then the girls probably didn't know what was up. Just gossip." Her sarcasm was lightened with amusement when she said to Barbara, "Every girl I knew was waiting for Babe to snag Roger, but he never noticed. Boys can be so goddamn dumb." She gazed at her brother and asked, "Why do you think old man Lynch began cutting you off the way he did?"

"That was over the pond," he said quickly.

There followed a long, involved discussion that verged on argument over a dispute about a holding pond for water. They talked on about growing up on a ranch, about being land rich, cash poor, about Vinny's law practice, how little it paid because he took on such poor clients and their causes. . . .

When it was drawing near time for Barbara to leave, she held up her hand to stop them.

"Look, I appreciate very much your talking to me like this, filling in some of the blanks. You realize that the state will want to question you also?" They both nodded. "Good. What they'll be getting at directly or indirectly is the question, Do you think Lara could have killed your father?"

"God, no!" Alene cried.

"No, never," Roger said firmly.

"Is it conceivable to you that your father committed suicide?"

They denied that just as quickly and firmly.

"Is it conceivable to you that if Lara had found him dead, she might have tried to arrange it to look like murder in order to collect the insurance?"

"No," Alene said. "That presupposes suicide again, and that's impossible. He never would have killed himself."

And that wasn't the question she had asked, Barbara thought. She tried again. "Do you think Lara would have done anything illegal or unethical or immoral in order to collect insurance, perhaps to guarantee security for her son?"

Alene studied her face for a time, then she asked, "Do you really think they'd pose a question like that?"

"I don't know. It's a possibility."

Roger said quietly, "It's hard to know what a parent would

do to safeguard her children. If you said the safety of her son, I'd have to say sure, Lara would do whatever it took to keep him safe. But financial security? No. She has a profession that she likes, she's a good, hard worker, she's young. And she's not money hungry. Nathan's financial security isn't an issue."

But Alene didn't answer the rephrased question, Barbara noted to her regret. Did that mean she saw financial security and safety as one and the same? She hoped that no investigator, or prosecutor, ever asked her the question in such a way that she wouldn't be able to answer it.

 **14**

Barbara was at her desk on Monday morning when Bailey arrived. "You first," she said.

"Scum off the top," he said, "on Curtis Stroh. First layer only, more to come, with any luck."

"Shoot." She leaned back in her chair.

"Okay. He's a charmer, a real ladies' man, a succession of live-in girlfriends since Lara left, but none of the new lovers stayed longer than a few months. The latest one, Sonia Delano, gave me an earful. It's in there," he said, motioning toward the envelope he had put on her desk. "When he and Lara split, he got the house, and he's kept it, but he's always hurting for money. Pretty good income doing private computer consulting. Sonia said he's after Lara, gunning for her, and always has been. He wants custody, not because of the kid but to get out of paying two-fifty a month support, and to screw Lara. Sonia doesn't know where he was the night Jessup got it. They had been fighting a lot, and she was off at the coast with friends. When the kid got there, Stroh took him to Indiana for ten days, and she packed up and got out while they were gone. But she also said that two detectives talked to him a day or two after he got back home; he called her and wanted to know if she had told them anything. And, Barbara, they talked to the boy, to Nathan."

"Curtis Stroh let them interview a child, his own child, without telling Lara?"

"So she says."

"Good God!"

"Right. Nothing but good about Lara from the hospital folks she worked with, but plenty about him. All stuff you already knew. I've just added names, people who'd testify if called. Nothing from motels, nothing worth talking about. A couple of people wondered why such a pretty woman was there alone, but no one paid any real attention. Cheap motels, a lot of activity, she was just a name in the book." He shook his head. "In short, nothing. Zilch."

"What about Jessup's car?"

"You might get something there. I didn't, not yet. A state helicopter salvage crew airlifted it out of the canyon and to their garage in Bend, where it's been ever since, under lock and key. The sheriff's bunch combed the mountainside for other evidence."

She nodded. "As soon as we're officially on the case, I want a real expert to go over the car." She glanced at the notes on her desk. "Meanwhile, the names of the Lynch crew keep cropping up. Thomas and Anna Lynch, and their daughter, Bethany, who answers to the name Babe. They say she was boy-crazy when she was a girl, but when Roger got himself a real girlfriend, she had a fit. See what you can find about them all."

"More history," Bailey said unhappily. "And mining in alien territory."

"That's right."

"You know people over there carry rifles, and they shoot them just like in Westerns?"

"So keep your head down. Anyone else on that mountain the night Vinny died?"

"Yeah. Eight families in residence. I'm still digging."

"One more thing. The turnoff on Lookout Mountain Road. Kids go up there and park, do a little stargazing. There may be something there."

After Bailey left, she began to pace, thinking about detectives interviewing a child, wondering what Nathan could possibly have told them, how influential his father was, how colored his statement might have been. She wished Frank would show up so that they could talk about it, how to handle it.

Across town Frank was at his desk, where he had just lifted the telephone. "Holloway," he said.

"Frank! Damn, I'm glad I caught you in. Don, Don Fleishman. I want to apologize about that contract. The contract department really messed up this time. I was just down there cracking the whip, and believe me, Frank, believe me, they're sorry. See, what happened is they sent you the wrong contract, and I should have gone over it, but I didn't. I trusted them to do their job."

"The wrong contract," Frank said. "Not your standard agreement?"

"For some people it's pretty standard. See, how it works is that we have some writers on the line ready to run with a late-breaking newsworthy story, a celebrity's mysterious death, a big bombing, something like that. We give one of them a call and assign the book, and he holes up for a few days and in a couple of weeks we have a book on the stands. Those guys get that contract. They aren't writing for posterity, or pretending to do a literary work. They're in it for a few quick bucks, a quick book to get out while the news is hot, the interest is at a peak. Then they're done with it. Finis. Kaput. Ready for the next assignment. You weren't supposed to get one of their agreements, no way, not your book. You have a book for all time, a book with a future shelf life, library life, a book that's going to be talked about and read by a lot of people. We have a big organization here, and somewhere along the line someone screwed up, that's all. Look, what I'll do is send you a proper agreement, Express Mail, overnight delivery, and believe me, Frank, you won't find it objectionable."

"More on the lines of the model contract I sent you?"

"Frank, Frank, that contract is a joke. It's the kind of thing teachers hand out to high school kids, no publisher would use it, no contract department or legal department would allow it to be used. But our contract is good, believe me, it's a good one that follows the highest standards in the publishing industry. As you know, every industry has its own standards, its own considerations to ensure a fair agreement to both sides. If there are a few things in the new contract that bother you, give me a call, and we'll discuss them and the reason they're in it, or even negotiate them out if possible. I'm sorry, Frank, believe me, I'm really sorry for this mix-up. I know it must have been a painful blow to you to think we'd treat you that way, and for you to have thought so for even a minute is painful for me, believe me. You'll get the new contract tomorrow or the next day. I've learned that overnight Express Mail doesn't always mean what it says, but it will be in your hands this week. And, Frank, call me if you have any questions. We're in this together. All the way."

Frank sat at his desk for a time after he hung up. He could

well believe a mix-up had occurred, it happened within his firm
often enough. They hadn't really meant him to have that agreement, that was certain; they wouldn't have sent such an agreement to an attorney, neophyte writer or not. Besides, Don
Fleishman wanted his book; from the way he sounded, he was
eager not to piss Frank off. . . .

By the time he rose and strolled out of his office to walk to
Barbara's office, he was grinning. At first he thought he would
tell her about the mix-up but then decided not yet. Not until he
had a decent contract duly signed by both parties, and then he'd
take her out to celebrate.

"Well, you ate the little yellow bird and found it excellent," Barbara said when Frank entered her office.

"Fine day, good day for walking," he said. "And I had a good
restful weekend." That was a lie; he had stewed and fretted all
weekend, but now he felt revived. That was more than he could
say for her, he thought; she looked frazzled. He was dismayed
when he found himself wishing that John Mureau would fall into
one of the deep holes he liked to poke around in.

Keeping his voice as neutral as possible, he asked, "Are you
all right? Not coming down with something?"

"Something I ate on the plane last night did me in, and I was
up late thinking about Lara and McReady." She frowned. "Dad,
what kind of blemish would it take to eliminate McReady from
a list of nominees for the Court? How serious would it have to
be?"

He sat on her couch and said, "Way I see it, there's going to
be two vacancies coming up, and deals will be struck. The ad-
ministration will try for someone left of center, and they'll be
turned down; then they'll settle for someone they can call a cen-
trist, but what that means is that he'll be someone that twenty
years ago, or even ten years ago, would have qualified as a con-

servative, but he'll be squeaky clean. Then the far right will put up their name, McReady more than likely, who will have to be clean, too. In the present climate, with so many scandals—moral, financial, ethical, name it—and both sides primed for a fight, they'll have investigated both of them from hell to high water, and they'd better come up clean, or the talk shows will tear them to pieces." He paused. "How clean? If he cheated on a driver's license test, it'll come out and damn him."

He regarded her soberly. "The problem is that presidents come and go; senators, congressmen, they all come and they go. Justices on the Supreme Court just come and stay. The next two people sworn in will be around for a long time, and the Court decides the laws of the land. If he has backers pulling his string, they'll have checked him thoroughly, and they'll be satisfied first how his opinions will read, and second that no one is going to uncover anything to sidetrack him. It appears that they've been grooming him for a long time, and they've seen to it that he minded his manners ever since Thomas Lynch clasped him to his bosom years ago."

"That's pretty scary," Barbara said after a moment.

"That's real scary."

She sat down opposite him then. "Well, what about Caesar's wife, then? How clean does she have to be?"

"Depends. What are you driving at?"

She told him about her long conversation with Alene and Roger. "A wild, boy-crazy girl, but she wasn't a girl any longer when Roger found his true love. And I keep thinking of what Vinny told Lara, that the land didn't change, and neither did Thomas or Anna Lynch, or Harris McReady or Babe. Did he know something to make him include her in the unchangeables?"

Frank shook his head. "It's a reach, Bobby. Too long a reach, maybe. Too far back, cat gossip, kid stuff. It wouldn't make any difference if she collected males as if they were postage stamps, just as long as all that was before she became Mrs. McReady."

"Dad, I don't have anything. Just Lara's denial. That's not enough."

"I know. I know that."

"Yeah. Okay, another little problem. Curtis Stroh's been spitting venom apparently, talked to detectives, the whole thing, and he let them interview the boy, Nathan. I have to warn Lara."

"Christ on a mountain! But whatever they got from the boy they can't use, not if they didn't go about it properly with the right safeguards. How old is he? Twelve?"

"He'll be thirteen in October. And even if they can't use that statement, if they call him, they can work it in one way or another, tie him in knots. If Stroh was prompting him or exerting influence, who knows what the kid might have said? I have to find out."

"Right. We have to meet him. Let's think."

For a time neither spoke, then Barbara said, "I could ask Lara to come down here to Eugene after she picks him up on Sunday, spend the night in town, let us all have dinner together, something like that."

"My place," Frank said. "Return her hospitality, that sort of thing. Dinner at the house, then after the boy goes to bed, we can talk it over." He gave Barbara a quick, sharp look. "I don't think it should be turned into a party, though. Just Lara and her lawyers. Okay?"

"Sure," she said, surprised. Suddenly she understood, not only the questioning looks he had given her from time to time, but the lack of invitations to dinner as well. "Dad," she said, "John isn't hanging around. He came by on his way to Canada and from there he'll go back to Arizona."

"Oh? You might have mentioned that."

"Oh? You might have asked."

"Well, if they fed you poison on the airplane, and I bet you skipped breakfast, maybe you're ready for a bite to eat now. I know I am. Lunch?"

"Sure. I'll call Lara first, though." Then she said, "Oh, damn. Maria." She hurried from her office to the reception room, where Maria was busy keystroking in something. "Knock off for lunch," Barbara said sternly. "Maria, I told you, if I forget what time it is, you have to remind me. Go, have lunch, now."

"Are you going now?" Maria asked. She was a year or two older than Barbara; she and her two children lived with her mother, and Barbara suspected that Maria's mother sometimes told her daughter when to eat, when to go to bed, and Maria automatically assumed that same role here in the office. She babied Shelley exactly the same way she did her children, the way she wanted to do with Barbara.

"I'm going in a few minutes," Barbara said; then in exasperation she added, "But, Maria, you don't have to wait for me to take off. That isn't how it works."

Maria smiled at her and turned back to her computer. "I'll just finish up this first," she said.

"Good God," Frank said when Barbara returned. "They cloned Patsy!"

"Sometimes she bugs the hell out of me."

He laughed.

She picked up her phone and dialed Lara's number.

On Thursday Manny called Barbara in the afternoon. "It's an official proposition," he said. He sounded very distant, almost toneless. "If Lara plays their game, takes the Alford about tampering, agrees to the verdict of suicide, she can pack up and leave. Five years' probation. Done. Otherwise, they'll go for murder one. The gun and note make it premeditated."

"Shit!"

Ignoring that, Manny said, "I asked about bail, and Shinizer said there's no problem. They don't want her in jail; we don't have a decent jail to hold a female prisoner for months, and it would mean out of county, which no one seems to want. He said if she happens to come across Vinny's papers, to come in and talk things over again, right up to the time a trial starts. After that, nothing doing."

They were giving her enough rope, freedom to search. . . . She said, "Lara's picking up Nathan on Sunday, and they'll come here to spend the night, then she'll be home on Monday. Did they give you a deadline for her decision?"

"Noon, Monday."

"She'll be back before that. We'll talk to her over the weekend, and you stall Shinizer. Okay?"

After she hung up, she remained motionless at her desk for a long time. They were missing something. In that big box of papers, there had to be something worth guarding, something Vinny Jessup had believed would keep Harris McReady off the Supreme Court. Something important enough to kill Vinny for.

She cursed Vinny Jessup with a fluency that would have startled her father if he had been there to hear. Why hadn't Vinny written it out, a brief like the one he had prepared for his son, just spelled it out in black and white? Suddenly she stopped in the center of the room. Maybe in the box were the accusations, his proofs, hidden like purloined letters in the mass of other material. And if that was the case, there might be some kind of identifying mark on the correct pages, a number, a star, a check mark, something.

She felt desperate for a hint about how to proceed, a directional guide, a polestar. She felt as if she were on a raft drifting in a black starless night, around and around and around.

✥ 15

Sunday was hot and sultry, the sky heavy with what the weather gurus were calling an inversion. Eugene, they explained at great length, cradled between two mountain ranges, would be subject more and more often to such inversions as the population increased, traffic increased, emissions from automobiles, from forest fires, from grass burning, from people exhaling all built up whenever the customary ocean breezes failed to cross the Coast Range. The ocean breeze had stalled out in the Pacific, near Hawaii maybe. No relief was in sight for the next few days.

And everything smelled of fireworks and citronella. Barbara had sat on a blanket with friends on her side of the river the night before, watching the fireworks from Autzen Stadium on the other side until the mosquitoes had driven her home, apparently unfazed by the coating of citronella she wore.

"There never used to be so many mosquitoes," she grumbled to Frank.

"Ah, the good old days. I remember when I was a boy and this was still called Skinner's Mud Flat, and the mosquitoes were so thick you couldn't see through the clouds of them. The Indians shot them out of the sky with bows and arrows." The doorbell rang, and he went to admit Lara and Nathan.

Lara looked strained, her smile forced as she introduced Nathan. And he looked almost exactly like her, the same coloring, same curly red-blond hair, freckles. Even his expression was as strained as hers.

"Hi," Barbara said. Nathan didn't look directly at her when they shook hands. He didn't look directly at Frank, either.

"What I thought we'd do," Barbara said, "is show you to your rooms, let you wash up or whatever, and then have a cool drink out on the back porch."

She led the way up the stairs to the bedrooms, one she had often used in this house, and a smaller one in which Frank had put the television. "Bathroom over there," she said, pointing. "Come down when you're ready."

In the kitchen Frank was arranging a tray with a pitcher of lemonade and snack foods. She had warned him that Lara didn't drink anything alcoholic and they had decided to join her in abstinence, at least until dinner. Lemonade with dinner would be carrying solidarity a bit too far, Barbara had said.

Frank took the tray out to the porch and stayed with it, to keep the marauding cats at bay, and she waited for their guests. Lara had told her that there was always a period of readjustment when Nathan spent more than just a weekend with his father. She had also said that Curtis had often told Nathan that lawyers were scum, which had led to difficulties at the beginning of her relationship with Vinny and later with Nathan's acceptance of Manny. Well, kid, Barbara thought as she heard their footsteps coming down, here are two more lawyers you'll just have to put up with.

On the porch Lara exclaimed over the beauty of the garden, and Nathan slouched down on the top step and said nothing. Lara took him a glass of lemonade, which he barely acknowledged and instantly put down on the step beside him. He appeared to be engrossed in a study of his sneakers.

They talked about the weather, about the drive to and from

Portland, how crowded I-5 was these days, the maniacs on the road, and all the while Nathan sat without moving, without touching his lemonade. Lara looked miserable.

After a few minutes of the inane conversation, Frank excused himself, went inside, and returned almost immediately. He went to the step and whistled, then waited. In a moment a cat appeared on the fence, walked along the top rail for a few steps, and jumped down. A second cat followed. They both trotted to Frank with their tails high in the air, beautiful monstrous golden coon cats.

"The rest of my family," Frank said. "Thing One and Thing Two." He gave them both a treat and rubbed their heads.

"Good heavens!" Lara said. "They shoot cats that size over where we come from, before they start stealing lambs or something."

Frank laughed. He squeezed a toy mouse that made a wheezing sound and threw it across the yard. Both cats raced after it. They tumbled over each other when they reached the toy, and had a mock battle for a moment before one seized the mouse, ran back to Frank, and dropped it at his feet. Their golden eyes were luminous as they watched him pick it up and then drop it into Nathan's lap. "Try it," he said.

Nathan held the mouse for a moment as if he wanted no part of any game, then he tossed it underhand into a flower bed where blue lupines and pink and white monarda were in bloom, their growth so luxurious that no ground was visible. The mouse vanished in the greenery. Lara started to move toward Nathan, obviously angry. His aim had been deliberate. Frank shook his head slightly and motioned her back, his expression equable, even amused.

Both cats ran to the edge of the flowers, then stepped in among them, not treading on a single stem in their search for the toy. One of them found it, and he leaped out from the flower bed onto the lawn in a motion that was as graceful as a Nureyev maneuver. He brought the toy back to Nathan and waited for the game to continue.

Frank returned to his chair. "You'll get tired before they will," he warned Nathan, who turned to grin at him.

They had dinner on the porch, grilled steaks and vegetables, everything done to perfection, as always. And while Nathan no longer seemed hidden behind a veil of wary hostility, neither did he say anything unless it was to answer a direct question. His gaze wandered again and again to the cats, both of them eyeing the steaks with intensity.

"If you don't want them piling up in bed with you," Frank said, "keep your door closed. They don't have the manners of a flea, and they think people beds are just fine."

Barbara knew that both cats shared his bed every night, and this meant that he intended to close them out, let them find Nathan.

"Do you think they'd come if I whistle?" Nathan asked unexpectedly. It was his first spontaneous utterance.

"Don't know," Frank said. He looked thoughtful; then said, "Let's try a little experiment. I'll go into the study and close the door, and you go to the living room and whistle. No guarantees, you understand. They've never had anyone but me whistle for them. Want to try?"

Nathan nodded, and they left together, with both cats following.

"He's wonderful," Lara said. "That's how Vinny treated Nathan. With respect. You were lucky to have a father like that."

"I know," Barbara said. She had never given it much thought, but it was true. Frank had always treated her with a kind of respect that adults seldom showed children. She knew very well that she could not have gotten around Nathan's self-protective silence, his distance the way Frank had done. She had become impatient with the boy, wished he would yawn and go to bed or go take a bath or something so they could talk.

"Let's clear stuff away," she said. "I know Dad has a dessert, but apparently it has to wait for the fun and games to end."

She had started the coffee before Nathan reappeared, looking triumphant, trailed by Thing One and Thing Two.

"I told them I'd give them some steak," Nathan said. "Are those really their names?"

Barbara handed him a plate of meat scraps. "You have no idea how two kittens can destroy a Christmas tree," she said. "They took it apart, ornament by ornament, practically limb by limb. They earned their names."

He nodded gravely, but his eyes were shining.

When Nathan went upstairs to watch television and go to bed, both cats galloped up behind him. He seemed very pleased.

As soon as he was gone, Lara said in a rush, "Curtis is going to petition the court for custody. He says they're going to arrest me and put me in jail, and he'll get custody."

"Did he say anything like that in front of Nathan?" Barbara asked.

"Not while I was there, but I'm sure he did. Nathan's been so tense; he's afraid. And he won't talk to me. Hardly a word. Did you notice that he won't even look at me? He's never come back like this before. Curtis must have told him terrible things."

"He's under a terrific strain," Barbara said. "He's told one thing by his father but experiences something altogether different. Few adults can handle a situation like that. It must be even harder for a child." Then, choosing her words carefully, she said, "Lara, there's something else you have to know. Apparently some investigators talked to Nathan while he was in Portland. I don't have any details, who they were, if Curtis stayed with him, or what he might have said."

Lara's face turned deathly white, making her freckles look artificial, as if she had painted them on. Her pallor was followed swiftly by a rush of color, and she jumped to her feet, both hands clenched into white-knuckled fists. "He wouldn't dare let them question a child! That's insane, inhuman! Nathan's just a child!"

"Sit down, Lara," Barbara said quietly. "It's done. He did let them, and we have to deal with it. In the morning, call your divorce lawyer and tell her what happened. That's the first thing. Tell her that Curtis is threatening to petition for custody. Tell her to inform the judge who handled the divorce and custody battle that an improper interrogation was conducted. Lara, are you listening to me?"

It was not at all clear that she was. She was staring off in a glassy-eyed way that suggested that she had heard nothing, that her mind was somewhere else altogether. Slowly she turned her gaze back to Barbara and nodded. "Yes," she whispered. "I'll call her."

"All right. So call her and let me know what she has to say. I'll want a copy of the entire divorce proceeding, the hearings, everything. Can you get the documents?"

"I have everything there was."

"Good. Now, Dad and I can't ask Nathan what they talked about, what they asked him, what he told them. He doesn't know us, and he has no reason to trust us. A child psychologist might get him to talk, but he or she would have Nathan as the client and be under no obligation to tell us anything. Or you, either. We don't know what Curtis told him, how much of it took root, or if he believed any of it. If anything was said that causes him anguish, you might have to bring in a child psychologist to help him, but only if you see signs of distress. If he's willing to talk to you, that would be the best thing, of course, but depending on the degree of guilt he might feel, it might not happen. You have to be prepared for that."

"I won't let Curtis have him again, not even for a weekend," Lara said in a low, vehement voice. "I won't!"

"Talk to the divorce lawyer," Barbara said firmly. "Be advised by her. Lara, I have to ask you this: do you know of anything that Nathan might have said that could hurt your case?"

Lara shook her head.

"It's important," Barbara said. "If he just repeated lies that Curtis fed him, that's one thing. We can call Curtis as a witness and show him for what he is. If there's anything that didn't come from Curtis, we have to know about it."

"There's nothing. Nathan loved Vinny; he loved living out there. He's been happy."

Barbara studied her for a few seconds, then said, "Okay, now about the official offer Shinizer made . . ."

They talked about the offer, and about what to expect in the weeks to come. "If you're out on bail," Frank said, "restrictions on your movements probably will be part of the court order. You'll have to make arrangements for Nathan's transportation to Portland and back when that comes up."

Lara's mouth tightened. "He usually goes by bus, but I'll talk to the divorce lawyer," she said grimly. "I don't want Nathan alone with Curtis ever again."

"Listen, Lara," Barbara said. "Whatever you do right now, don't dismiss a court order or try to get around it, or do anything else to add to your problems." She waited for Lara's reluctant nod. "In the morning before you take off," she said, "I think Dad should talk man-to-man to Nathan and tell him that you might be in trouble, and if you are, we'll take care of you. I think he might need a little reassuring. We don't want him to get the idea that plots are taking place behind his back or that anyone doesn't trust him."

Lara nodded miserably.

In her own apartment later, Barbara paced unhappily, and

after several minutes she stopped, and said under her breath, "She's lying."

Nathan knew something, might have told something damaging, and if life had been as great before Vinny's death as everyone was suggesting, that something might have to do with the night of his murder. And what can you do about it if your client lies to you? she asked herself mockingly. Diddly, she answered.

Everything happened almost exactly the way Barbara and Frank had predicted. The grand jury handed down a true bill; Lara was asked to present herself at the district attorney's office, and she and Manny checked in. She was escorted to the police station, where she was fingerprinted and photographed, and she and Manny appeared before the judge where she said in a whisper, "Not guilty," the only words she spoke. Trial was set for the first week in January, and the charge was murder one. Bail was granted, one hundred thousand dollars, ten percent of which had to be presented to the bail bondsman within twenty-four hours. And it was done, another reel of the continuing nightmare. That night Lara cried herself to sleep.

At her desk, Barbara and Frank were bent over a group of clippings with a bright light trained on them. "What do you think?" she asked.

"Not sure. Could be. But what for?"

"I don't know."

Some of the clippings were actual newspaper clippings; others were photocopies of newspaper articles. There were seven in all, and in the upper right corner of each one, there was a single dot made with a black felt-tip pen. The dots were hardly visible, certainly not a distraction; neither Barbara nor Frank had even noticed them until they went back through the box of papers again, searching for anything out of the ordinary.

Frank straightened up and groaned. "You know what that means? We've got to go back to the beginning and search for those damn dots, see if they're on the judicial decisions, if they're anywhere else."

In the box they had found a large folder stuffed with speeches by dozens of legislators, laws argued for or against, and talks by other right-wing extremists, supporters, and backers. Barbara and Frank had ignored them. No longer, she thought grimly. Each and every paper would go under the microscope now. She felt as if a two-ton weight had been molded onto her shoulders.

So far they had found nothing else of interest, and neither of them was certain the tiny dots were, either. Random? Reading with a pen in hand? Marking things to be filed? It could mean any of those things, or something they hadn't thought of, or nothing.

Neither of them had suggested they hire someone to do this tiresome job. No one else could be trusted to spot an anomaly, they said, but in fact they were afraid no one else could be trusted, period. They did not want to subject Lara to a media frenzy, and that meant they had to keep McReady's name out of it until they had something solid.

"I'll carry on while you make your appearance over in Salt Creek," Frank said with a grimace.

She would drive over the following day, meet Manny's secretary, inspect Manny's office, talk to Lara, meet Shinizer, and generally look around. Bailey would drive over the day after her arrival. Two or three days, then back home, back to her office, back to work here.

She was not looking forward to Salt Creek and Bend in July. Nor, she thought bleakly, was she looking forward to it in December on into January. Too damn hot, or too damn cold, what good was it?

Manny had already written his motions to the court, one for

the judge to recuse himself from the case, one to change the venue. He predicted that both would be turned down out of hand, no waiting period required.

"In that case, wait until I get there to hand them over," Barbara had said. "I'd like to see your judge in person in action."

"You should see him," Manny had agreed. "But you won't like it."

Old-fashioned hanging judge, she mused, who decided guilt or innocence by the skin color or the sex of the defendant. In this case a female defendant, female lead counsel, Native American second counsel . . . She suspected that before this trial was over, she would have found many, many grounds for appeal; she also suspected that the judge had already decided the entire thing and could just as soon skip to the sentencing phase as not.

✥ 16

The combined population of Bend and Salt Creek was about thirty-three thousand, and twelve hundred of them lived in Salt Creek, but the fifteen miles separating the two towns was already showing signs of surrender. Strip malls, gas stations, residential areas, a church or two . . . First the highway would yield to nonstop commercial growth, then the land behind the highway would become subdivisions, neighborhoods, and the two communities would be one. A bypass highway, more schools, more stores, more everything. A new Phoenix rising?

Manny's office was on Main Street, which was also Highway

97, much too busy and high-speed for a downtown street, and although the buildings were set well back with parking spaces in front, it was much too noisy for comfort in the office situated on it.

Barbara stood in the center of Manny's office and gazed about unhappily.

"This is where I hang out," Manny said. "Your office will be in the back of the building." He had the second floor of a two-story frame building; below was a hardware store and a Realtor's office. He led Barbara across a once-painted wood-floor hallway, with traces of green, no more than that, to another office; their footsteps echoed and reechoed throughout the second floor; the room he led her to overlooked a small subdivision across a street, and then the desert. He closed the door, and the street sounds faded to white noise.

"Ah," she said in relief. "Much better." There was a desk, several straight chairs, three overstuffed Naugahyde-covered chairs, and a dining table with the legs cut short to turn it into a coffee table. It would do. A computer was set up on the desk, but she already had decided to use her own laptop. She had not yet grown used to the idea of working with strangers, and to put confidential material on someone else's computer was unthinkable.

"One more room," Manny said, motioning toward the door. "Conference room."

That room adjoined his office, with a connecting door, and served as a multifunction room; there were many file cabinets against one wall, and boxes of files stacked up near the cabinets. The files from Vinny's practice, Manny said. One wall had bookshelves from floor to ceiling, filled to overflowing with law books, for the most part. A round table with many marks, scars, gouges, and little varnish or finish of any sort was centered in the room with a half a dozen mismatched chairs around it.

Apparently this was also his secretary's room; at least a woman was there now, at a desk against the wall opposite the files. Barbara suspected that she had been moved from across the hall for the time being.

"Nadia Walker," Manny said. The woman stood up and came to shake Barbara's hand. She was in her thirties, thick in the middle, about five feet tall, with lustrous black hair, beautiful brown eyes, and the longest, thickest eyelashes Barbara had ever seen.

Barbara and Manny returned to the room she would call hers, and she sat on one of the Naugahyde-covered chairs. She didn't get up instantly or comment about the chair, but she would pick the wooden chairs in the future; the plastic was cold and clammy against her skin. Robert Sheffield was due any minute. Both Manny and Lara wanted him to assist on the case.

"Vinny and I used to work together quite often," Manny said, seating himself across the coffee table from her. "Sometimes on one of my cases, sometimes on his, didn't make much difference where it started. See, there are folks who will talk to me who wouldn't give you or Robert or Vinny, either, far as that goes, the time of day. And folks who'd talk to him and never see me standing in front of them. That's how it goes; you work with it. Robert and I are falling into the same sort of pattern, and it's working pretty well. I trust him, and Vinny did, too, or he wouldn't have turned over his cases to him."

He had read her hesitation correctly; she had planned to keep Robert on the fringe, busy work at the edge, things that always needed doing but that wouldn't matter too much if he talked about them outside.

"Okay," she said. "Does he know about the box Vinny left for Lara?"

"No. I haven't told him anything about this case. That's your job."

"Good. For now, let's put those files aside. Dad's going over everything one more time, and meanwhile there are several other lines to follow up on."

They were still discussing the investigation by the state as well as by the sheriff when Robert Sheffield arrived. Manny finished what he was saying. "If the state investigators ask questions, take statements, chances are good there will be copies on file; you'll get them as part of discovery. If the sheriff's office handles statements, or anything else, maybe you'll see the results, maybe not."

Barbara knew that her surprise and dismay showed. She looked from Manny to Robert, who nodded and shrugged.

"Jesus Christ!" she muttered. "You try filing a complaint?"

"Several times," Manny said. He shrugged as expressively as Robert had done.

She leaned back in her chair. After a moment she said, "Okay. So we go with it for now. But, gentlemen," she added, "I want you both to keep absolutely thorough notes, memoranda of every request, every word said, from right now on through."

They both nodded. Robert pulled a chair in closer and sat down, and their team went to work. Robert had looked awkward standing, but he was even more awkward sitting. Poor boy, Barbara thought, he needed custom furniture for his long legs.

"We'll let Bailey oversee the whole investigation," she said. "Robert, I'll want you to go through all the files Vinny gave you, just in case there's someone in there with a real grudge, or in case there's something hidden among those files that could prove helpful. Okay?"

She outlined the various approaches she planned to take: Manny would ride the district attorney, try to get everything turned over to the defense in a timely manner, file the proper motions. Robert would start the search for possible suspects for Vinny's murder, or for anything out of the ordinary in the files.

She admitted to him that she didn't know enough to tell him exactly what to look for. Bailey would follow up on everything that came along.

"We want the dope on Vinny's car, on whoever else was on the mountain that night, the servants in the Lynch house, people who work on the ranch or left recently, the murder weapon. . . . I want the typewriter the suicide note was written on," she said when she was nearly to the end of the notes she had made.

"I think if I come over here on Wednesdays, we can meet and discuss our progress, if any. I'd rather not trust anything of importance to the telephone, or the post office, either. So, I'll come over on Wednesday, and stay for as long as it takes to read reports, meet people here, talk to you guys."

"You have any objection if we talk things over ourselves?" Robert asked.

She shook her head. "None. Just keep in mind that I like to know everything that's going on in a case I'm handling."

That afternoon she walked to the courthouse with Manny. The courthouse was a pretty little frame building with beveled lead-glass windows, prisms for the light entering the building, creating rainbows on the interior walls. Six steps up, double oak doors with the fancy glass lights, nice oak flooring, two simple chandeliers in the anteroom, and a wide, curved staircase to the second floor. Two desks, one of them occupied by a lean man who glanced up, nodded, and turned back to a paperback book he was reading. Two courtrooms, one on each side of the anteroom. Manny led the way to one of the courtrooms, small and bright with more of the pretty glass windows, benches for perhaps twenty-five spectators, nice padded chairs for the jurors, and a very high judge's bench with two flags flanking it, the Oregon flag and the U.S. flag. Identical tables and chairs for the prosecution and defense, high-backed chairs that looked uncomfortable.

Judge Herman Henkel entered from a door behind his bench and took his chair. He was not wearing his robe, just blue pants and a blue-and-pink plaid short-sleeved shirt. His hair was bone white and rather dull, his cheeks and nose very pink and shiny. He was overweight, with dewlaps and double chins; his eyes were small and deep set.

Suddenly in Barbara's head was the tinkly music of "The Farmer in the Dell." She blinked, recalling all of a piece the house she had lived in when she was no more than five or six. A nice house in a good neighborhood of middle-class houses in the south end of town, not ritzy or rich, but comfortable. A neighbor, Mr. Gorman, had been fanatical about his lawn, his yard, his house trim, car and about the sidewalk in front of his house. She could see him clearly in her mind—Herman Henkel was so like him, they might have been brothers. Barbara had run out of her house when she heard the ice-cream truck; she had been waiting with her quarter in her hand, and she ran out and bought an ice-cream stick, vanilla with chocolate coating. She had not waited for the ice-cream man to get in front of her own house; he was still at the curb by Mr. Gorman's. And then, walking home, two doors down the street, she had been drenched by a hose. In astonishment she had dropped her ice cream, and stood paralyzed as Mr. Gorman adjusted the flow of water to a hard stream and washed the ice cream off the sidewalk into the gutter. Wordlessly he returned to his yard, past the front hedge, out of her sight.

She had no memory of what Frank had done about the incident; no memory past her immobilization in shock at the sudden drenching. After that day she had hated Mr. Gorman with a passion only a child could sustain.

Looking at Judge Herman Henkel, she felt that old hatred stirring undimmed by the intervening years; she had not thought of Gorman from the time she was eight or nine, when her family had moved to a different house, until this minute in court.

"Now, Manny," the judge was saying, "you know I don't intend to recuse myself. No reason to. We'll have us a fair and square trial like always. And I don't intend to have a change of venue. So, let's get on with things. That your new partner?"

"Yes," Manny said, and motioned to Barbara, who stepped forward to meet Judge Herman Henkel.

The judge frowned at her, and deliberately looked her over, up and down, back up. "I don't allow any theatricals in my court," he said. "No grandstanding, no politicking. You understand what I'm telling you?"

"I'll make a great effort to control myself," she said coldly.

His scowl deepened; he stood up and left the bench, walked out through the door he had entered by.

Watching him exit, she thought at least she knew why she disliked him intensely, fair or not fair. But there was little reason she could see for him to have shown an equal dislike for her, not this early in the game, anyway. If he was that openly sexist, that could be good for her side, but she knew too many people in the field who were blatantly sexist, off the record, and goody-two-shoes on record. Some of the worst racists she had ever known never said a word on record to indicate their true inclinations. Just a datum, she told herself then, leaving the building with Manny.

"Mistake, I guess," she said to Manny, on the way back to his offices, just around the corner.

"I doubt it. You both know where you stand; that never hurts, to have it out in the open."

That afternoon she walked all over Salt Creek—into the hardware store, both banks, two supermarkets, one mom-and-pop

grocery, two gift shops, one with very nice, pricey knickknacks
and kitchenware. . . . She felt certain that everyone in town knew
who she was, why she was there; no one quizzed her, or stared
much, but it was in the way they treated her, the quick looks at
her, then over her shoulder, a certain wariness that seemed to
enter the establishments along with her.

Thoughtfully she got into her car and drove the fifteen miles
to Bend. There were so many new people in Bend, new construction, new subdivisions, people coming to look, to visit, to
browse in real estate listings. Bend was too busy with its own
growth spurt to pay any attention to her. She found a sidewalk
telephone and called Bailey to tell him to hole up in Bend, not
in Salt Creek, where he would be under surveillance day and
night.

She had discussed housing arrangements with Lara, and they
had decided that Barbara would stay at Lara's house the days
she was in the area until the trial started. After that she would
have a hotel room. Alene and Roger planned to come and stay
during the trial, but aside from that, Barbara felt it would be too
constricting to be with Lara all day in court, and then with her
all evening as well. And she, Barbara, needed time out, time to
pace and think, plan the coming day, go over the present day—
without the distraction of Lara and Nathan and the others.

Barbara and Lara had laid down ground rules for the present,
when she would be a guest at Lara's house. No talking about
the case, any aspect of it, in front of Nathan or at dinner, and as
soon as dinner was over, Barbara would be free to vanish into
her own room or Vinny's study, which Lara had offered her.

Barbara had said, "I won't share cooking chores with you,
and in fact it might be best if you and Nathan just go ahead and
have your meals as if I'm not around, and I'll fend for myself
when I get ready."

"Please, don't do that," Lara had said instantly. "I'd feel terrible, and it would be so strange not to have you eat with us. I have to cook anyway, and one more doesn't make a bit of difference."

They compromised: Barbara would pay half the grocery bill for the days she was a houseguest, and Lara and Nathan would shop and cook.

That day Lara had to work at the hospital until six; Barbara got to the house at six-fifteen, closely followed by Lara's car, and Nathan came out to help with a bag of groceries. They all went inside through the lower-level garage; Lara closed the big door, which clanged and banged, and they went up the stairs to the entrance hall, on to the kitchen. Barbara had stopped for a bottle of wine, and Nathan was prying in Lara's bag, looking, he said, for a soda or something.

Dinner was a simple, quickly prepared meal, to Barbara's relief. There was a salad, tortillas, a fast stir-fry shredded-beef filling with canned salsa, refried beans, rice, and it was on the table within half an hour. Good, fast, and satisfying—what more could anyone want?

Nathan ate quickly, then excused himself, a program on television, he said, looking out through the window, looking anywhere but at Barbara or at Lara. He had not spoken throughout the evening after asking if there were any sodas. He had been out on his bike, apparently, his face was sunburned, his freckles thick and dark. As he left the room, Lara called after him, "I have ice cream."

"Maybe later," he said, and kept walking.

In Vinny's study late that night, Barbara had to admit that for her this arrangement was more than satisfactory. She hated hotel rooms, and motel rooms even more so. With the house on several different levels, no sound from Lara or Nathan seemed to escape the tier that held their bedrooms, and Barbara felt free to roam about the downstairs, to her room on the top level, here to Vinny's study just a few steps up from the entrance. It was a clever house, she thought with approval. The hall outside Vinny's door was carpeted; even if Lara or Nathan or both were up and down, back and forth to the kitchen and living room, to their upper-level rooms, their steps were inaudible.

Now, seated at Vinny's desk, Barbara was sifting through a box of personal effects that Vinny's secretary had brought to Lara several weeks after his death. A few books, some pieces of pottery, a calendar with various dates circled, small notes here and there, an engagement book, another calendar, a day-planner type, with large blanks below the numbered days . . . All this stuff, Lara had said, indicating the box, were things that Serena Batdorf, Vinny's secretary, had not allowed the sheriff to take away; she had boxed up these things and hauled them over to Lara after the sheriff had finished his search of Lara's house.

Barbara had an appointment with Serena Batdorf on the following day, but for now, she was simply leafing through the calendars. Dentist appointment, tune-up, "HH is an ass" written in the margin of February. "Call Manny" in March. The kind of messages you leave yourself, she thought, then picked up the day planner. It wasn't much more informative. Court dates, names she was not familiar with, reminders: "Look up deed, Meyers." "Delia's will." A telephone number or two.

For June he had penciled in; "Coast—weekend." For July: "Leslie Gulch."

Other people's appointments were meaningless without interpretation, and tomorrow she would take the calendars when she went to talk to Serena Batdorf. She left Vinny's office and walked to the kitchen for a glass of water, then carried it out to the deck; the night was very cool, with a slight wind falling down from the mountain. She could hear coyotes yipping, and wind in trees, an occasional distant automobile or truck sound so faint that it was not intrusive; it was very dark except for a few lights

that apparently were down in Salt Creek, three miles away.
Gradually she became aware of a closer glow, and she walked to
the far end of the deck, and from there she could see a house
light flickering through shrubs.

She wondered how visible this house was to the neighbors.
In the daylight it appeared isolated, screened off from everyone
up and down Salt Creek Road, but seeing the other house lights
made her realize that the isolation was illusory; if she could see
other house lights, people around here could just as well see
these lights.

From where she was standing now, overlooking the driveway
and the road, she turned to survey the house, garage lights, bedrooms on the upper levels, part of the deck visible from the road.
Someone might have seen Vinny leave that night, might pinpoint
the time, confirm Lara's story.

She visualized the interior of the house; the room overlooking
the driveway was Nathan's room, Lara's was in the rear with a
desert view, as was the room Barbara was using. Nathan could
have seen Vinny leave that night, she thought, disquieted. Was
that what the detectives had drawn from him, that he had seen
Vinny leave? But that would not have left him with a burden of
guilt. Slowly she walked back to the study and dug out from her
briefcase the transcription of Lara's tape-recorded statement.

Q: Then what did he do?
A: He picked up his briefcase and walked down the stairs
   to the garage. He got in his car and drove out.
Q: Did he close the garage door?
A: Yes. I heard it close.

All out in the open; no one was disputing that Vinny had left
a few minutes before ten that night. Earlier, Barbara had heard
the garage door close; it was not a quiet door, it banged.

So Nathan probably had heard him leave, even if Lara had thought he was already asleep. And then what had he heard? What happened from the time the Corning family left until Nathan really fell asleep, something that he might have told detectives, something that was haunting him now, making him avoid looking at his mother, making him nervous and jumpy at any sudden noise, making him silent and withdrawn?

She made a note to tell Manny to get a copy of Nathan's statement as soon as it was available. Sheriff's men, or state detectives? Who had they been? She understood now what Manny had been warning her about: it could make a difference who had questioned Nathan.

✥ 17

Serena Batdorf was fifty, with hair dyed a strange color that made Barbara think of cantaloupes. She had light blue eyes and deep squint lines. Since Vinny's death, she had been working in a Realtor's office in Bend, but she was quick to say she didn't like it. No challenge, no excitement, just tedious. She had worked for Vinny for six years, she said in a melancholy voice, after he came home from the hospital the first time. "Such a good man, it's a shame. The good ones seem to go first, don't they?" She sighed. She had sighed when Barbara called for an appointment.

Barbara was seated in the real estate office with her. Serena

Batdorf had said she could spare half an hour, but no longer than that. Real estate was booming, she had added with a sigh.

"Was it exciting, working for Vinny?"

"Well, I don't mean the kind of excitement you see on TV, you know, big dramatic scenes in court or people shooting at you, nothing like that, but always different. Every day, it looked like something new and different would come along. He did everything, you see—trusts, divorces, but he didn't like doing them, land deals, civil cases, criminal cases, all of it. That's how it is with a country lawyer, they get to do everything."

"What was he like to work for? Demanding, easygoing, what?"

"Oh, real easygoing. You couldn't have found a better or more considerate boss. If we didn't have much going on, he'd say, Just take the day off, take in a movie. It didn't happen too often because he had a lot of clients, you understand, but now and then things would ease up, and he'd give me the day off, or afternoon, with pay, I mean."

Her sighs were coming closer together, more heartfelt than ever, Barbara thought with a touch of cynicism. If Vinny had put up with her sighing like this, he must have been a saint or deaf.

"Did you keep his appointment calendar for him?" she asked.

"Yes. He wasn't really very good with dates. Names and faces and what happened in court, things like that, steel-trap kind of mind, but for dates . . . Well, I kept all that information for him. Part of my job."

"Lara gave me the things you packed up from the office," Barbara said then. "I didn't find a real appointment calendar, though. Do you still have it?"

Serena's lips tightened, and she sucked in her cheeks. "That sheriff, Silly Gooey, he took it. He came the very day they found

Vinny's body and he took it. He wanted to go through every-thing, but Robert Sheffield came in and told him to get a court order or something. But he kept all the stuff he already put in his car."

"Did he give you a receipt?"

"Not a thing. And I was too upset to even think about de-manding one, or anything else. If Robert hadn't come in, that sheriff would have cleaned out the whole office, I imagine; I was too upset to stop him." She shook her head and sighed deeply.

Barbara's impatience with this woman was becoming more strained; she found herself sighing and nearly laughed aloud. In-stead, she asked, "When did you box up the stuff you took over to Lara?"

"That afternoon. Robert said I should put them in a box and in a few weeks just deliver them to Lara because anything Silly Gooey took away probably would never come to light again. So that's what I did."

"I have the calendars you put in the box," Barbara said. "Do you think you could make any sense out of the few things he jotted down on them?"

Serena Batdorf looked like a candidate for martyrdom. "He wasn't good about making notes about dates," she said help-lessly. "I can try, but I usually did all that kind of thing, not him, and any notes he made I might not have known anything about."

"Let's try," Barbara said. Together they looked at the first calendar.

"I know who HH is," Serena said, and whispered the name: "Herman Henkel. And he is an ass." She pointed. "See this, den-tist appointment, no date or anything. Just to remind him to ask me to set it up for him and remind him when it was coming around. That's how he did things. He, poor thing, never knew if he was coming or going."

"What about Meyers, this note about a deed?"

Serena thought a moment, then said, "Right-of-way problem. Just a little job, clear up who owned a strip of property, something like that. No big deal. I had an appointment with Meyers in my book, but I can't remember just when it was. Like I said, no big deal."

"And there aren't any dates for the coast trip or Leslie Gulch, either."

"No. He would have had me arrange a timetable for them, but he wasn't making plans for the rest of the summer, not yet, nothing after the middle of May. At least nothing definite. His checkup, you see. He knew he'd be away, and maybe they'd even keep him again, like before."

"Did you have the checkup date in your book?"

"Not yet. I kept after him to tell me, but he kept forgetting. I intended to ask Lara and never got around to it."

Barbara looked over the calendar and the day planner. "These court dates, did he keep all those dates?"

"I think so. But without my book I can't remember exactly. Probably he did. But you know how it is, things get canceled or someone doesn't show up or something else happens, so I can't say for sure."

Barbara knew all about that. She pointed. "And this one, Delia's will? Is that a routine matter, too?"

"I don't know," Serena said. She peered at it closer, then pursed her lips. "Delia, Delia . . . Oh, Delia. He wrote her will a few years back. I remember that I had to ask if that was a real name and how to spell it. Maybe she wanted some changes made, and he just forgot to tell me. It was hard, planning dates with him, he kept forgetting them or he'd forget to tell me, or something. I never complained, of course; that was just his way." She shook her head. "What you really need is to make Silly Gooey hand over my appointment book and go over that with me."

"I expect you're right," Barbara said. They talked a few more minutes, but she felt that it was all a waste of time, and she knew no more when she left Serena Batdorf than when she had come in. According to Serena, Vinny had had no real enemies; even the people he beat in court, or forced concessions from, ended up liking him. Everyone who knew him called him fair, a straight shooter, a good man. Right, Barbara thought. Right. But someone out there had not liked him; someone had shot him in the head. She sighed.

A little early for her meeting with Bailey at the Vista Motel, she sat on a terrace with iced coffee and brooded about Silly Gooey, Sheriff Sylvester Gouin. Maybe Sheffield could get the appointment book from him; at least Robert Sheffield had been a witness to the sheriff's taking it. She had no real idea of what she might find in the book or why she even wanted it, but a matter of principle was involved; the sheriff had no right to it, not without a court order, and then forking over a receipt.

She nodded to herself; next on the agenda, meet the local constabulary—sheriff and district attorney both.

Bailey appeared, slouching along in no hurry apparently, just taking in the sights. His ambling gait was pure deception, she had learned years earlier when she had found it a challenge to keep up with him. But anyone describing him would, no doubt, say he was moseying along in nearly slow motion. She waved, and he made his way to her table.

"Hiya," he said, eyeing her iced coffee with disfavor. "They serve cold beer here?"

"I don't know. Ask." The waiter came and he asked and was treated to a minihistory of the microbrewery business in Bend. He ordered a beer.

"I've been thinking of the problem you mentioned before,"

Barbara said while they waited for the waiter to return. "About standing out over here. What you might do is talk to a real estate agent and see if you can rent a furnished house, or even an apartment. You can use it, I could use it from time to time, and when the trial starts, we'll really need it."

"Be cheaper than a hotel room," he said noncommittally. "But, Barbara, I'll tell you up front, I don't aim to put in a lot of time over here. I'd rather drive back and forth every day. Too hot, too dry."

She could not deny the heat or the aridity; she felt parched, as if her skin were ready to peel off in long strips that, no doubt, would look like meat jerky. "Well, if not right now, a couple of months down the line. You probably couldn't get one right now anyway. Try Serena Batdorf," she said. "I think she's a talker, and she worked for Vinny for six years. A long shot, but she might come up with something useful." She gave him Serena's address and telephone number at the real estate office. "Bailey, do you suppose sighs are contagious, the way yawns are?"

He gave her a suspicious look, but before he could comment, the waiter brought his beer, and she got out her notebook, and for the next forty-five minutes they made plans; he reported what little he had found out so far, and she filled him in on what little she had learned. Neither had a lot to give the other, but she had known that already; it was too soon.

After Bailey left, she thought about Shinizer and Silly Gooey again. Shinizer had an address in the same building as Robert Sheffield's office; probably the sheriff was not too far from there. She had spied a telephone near the women's room, and used it now to call Sheffield. Since she didn't need an excuse to talk to one of the counsel in her case, she offered none, and merely asked if he would be around in an hour or so, and would it be convenient for her to drop in. It was nearly two; they agreed that four would be a good time, and she hung up. A couple of hours to kill.

She drove around Bend, through the new developments, past the new strip malls, down to the river, where she left the car and sat in the shade of a cottonwood tree for a long time. The tree was a hundred feet tall, at least, four feet through the trunk, and it rustled and whispered in a breeze so faint that she could barely feel the movement of air. The Deschutes River was below the bench where she was sitting, a pretty little river with a rocky bottom, rocky shoreline, and clear, flashing water that didn't look to be more than a foot or two deep here, a little sister to the Willamette River in Eugene, but with the same restorative powers. When she left the riverfront park, she felt refreshed and not quite so depressed, and she realized with a shock how depressed she had become.

She sat in her car with her hand on the key, but didn't turn it on yet. Why depressed? It was too early in the case to feel defeated yet, she told herself severely, but the words didn't stick. She simply didn't see a decent defense taking shape for Lara Jessup. Usually the bits and pieces being gathered began to adhere, a form began to reveal itself, but nothing like that was happening yet. Bits and pieces were like fluff, lifted, swirled about, dropped, each particle isolated, repelling and being repelled by all the other particles.

It was not yet four when she parked outside the office building in Salt Creek; it was on the same street as the courthouse, part private offices, part public, even the sheriff had an office here in the Lynch Building. It was a two-story, concrete-block structure with river-stone facing in front, broad stone steps, high windows, a small lobby with stairs, and an elevator. No one was in the lobby; there were four glass-front doors, attorneys, and farther down, the sheriff's department. She went up the stairs.

All the doors on this floor were wooden, no glass fronts, nothing fancy, just solid doors. She walked the length of the hallway; the district attorney's rooms were at one end. Retracing her steps, continuing on down the other way, she came to Sheffield's name. She knocked on the door.

A stout man with very little hair and not much neck opened the door to admit her to a tiny anteroom that held a desk with a computer, file cabinets, and two extra chairs against the wall. The stout man nearly filled the space all by himself.

"Barbara Holloway," she said. "I believe Mr. Sheffield is expecting me."

"Oh, yes, right. I'll just give him a call. Please have a seat; he'll be right here." He went to the desk, picked up the telephone, and hit a button. He didn't shift his gaze from her.

Barbara did not sit down, but went to the door again and stood in the doorway gazing down the hall. Sheffield came from the district attorney's office and hurried toward her, followed by another man, who she assumed was Carl Shinizer.

Sheffield was pale, apparently angry; Shinizer was beaming at her in a jovial way.

"Ms. Holloway, Carl Shinizer," Sheffield said. "He wanted to meet you."

"And I wanted to meet him," she said easily. She shook his hand. She knew he was forty-eight, married, with four children, a graduate of Ohio State. He was of medium height, and wiry, with sinewy hands and arms, and sharp features. He was wearing nice slacks and a short-sleeved shirt unbuttoned at the collar. His hair was wavy and dark brown, almost black, his eyes dark brown; although very tanned, his skin didn't have the baked look she had come to expect from desert people. He looked like a runner. Maybe he ran at night and used a tanning salon.

"I hope you're not finding our climate too extreme," Shinizer said. "People from the valley sometimes have trouble adapting."

"It's fine," she said. "Mr. Shinizer, I understand that you have offered a deal for Lara, but since I got it secondhand, I wonder if you would repeat it, just to keep the record straight."

His eyes narrowed and he nodded. "My office?"

"Since we're all here, why not Mr. Sheffield's office," she said, and without waiting for a reply, she turned and walked through the anteroom to the door on the opposite wall. The stout man rushed to open the door and then move out of the way. "We haven't actually met," Barbara said nodding toward him; she turned to Sheffield.

"Jay Balmer, clerk, secretary."

"How do you do," she said, and entered the other office. It was big enough for several chairs, a large desk, more files, another computer, and little else. Bare-bones operation, exactly what her office would have looked like if her father hadn't taken a hand in the furnishings.

Shinizer pulled a chair closer to the desk, then waited for Barbara to be seated before he sat down. Sheffield went around the desk and sat in a swivel chair that creaked and squealed.

"My offer," Shinizer said, "was simple. By taking the Alford, Mrs. Jessup accepts the responsibility for her actions, tampering with evidence, arranging the suicide note, taking the papers Vinny was carrying, and my office will go easy on her. We don't want to prosecute her, you see. Vinny was dying, she was desperate; she did a foolish thing. Her confession, her acceptance of probation, relinquishing any claim on the estate, and quitting the area, that's all we'd ask for. If she comes across the papers Vinny was to deliver to Judge McReady, that would help her case considerably, of course."

"Or?"

"Murder one, premeditated, as proven by the gun and the

note, as well as the amount of codeine in his system, furnished
by her, and witnesses who will put her on the mountain that
night. We can accept desperation, a panicky woman who made
a serious mistake, but if she refuses to accept responsibility, we
have little choice but to pursue the murder charge." He looked
very mournful and sincere.

"I see," Barbara said; she stood up.

Then, moving with a surprising swiftness, Sheffield left his
desk and crossed the office to pull open the door to the anteroom. Jay Balmer was standing in the doorway.

"I wondered if you'd need me anymore today," he said after
a second.

"Hang around a few minutes," Sheffield said. "I think Carl is
leaving now."

Carl Shinizer was on his feet, on his way to the door. "It's
been a pleasure, Ms. Holloway. Perhaps later, when you've had
a chance to get your bearings over here, we can share a cup of
coffee, or even a glass of wine."

"Perhaps," she said. She watched Sheffield escort him to the
outer door, close the door behind him, and continue to stand
there.

"Get your stuff together and clear out," Sheffield said to Jay
Balmer.

"What do you mean?"

"You're fired. Beat it."

"You can't do that, not without cause. Not without a couple
weeks' notice. You can't just fire me."

"I can, and I did. Sue me."

"Don't think I won't!" Balmer said harshly. "You'll hear
from me."

He rummaged in his desk and brought out a few odds and
ends, and then looked around the office. "You'll hear from me,"
he said; he stamped out and slammed the door behind him.

Silently Barbara walked to Balmer's desk and studied the telephone for a second; she pressed the REDIAL button. A woman answered on the third ring: "The district attorney's office. Can I help you?" Barbara hung up.

"He wasn't in when you called," Sheffield said in a wooden tone. "About half an hour ago he returned and I told him you were coming and to just bring you on in when you showed up. Then, I overheard him on the phone to Carl, *reporting* might be a more accurate word, and I went to Carl's office to try to find out who the primary employer of Jay Balmer is. You saw the rest."

She nodded, still silent, and then picked up her purse and briefcase, prepared to leave. She was not leaving the briefcase in the car for fear of melting the computer, and it was a nuisance to lug it in and out with her everywhere she went, but, she thought unhappily, she saw little reason to trust it anywhere except at her side.

"Ms. Holloway, let's get out of here and have a drink or something. I'd like to talk to you, but not here."

"Okay. Where?"

He went to the inner office and turned off a lamp on the desk, closed the blinds, and glanced around. "Nowhere in Salt Creek," he said after a moment. In the anteroom, he glanced around in a cursory manner, shrugged, and locked the file cabinets. "Little point in locking up these files, not if Balmer's been at them." He locked the door to the hall after they left the office, and they walked down the stairs, out to the front of the building, and paused. "I don't have a car here; I walk back and forth," he said. "There's a place a few miles down the road toward Bend, a tavern. Luke's Place. I could meet you there, or you could drive us both there."

"I'll drive us," she said.

Of course, her car was superhot again, she opened the windows all the way, not a great deal of help since the air coming in when she started was almost as hot as the air already present. In just a few minutes Sheffield told her to take the next turn off to the right, and ahead was a sign with a big arrow for Luke's Place. She turned, drove on a dirt road for several hundred feet, then parked in the shade of a juniper tree.

The tavern was dim and cool; business was good, a lot of people were there, all locals, apparently. It wasn't the sort of place tourists would come across on their own. She ordered a gin and bitter lemon, and he said beer, and they waited in silence until their drinks were before them. She was very aware that he was studying her as they waited. Neither spoke until the waiter came and left again.

"Ms. Holloway, I know how that looked back in the office. And you are well advised to trust no one over here, except your client and Manny. I think you're safe with both of them. I'd like to add my name, but I understand this might not be the best of times to push myself forward."

She sipped her gin and lemon; it was excellent, cooled almost to freezing, exactly right. "Tell me about Shinizer's offer," she said. "I have the feeling that every time I hear about it, the terms have changed, or the premises, or something else."

"You're right. This is the first time I've heard anything about witnesses who can put Lara on the mountain. I don't know what that means. And they're saying she got the codeine at the hospital and was doping him with it for weeks, either with or without his knowledge and cooperation. She says she didn't. They have a number of people who will testify that Vinny was dying. Some of them might even quote him, last-days kind of thing." He drank his beer, frowning. "It's all still malleable," he said slowly. "They really prefer to label it suicide, and be done with it. But unless someone confesses to tampering with the evidence, they have to go for murder. No middle ground. No fingerprints on the gun or the briefcase. The suicide note obviously a fake."

He looked at her for a second, turned away, and said in a harsh low voice, "I'm afraid for her, for Lara. I don't think she should be up there alone, or driving around alone. If they decide she's really going to tough it out . . ." He looked at her again, and leaned in closer. "I've read every word I could find about Lewis Jessup, about the charges, about his disappearance, and how the case was closed instantly when he vanished. That's what I'm afraid of, that it could happen again, just like that."

"Good God!" But this was different, she wanted to say, and found that she couldn't say that. It was no different, after all. Vinny had brought in outside help, Lester DeFeo, a really high-profile, high-powered attorney, and the boy had vanished anyway, and nothing had been done. There was little difference. Lewis Jessup had been out on bail, ordered not to leave the county; Lara had the same orders, the same illusory freedom. If Lara vanished, if she had a fatal accident, would this case be closed summarily?

Then the thought came to her, Was Robert Sheffield to be trusted even in this warning, this voiced apprehension? Or was he playing a part in the game, his role meant to deepen the fear, add a new scare tactic in an effort to make Lara disclose the whereabouts of the missing papers?

If Sheffield was merely a pawn, a messenger boy, what difference did it make? The threat was there, too plausible to be ignored. History did repeat itself more often than not.

18

Robert Sheffield was an enigma, Barbara decided, sipping her icy drink; he looked like a boy still unsure about his table manners, and yet she knew he had been an honor student at Columbia, had gone on to law school at Northwestern, had worked for a major Chicago firm for less than a year, and settled in here to start his own office in the tiny godforsaken end of the world that Salt Creek must have seemed to him.

And now he was warning her that Lara might be killed, made to vanish—something. If his fear and anguish were not real, he was a world-class actor. "What do you suggest we can do to protect Lara?" she asked.

"I don't know. Get her a boarder, someone to stay in the house with her, for openers." Almost instantly he added, "But that wouldn't do it, not if she's out driving to work at god-awful hours the way she does."

Barbara took another sip, and then, coming to a decision, she asked, "Robert, what's your place here? What are you doing here? Why here?"

"You've looked me up, asked Manny about me, the usual, I assume," he said, and turned his gaze past her, out the window. "I had a job, you know, pretty good job, pretty good law firm. And one day I just didn't go to work. I got up, shaved, dressed, made coffee, and then sat down at my kitchen counter and stayed there for an hour, two hours. All morning. They called and I let the phone ring. I went for a walk, and that night I packed some things, put some things in a mini-storage place, loaded my car, and started driving. No plans, no destination. West and somewhere else, mostly somewhere else."

He glanced at her, then quickly away. "It doesn't matter what the case was I was assigned to. I doubt that it was a particular case, just the whole scene. I stopped at half a dozen towns across the country, hung out a few days, drove on. Then I came here, and stayed. No particular reason for this place over another, except I'm partial to the desert, I guess. I didn't know that until I got here."

He had family back East, she knew, two brothers and a sister, parents in New Jersey. The problem was, she thought, if he wanted a share of the kind of power Lynch wielded, wouldn't it have been more likely to fall into his lap with the big prestigious firm he had walked away from? She studied his lean face and found no answer to her real question: why was he here?

Both Manny and Vinny had come to know him and to trust him, she reminded herself, and she doubted that either of them would have been easily duped. But still she kept hedging, uncertain. He continued to be an enigma.

"I wonder if Lara has a gun, if she can shoot it," she murmured, and finished her drink.

"Yes, to both parts. Vinny taught her to shoot. But Lewis Jessup could shoot, too, and he had a rifle in the truck the day he vanished."

"But he didn't know he was in danger. I'm going to make sure Lara understands the situation." She looked at her watch. Nearly five. Manny might still be at the office, and she wanted to scrounge up a map or two of the local area, especially Vinny's old ranch.

They left the tavern soon after that, and she drove Robert to his office building and then went back to Manny's building. The first-floor Realtor's office was closed, and the hardware store was deserted; the owner, Len Preston, was sweeping the sidewalk. He nodded to Barbara and continued to sweep as she passed him.

Plodding up the stairs, enervated by the heat, she was worried about the problem of keeping Lara safe, of bringing up the topic in such a way that she wouldn't cause panic or alarm Nathan. . . . Manny appeared at the top of the stairs.

"Oh, Barbara, glad you got back today. Someone wants to meet you. Judge McReady." He nodded toward his office.

She could not read Manny's expression at all. She followed him into his office and set her briefcase down. "Barbara, Judge and Mrs. McReady. Barbara Holloway," Manny said very properly, and he sat at his desk.

Babe McReady was dressed in cream-colored Bermuda shorts and a tank top, and she wore sandals. She was very tanned and muscular, her hair not quite platinum blond, but a warmer honey blond, the kind of color a good salon could produce. Her face was unlined, her eyes a clear brown; she wore hardly any makeup, a touch of lipstick, a hint of eye shadow. She looked cool and capable. Barbara knew she herself was red-faced from the heat, from climbing the stairs, lugging her briefcase and laptop everywhere she went; her clothes were wrinkled and felt dirty, gritty. When she shook Babe's hand, it was cool. And, she realized, that hand was hard and calloused.

McReady was as fit and trim as Babe was, and as tan. He had pale hair cut short, with streaks of gray at the temples. His eyebrows were heavy, shaggy and straight across, giving him a serious expression. He wore eyeglasses with black frames, adding to his look of earnestness and sincerity. He looked like an actor who might come on late-night television and pitch insurance.

"A pleasure, Ms. Holloway," he said in a deep voice, a good baritone, good in court, for speeches, television pitches. "I've followed some of your cases with a great deal of interest."

"Do you ride?" Babe asked. "You want to come out to the ranch for a ride? Any day this coming week."

Her voice was husky, her words too fast, and she looked at Barbara when she addressed her, then away so quickly, it was disconcerting, as if she was not at all interested in the answer to her invitation. She reminded Barbara of a child she had known many years before, a girl whose room had looked like a toy store. Sonia? Sunny, that was it. Sunny had stood gazing about with exactly the same expression Babe had, of bored indifference.

"Afraid not," Barbara said.

"We dropped in to meet you," McReady said, cutting off anything else Babe might have said. "And to invite you to the house for a cocktail, to get acquainted. New faces are so rare in a town this size, I'm afraid everyone will be trying to lure you away. Actually, you don't have to ride. It's too hot for that unless you go out at dawn."

"Maybe another time," Barbara said. "I'm only going to be here a day or two, and I have a lot to do in a short time."

"Of course," McReady said. "I understand how that goes. Ms. Holloway, I would like a brief chat with you, however. Do you have a few minutes?"

"Yes, of course. My office?"

"That's fine," he said. Babe was moving restlessly about the office; she stopped at the window and pulled the blind aside to gaze out. "Babe, why don't you go on to the house. I'll get a ride up in a few minutes."

Babe turned to face him, smiling. "A ride at dawn! That's what I'll do. It's been years since I've ridden at dawn. I'll go to the ranch, not the mountain house."

"They're expecting us at the house. Come on, I'll go to the car with you. Ms. Holloway, I'll just be a minute."

"A ride at dawn is lovely," Babe said to Barbara. "It's the best time. The shadows are weird, too long and too black, and the meadowlarks start singing at the first light of dawn."

McReady took her by the elbow, and they left the office.

Neither Barbara nor Manny moved until the sound of their footsteps receded, was gone.

"Is she ill?" Barbara asked.

"Not really. She just doesn't pay a lot of attention to what he's saying, and he never pays much attention to what she's saying or doing. Two separate worlds." He glanced around the office, then said, "I think I turned off the air conditioner a bit early. I'll turn it on again and hang out in here until he's done, and offer him a ride home afterward."

She walked over to her own office and entered, leaving the door open behind her; she pulled the cord to the overhead fan and sat on one of the wooden chairs to wait.

Sounds were magnified in the old frame building, through the echoing halls, up and down the wooden stairs; there was not a carpet in the upper offices to muffle the noise, no drapes, just metal blinds that added to the effect of sound waves bouncing from one hard surface to another, growing. She heard the outer door open, heard McReady's steps in the lower hall, then on the stairs, in the hall, heard Manny murmur, "That way, the open door," and then McReady came in.

He looked over the office with a neutral expression, selected one of the wooden chairs and drew it closer to the coffee table and sat down.

"Thanks for waiting," he said. "I know you're hot and probably tired out from the heat. It does that to people not used to it. I appreciate your kindness and generosity. The gift of time usually is the greatest gift of all."

She shrugged. "You're welcome. I'm curious, that simple."

"I understand. Ms. Holloway, I've talked to an oncologist, a specialist, who tells me that there is no doubt that Vinny's cancer had invaded his brain, that he suffered from a kind of terminal dementia during his last few months. It's very sad, of course; he had been quite brilliant." He spread his hands and then put them on his knees and gazed at the floor for a moment. When he raised his head, he drew in a deep breath.

"This is difficult. My position is a difficult one, a delicate one. Ms. Holloway, Vinny had no papers of any interest to me. I didn't know what he was talking about the night he died, and I still don't. There simply were no documents of any kind that could have concerned me. I waited for him with my wife and her parents until after eleven, and that's all I know about that night."

She watched him closely. He was so sincere, she wanted to vote for him then and there, for whatever office he chose to run for. When she did not speak, he gazed directly at her with a very serious expression.

"I understand what I'm about to propose could be considered highly irregular," he said in a low voice, "but I think it's important enough to articulate it, to discuss it with you. When Lara Jessup's case comes to trial, the Ninth Circuit Court will be in session, in the middle of our winter term. This poses a very awkward situation. For a federal judge to be called as a witness in a murder trial during a court session is unprecedented, of course. What I am saying, Ms. Holloway, is that I must not be called as a witness, nor do I want my wife or her parents to have to endure that kind of exposure. There's no point in it, nothing at all to be gained, and a great deal of harm could be done."

"I see," she said noncommittally.

"What I suggest," he said, almost as if following a script that had not included any interruptions from her, "is that we set a date for depositions *de bene esse* to be taken from all of us this fall. My wife, of course, will be in California with me in the winter; Mr. and Mrs. Lynch are elderly and do not spend their winters in this climate any longer. None of us will be available at the time of the trial. I understand you'll want our statements, of course, and I'm sure we can arrange a time that will be convenient to all the parties concerned."

"And then?" she asked.

"And then, at the trial, both you and the prosecuting attorney stipulate to the accuracy of the depositions, and that's that. There are others from the house to verify our statements, of course, servants who know when we absented ourselves from the sitting room, when we went upstairs and to bed. We will arrange for them all to be available, for their statements to be taken."

When he smiled, she decided to vote for him twice, maybe three times. "I understand your reluctance to appear at a trial," she said. "But you realize that this is only the beginning of what could be a long investigation. It would be premature to agree to such arrangements at this early date." She smiled slightly. "Of course, we all understand that depositions are not used in criminal trials. What you actually mean is your sworn statements, is that correct?"

He shrugged. "Judges have a great deal of leeway, criminal trials or civil. I'm sure Judge Henkel would see the logic of my proposal. Depositions *de bene esse* simply means that if it happens that we cannot appear at trial, then the depositions would be available. We, of course, would make every effort to appear if called upon."

"I'm certain Judge Henkel would understand," she said. "What I would suggest as a counterproposal, however, is a perpetuation of testimony."

For a moment his face became masklike, an expression so fleeting that it was possible to deny any change had occurred. Then he smiled again.

"Of course," he said, rising from his chair. "I really do hope you'll find time to visit us either at the mountain house or the ranch. We have a few very gentle horses that even novice riders manage very easily. It would be our pleasure."

She walked to the door with him and shook his hand when he offered it. His handshake was exactly right, not too hard, not too long, certainly not a caress, but with a practiced pressure that communicated warmth and concern, interest in her.

She watched him walk down the hallway to Manny's office door, pause, and, it appeared, turn down the offer of a ride. He went down the stairs, his footsteps echoing hollowly throughout the upper floor.

Manny came from his office and headed her way. "He said Babe's waiting for him. No ride needed."

"Well," she said, then listened to the outside door close on the first floor. "Whatever he's selling, I'll buy half a dozen of." Manny laughed, and they entered her office.

After she told him what McReady had proposed, they sat in silence for a moment, then Manny said, "What's he after? He knows you won't go out to ride or party with him and his crew."

"I think he wanted to make sure I understand that Vinny was insane, that he has experts who will swear cancer had invaded his brain, that there were no papers. And that he'll have an army of people to back up that he never left the Lynch house that night. How's all that for one tiny, teensy, friendly chat?"

Manny nodded. "My father used to say choose your friends with great care, and your enemies with more."

She decided that it was not a non sequitur.

❧

That night she pored over the map Manny had provided, and the following day she and Bailey left Bend at ten o'clock and started the drive to the ranch that Vinny and Marilyn had owned, now part of the Lynch spread. Bailey was not happy. He made no secret of his dislike of the heat and the aridity. "God, where are the people?" he muttered after leaving U.S. 97 and heading east toward the ranches.

The highway had been busy, but the secondary road they were on was deserted, narrow, unmarked, and now and then turned into a gravel road, then back to concrete for no apparent reason. And this was open range country. Cattle roamed freely from one dead-looking field to another equally dead-looking field on the other side of the road. "Imagine this on a bitter-cold December night, dark already, black ice on the road, possibly," she said. "Would it be faster or slower going than now?"

"Maybe faster," he said, slowing down while a calf tried to make up its mind where it wanted to be and awaited inspiration in the middle of the road. A big cow bawled at it, and it scampered like a kitten to her side. "No cows late at night, I bet." Morosely he added, "Deer out at night, cows by day. Maybe not faster."

"Cattle," she said. "Back home they're cows; out here they're cattle." He gave her a look that was decidedly unfriendly. "But you don't say a cattle, you have to say a head of cattle, sort of ignore the legs, tail, steaks on the hoof—"

"Barbara," he said, "shut up." He glanced at her and said, "By the way, your client lied to you."

She stiffened.

"Her name's Clara. She dropped the C after she married Stroh."

This time her look at him was decidedly not friendly. He grinned. "I would have done exactly the same thing," she said.

"Thank you, Momma; thank you, Daddy. Clara. I bet her brothers called her Clara the Cow."

Altogether it took an hour and forty-five minutes to reach
the turn to the Lynch ranch. The buildings were not visible, just
a dirt road that wound back to a hill and out of sight. They did
not turn onto it. Jessup's old ranch was four miles farther down
the county road.

"Too far," Barbara said unhappily. Nearly two hours out,
then two hours back, plus time spent somewhere out there.
From the map it appeared that the ranch houses were another
mile or two from the road they were on. "Too damn far."

Bailey grunted and then swore at a pothole. He slowed down
even more. "Okay, McReady was seen at about eleven-thirty
that night, and again before six the next morning, but that would
leave time enough to get out here and back."

"Not long enough to do much more than drive out and drive
back in. What for?"

They reached the turn for the Jessup ranch. "You want to
look at anything back there?" Bailey asked.

"No. No point. But pull over a minute, will you?"

He stopped in the middle of the road. There was no reason
not to. A trailing dust cloud caught up to them and enwrapped
the car. Bailey hurriedly closed the air-intake vents.

Barbara waited for the dust to settle again, and then got out
and looked at the road, looked at the driveway to the house,
studied the land all around. It was rocky with sparse growth of
grasses and sage, a juniper tree in the distance with a cluster of
cattle crowded together in the shade. Everything was grayed
with dust; even the sky looked dusty, a pale blue. Bailey stayed
in the car.

At last she got back inside and opened a map. "Look," she
said, pointing. "This is how they checked the water, out the
driveway to the road we're on, then a little track that heads back

toward the hill there, the boundary between the two properties in those days. Manny said he must have made that turn, that he was in there somewhere in the truck when Vinny and Roger went out to look for him."

Bailey shrugged. "Okay."

"The problem is that Vinny and Roger turned in there, too, and didn't come across the truck. Vinny had been in town at his office, and was on his way home when the boy left the house. Vinny didn't spot him on the highway. And he didn't spot him on this road. He was back in there somewhere." She traced a line that Manny had drawn on the map. "The track splits here, this part goes to the Lynch house, this part to the hills and finally back to the Jessup place."

Bailey was surveying the desert; he said reasonably, "You could drive off the road in any direction and be lost to sight in a few minutes that late in the day, light failing, night coming on. The fact is, no one knows what the kid did, where he went, if he met someone out here and when, if it was a planned meeting, or if he was halfway down to Bend and his old man simply missed him."

"No, we know a little more than that. The cattle had gathered at a trough about four miles back in. Manny said that probably meant that water had been deiced there. It was frozen farther in the next day when they checked. The ground fault interrupter had been tripped and hadn't been reset. He said the deicers weren't as reliable then as they are now; power outages took them out and they didn't come back on automatically. Someone had to go out and do it."

Bailey shrugged again and turned the key, started the engine. "Done here?"

"I guess so. He left the house at about three-thirty and drove out to the road here, up four miles to that water trough. Say half an hour. Then what? That's the question. A date with someone?

On back toward the hills? The left fork to the Lynch place?" She folded the map slowly and stowed it away in her briefcase; Bailey started to drive.

She told him what Robert Sheffield had said, that Lara was in danger, the same kind of danger that Lewis Jessup had been in. "Before you take off, I want you to talk to her, tell her what steps she can take to safeguard herself, you know the kind of thing."

"And you know it won't be worth more than a safety match in hell," he said grouchily. "Right now, if you got a flat tire out here on this road, what would you do? Sit and wait for a Triple A savior to come along and fix it? And if I wanted to pot you, I could sure arrange for a flat tire out on a lonely road, and sit and wait with my trusty cannon."

"But it's not really quite that simple," she said after a moment. "You'd have to be sure I was on the right road, and there's the problem of a body with a slug or two in it, and your trusty cannon that everyone knows you own might be hauled in for examination. Anyway, do what you can. She looked as if she had gone deaf when I suggested she might be in danger."

Actually, Lara had looked as if Barbara was saying something that was so obvious that to voice it at all was a waste of time, and to respond to it a bigger waste.

Now that they were driving west, the view ahead was of the Cascade mountaintops glowing white against the pale blue sky; a few thin clouds rose over the sharp peaks, looking more like a mist falling upward into the sky than like serious clouds. And nowhere in sight beyond the car was there anything human to be seen. No person, no other car, no building, fence, not even a contrail in the sky. She thought of the expression on Babe's face when she talked about riding at dawn. And she found herself nodding; a ride at dawn in this vast empty land would be lovely.

✦ 19

"You're pretty quiet," Frank said. It was Sunday evening, the air cool and fresh, the hour when shadows vanished one into another and everything visible was softened and without hard contrasts.

"I was thinking of a time when I drove up from California," Barbara said. "Leaving Sacramento was like feeling the devil's breath on my back pushing me. Then Shasta, and the Siskiyous and things began to change, until up and over the pass, and it was like stepping into the land of Oz, the emerald world, everything green and vibrant. I stopped the car and got out just to stand and take one deep breath after another. Green is pretty swell, don't you think?"

"I think," he said gravely. And she, he also thought, had had her fill of the heat of east Oregon for a while.

She had told him about her days in Salt Creek and Bend. He had agreed that if Shinizer opted for depositions, or even if he agreed to perpetuation of testimony from the Lynch crew, she had little choice but to go along with it, especially since she had been warned that McReady and the others planned to be out of the state during the trial. She had no way to force them to return in order to get them on the witness stand.

"About those dots on McReady's decisions and speeches," he said, "they correspond within days to speeches made by about half a dozen select people of the far right persuasion, laws argued for or against, things of that sort. McReady just gave them more ammunition for whatever cause they were campaigning for. He's their boy. Choreographed by Balanchine. But you can't hang a man for agreeing with his associates. Just interesting. The only other interesting thing I turned up," he said morosely, "is that Vinny stopped gathering material, stopped the clipping services, stopped adding to the files altogether a few years back. Nothing's more recent than four years ago."

"Wonder what happened four years ago to make him give it up," she said after a moment. Frank simply grunted. "It's going to be a bare-bones defense," she said after another pointless consideration of events four years ago. "Lara will be her own best witness, but it's shaping up to be a yes-you-did, no-I-didn't kind of dialogue." The worst kind of trial, she was thinking, especially when the judge was biased. But it couldn't be helped; there it was.

She didn't linger long that night; she was tired and dehydrated, she said, getting ready to leave. Frank didn't protest. "You're also sunburned," he said.

"Skin cancer," she said darkly. "How do they survive over there? See you in the morning?"

"Sometime before noon."

Actually, he was eager to get back to his study, and the contract spread out over his desk. It had arrived yesterday, Saturday, and was postmarked Thursday. So much for Donald ("Call me Don") Fleishman's word about overnight mail. Yesterday he had cursed as he skimmed through the contract, but that Sunday night, he was humming softly and tunelessly as he approached it.

"You son of a bitch," he whispered as he sat down, and whether he meant the printed contract or the editor who had sent it, he couldn't have said, but overnight his fury had changed to determination mingled with amusement. He would go to the

wire with them over the damn contract as many times as it took
to get it right, even though he no longer believed that it would
ever be made right. Just better. How much better would be better enough? He had no answer.

While waiting for the revised contract, he had done some
homework, a little research into the corporation behind Arrowwood, and had found that C and M owned two television series
that featured lawyers. And a talk show that featured attorneys
and current celebrity cases. And one of their several publishing
houses had published a few popular novels with lawyer protag-
onists. All fuel for the rage that had surged when he saw the new
contract, which would let them buy his book, which they now
said they would publish, but without a time limit on when. Under the contract terms, the corporate bigwigs would still have
the right to use his material any way they chose. They would
own all rights, television, CDs, movies, stage, sound reproduc-
tion . . . in perpetuity throughout the universe. And he would
agree to hold them harmless in the event of a lawsuit for any
reason; he would pay the attorney fees, theirs and his, and
grant them the right to settle out of court at their discretion,
with him paying whatever figure they arrived at for a settlement. He had regarded the new contract with amazement,
rage, awe, disbelief. . . . And now he was humming as he
wielded the highlighter.

A few minutes later, he put the highlighter down and leaned
back in his chair with his hands clasped behind his head, con-
templating the ceiling. He suspected that Wanda Doolittle was
right; they wanted his manuscript to cannibalize for their other
projects, not as a book in itself. But what did he want it for? Not
a general public, that was for certain; it was too technical for
casual reading in an airport terminal. For other attorneys? Students? An educated lay audience? All of the above?

"All right," he said softly. "All right." He would wrestle with the contract as long as Donald ("Call me Don") Fleishman wanted to play that game, and meanwhile he would photocopy the manuscript again and submit that copy to a university press. He nodded and sat up straighter, picked up the highlighter once more, and returned to the contract. He almost hoped they had already extracted some of the dialogue, a scene from a trial or two.... He realized he wanted to sue the bastards, and he began to chuckle.

In her apartment Barbara was glancing through the mail delivered there instead of to the office. Personal stuff, bills, a dental-appointment reminder. Two postcards from John.

She sat at the table with a cup of coffee and studied the postcards from Canada—mountains, a stream, a waterfall, a sunset, a bear.... The messages were brief: *Miss you. Love you. Wish you were here.*

She could have gone with him, she thought bleakly. What little she had accomplished here could well have been put off a week or two without any harm. She blinked hard, and suddenly wondered if all her work was like that, something she could do immediately or later with little difference, if the only urgency involved was artificial, imposed on the material, not inherent in it. Restless now, she stood up and walked to the window to look out at the pool, lighted with underwater lights, and a pole lamp or two; mysterious-looking, the water appeared to be blue, black, and silver. Swarms of insects circled the pools of light at the lamps endlessly, feeding ground for the bats that swooped now and again, without a beating of wings or hunting cries that carried to her ears.

Her face was hot; she had to shower and trowel on cream, and then do a little work. With a quick motion she returned to the table and swept up most of the mail to go to the recycle bag.

She hesitated at the dentist's reminder, glanced at her wall cal
endar and saw that she had penciled in the appointment, and
tossed the card. Then she found herself thinking of Vinny's calendar and the cryptic notes on it, with nothing firm after the
middle of May.

She forgot the shower and face cream and wandered to her
office, thinking hard. There was something, something. . . . She
began to jot down notes.

On Monday when she brought in the newspaper, she stood at
her table staring at the banner headline about the weather in the
Southwest, where a heat wave was in its second week and going
strong. One hundred fifteen degrees yesterday in Phoenix, overnight low eighty-nine, hotter today. . . . She turned the paper
facedown and poured herself coffee.

Bailey had left a message on her machine: he was headed for
Bend with Gary Greening to look at the Jessup van. She nodded
in satisfaction. Greening was recognized as an expert in automobile wrecks and follow-up investigations.

She walked to her office, got the files from the safe, and settled
on her couch to begin working on the Jessup material again,
without any hope of spotting anything that Frank had missed,
but because she wanted to see for herself the last things Vinny
had collected before he called it quits. Frank had said nothing of
interest or different from what he had gotten before, but still . . .
One of the leads had to go somewhere, she told herself glumly.
To date, it appeared that no matter which road she traveled, it
turned into a dead end.

A short time later there was a tap on her door, and she had
to admit that she welcomed any interruption. "Come on in," she
called. It was either Shelley or Frank, she knew; Maria wouldn't
let anyone else back without calling first.

Shelley entered. And she looked as woebegone as possible for a pretty doll to look.

"Problem?" Barbara asked, patting the couch next to her.

Shelley sank down into it and nodded. "There's nothing for me to do," she said. "I've straightened out my files, rewritten a few reports so many times I've memorized them, researched fences until I think I'm some kind of expert, and now what? Two, count 'em, two people came to Martin's all last week, and how many hours can I spend over a fence problem and a loud radio that plays after nine at night?"

"It's always slow this time of year," Barbara reassured her. "Too hot to complain about silly neighborhood arguments or wills."

"Yeah, well, there's also the fact that they don't trust me, or even like me over there."

"They're just used to me. I spoil them." Suddenly it occurred to her that there was something Shelley could do that she probably couldn't. She stood up and walked to her desk, thinking. After a moment she said, "How would you like a change of scene for a couple of days?"

"You're firing me," Shelley said, then groaned. "I don't blame you, either. I'm sure not earning my keep."

Barbara laughed and returned to the coffee table, and now she sat opposite Shelley and leaned forward. "Curtis Stroh is a chaser," she said slowly. "He absolutely would not talk to Bailey, and I doubt he'd give me the time of day. I'm not his type."

Shelley was sitting upright, all traces of defeat banished. "I'll get him," she said.

"I suspect you will," Barbara said. "Let's talk about it. You realize you can't lie to him, if he wants to know who you work for."

"So he won't think to ask anything like that," Shelley said, brushing it aside. "What are you after?"

"A couple of things. Who interviewed Nathan, for openers. The sheriff is stonewalling, or maybe it was the state detectives and they're stonewalling. What did Nathan tell them? Was Curtis in on the interview? A general reading of him. Where he was the night Vinny died. If the D.A. has had an interview with him, he's keeping it under wraps, and they might not have talked to him formally at all. He could have a perfect alibi for all I know. Game?"

"You bet! I'll go today! Shove some stuff in a bag and take off."

The last court decision Vinny had collected about McReady had to do with a recantation of a confession: McReady was against it. Barbara realized she was only skimming through the text and put it down. "Pompous ass," she muttered under her breath. But Frank had been right; all the late stuff was just about like all the early stuff, with nothing that she could spot to have made Vinny decide he'd had enough at that point. Unless it was tedium, boredom.

On Tuesday Manny called her. "We've got the names of the folks who claim they saw Lara and Vinny on the mountain," he said in a nearly flat, uninflected tone.

"What do you mean? Together?"

"They stated that going home from a movie, they saw his van and her car parked at the turnout."

"Shit," she said. "Okay. Give me their names for Bailey, let him start digging."

"Greg and Melissa Freelander," Manny said. "They have a summer house on the mountain, live in Portland. He's in television. Sales or something like that. Upper management, I guess."

They talked for another minute or two, and before they hung

up, Barbara said, "Manny, do me a favor, will you? Get hold of Lara and ask her to try to think of anything that might have happened four years ago, say from February through May, that could have been a reason for Vinny to have stopped adding to those files."

Maybe overnight something would come to Lara, Barbara thought after hanging up. The last clipping was from April, four years ago; after that, nothing. Why had Vinny stopped then? Had he learned something that made it worthless? Decided there was no point after all? Given up trying to get even with Mc-Ready? She felt almost as if Vinny were standing in the shadows nearby, taunting her, leading her by the nose onto one dead-end avenue after another.

It was still early in the investigation, she reminded herself. A whole field of stones lay ahead to be turned over one by one. The fact that most of them would simply reveal beetles did not mean that at least one would not reveal the gleam of pure gold.

When Frank arrived, before noon as promised, he said maybe he'd mosey over to Bend and Salt Creek with her the next day, if she wanted.

"Sure. But what for?"

"Oh, I don't know. Renew acquaintances with the Lynches. Say howdy to Thomas. Have a look at their house on the hill. Keep you company. Keep me company. Let folks get used to seeing me around now and then." He shrugged, then grinned. "I was thinking that maybe Nathan and I could do a little roaming."

Of course he would know Thomas and Anna Lynch; he knew everyone in the state. She nodded. "Thomas Lynch will know that you're acting as a spy."

"Well, sure he will. But I reckon he'll be curious, too. Two old pros prying, neither of us likely to get a grain of useful stuff, but who knows? Maybe I'll get lucky."

He was thinking that if he stayed in town, that damn contract would prey on his mind day and night until he got it in the mail again, and he was determined not to rush anything, but to find each and every snag and snarl in it and demand each and every one of them be fixed. It would take time, but aside from that he was in no rush now to return it; let Donald ("Call me Don") Fleishman stew about what he was up to. That morning he had made a copy of his book and had mailed it off to the University of Illinois Press. If they sent it back, then on to Pennsylvania, Indiana, Ohio.... There were a lot of university presses out there.

Barbara was saying, "Manny tells me that Shinizer has begun to release some of the statements, so there's a stack of stuff to get started on. And Bailey's starting to bring in stuff. And I'm sick and tired of these files on McReady."

Frank was, too. "So heigh-ho, tomorrow the yellow dust road. What time?"

"Nine, ten?" She eyed him suspiciously; he was too cheerful, too high, like a boy who had successfully stolen second base. His lady friend? Was she responsible for that sparkle? Or, she thought darkly, maybe he was into sniffing glue or something these days. He left then, errands to tend to, he said.

When Bailey called, she gave him the Freelanders' names, and he said he would be in touch at Lara's house the next afternoon, but not to expect anything from Greening about Vinny's van for a couple of weeks.

"Did you get a look at it?"

"Yep. Tell you tomorrow. I've got pictures, too."

Then, with great reluctance, she began to pull out the files from the time Lewis Jessup had been arrested for murder until he had vanished.

And none of it made any difference, she decided late that

afternoon. She could account for much of McReady's time during the months following the arrest of Lewis Jessup; she knew he had taken two days to drive from Bend to Spokane, a one-day trip at most, at the time Lewis had vanished. She knew he had spent New Year's Eve with Babe and family at a party at their ranch and that he had married Babe in June the same year. He had tried thirty-one cases, won most of them. She was thankful that Vinny had not detailed each and every case along the way—petty stuff, most of it, shoplifting, car theft, sticky fingers in a till, DUI cases. . . . Facts, data, all of it meaningless.

She had no illusions about the possibility of dragging in anything about McReady unless she had hard evidence to back up whatever she accused him of. And she felt certain that her defense was going to come down to trying to raise enough reasonable doubt to convince a jury that although Lara might have killed her husband, so might someone else have done it. The worst possible scenario, she thought darkly, and again she was grateful that Lara would be a good witness in her own defense.

 20

"First, Robert Sheffield, and maybe Shinizer," Frank said, driving to Salt Creek the next morning. "It's going to be hotter than hell, so let's not rush anything."

"Right."

"What I thought we might do," he went on, "is let me meet

folks, have a look around, have some lunch, and after that, while you're tackling the discovery material, I might take a little walk around town, see what happens."

She knew that he would spend hours in town, chatting with people up and down the streets, and by the time he was done, he would know most of the shopkeepers, their clerks, the waitresses and waiters in the restaurants, what was on the menus. . . . And people who would later swear they hadn't told him a thing would confide a tidbit here, another there.

Three hours later Frank felt that the day was unrolling exactly as he had planned it. He had met Robert Sheffield and Manny and Manny's secretary; the four attorneys had eaten lunch together in Dorothy's Bar and Grill, and it had been excellent; and now, strolling down the street toward the post office, he was not at all surprised to hear someone call his name.

"Frank? Frank Holloway? For God's sake!"

He turned to see Thomas Lynch at the wheel of a Bronco, grinning at him. He grinned back. "Thomas! It's been a long time." Thomas was very brown, sun-and-wind-cured, his face crisscrossed with seams; his hair was thin and gray, his eyes dark. He looked older than his sixty-five years.

"Too long. What are you doing out in this heat on foot? Want a ride somewhere? Get in."

"Actually, I'm just killing time while my daughter does a little work in Manny Truewater's office. But I will get out of the sun." He stepped into the shade of a dusty juniper tree. Lynch pulled to the curb and turned off the motor. "How are you, Thomas? How's Anna?"

"Good, fine. Look, I'm on my way home, in from the ranch, a long and thirsty drive. Join me for a little cool something to drink. I'll bring you back down when you give the word. It's a hell of a lot cooler up at my place than here in town."

Frank looked up the street where a water mirage had formed. "You're on," he said, and got in the Bronco.

Thomas Lynch was five feet nine or thereabouts, but he looked shorter than that and thick through the chest and shoulders. He hunched over the wheel as if he had to get closer to the windshield to see out. At the intersection with the highway, he drummed his fingers on the steering wheel impatiently; it was a long wait to get out into the traffic.

"I remember when we used to go over to Bend to shop," he said. "An all-day excursion then, and I used to gawk at the automobiles, when we saw any. Some days not a one."

Frank nodded. "Yeah. Bend was what, two, three thousand? And Salt Creek? Forget it. You had to know it was here, or you'd never see it at all. Just a dust devil on the side of the road."

Lynch pulled onto the highway with a squeal of tires and almost instantly slowed down and then stopped, to the blare of a horn from a truck behind them. He made the turn onto Salt Creek Road, and after a short drive turned again, onto the red lava road.

"Pretty," Frank said, gazing at the road, approving of the contrast with the pale earth and the gray-green sage, the shadows that appeared and vanished as the car manipulated curves. The pine trees and their red trunks added just the right touch.

When Lynch passed the place where Vinny had gone over the side of the mountain, neither of them commented or gave it more than a glance. He turned onto his own driveway and drove past the white-gravel parking area, followed a black road up and around to two stone pillars and the final approach to the house. Big, six thousand square feet, Frank had read, with beautifully planted and tended gardens. And there they were, borders of shrubs, a native grass area, a larger green lawn that looked golf-course immaculate, and flowers on a terrace in pots, in hanging pots, massed in beds. . . .

The drive was wide enough for parking on the side, with plenty of room for a car to pass. Two cars were parked under a covered section at the front terrace, a Cadillac Seville and a BMW convertible. Lynch parked there, too.

"Home," he said, opening his door.

"And pretty damn impressive it is," Frank said. The house appeared to be two stories high, but he had read that it had three floors; one must be partly underground, he decided. Lynch led the way inside to a spacious foyer with a red Italian tile floor, wide stairs, open doors on both sides, and not a person in sight, not a sound to be heard.

"Straight on through to the patio out back," Lynch said, motioning Frank to come along. He paused at the foot of the stairs and yelled, "Anna, I'm home!"

They walked through the hallway, past intersecting halls, past rooms with open doors—a living room, a game room, dining room . . . and some with closed doors. Then out to the rear patio, and down below lay the desert. The view was magnificent, from here to infinity. This part of the patio was covered, and it was cool, with a fresh breeze coming off the mountain. There were half a dozen groups of rattan furniture—chairs, sofas, coffee tables, end tables—and the patio was large enough that there could have been half a dozen additional groups of furnishings; there were steps going up to a higher level, and other steps going down.

A young Mexican woman appeared from a doorway and approached them. "Mr. Lynch, can I bring you anything?"

"Beer," Lynch said. "Frank?"

"That sounds good," Frank said.

The young woman left as noiselessly as she had come, and Lynch motioned to the chairs near the edge of the patio. They went to them and sat down.

"You said your daughter has some work to do with Manny,"

Thomas said after a moment. "You know where my daughter is at this very moment? Out at the ranch, helping out, searching for a lost calf or some damn fool thing." He cast a sidelong glance at Frank. "Has your daughter taken over your office?"

Frank laughed. "Pretty much. Course, I have little use for it these days."

"Yeah, me too. I hire people to find the strays. God knows I don't want to be out there looking for them anymore. Been there, done that. Babe wants to do it."

He frowned, gazing out at the desert. Then in a low voice, as if thinking out loud, he added, "Thing is, she's a better rancher than I ever was."

"And my daughter's a better attorney than I ever was. How do you figure?"

"I don't. I never could figure out Babe, still can't. She's happier on the ranch than any wrangler I ever met, and she's a damn good hand, good manager, good foreman. She could live anywhere—Paris, London, San Francisco, New York, and she does live in all those places from time to time—but she always comes home to the ranch. I can't figure her out. You have any grandkids?"

Frank shook his head.

"What he means," a woman said, coming to the patio from the house, "is that he had trouble keeping me on the ranch, and more trouble keeping our daughter off it." She advanced toward Frank, who had risen at the sound of her voice; as she drew near, she extended both hands. "Frank Holloway. It's been twenty years, and you look almost exactly the same. How do you manage that?"

"You look wonderful, Anna," he said truthfully, taking her hands. She was tall and slender, willowy, with shoulder-length hair that could have been blond, or even colorless, but was not white or gray. He couldn't understand that color, he thought, or lack of color. There were a few wrinkles on her face, not noticeable from a distance of more than four feet. She was wearing ivory-colored silk pants and a matching shirt, and sandals with no stockings. Her toenails were bright red, although her fingernails were almost exactly the same color as her clothes.

"What happened with Babe," she said, sitting down on one of the lounge chairs, "is that he insisted on treating her like a son; she had to ride like a boy, shoot, fish, all of it, and now she behaves more like a man than a woman, and he complains."

"Not complaining," Lynch said. "Tell the truth, I'm damn proud of her. Ah, here's our beer. You want anything, Anna?"

The young woman who had taken their orders put a tray down on a table, poured out two pilsner glasses, and put one on an end table by Thomas, the other at Frank's elbow. She looked at Anna, who motioned her away.

"No," Anna said. "I have to leave in a few minutes. Remember? We're due at the Gregory house at five. I told Valerie Fields I'd pick her up and drive her over. You don't have to get started yet."

Frank glanced at his watch. It was five minutes before four. "I should be on my way," he said.

"Nonsense. You haven't even touched your beer," Lynch said. "God knows I don't want to get to that damn lawn party any earlier than I have to. Lawn party! In this heat."

"Your daughter is going to defend Lara Jessup, isn't she?" Anna said then, as if the thought had just this second occurred to her.

"That's right."

She shook her head. "That poor girl. Lara, I mean. Obviously she panicked that night when she found Vinny dead. I can't imagine what that must have been like for her. Horrible!" She shook her head again. "Frank, six or eight people in this house will testify that no one came up here, and no one left. What possible defense does your daughter see for Lara? Why doesn't that poor child simply admit what happened and be done with it?"

Before Frank could say a word, Thomas Lynch snapped, "For God's sake, Anna! You know that's not a proper thing to say to Frank! Butt out!"

"It's exactly what everyone else is saying, and you know it."

Deliberately Lynch picked up his beer and took a long drink, turning to face out toward the desert again.

Anna stood up. "As I said, I have to leave. Frank, perhaps you can visit us again. Lunch, or dinner?"

"Maybe," he said, standing up. "I don't expect to be spending much time over here."

Lynch didn't move when Anna left them and vanished into the house. After a moment he muttered, "That damn woman. She drives me crazy! I'm sorry, Frank. That was improper, uncalled-for. She never could hold her tongue."

"Is it what folks in these parts are saying?"

"If she says so. She's the one who gets the local scuttlebutt. But it's true enough, what she said about the folks in the house here. Harris was with us all that evening; it was well past eleven before I turned in, and he was still here. See, our security system gets turned on at ten, so we know no one left. I turn it on and off every night myself, if we're home. No one in, no one out. I'm afraid Lara Jessup is in for a tough time if she insists on going to trial."

"The defendant is always in for a tough time during a trial," Frank said.

"A rumor I did hear," Lynch said then, still gazing out at the desert, "is they've offered her a deal of some sort. Ever do any horse-trading, Frank?"

"Nope. Never owned a horse, or really wanted to."

"How it works is, you start out knowing pretty much what

you want and the other guy, he knows, too. But there's always a certain amount of posturing to get through. You back off, he backs off, you both come forward, do a little cussing maybe. It's like a dance that you both understand. Thing is, if you're good at it and he is, too, you both end up satisfied."

Frank took a long drink of his beer and set the glass down. "Uh-huh," he said. "I think it's time to get a ride back to town, let you get on with your evening."

Lynch did not insist on keeping him, and soon they were back in the Bronco heading back down the mountain. It was still very hot when they left the mountain road and drove into Salt Creek.

"Anywhere's fine," Frank said. "That's a lovely place you have up there."

Lynch drove to the Lynch Building with the real estate office and hardware store on the first floor, and Manny's offices on the upper one. "I'll give you a call," he said. "Lunch would be good."

Frank opened his door and got out; for a moment the two men regarded each other, a measuring examination, assessing each other's strength, his weakness. Posturing. They didn't offer to shake hands. He waved good-bye then, walked into the stairwell, and started up. The Bronco pulled away.

Upstairs, the air conditioner was making a noisy effort to overcome the rising heat in the building; it was a losing battle. Barbara was sitting at the desk, which was covered with papers; it looked as if a wind storm had dumped a wastebasket on the desk.

Frank paused in the doorway and surveyed the mess. He made no comment, simply crossed to one of the wooden chairs and sat down. Barbara was flushed and she had drawn her hair up in a ponytail.

"I'm looking for something," she said, scowling at the desk.

"Not finding it, either, looks like."

"Not finding it. Goddamn it. Where've you been?"

"You first. What did you lose?"

"Not me. Robert, and maybe he didn't lose it. He thinks he saw a paper in Vinny's files that had been typed on that typewriter that the suicide note was typed on. There are dozens and dozens of typed letters, printouts. . . . We're going over them all, looking for an Underwood portable typeface, vintage sixties, maybe even fifties, some letters out of alignment, smudged lowercase *e*." Her scowl deepened. "Manny and his secretary are doing the same thing in his office, and Robert's going through the files he inherited from Vinny. Your turn."

He told her about going up to the Lynch mansion. "Don't underestimate him," he said thoughtfully. "He's a horse trader. I mentioned that you were up here working, and that instantly became the theme of our visit—our wayward daughters. If I'd complained of arthritic joints, we would have commiserated with each other over health. He and Anna staged the little charade, perfect timing, not a missed cue."

She was listening intently. "What was it all for?"

"To let me know about the security, I guess, back up McReady's story, gauge my involvement in all this, pass on the words of wisdom about Lara admitting her guilt. Maybe demonstrate that he's just a harmless old man, getting on in years, lonely. Forge a little understanding between us—two old guys who can talk to each other, who've been around a bit. All of the above. But I suspect the real purpose was to let us know we can still make a deal."

She began to shuffle papers together, stack them. "Dad, they could be running a little scared."

"Doubt it," he said after a moment. "Bobby, they have a houseful of servants who will testify that the security gets turned on at ten, and who will testify that the Lynch-McReady crew were all in and accounted for all evening; I don't think they have a damn thing to scare them. I think they just don't want any hassle."

"Or publicity," she said after a moment. "The wrong kind of publicity, at that."

"It's hot as hell up here, you realize that?"

She rolled her eyes. "Really? I asked Nadia to make copies of everything that comes in every day, so we can read at home or in Vinny's home office, anywhere but up here. Bailey's going to show up at Lara's at about five-thirty, and then he's heading back home. Let's beat it. I'll get back to this stuff in the morning."

She shoved file folders into the desk drawer and locked it. "Ready?" They walked into the hallway, and she locked the office door after them. They looked in on and waved good-bye to Nadia, who was at a long table in the conference/all-purpose room studying typed papers; then they looked in on Manny. It appeared that the tornado that had dumped papers on Barbara's desk had visited his office, too.

A little later they were on the deck at Lara's house, relishing the breeze off the mountain, when Bailey arrived. Frank said beer and wine were both in the fridge, and Bailey helped himself to a beer.

"Not much yet," he said when he rejoined them. "But it's kind of interesting that there were no prints on the van door, not Vinny Jessup's, no one's. Briefcase wiped clean. Smudges on the gun. And the staties found a napkin just inside the door, powder burns on it, and blood spatters. The staties are pretty good, by the way, the special investigations bunch. They hauled the van in, did the workup on it, and kept it in their possession from day one."

"Back up," Barbara said sharply. "What about a napkin?"

"Oh, didn't I finish that part? Seems it's from the Lynch

house. Monogram TL." He drank beer from the bottle and then grinned at Barbara. "Whoever shot Vinny Jessup held the gun wrapped up in the napkin, from all appearances. Lots of blood inside the van, none on the outside. Napkin was between the door and the seat. Looks like he was shot in the left temple, fell over sideways, and blood was spattered around everything. Point-blank range. The killer probably got blood on him. No one examined the parking turnout for blood before it was pretty thoroughly messed up by the sheriff's crew and others. The van was in the Lynch parking space; white gravel from the tires matches the gravel there. And that's just about all I have to date. Babe's at the ranch; apparently she spends most of her summers out there, maybe most of the time, period. McReady's gone down to San Francisco. Nothing yet on the Freelanders, the ones who claim they saw Lara on the mountain that night. Working on them. And now I'm going home."

"Put one more little job in your basket," Barbara said. "Underwood typewriter, portable, circa fifties or sixties. The lowercase *e* is dirty, filled in, and the *a* and *i* are misaligned."

He nodded. "What's the population of Salt Creek, a thousand? Won't take more than a month to go from door to door asking about it."

"I want it," she said. "Bad."

"Okay. Okay. See you tomorrow, about this time?"

"Sure. Same place, same time."

Lara and Nathan drove in as Bailey was driving out. Nathan came straight up to the deck and kicked a pinecone around; then, watching it, he asked, "Is he a private detective? Mom said he is."

"He is," Frank said.

Nathan kicked the pinecone off the deck, sent it sailing down the length of the yard. "Cool," he said.

Frank asked him for some advice about good fishing spots, and they went inside together. Lara stuck her head out the kitchen door long enough to say hi, and withdrew again. And Barbara sat in the shade, watching faraway dust columns form, dissipate, reform.

If McReady shot him holding the gun wrapped in a napkin, why had he left the napkin behind? Had searching for Vinny's papers made him forgetful of the napkin? Rushed? Afraid of an interruption? She visualized the mountain road with its switchbacks; car lights would show up well in advance of an approaching car. McReady might have seen a car coming, acted too hastily, looked for the papers, wiped off fingerprints.... And then forgot the napkin. She frowned at one of the dust columns that looked substantial and solid.

That night Lara prepared dinner for them all, grilled steaks done on the deck, baked potatoes, and vegetables. It was all very simple, efficient and without fuss, and good, but nowhere near Frank's standards. Afterward Barbara went to Vinny's study and started to read the various bits of discovery the district attorney had turned over.

Frank tapped on the door to tell her good night and to inform her that he and Nathan and a friend of Nathan's were leaving early in the morning to go fishing. The boys knew a couple of good spots. And later on, Lara tapped on the door and slipped inside the office when Barbara called out, "Come on in."

"I wanted to wait until Nathan was in bed," Lara said hesitantly. "I have to ask you something and tell you something."

"Well, sit down, and tell me what's on your mind."

"What happens if they bring in an eyewitness who swears he saw me and Vinny at the turnout? It's all over the hospital, people are giving me pretty funny looks."

"Eyewitnesses are notoriously unreliable," Barbara said. "Could anyone have seen you and Vinny parked at the turn-out?"

"No!"

Barbara shrugged. "So I find a way to discredit the witness. Don't worry too much about that."

Lara looked past Barbara at the bookcases. Silently she pulled a folded sheet of paper from her pocket and pushed it across the desk. It was a printout. Barbara read: *Why don't you come clean. I saw you on the mountain the night you killed Vinny. I don't want to testify, but if you don't come clean, I'll come forward.*

"Crank letter, crank calls, you might get them, too," Barbara said, studying the note. It was ink-jet print on Xerox paper, available in every discount warehouse, every office-supply company, stationery shop, copy shops. . . .

"Did you keep the envelope?" she asked, finally looking up from the note.

Lara was very pale; her freckles looked garish. She shook her head. "I tossed it in the kitchen trash. I can get it out again."

"Okay, do that. We'll give it and the note to Bailey, see if he can recover any fingerprints. . . . Lara, what's wrong?"

Lara was staring at the note as if hypnotized by it. "People saw me. I was up there that night," she whispered.

✧ 21

In Eugene after the sun set on the hottest day, the temperature dropped five, ten degrees, even more, Barbara mused on Lara's deck, huddled under an afghan, but out here in the desert it plummeted; it felt almost as if there might be a frost. Incredible, it had been at least a hundred degrees that afternoon. It was so dark, she might have been the last person awake east of the mountains. She had watched the glow from Salt Creek diminish, fade, vanish, and another glow from the south that must have come from Bend, gone now. A few dogs that had been barking earlier had become quiet, and the silence was complete. No wind blew; nothing stirred. Nathan said you could hear the coyotes just about every night, but she had not heard them yet. Behind her, Lara's house was dark, with only a pale night-light in an upper hall, and the trace of light from the office door, which Barbara had left open enough to be a beacon when she was ready to go back inside. Neither light made it all the way to the deck.

She shivered in the chill black night, and thought finally: *There's no defense.*

She had asked her father, What next? after the two warnings, one from McReady to her, one from Lynch to Frank. Now she knew what next. An unidentified witness to put Lara on the mountain. Not the Freelanders, someone else, and the probability that what Nathan had told the detectives was that he had heard or seen Lara go out that night after Vinny left.

Well, Barbara thought bleakly, she had suspected from the start that Lara had lied to her; now she knew. Were there more lies to be aired little by little until the trial began, one story after another to deal with?

Lara hadn't told anyone else yet, and Barbara had ordered her not to breathe a word about it, not to anyone at all.

"It's bad, isn't it?" Lara had asked, after her confession about following Vinny up the mountain. "How bad?"

"It means you can't take the stand and defend yourself," Barbara had said bluntly. She had not added that the only defense she had counted on was Lara's presence on the witness stand on her own behalf.

And now she had to consider the implications: Robert Sheffield would want to go for the Alford plea, she felt certain. No matter what incriminating evidence they found against McReady, he would be virtually untouchable with a houseful of reputable witnesses who would alibi him. Robert could argue persuasively that in this county, with this judge and this prosecutor, McReady was absolutely safe, and Lara was as good as convicted before a jury was even seated. Barbara could not refute that.

She couldn't guess where Manny would alight. Frank probably would side with Robert. Not instantly, not until they did a lot more digging, but eventually. He was too pragmatic not to grasp the dangerous situation Lara was now in. There was too much to lose, and the possibility of winning had just taken a sharp turn for the worse. His first concern would be for Lara's life, her safety, which was right and proper, of course. And how would she, Barbara, vote? She didn't know.

Lara had said that she would go to Shinizer and tell the truth, tell her reasons for lying before, her fear and confusion, the sheriff's first saying that there had been an accident, then a suicide, and finally murder had kept her confused and frightened.

"Don't even consider it," Barbara had said sharply. She had seen prosecutors destroy suspects who changed a statement, especially when it appeared that the altered statement was a direct result of another's testimony. If Lara had admitted the truth early, before other evidence came to light, perhaps it might not have been so deadly; it was too late now. A confession about lying in her statement to Shinizer would be tantamount to a confession of guilt, either to murder or to tampering with evidence of a suicide. And would that be such a terrible thing to admit to? Barbara drew the afghan in closer, and was still cold.

She felt confident that she could have handled the Freelanders, whoever they were; since they were wrong about seeing Lara and Vinny together, she would have backed them down one way or another. But an unknown witness, and now Lara's admission, that put a totally different light on it. She could not be a party to Lara's perjury, allow her to testify knowing the lie, especially now, since it was almost certain that Nathan had seen her leave and had told that to the investigator. Lara had to keep quiet; she couldn't take the stand and deny the truth, deny her son's statement, or force him to lie under oath.

Barbara heard a coyote then; distant and indistinct, it sounded terribly lonely until it was answered by a second one, then another in a series of barks, yips, howls—a desert chorus.

If you think you're likely to win, use strategy A; if you think you could lose, go to strategy B; if you feel almost certain that you will lose, skip to strategy C as soon as possible. One of her instructors had said that. Good advice: prepare three cases simultaneously, be prepared for the worst at all times, be ready to do a quick dance to a different tune. . . .

The next day she told Manny and Robert that she was going to be away for a week or so, that she would visit Lester DeFeo, just to touch base with him, and then take care of a few other things. She conferred with Bailey, and that evening, on the way back to Eugene, she told Frank that she intended to take a short vacation for a few days, after talking to DeFeo.

"I'm going down to Phoenix," she said, looking straight out the windshield at the car-clogged road winding up and over the high Cascade pass. Frank did not say a word.

The next day she flew to Denver's sprawling new airport and walked a mile from one plane to another, then caught a commuter to Cheyenne, Wyoming, where a rental car was waiting for her. By three she was seated in the living room of Lester DeFeo on the fourteenth floor of a condominium on the eastern side of town, the prairie side. His apartment was the entire floor, apparently, with windows overlooking mountains to the west and the prairie to the east.

DeFeo was a slightly built man, eighty-two years old, bald, and almost totally blind. His eyes appeared milky. Although the apartment was large and rambling, the room they were in was small and crowded with furnishings, too many chairs, too many tables, too many lamps, as if more light would solve his problem. There were a lot of books on shelves, in bookcases, but she noted sadly that the books were covered with a fine dust.

She had told him her purpose for the visit, and he had shaken his head.

"Wasted a trip out here, Ms. Holloway. You saw my notes, the letters Vinny and I exchanged. Nothing I can add to them." He shook his head again. "Goddamn shame about Vinny. I was sorry to hear about it."

"I'm not looking for anything official," she said. "Your impressions maybe of Vinny, Lynch, McReady, the whole cast of characters. The Jessup children aren't very helpful; they're part of the scene, too close."

"Tell you who to ask," DeFeo said. "Manny. Manny Truewater. He knows more than anyone in the county about the whole crew."

"I imagine you're right," she said. "The problem with him is that you have to know the exact question to ask. He doesn't volunteer much."

DeFeo chuckled. "I remember Manny. Okay, thing is, there's little for me to recall. It never got to trial, as you know, and I met the principals only a couple of times. Vinny was putting the case together; I was to be the first trial attorney, he'd have been the backup. There wasn't a case, but even so, there were several mysteries, and the first and biggest one was how the whole damn business got as far as it did. Of course, the mystery of who killed those two kids was never solved, never seriously investigated, far's I could see. And finally, the mystery of what happened to Lewis Jessup was never solved."

He stopped talking, and turned toward the windows overlooking the seemingly endless prairie. "Vinny came out here to talk it over in the spring after Lewis vanished. I was at the ranch in those days, haven't been out there in nearly a year. . . . Anyway, that's where we talked, and a chinook was blowing down from the mountain. Hot wind that doesn't let up, day after day. Drives some folks crazy; nervous breakdowns, psychotic episodes, divorces, murders, they all happen during chinook weather.

"His wife was in the hospital, Lewis gone, the ranch was going, and he got it in his head that he had to destroy McReady, that he was to blame for it all. I tried to talk him out of that crap, but it didn't do any good. He believed what he believed."

"You didn't share his belief that McReady was behind the disappearance of Lewis Jessup?"

He shook his head. "No. Never did. I've known a lot of men like McReady—opportunists. If you dropped a dime, he'd put his foot on it and pick it up later, but he wouldn't put his hand in your pocket and grab a dime. That's the difference. And besides, he just didn't have the opportunity that day or night. He was covered by people who didn't give a damn one way or the other about him, up till midnight, and his radio came on at five the next morning, his neighbor heard it, heard him up and about. The neighbor would have heard his car start during the hours he was in bed sleeping, and it didn't happen. In those days McReady couldn't afford a pot to shit in, cheap apartment, cardboard walls. Like that. He was covered. But Vinny was blind to all that."

"You said Vinny came over here to talk to you about it. What for? What did he want you to do?"

For a time DeFeo didn't answer. He was still turned toward the windows; she wondered how much of the vista he could see, or if he had only his memories of what was out there.

Finally he said, "He wanted us, together, to bring charges against McReady and Thomas Lynch. Obstruction of justice, subornation of perjury, conspiracy . . . I don't know what all he was prepared to charge them with. I think he was insane for a brief time, Ms. Holloway. I don't think it lasted more than a few weeks, but during those weeks he was crazy as a bedbug."

She felt baffled. "But what for? Why you? Why come all the way over here to talk about that?"

"Because I was the one who had detectives look into Lynch and his connection to McReady. I wondered why he gave McReady the green light to go after Lewis Jessup. Lynch was what they used to call a kingmaker, the power behind the scenes, the puller of strings who manipulated people and events for political ends and had friends and debtors in many high places. His father had been kingmaker before him; he was heir to the power. The line stops with him, no son to carry on after he's gone; all McReady wants is his seat on the Court, and Babe isn't interested. She was traveling a lot, last I heard, improving their beef stock, buying from around the world. I never met her, but what I heard was that all she wanted from life was to be a good rancher, run a good spread. So Lynch is the last kingmaker in that family. And he picked a rotten apple when he could have had the best.

"But this situation with Lewis Jessup and McReady was all wrong, too open, too visible. You never see the puppeteer at work; you just see the end show, and in this situation Lynch was present from the start. He's not devious, not like McReady, just invisible, working behind a screen at all times. Straight to the point when necessary, and always out of sight. So this situation just didn't work, and I didn't believe they murdered Lewis Jessup for a minor political victory. Having McReady win or lose that particular case was in the category of minor league. It didn't make a damn bit of difference to them."

"Lynch wanted the ranch," she said after a moment. "At least, that's what I've heard."

DeFeo shrugged. "Maybe enough to marry off his daughter to a Jessup boy, but enough to kill for? I don't think so."

She should not have come here, Barbara thought fleetingly; DeFeo had been an outsider, had met most of the principals only a few times, and had little reason to have strong opinions about any of them. But, she argued with herself, as an outsider, his vision of them all might have been sharper, clearer. Still, she almost wished she had not come here.

"Ms. Holloway," DeFeo said then, "all I know, of course, is what I read in the newspapers about Vinny's death. But I have to warn you that he was a man possessed by a belief that could not be demonstrated and was not warranted. I doubt that he had anything of interest for McReady that night, and if he had found out anything, it had to have been something readily available to the public, something on record, not something hidden from seventeen years ago. I didn't believe it then, that there was anything to link McReady to Lewis Jessup's vanishing act or his death, whichever it was, and I don't believe it today. That's simply not his style. Too direct." He smiled, "You see, Ms. Holloway, Harris McReady is a scheming, lying, backstabbing, opportunistic son of a bitch who's never taken a direct path in his life, and that would have been a direct path toward his goals. Not his style."

He laughed suddenly and leaned back in his chair. "Sorry," he said. "Just wanted to make sure you understand I haven't joined their camp. Nothing like that." He sobered again quickly. "I am sorry. I understand this can't help your case for the young widow. But like I said early on, I can't help you. Vinny was a man with a wild hair up his ass, or maybe more like a mad bulldog. He couldn't let go, and now he's dead, and McReady's a step closer to the Court than he was six months ago. And that's the way of the world."

That night in her motel room, making her notes on the laptop, she paused and reflected: but Vinny had let go. Four years ago he let go. Why?

The next morning she drove from Cheyenne to the Denver airport, a long, straight shot, billiard-table level all the way, and crowded with traffic that averaged eighty miles an hour.

At four-thirty she watched Phoenix rise from the sand and rocks of the Arizona desert; her chest felt tight, her hands clammy. Her heart was racing, its beat erratic. As the plane descended in a smooth landing, she closed her eyes.

Praying? Maybe she was, she thought. Maybe she was. Maybe this time they would work things out.

Later she could not have said how the fight started or who started it. Not on the first day. That had been lovely. Not on the second day, almost as perfect as day one. On the third day John took her out to look at several houses he was considering; only one of them was vacant, two would be vacant by September, and the occupants had agreed to show them now.

Barbara sat in his air-conditioned car and took a deep breath before leaving it. The temperature was 106 degrees, the glare on the highway had given her a headache, and she hated this particular subdivision with manicured lawns and tropical plants, and as deserted-looking as a mausoleum.

"If they want bluegrass, why don't they move to Kentucky?" she muttered, walking to the front of the house. It was pleasant enough looking, soft blue with white trim, sparkling clean everything, inhuman. A magazine illustration.

She had not meant anything really by her remark, but John took it personally, as if she had found fault with him, not with the attitude that made people try to pretend the desert was a lush oasis.

That had been part of the argument that escalated into a real fight later on. It might have started that night when, leaving a restaurant at ten-thirty, she had groaned; it was still eighty-nine degrees outside, and she had been chilled enough inside to have wanted a sweater, which, of course, she had not brought with her.

Or maybe something else that had completely slipped her mind. Most people, he suggested, came in the winter and stayed so that as the seasons progressed, they acclimated to the change in weather. Most places, she had said, reasonably she had thought at the time, didn't require a six-month period of adjustment.

Eventually he had snapped, "Why did you come here? You're in another messed-up case, aren't you? You're taking it out on me. If your work isn't going well, at least forget it for a few days. Can't you manage that?"

She stared at him, aghast. She had been trying hard, she thought aggrievedly, really hard; she had not mentioned the weather all that evening except for that one involuntary groan, and had gone with him to look at houses that obviously would not do for anyone who valued privacy. All she had said was that the architects down here believed in open planning, didn't they?

"How on earth did my work become a topic suddenly?" she asked furiously. "I haven't brought it up. Haven't tried to overburden your sensibilities with such sordid matters at all."

"I'm sorry," he said instantly. "I didn't mean it like it sounded. You get that faraway look, a distant look as if your mind is fifteen hundred miles away, and I . . . Let's go get something cold to drink."

But there it was, she thought. His hatred for her work, his jealousy of that part of her life. That night she said she was flying home the next day, and that's when the real fight started. He wanted her to help find the perfect house for them, for her, him, and his children. He thought that was what she had come down for, to help find a house, to make a commitment.

She pointed out that she had not said anything to that effect. "You're acting as if what you want is the only thing that counts," she said. "I said I was coming for a visit, no more, no less."

"You want everything on your own terms," he said bitterly. "Your way, your place, your cozy little apartments side by side, your life exactly to suit you. When it's convenient, you'll remember me, our life, but only when it's convenient."

"And exactly what is it you want?" she demanded. "You'll

have your university, your consultations all over the world, your excursions, your children, your house. All your way. And know I'm home, waiting. Take a case now and then when there's free time, but nothing messy, nothing sordid, nice cases with nice people. It won't work, buster!"

"You don't want it to work!"

"You better believe it. I have a life. You think I'm going to toss it all out the window to be Mrs. Faculty Wife? Attend the meetings, have teas for the ladies, listen to pompous academics make speeches to one another? Think again!"

The next day she flew to Eugene, home.

 22

It was October, a beautiful day, but Barbara had little eye for the spectacular autumn scenery. When Frank drew in his breath and said, "Ah, vine maples are turning," she hardly even glanced out the car window. Sumac and vine maples had turned crimson; scarlet poison oak announced its presence, yellow poplars and aspens. . . .

Early that morning, Manny had called: "Barbara, if you can make it over today, that would be good. Things are happening. We need to consult."

And here they were, not yet eleven o'clock, and they were pulling into Sisters already. She had made this trip so many times since summer that she felt she could drive it sleeping; so far, until today, she had stuck with her schedule, Eugene from Sunday until Wednesday, then over to Lara's house for several days, back home. Actually, it hadn't been bad at all, she had to admit; she had enjoyed the drive most of the time, and during the past four or five weeks, the weather on both sides of the mountains had been very fine.

She also would have to admit, if pressed about it, that Lara's case had come to a standstill, stalled right out, and she had not found a single way to remedy that. She had tried to convince herself that this was not unusual; cases often seemed to stop moving for weeks, or months even. But it was a worry.

She glanced at her father, who was driving happily, not very fast, taking time to enjoy the view that changed with every curve. And he was up to something, she thought, not for the first time. She suspected that his lady friend was the reason for his distracted air these days, going on months now, but he was not talking about her, and Barbara would have bitten her tongue all the way off and sewn her lips together before she would have asked. He didn't ask her personal questions; she didn't ask him any. That's the way it was, had been, would always be. Either of them might drop a hint now and then that if the other wanted to talk, it was okay, go ahead; she had dropped the hint a few times, lazing around on his back porch, or at his table, and he had hinted the same thing. He had made it clear he could listen and chop vegetables or slice meat, or just sit back and close his eyes and listen if she wanted to talk. Neither of them had heeded the broad hints.

She couldn't have said why she was so reluctant to tell him that she had cut short her vacation in Phoenix, that she had left so abruptly that John had been stuck going alone to a luncheon with some people he particularly wanted her to meet, a luncheon she had been planning to attend that included a dean or two, the head of his department, important people in the university, people she'd like, he had said. And she couldn't have said why the

idea of socializing with his colleagues had been so daunting, re-
pugnant even. Possibly because she had been wrapped up in a
case, she had reasoned; she had not been willing to break her
concentration with small talk that to her would have been meaningless. That would have been a lie, but it had sounded like a
reasonable explanation on the plane flying home. Even then, trying to convince herself, she had known that it was not the real
reason for her leaving the way she had done, although so far she
had not found the real reason. She would know it when she saw
it, she told herself, and put it out of mind as much as possible.

Frank turned onto the bypass road around Bend, and she said,
"I told Manny we'd come directly to his office. He'll be waiting
for us."

Frank nodded. "Could be ultimatum time, you know," he
said mildly.

She knew. They had all four discussed Lara's admission about
following Vinny up the mountain, and Robert had come down
hard on the side of taking the Alford plea sooner rather than
later. Manny had hesitated and agreed to give it some time, see
what developed, and it could be that now time had run out.

A few minutes later Frank was slowing down in Salt Creek.
Since school had started the fall semester, traffic had eased up,
and they had made very good time, although she had felt he was
dawdling all the way through the mountains. He parked outside
the real estate office, and they mounted the stairs.

Manny met them at the top. He didn't look any more anxious
than he ever did, or any less grave; he looked exactly the same
every time she saw him, and she still could not read his face
worth a damn, she thought with some amazement.

"Conference room," Manny said, taking her hands and pressing them lightly. "Robert's waiting."

The conference room was ready for them; chairs had been
drawn up to the large, much-scarred table. There was even a

pitcher of water and glasses, coffee cups and a carafe. Robert stood up to greet them when they entered. Nadia Walker, Manny's secretary, was not in sight.

"We have a problem," Robert said bluntly as soon as they were all seated. "Shinizer petitioned the court for permission to bring in a child psychologist to question Nathan."

Barbara let out a long breath. "Shit."

"You said that you could fight having a statement presented if it wasn't properly handled from the start," Robert said. His voice was low and intense, and she had no trouble reading his face; he was angry and frightened for Lara, badly frightened. "And we all know that if they start over with a psychologist doing the questioning, there's nothing we can do to stop them."

"Has the petition been granted yet?" she asked.

"No. They did it yesterday, late. How long do you think it'll take Judge Henkel to sign on the dotted line?"

"We can stall them," Frank said. "Lara's divorce was in Portland; the judge up there has jurisdiction over Nathan's welfare. I'll take care of that. At least we don't have to let them get to the boy immediately."

"What good that will do?" Robert demanded. "That's the first hassle. Next, they notified us that they intend to take the perpetuation of testimony as soon as possible."

"Thirty days," Frank said. "We can demand our thirty days' notice."

Robert shrugged. "So around the first of November." He looked at Frank with a helpless expression. "What good will that do anyone? It's just putting off the inevitable. Frank, there's no defense. It's putting Lara deeper in debt, putting off the only decision she can come to, keeping her in a state of tension and suspense that's bound to be hurting her psychologically."

Barbara started to say something hopeful, something optimistic, something she didn't believe, but Robert turned his bleak expression on her and said vehemently, "Manny and I've been over all the statements, all the evidence, every bit of it. Listen to how it sounds, Barbara. Take notes, and if you think of anything we've missed, for God's sake, let us in on it. Okay. Vinny had papers to deliver to McReady."

Manny spoke now, in his quiet, measured way, "No papers have been found. McReady knows nothing about papers. He doesn't know why Vinny called him that Sunday night. They had no business with each other. The Corning couple can't be certain they even heard Vinny mention any papers; all they can swear to is that he said he would go around to the Lynch place at about ten. Folks up there waited for him until a little after eleven; he never showed up."

Robert nodded, then said, "We know Vinny went to the Lynch property that night, because there was the white gravel and gravel dust in his tires. The only place he could have picked it up was the Lynch parking area."

Manny said, "So he went in there to turn around. A lot of people do that. We know from the direction of the wheels on the edge of the cliff that he turned somewhere and was heading down when he went over."

"There were no fingerprints on the briefcase, the gun, the car door, or the note in his pocket."

"We agree that someone wiped everything clean. That someone was Lara."

"The fake suicide note was typed on a typewriter the servants all used in the Lynch house. McReady had access to it, and would have known about it."

Manny spread his hands in a gesture of dismissal. "No one can prove Lara didn't enter the house the day of the open house reception. She spotted the typewriter and wrote that hasty note. It would have been too stupid an act for McReady to use it; he knows how easy it is to trace type."

Barbara shut her eyes hard. They had all been so excited the day Robert found Delia Kersh's will among the Jessup material he had inherited, a will that Vinny had drawn up, and Delia's letter to Vinny, written on that typewriter. Set up, and knocked down this easily. Delia Kersh, a former cook at the Lynch house, was retired now, living down at Klamath Falls.

Inexorably, Robert went on, "The napkin the killer used to hold the gun was from the Lynch house. McReady had access to it."

Just as relentlessly, Manny continued, "Lara swiped it the day of the reception."

"She had no reason to kill Vinny."

"She wanted out of a May/December marriage. She wanted the insurance money now, not at some unforeseeable future time. She didn't want to nurse a dying man for months to come. She's young and beautiful, and she wants her own life, people her own age, dancing, parties with young people."

"In her statement she swore that she did not leave the house that night after Vinny left."

"She lied. Her own son will testify that she went out. A neighbor saw her car leave. Another witness saw her on the mountain. Mr. and Mrs. Freelander saw her car and Vinny's van side by side by the turnout on the mountain. Afterward she went back home and did laundry. At eleven at night she did laundry to wash blood from her clothes, and she took a bath to wash blood from her hands and arms. Then she went to sleep on the couch." He looked out the window and added, "A suspect who lies under oath is not to be believed; if one statement is false, all must be considered false."

Robert looked at Barbara with a desperate expression. "You might be able to impeach the Freelanders; he was probably stoned out of his head, and she could get tangled up in her own statements, but what about the other neighbor who saw Lara leave? What about Nathan?"

The question hung there: what about Nathan? Frank cleared his throat; he and Nathan had become friends, fishing buddies, a pair of rock hounds, hiking pals. He had not asked the boy a single question, and he wouldn't, but he felt certain that in the near future Nathan would shuffle his feet, cast a lure into a river, give him a sidelong glance, and then open up. He knew the signs, knew that Nathan was desperate to talk to someone he could trust, someone who was not his mother, whom he felt he had betrayed.

What about Nathan? That was the question. "Let's leave it for a minute," Barbara said. "Manny, how much would it take to bring McReady into the picture? What kind of evidence?"

"More than you have. A solid denial by everyone in that house, that's all they need, unless you come up with the papers Vinny said he had or a witness or his hand on the smoking gun. And you don't have any of those things."

"All the evidence of the van, that it was pushed over, the gravel in the tires, no prints on the door, none of that will sway a jury?"

"Barbara, we've been over it all time and time again," Manny said. "You can't introduce anything Herman Henkel wants to keep out. You say the evidence points to McReady, they say it points more directly at Lara. The jury picks one, and the jury will do pretty much what the prosecutor and the judge tell it to do."

"They can make a case and you can't," Robert said harshly. "Without her testimony, there isn't a case! You can't even establish a reasonable doubt, not even that much. As far as the folks around here are concerned, there's no doubt whatever. You try to bring in McReady's name at the trial in any way beyond whatever his testimony offers, you'll be accused of using him, of malingning his reputation for some political end. It isn't just McReady and Babe, it's the Lynches, both of them, and several live-in servants. People here know them all; they'll take their word, not yours."

"Have you told Lara about the psychologist?"

Robert shook his head. "We wanted to talk it over with you first. She's coming here from work, around four-thirty."

"Well, what I suggest," Frank said then, "is that we bat it around a bit and then split up, go out and have some lunch. Give us all a chance to think it over before Lara gets here. Agreed?"

Reluctantly Robert nodded; Manny shrugged, and they talked it over for another forty-five minutes. Curtis Stroh was out as a possible suspect. Shelley had found out that he had an alibi, and she had checked it out thoroughly. A stranger and happenstance had never been seriously considered by anyone. On that mountain? With the fake suicide note in Vinny's pocket? The car wiped clean? No way. No one had pushed for a defense that would include such a remote possibility.

Barbara had reported what Lester DeFeo had said, that Vinny could not link McReady to Lewis Jessup's disappearance years ago, and no one could now. Manny had looked stubborn and had shaken his head; he still knew what he knew, but there was no way to prove anything, to make the connection in any meaningful way. And Judge Henkel certainly would not allow any ancient history or rumors or innuendo to creep into the present-day trial; they all understood that quite well.

Through the talk, the question continued to hang in the air, to fill the air, *What about Nathan?*

Shortly after twelve Barbara said that she wanted to take Frank down to Bend, to a restaurant where they wouldn't see anyone they knew or who knew them, and they would be back by two.

There, waiting for their orders in a quiet little restaurant, she said, "It's a fuckup, isn't it?"

He nodded. "It surely is that."

A waitress brought salads and sandwiches, asked politely if they wanted anything else, and left again. They began to eat in silence.

After a few minutes Barbara said in disgust, "I feel as if I've gone brain-dead. I can't come up with a thing to run with."

"Honey," Frank said soberly, "that could be because there isn't anything. What you have is all you get."

She ate another bite or two of her sandwich, then pushed her plate back. "I think I can understand Vinny's frustration from years ago. It would be really satisfying to get a gun and go shoot McReady right between the eyes." She sipped some coffee, which was very bad, and pushed it away. "He's going to pull it off again, isn't he?"

"And take another step toward the Court," Frank said. "Talk about Teflon! That's what he is, through and through, not just surface-coated."

Lara was being backed into a corner, step by step, with an inevitability that was like the approach of death for a ninety-year-old, or the coming birth scene for a woman in her last trimester. No one, not even Robert, whose judgment was sometimes suspect when it came to Lara, not even he had suggested that Lara go to Shinizer and correct her statement. There was murder and then there was slow murder; no one would suggest it later in the day, either. And where did that leave Lara? She couldn't change her statement, she couldn't prevent a formal interrogation of her son eventually if the judge ordered it; she couldn't testify in her own trial. Step by step being forced to retreat, and not very far from her the abyss yawned wide. It left her up shit creek.

⟡

"What I'd like to do," Barbara said that afternoon, back in Manny's conference room, "is put off making a decision until after we have the testimony from McReady and the others. Then decide."

"Why?" Robert demanded. "What's it for? I tell you, Barbara, this is too hard on Lara. She's putting a great face on it, but the cost is too high."

She could feel her own tension mounting as she watched Robert Sheffield. She couldn't really blame him; he was in love with Lara and he was very frightened for her, but this was her case, Barbara's, and she would not let him or anyone else run it for her. Keeping her voice cool and calm, she said, "I want their sworn statements so that if something does break for us, they will impeach themselves. A few weeks won't make that much difference to Lara, not at this stage."

Surprisingly, Manny agreed with her. "A few weeks won't make any difference. No decision until after the testimony."

She looked at Frank, who had become as unreadable as Manny. After a moment he nodded. "I accept that." Then he asked mildly, "But will Lara? That will determine the issue."

"She'll accept it if we are agreed here, if we're all in agreement," Barbara said. She looked at Robert and waited.

Abruptly he stood up and walked to the window, where he stood with his back to them for a minute. Finally he turned and said, "On the condition we can keep them away from Nathan that long."

"Fair enough," Frank said. "My department."

Barbara nodded. "One way or another we'll keep them off his back."

They were still talking when Lara arrived a little after four. "I got off early," she said, entering the conference room. "What's happened?"

Frank pulled a chair away from the table for her, and Robert took her jacket. Lara was very pale; her freckles had nearly vanished by now, and her skin was the color of milk.

Barbara told her. "They want to bring in a child psychologist to question Nathan."

"Can't you stop them?" Her face had gone from pale to ghost-white; even her lips lost their color.

"For a time we can, but not forever. The judge will order it done eventually, but there are legal maneuvers we can take before that happens."

"He's just a child," Lara whispered. "Can they make a child testify against his mother? Don't they know what that would do to him?" Suddenly she jumped up, knocking over the chair behind her. "I'll go to Shinizer and tell him. Now, today! He can't do this to Nathan. I'll tell him about that night!"

"Lara, that's exactly what they want, to break you, to force a confession from you. That's their game." Barbara caught Lara's arm and pulled her around when the younger woman started to walk toward the door. "Listen to me! Sit down and listen to me!"

Robert picked up the chair and righted it, and Barbara nearly pushed Lara back down into it.

"If you admit to being on the mountain that night, they'll convict you of murder, Lara. And if they convict you, they'll put you in prison. An appeal would take years, two, three years at the very least, and you would spend that time in prison. Do you understand what I'm telling you?"

Lara looked as if she might faint.

"All right. What we want to do is stall for time, long enough to get testimony from that whole crew up at the Lynch place. We'll keep them away from Nathan until then, I promise you. And after we have the testimony in hand, we'll decide what to do next. Meanwhile, no confession, no admission of anything, no talking to any of them without one of us at your side. Will you agree to that?"

"How will you keep them away from Nathan? They got to him before. What do you mean, until then? Eventually they'll question him, won't they?"

"Lara, I'll talk to Nathan," Manny said then. "I'll tell him that from now on, I'm his attorney, and if anyone wants to talk to him, to refer them to me and then keep his mouth shut. He's seen enough movies to think that's cool, I expect. We'll take care of it. And when the time comes, we'll make absolutely certain the psychologist is a children's advocate, not a stooge for the prosecution."

"If they break the law and get to him under any pretext, they won't be able to use his testimony," Frank said. "I'll see to it that they understand that simple legality. We will protect the boy, Lara, all of us."

Barbara felt as if she could see Lara's mind racing ahead, to the day after the testimony was taken, and as if on cue, Lara said, "And afterward, then I'll have to do what they want, won't I? Accept that plea, agree that they can prove whatever they say they can. . . ."

"Not whatever!" Robert cried. "It's not like that. Just that you came across Vinny's body and tampered with evidence, not murder or anything more criminal than that. You arranged the evidence to look like a murder. That's all they want you to admit to."

"That's all," Lara said bitterly. "It's a lie, but that's all they want. No matter what I do, I'll lose my son. Curtis will get him if I'm on probation; he'll get him if I'm in prison. And if Nathan has to testify against me, it won't matter if Curtis has him, or who has him; he'll be destroyed. A boy can't do that to his mother and survive in one piece."

✧ 23

That evening Frank asked Nathan to be his guide, steer him to various stores in Bend, and later they would prepare dinner together.

Nathan looked at him as if he had been asked to put on a dress and some makeup. "I'll show you where the stores are, but I can't cook, except things like hot dogs or hamburgers or instant oatmeal," Nathan said very positively.

"Well, let's talk about it while we shop. See, I want a good meat market and a specialty health-food store, something like that, and a good place for veggies. . . ."

They left together, and Lara seemed to sag as soon as Nathan was out of the house. Barbara marveled at her self-control in front of her son. "And you," she said, "should go take a long, soaking bath and leave the cooking to the pros. Dad's a genius in the kitchen. He likes to cook. I relax with a glass of wine, and I guess the best way for you to get rid of tension is a bath."

Lara nodded gratefully. She looked as near tears as Barbara had ever seen her; that wouldn't hurt a thing, either, Barbara thought, if Lara had a good cry while she soaked. But she knew it wouldn't happen. Maybe very late at night, but not now. She went to pour her wine, and Lara went up the stairs to her bathroom.

✧

Barbara wandered upstairs, down, to Vinny's study, to the living room, back. . . . She was missing something; it was like waking up knowing she had just had a powerful, meaningful, important, necessary dream, but nothing else came with the thought, no content, no context, just *red alert, red alert*. She cursed and paced.

Frank and Nathan returned with bags of groceries, and when she drew near the kitchen, she could hear her father's murmur explaining the mysteries of risotto. "As soon as it starts to get dry, you add a little hot broth, half a cup or less, and keep stirring. Now for salad . . ."

Dinner, of course, was delicious, garlicky, fragrant with fruity olive oil, everything exactly right.

"Nathan did the risotto," Frank said when Lara praised the food. "That's the only hard part of this meal, and he did a fine job. He's going to be a good cook, got the knack."

Barbara rolled her eyes. She was a kitchen klutz, no matter how many instructions she received. Nathan was very pleased.

That night, after everyone else had gone to bed, she stopped pacing and decided to search for whatever it had been that made Vinny stop collecting material on Harris McReady four years ago. Something had happened, she thought, something important enough to sidetrack him. Lara had not been able to think of anything it might have been, but there was something, Barbara told herself firmly.

She went back to the study and began to sort through reports, through discovery, Robert's notes, Manny's notes. . . . Robert had proven to be an asset, after all; he had been very good with Vinny's old files, noting everything that might be of interest, although aside from Delia Kersh's typed letter about her will, nothing had been. Still, he had been methodical and meticulous.

With anyone but McReady, there would be plenty to cast a

doubt with the jury, she brooded; the typewriter, the napkin, no fingerprints on the car or briefcase, or anything else, the phone call to McReady mentioning mysterious, missing papers, the Lynch gravel in the tire treads of Vinny's van . . . Plenty, more than enough to raise a reasonable doubt, but not here, not in Loomis County. Manny and Robert had done a good job explaining away the evidence piece by piece; a prosecutor would do a better job since he wouldn't have any sympathy for Lara, wouldn't have heard her story, and wouldn't have believed it if he had.

She picked up a copy of Delia Kersh's letter to Vinny. Any expert would be able to identify the typewriter with no more than a glance—uneven letters, heavy pressure and light, indicating an inept typist, not a touch typist. . . . Suddenly Barbara stiffened as she regarded the letter. They had all been so preoccupied with the typeface, she had not paid any attention to the date. Now she saw it, and now it registered in her mind. February, four years ago. Something Kersh had told Vinny? Something she had said unintentionally? Something he had found meaningful even if she had not?

Barbara closed her eyes, bringing to mind what Bailey had reported about Delia Kersh. About seventy, a cook for the Lynch group for thirty-four years, retired three years ago after she trained her replacement, lived in an adult community in Klamath Falls, and she had clammed up. All she admitted was that the typewriter was up at the house, in a little room off the kitchen that the servants used as a lounge. Babe gave it to them years back when she got a computer. Kersh was a widow; her husband used to work for the Lynch gang, yardman, mechanic, all-around handyman sort of job. She had a sister somewhere— Barbara couldn't remember where—and some nieces and nephews, no kids of her own.

And that was just about all. Kersh had not been willing to

talk to Bailey, to gossip, to say a word about the Lynches or McReady or anything except the typewriter, which she couldn't very well deny since the state investigators had also uncovered it.

"I'll go talk to her myself," Barbara said aloud.

The next morning they made plans: she would take the car down to Klamath Falls, be gone much of the day; Frank would walk to town later on and do some research in Manny's law library. He had phone calls to make; he would be busy most of the day also. Then after school was out, he and Nathan would borrow Lara's car and dinner shop. Nathan, he said, was willing to give another dinner a go.

Barbara left right after breakfast. It was a long drive, a hundred and fifty miles due south on Highway 97, almost to the California border. Most of the road was only two lanes once the Bend area was left behind, and now and then traffic crawled in a snarl of horns and ill-tempered drivers caught behind a slow-moving vehicle. On the left there was a scant pine forest, then a marsh, more skimpy woods, few roads, few ranches or houses, an occasional vista of high desert from the road to the eastern horizon. On the right the Cascades rose with snow on the higher elevations already; now and then the heavier forests came down to the road, then retreated, following the contour of the mountains.

At the town of Klamath Falls, with the broad expanse of Upper Klamath Lake dominating the landscape, she had to ask directions to find the adult community, which turned out to be a gated subdivision of mixed housing. A few individual houses, some town houses, several condominiums and apartments, and a lot of young trees and shrubbery that didn't look established yet. The subdivision had a vulnerable look to it, not helped by a dead rhododendron or two and a few diseased and dying pine trees.

Delia Kersh lived in an apartment building, first floor, with an outside door and no view of the lake. Barbara parked, picked up her briefcase and a clipboard she had brought along, and walked to the door. She had not called ahead for an appointment, and as she waited on the stoop after ringing the bell, she began to examine a list of names on the top sheet of paper on the clipboard, and checked off one of them.

"Yes, what is it?" a voice asked from inside the apartment. The door opened an inch or two on a chain.

"Mrs. Kersh? Mrs. Delia Kersh?"

"Yes. What do you want?"

"Thank goodness. I'm an associate of Robert Sheffield up in Salt Creek. He's taken over a lot of Vinny Jessup's law practice, including some work Mr. Jessup did for you. We're trying to verify that the clients are satisfied with the new arrangement."

The door closed a bit, then opened wider. Delia Kersh was about five feet four and twenty pounds overweight, with snow-white hair and a florid complexion. She was dressed in pink sweatpants and a sweatshirt, pink with big white daisies on it. She wore glasses with pink frames, and was examining Barbara skeptically. "You came down here to ask that?"

"Well, not just you. I'm also looking for Janet and Harvey Dunhill, but I haven't found them. Since you were in the same area, I decided to come by here, too."

"Never heard of any Dunhills, not here, not from Salt Creek."

"No, they weren't from Salt Creek, but from over at Christmas Valley, one of those new developments over there. I don't think anyone ever heard of them."

Delia Kersh shook her head. "Lots of people came and left over there. Nothing but sand."

"I know. Anyway, the lead we have, the last address is down this way, but no one answered our letters, and eventually they came back. And we couldn't find a telephone number. I bet they went back to California, but we have to try to find them. You got Robert's letter, didn't you? Asking if you were satisfied with the new arrangement?"

"It said I didn't need to answer if I was satisfied, so I didn't."

"I know," Barbara said glumly. "That was a mistake. We have no way of knowing if people got the letters or not." She looked at her clipboard again, made a check mark, then said, "Anyway, since I had to be in the area, I came by just to tell you that if you need any changes in your will, Robert will be happy to take care of it for you without any additional charge. He feels that since you were Vinny's client, that's only fair."

She began to fumble in her briefcase, and dropped the clipboard. "Oh, dear, I know I have his card. He's moving his office and wants to make sure you have the new address, just in case you want to make changes in your will. I'm supposed to write it on his card for you. He doesn't want to get new cards printed until he actually makes the move, right after Thanksgiving."

"Well, I don't want to change a thing," Delia Kersh said. "Vinny wrote me a up a good will."

Barbara continued to grope in her briefcase. When she found the card, she dropped a few other papers, trying to juggle the briefcase, the clipboard, a pen, and her purse all at once.

"Why don't you come inside and put your things down," Delia Kersh said somewhat caustically.

"Thanks."

Inside the apartment, Barbara stopped and gazed about. "How nice this is," she said truthfully. The furniture was very good antiques, and not too many pieces. A Kirman carpet glowed, spotless, perfect-looking. Two blue-green glass bowls held plants on a low table at the window, and there were several bookcases with hardcover and paperback books, not for show, for reading. "Depression glass?" she asked, pointing to the glass bowls. "They're perfect for plants, aren't they?"

Delia Kersh flushed slightly and nodded. "I like it," she said. Then surprisingly, she asked, "Do you want a cup of coffee? I was just about to have a cup when you rang."

"I'd love one," Barbara said. "But I don't want to take up too much of your time." She looked again at the clipboard, as if counting the names on the top sheet, as if her own time was in need of watching.

"Oh, I have plenty of time," Delia Kersh said. "Here, make yourself comfortable on the sofa, and I'll just get our coffee and bring it out."

After that, every time Barbara made a motion to leave, Delia Kersh wanted to give her more coffee, to give her a cookie, wanted to talk.

"I went to normal school over in Idaho, prepared for a career in teaching, you see, but then Mrs. Lynch offered me a job, and I wanted to marry Kersh, and in those days they didn't approve of married teachers, so I took her up on it. My father and mother were furious. A domestic servant! It was scandalous. But I'll confess, Ms. Holloway, it was a better-paying job than teaching would have been, and I had my room and board, and Kersh had a good job, too, with them, so we were quite content. We even had our own apartments, both at the ranch and at the mountain house after they bought that."

She looked about her tidy living room with satisfaction and nodded slightly. Life had worked out fine, everything about her suggested.

Now and then Barbara guided the conversation to Vinny Jessup or Babe or the ranch, but it didn't need a lot of guidance, and once started, Delia Kersh was harder to stop than to direct.

"Oh, it was lonesome sometimes," she admitted when Barbara asked. "Not as bad as you'd think, though. I had Kersh, and the Lynches entertained a lot, and Babe loved it out there, riding with the hands, doing a real day's work most days. And of course the Jessups were nearby, and Babe and Roger were the best of friends. It wasn't at all bad for her. In fact, she stayed quite often when her folks left for weeks at a time; they'd go to New York or San Francisco, over to Portland, but she was happy to stay put."

"It must have been a blow to the Jessup boy when she dropped him and started going out with Harris McReady."

Delia shook her head. "It wasn't like that at all. He got a girlfriend, and Babe was left out in the cold. Took it hard, too. She was so hurt and mad, she tried to run him down with the Jeep they had in those days. Can you believe it! That's how mad she was. Mrs. Lynch packed her up and they went off to Europe for months, and when they came back, that winter, a few weeks before Christmas, or soon after that, that's when she started seeing Judge McReady. She never would have dropped Roger, never."

Barbara remembered Alene's words: Babe threw a fit when Roger brought Janice home the first time.

"I heard that the Jessups lost their ranch and everything because the younger boy ran away," Barbara said. "Skipped bail, something like that."

"He did that. I never knew him well, not like Roger; he was younger than Roger, too young to be in the same crowd with Roger and Babe, so he didn't hang out at our place. But he took off instead of facing a trial, and they lost it all. He killed two youngsters, or so they said. I guess he must have done it, or why run away like that?"

Barbara finished a cookie and said it was delicious. Delia had served a variety of homemade cookies, all of them delicious, and Barbara had tried one of each. She was trying to think of a good way to bring in Vinny's belief that McReady and Lynch had conspired to get rid of Lewis when Delia said in a hushed voice, "Poor Vinny Jessup! You wouldn't believe how that man suffered that year! Lost his son, wife went mad, lost the ranch, and for a while Vinny was out of his head with grief. He wanted to blame someone for his troubles, and he picked Mr. McReady, Judge McReady! And Mr. Lynch, even. Why he thought Mr. Lynch would want to harm his boy is beyond me, but he got the idea in his head and for a long time that's where it stayed."

"I heard that Mr. Lynch helped Judge McReady, gave him a boost up in his career. And it worked. Look where he is now!"

Delia made a rude sound, not quite a snort, but close. "He didn't have a bit of use for the young Mr. McReady, and Babe couldn't bear to have him around until after Roger dropped her. No one in that house cared a fig for Mr. McReady in those days, and Mr. Lynch wouldn't have helped him run for dogcatcher, at least not until Babe took up with him. Of course, it all changed then. You never saw a man as crazy about a child as he was about Babe. Never. He would have done anything for her, and he's still pretty much like that."

"You think Vinny Jessup got over his notion that Judge McReady did something to Lewis?"

"Well, sure he did. He wasn't a stupid man, you know. And he was a good man, not stuck-up, or highfalutin, as we used to say, nothing like that. He treated me like an equal, the same as he would have treated Mrs. Lynch or the queen of England or any other lady. He was a gentleman."

"Well, you were a client, and lawyers tend to treat their clients well," Barbara said with a little shrug, as is she doubted that Vinny had shown unusual behavior.

"Lawyers also tend to charge by the minute," Delia said tartly. "Vinny Jessup said it would cost me fifty dollars, and that's what he charged, and he spent hours with me, chatting, drawing up the will, making sure it was exactly what I wanted. Just being a gentleman. He wanted to know how things had been going out at the ranch, if things had changed. We talked about the good old days when Babe and his children were growing up out there. We had a little laugh at the idea of Babe trying to run Roger down because he got a girlfriend." She sighed deeply. "We talked about a lot of things, how the roundup stopped everything else each year, the hot springs where the kids would go skinny-dipping and the grown-ups had to pretend they didn't know. Couldn't stop them, you see, and we all knew it was innocent. We talked about how things used to be, and how little difference money used to make; no one really cared how much money anyone else had then, not like now. . . ."

She talked on, and eventually Barbara really had to leave if she wanted to get back to Salt Creek in time for dinner.

"I've taken your whole day," she said. "I'm sorry. I intended to ask you a simple question and be on my way. It was those wonderful cookies that did me in, I'm afraid."

Delia smiled complacently. "I didn't mind in the least, Ms. Holloway. It was good to talk over old times with someone."

As soon as she was on the highway heading north, Barbara dug her tape recorder out of her purse and started talking into it, about the whole three hours she had spent with Delia Kersh, trying to remember every word the woman had uttered. She would be up hours transcribing it, but for now, she simply wanted a record. She felt a strange sensation, a feeling that was indescribable, originating somewhere within her in a place she felt certain could not be located on an anatomy chart. But it was there.

✦ 24

Overnight the weather changed; the temperature dropped to the low twenties, frost outlined every blade of grass, every rock; although frost sparkled in the sunlight and vanished by ten, it still was bitter cold outside, and a harsh wind blew in from the North Pole. The weather could change dramatically over in the valley in a short time as well as here, Barbara told herself when she looked out and saw what appeared to be snow; the thought was followed swiftly by a denial: it never went this far this fast. No one could say the frost melted; melting ice left a residue of moisture. This frost just disappeared into thin air.

Lara's house was warm and comfortable, but when Barbara and Frank entered the office building and Manny's upstairs rooms, it seemed the wind entered with them, and stayed. Every crack that had admitted summer heat and leaked the air-conditioned air to the outside now was a passageway for toe-numbing drafts.

"All right," Frank said in a growly voice inside Barbara's office, "what are you up to? I don't think you closed your eyes all night."

"Hardly at all," she said. "I was listening to the wind blow in, and thinking." She had not talked much about Delia Kersh, and she had spent hours transcribing her tape, as she had known she would, and had not finished by a long stretch. Then she had become sidetracked by an idea that threatened to throw the entire case off the rails.

"I have to talk to Roger," she said. "Afterward I'll tell you what I'm up to. I want to try to catch him before he gets tangled up in things today."

She sat at her desk and dialed, then looked at Frank appraisingly. "How do you know I was up all night? Did the wind keep you awake?"

Actually, he had been up late working out a new letter to Donald ("Call me Don") Fleishman, but he simply nodded, and she turned her attention to the telephone, which someone had answered.

She had to go through two people before Roger Jessup came on the line, and when she said she had some questions to put to him, he said, "Let me call you back. What number?"

She read off the number on the telephone, hung up, and leaned back in her chair. "Kersh threw me a real curve. I was looking for a gold mine, and blew up everything instead with a land mine," she said. She had already told him that Delia Kersh had stuffed her full of cookies and coffee, and had talked freely after she got over her suspicions. "She put a whole new spin on things," Barbara said just as the telephone rang.

"Sorry," Roger said when she answered. "I had people in my office here. What's up?"

"A few questions," Barbara said. "When you and Babe Lynch had a falling-out, exactly what happened?"

He was silent too long, and she said, "Roger, I'm not looking for gossip. It could be important. What happened?"

"Well, like Alene said, she threw a fit. She seemed to have taken it for granted that we were a thing. You know? And she had a fit."

Patiently Barbara said, "Okay. She had a fit. What I want to know is exactly what happened."

He cleared his throat, then said in a rush, "She tried to hit me with her Jeep. And she ran it into a boulder and had hysterics. I loaded her in my truck and took her home. Mrs. Lynch took

her to England after that, or someplace. And Mr. Lynch told me
to get out and stay out."

"Was it a serious attempt?"

"God, Barbara, I don't know. I thought it was at the time,
but now, after all these years, I don't know."

"When was that? When did it happen? When did she leave
the area? Do you remember?"

"Sure. I took Janice home with me the first of June; she stayed
a week, and the day after she left, Babe tried to run me over.
Babe and Mrs. Lynch took off the following day and stayed
away for five or six months."

"Did you tell your father, or anyone else?"

"No. I was pretty surprised. I thought of her as a pal, a buddy,
not . . . not that way. And I wasn't real proud of that whole
scene. And, of course, that's about when Lewis was arrested, and
things generally were going to hell. I didn't tell anyone. A few
years ago Dad brought it up, and I don't have a clue how he
knew or when he learned about it, or anything else. But even
years ago, when Lewis disappeared, I knew the reason Lynch
was gunning for us, all of us; he was out to get even with the
Jessups. See, it was my fault, for not realizing how Babe felt, for
not understanding how it hurt her when I turned to someone
else. Alene said it, boys can be so damn dumb, and she was right,
more than she knew. I was so goddamn dumb. And the way her
father treats her, Babe, I mean, and always did treat her, it was
a sure thing that he would get even with anyone who hurt her."

"Do you remember when your father brought it up? In what
context?"

"Yes. He said he had come across some old snapshots of Babe
and me, and asked if I wanted them. I said no, and I guess he
tossed them out. He said they had been taken when we were
kids, before she tried to run me down. Surprised the hell out of
me. He and Lara had been married about a year, I guess. I re-

member that I was glad we were both getting rid of past hurts."

Barbara didn't keep him long after that. After she hung up, she looked at Frank and said, "I think I know why Vinny stopped gathering material about McReady four years ago."

"Tell me," he said gruffly. She looked dejected, and he was not really certain he wanted to know the reason.

"Right. Roger was the chosen one for Babe for a long time, apparently. She thought he was hers, but he found his wife, Janice, and that was that. Babe tried to hit him with a Jeep, missed, and ran into a boulder instead. He bundled her home in hysterics, and Lynch ordered him out, told him to stay away. The next day Anna Lynch took Babe off somewhere. They said to Europe. They were gone for months. And in that period Lewis was arrested, and almost immediately following the return of Babe and her mother, Lewis vanished. Probably Babe would have known only what her father told her about Lewis's arrest, all of that. And I doubt he told her much; I suspect that the Jessups were a topic they tried to avoid."

Barbara watched her father as she talked, and she could tell almost to the second when he leaped to the same conclusion she had reached. His eyes widened just a little, then narrowed, and a frown wrinkled his forehead. He nodded almost imperceptibly.

"You think Babe did it," he said after a moment.

"Yes. I think she saw Lewis and thought it was Roger out tending the stock, and she shot him. All bundled up, heavy jacket and hat, in the Jessup truck, Lewis would have looked like Roger, and she would have expected to see Roger, and probably never gave Lewis a thought. Delia said that up until then she'd had no use for McReady, and neither had Lynch. Tolman said it, too, remember? Lynch told him to give the case to McReady, teach him a lesson, let him get egg on his face. But after that, McReady was the golden-haired boy. I'd bet he cleaned up for them, probably loaded the body in his car, got rid of it on his way to Spokane; he got the girl, the gold watch, the ranch, the case all wrapped up, a boost up the ladder, all of it. Negligible risk for him and lots to gain. A real opportunist." She remembered what DeFeo had said and nodded. He might not hold up anyone for a dime, but he'd grab it if he saw the chance.

"Christ on a mountain!" Frank muttered. "Delia Kersh steered you in that direction?"

"Yes. She and Vinny had a nice long chat when she had her will drawn up, talked about old times, laughed about Babe's trying to hit Roger with the Jeep, silly girl. . . . Vinny confirmed it with Roger, and he realized that likely the wrong person had been killed, that the killer was more than likely Babe. And he stopped gathering material on McReady."

For a time neither spoke; Barbara stared at the wall, an ugly tan color that was depressing; a gust of wind rattled the windows, and papers on her desk stirred in the new draft. She waited while Frank went over the scenario she had sketched, nodding now and again. Finally he sighed heavily.

"Okay, it works. You know what it means, though?"

She knew. The case against McReady, feeble as it was, was down the drain. Vinny might still have despised him, even hated him enough to want to see him dead, but not because he suspected McReady had murdered his son. It meant that there was no real reason for McReady to have killed Vinny, unless Vinny was going to accuse him of dullness, of being a bore. Certainly not to protect Babe. From what? Who at this point would bring a charge against her? Any novice defense attorney would kick a charge aside without missing a step: Where was the body? Why would Babe have killed Lewis Jessup, who had been little more than a kid, one she had had nothing to do with, and in fact hardly even knew?

They were both silent for several minutes; then Barbara said, "Well, I have a few things to sic Bailey onto. I'll give him a call."

Frank stood up. "And I'm finding new and ingenious ways to keep Nathan free of interrogators."

"Dad, I don't think I'll air this theory to Robert, maybe not to Manny, either, yet. Certainly not to Lara. It's just a theory, not new hard evidence."

"Exactly. Maybe just a hypothesis, in fact." He knew as well as she did that Robert was on the edge of going ballistic; this development, having what little case they were putting together explode, might drive him right over. He was too much of an unknown factor, too unpredictable. If he blew, where would the fallout land?

He walked from her office, and she dialed Bailey's number in Eugene. She didn't expect to reach him, and that was how it worked; he would call her in half an hour, his wife, Hannah, said.

Barbara was reading and rereading her printout of Delia's monologue when he called back.

"Just one more thing to put on the list," she told him. "I know you've done some digging about Babe Lynch McReady, but I want you to concentrate on her. From the time the kids here were killed and Lewis was charged, until the recent past. Bailey, I want to know if she was ever in an institution, if she was in Europe that summer when Lewis was arrested. Not just newspaper clippings, deeper."

For a moment he was silent. "She isn't a public figure, not like him," he said. "She's pulled the shade down, kept behind cover, taken precautions. It's going to take a little time."

"Not too much time. We have thirty days before they testify. I'll need it all by then."

Bailey made a rude noise.

After they hung up, Barbara watched a few papers stir in the draft, and she thought, wool socks, heavy wool socks, and lined jeans. If she was going to work in this office, she had to dress for it.

✦ PART THREE

THE

KINGMAKER

✦ 25

Barbara sat at her own desk in Eugene and drummed her fingers. To date, every single lead—fat and glowing and ripe for plucking at first sight—shriveled, turned to dust, and blew away when she tried to reel it in for a closer look. She cursed bitterly. Solving the mystery of the disappearance of Lewis Jessup didn't do a goddamn thing to help Lara.

And that meant she would have to go for the best possible terms of probation, try to soften Lara's exile from east Oregon, sound out Lara's divorce lawyer about the possibility of winning if and when Curtis got serious about getting custody of Nathan. She understood very well the schedule Shinizer was following. Let Lara worry until sworn testimony proved beyond a doubt that Barbara could not drag McReady into the case through a loophole, a back door, a trapdoor, a transom, or any other way; afterward hit her with a court order to permit a psychologist to question Nathan, then sit back and wait for the deal.

Suddenly she wondered if any of them really understood the emotional cost they would exact in forcing a child to testify against his mother. It was their strongest card, but did they know enough about parental love to grasp how impossible Lara would find that? McReady and Babe were childless. He might understand the concept of blind parental love for a child, but only in an academic way, not experientially. Not like Frank's love for her, or Lara's love for Nathan. Or John's for his children, she added. She had not even understood that until it had been demonstrated in a way that separated her and John. But if McReady was unprepared to understand the turmoil that testifying would arouse in Nathan, the scars it would leave, who was masterminding the prosecution? Shinizer? It was possible, she decided, and did not believe it. Lynch? Slowly she nodded and mouthed the name: "Thomas Lynch."

She stopped drumming her fingers as a new thought occurred to her: Why hadn't McReady and Babe had children? Mutual consent? Or one of them infertile? There was a gigantic estate to pass along, and Babe was the end of the line. Why?

She was still without motion, thinking, a few minutes later when Maria buzzed to say that Bailey was on the phone.

"I was just going to call you," she said when he came on the line.

"Me first. My call."

"You have something?

"Maybe, maybe not. You know I was running down folks who used to work for the Lynch bunch. They're all in my reports. Anyway, one of them was a guy named Carlos Miranda, a ranch hand. I talked with him a month ago. Zilch. So that was that. Anyway, Carlos called me this morning. Seems his wife wants to talk to you. I said I could come by, and he said no way; she'll tell you what's on her mind, or no one. So. She'll go to Martin's at one this afternoon."

"Did she work for the Lynch gang, too?"

"Nope. I think Carlos sort of persuaded her to talk about something. Her name's Beatriz, and that's all I know."

"Okay. Okay, I'll be there. And I have to discuss something with you later on today."

Promptly at one she entered Martin's restaurant. He waved her to her usual table, where he already had placed a carafe of coffee and two mugs. Binnie stuck her head out from the kitchen door and blew a kiss, then vanished again. Martin was as big as a mountain; Binnie looked like a tiny jewel next to him, all sparkling eyes and bright teeth.

Barbara did not have to wait long. Beatriz Miranda arrived before Martin closed the kitchen door; at the sound of the bell, he detoured to open the front door for her. She was a heavyset woman who looked around the restaurant warily, as if suspecting a trap. Her hair was gray, pulled back in a severe bun at the nape of her neck; her skin looked as tough as a boot, dark brown, with deep creases on her forehead, vertical creases along the sides of her mouth.

"Miss Holloway?" she asked, just inside the doorway.

Barbara walked over to greet her. "I'm Barbara Holloway. How do you do, Ms. Miranda."

"Not too bad. Not too bad." She cast another sweeping, searching glance at the restaurant, at Martin vanishing into the kitchen, then held out her hand to shake.

"What can I do for you?" Barbara asked, leading the way back to her table.

She shook her head. "No. No. What I can do for you."

Barbara poured coffee for them both, and Miranda helped herself to cream and sugar, a lot of each. She kept her gaze on her mug now and stirred and stirred without speaking, as if gathering the words together in a proper order.

Finally Beatriz Miranda looked up. "A man, a detective, he come asking Carlos questions, but Carlos don't know nothing for him. Carlos say the man work for the lawyer who work for the Lara Jessup girl. He say it's in the papers. And we talk about it, and we don't want to get mixed up in nothing, but Carlos, yesterday, he say maybe I have to. Maybe I have to come here and tell you. Okay? Carlos, he say you come here to restaurant to help some people he know."

"It's about Lara Jessup?"

"No. No. About Thomas Lynch and Babe Lynch."

Barbara felt her stomach do a fluttery spasm that was a lot like a fear reaction, a quick rush of adrenaline to the midsection. She leaned back in her chair, holding her coffee mug in both hands. "What about them?"

"See, my sister, she has three daughters and two sons and the girls worked for people over around Bend for many years, many. Lolita, she work for Mr. and Mrs. Lynch a long time ago, fifteen, eighteen years ago. She there when Babe Lynch have nervous breakdown. And she there when Babe Lynch try to run down the Jessup boy, and then try to kill herself. She help Mrs. Lynch put Babe Lynch to bed, and next day get her dressed and put in car to take someplace. She don't know where they go, but when they come back in winter, Babe different, quiet and mean, and she don't talk to nobody, just out riding every day on her horse, day after day, and then she come in one day and say it done, over, and now she can rest."

Barbara didn't move as Beatriz told the story. Lynch made Babe go out with him to see what she had done. They came back with Babe unconscious in the car, and Thomas Lynch angry and more than a little crazy. He drank down a glass full of whiskey, and he swore and knocked things off a table, mad, wild. Leaving Babe in her room, Thomas and Anna went back out, and when they came home, he was driving a truck and Anna the car. Inside the house once more, they found Babe on the phone to Mc-Ready; Lolita was on the other side of the door, listening in terror. Babe told McReady she had shot Roger and wanted to be executed for it. Then Lynch took the phone away from her, and Anna Lynch and Lolita took Babe to her room; Lolita didn't know what Lynch said to McReady.

"Mrs. Lynch give Babe pills to make her sleep, and in night Mr. Lynch and Mrs. Lynch drive truck and car away, drive back in car, and next morning before light Mr. McReady come and they all talk and talk, and he leave in his car."

Lolita had been ordered to her room the night before and told to stay there until someone called her. But from her window she had seen McReady drive in and then drive out again. She was sixteen, Beatriz added softly. A child, very, very afraid. She never did see the body, and knew only what she had heard and the condition Babe was in on both occasions and Thomas Lynch acting crazy. Anna Lynch had not stopped crying for hours.

"Mr. Lynch, he say to Lolita if she tell anybody, she has to be killed, and her mother and father and sisters and brothers, all of them have to be killed, and she believe him, so she run away from that place and never go back."

Back in the office, Barbara outlined to Shelley what she had been told. "So," she finished, "Lolita Juarez lives down in the Taos area with her husband and three children. She never talked about any of this until her mother died a year and a half ago. Her father died five or six years ago, and the rest of her family has scattered—the girls are married with different names, the sons gone from Oregon—so she isn't living in fear for herself and her family anymore. She told her aunt, Beatriz Miranda, about it when Beatriz went down there for the funeral of Lolita's mother. None of them thought anything could be done after all these years, and there it stayed until Bailey stirred up Beatriz and her husband with his questions when he was tracking down former employees at the ranch."

Shelley was listening carefully, taking no notes yet. Barbara sat opposite her at the coffee table and said, "The first flight down you can get, and have a car waiting at the other end. I'll call her from here, and you should call again when you arrive at Taos. Don't push her; she works and might have trouble finding time, but help her find it. I want a statement from her, on tape, attested to by her. She might scare off easily, so play it by ear. And reassure her that she has nothing to fear, that we won't call her without her permission, but we need her statement."

"What for?" Shelley asked after thinking about this for a moment. "It wouldn't be admitted, would it? Not at Lara's trial, I mean. Haven't you been saying that nothing from that time would be allowed in? Besides, it would be easy to discount her story after so many years of silence."

"I know," Barbara said, pleased that Shelley had seen the problem so quickly. "But get the statement, let her talk as long as she wants to about them all, the Lynch crew, McReady, the Jessups, all of them. Sometimes," she added, "if the enemy knows you have equal firepower, neither side has to fire a shot."

They were still talking about Shelley's interview with Lolita Juarez, with Shelley taking notes now, when Bailey arrived, and Barbara told Maria to send him on back. He slouched in, wearing a new cap. Shelley and Barbara both stared at it in wonder, a bright blue woolen knit cap.

"Give me a call when you get back," Barbara said to Shelley. "Don't come over to Lara's, just call. If I'm tied up, I'll call back."

Shelley nodded. "Right. Bailey, that's a really neat topper. Looks good on you."

"Goodwill special," he said. "Buck and a quarter. Warm."

Shelley left, and Barbara eyed Bailey suspiciously. "Are you in disguise?"

"Nope. New leaf. Hannah said I get some new duds, or she'll do it for me and toss out everything I own. Been shopping." He did not sound happy.

"Your mad spree started and stopped with a cap?"

"Only thing I've seen yet that I liked. I'll try again later, tomorrow, next week, sometime. Hannah gives me credit for trying."

Grinning, Barbara went to her desk and sat down. She folded her hands on the desktop, and looked over Bailey's head at the wall. "I've heard," she said thoughtfully, "that people can get into anyone's medical records through the Internet if they have the right know-how."

As dispassionately as she had said this, Bailey said, "I've heard the same thing."

"A hacker, someone like that, could probably do it in an evening and have time to play a couple of computer games on the way."

"So they tell me. I've also heard that it's pretty illegal to do a thing like that."

"I don't doubt that," she said, nodding. "It's a scummy thing to do, invasion of privacy. Like breaking into an office—illegal forced entry—and stealing secrets—proprietary matter."

She continued to study the wall behind his head, and he continued to look sleepy, a touch bored, and distant. "Babe Lynch McReady," she murmured. "Where, when, what for, how long, cured or in remission, or what?"

"I've heard that Thomas Lynch has a special gun he uses on people who bother his kid."

"Bailey, come on! I would hate for you to bother her!"

He looked at the papers on her desk, and nodded toward them. "There's stuff in there."

"What we have are rumors, hints, suggestions, gossip. . . . Make it specific, Bailey. Doctors' names, diagnoses, hospital admissions, you know, specific."

Bailey sighed dramatically. "You're talking hospital files, doctors' files."

She spread her hands in a helpless gesture. "When you need an egg, a pickle just won't do." Then, shuffling papers, she said, "I want dates, when she and McReady got married, where they went for a honeymoon, how long, where they ended up afterward, when they left for Portland, then later for San Francisco. Where they live in the San Francisco area. Dates, specific dates."

"Public records for that kind of thing," he said. "A lot of it's already in there." He pointed to his own reports on her desk.

"And a lot isn't. For instance, how much time does she put in at the ranch, and how much time does he, and is it at the same time?"

When he said philosophically that he would do what he could, she said, "ASAP. Tomorrow. Yesterday would be better. Time's running out on us. One more thing, pictures of the Jessup kids in heavy winter gear. Lara might have some snapshots, or Alene or Roger might. I'd consider a picture of Babe and Roger together a Megabucks winner. Maybe you can put off shopping for a couple of weeks?"

He laughed and stood up. "I'll tell Hannah it's your fault. I'll be in touch. See ya."

After he left, she sat on her sofa and thought. Presently she found herself pacing back and forth, back and forth. The rich burgundy carpeting, a gift from Shelley's father to help them get the office up and running the year before, muffled her footsteps so that even she could not hear them. The furniture—desk, chairs, sofa—was a gift from her father to get things up and running and looking good. And the office looked very good, rich and successful. Then she remembered she was supposed to call Frank, and she did so; they agreed that whenever she was free, she would wander over to his house.

After dinner he said, "You understand, of course, that you can't use a statement about a crime committed so many years ago even if you could find a way to relate it to the present trial. You have a judge who would toss you off the case before he would let that happen." He waited for her nod. "You don't think it's a waste of time sending Shelley off on what could be a wild-goose chase?"

"I don't think so," she said. "You know, we get used to think-ing of what we can use at trial, and sometimes I believe we over-look things we could have used because they don't tell us what we want to hear, but just irrelevant facts instead."

"Such as?"

"Well, everyone has made it clear that Thomas Lynch is pretty crazy about Babe. She's the last of the line. It appears that he covered up murder for her. What if Vinny had something about Babe after all? McReady might not get too hot under the collar about it, but what about Thomas Lynch? How far would he go these days to protect her?" She smiled at him. "How far would you go to protect me?"

Frank poured more coffee, his eyes narrowed in thought. Fi-nally he said, "In some ways it's a better fit. Thomas wouldn't hesitate to act if he decided action was called for. It was hard to see McReady doing anything as positive as shooting someone. Poison pills, maybe, to be taken when he was elsewhere, but not a close-in shooting. No matter, there's still no way to bring it in, not without whatever it was that Vinny found, not without hard evidence of some sort."

"I know," she murmured. "I know."

Then Frank shook his head regretfully. "It's a better fit, but it won't quite work. Vinny was obsessional about McReady. I saw him, talked to him briefly last year, remember. He was gunning for Harris McReady, not Lynch."

Barbara had been gazing off into space; suddenly she jerked and shook her head.

"What?" Frank asked.

"I don't know for sure. Gunning for McReady. Obsessional. Let me think about it. Something . . ." Something too elusive to catch, something just out of sight, just out of reach, just beyond comprehension, but something real, she thought.

It was no use, she decided minutes later; she felt the way she sometimes did when she tried too hard to recapture a dream, determinedly keeping her eyes closed in bed, forcing herself to lie still, to will a dream back, and all the while getting more and more awake, further and further from the dream images.

"Well, I have work to do," she said, carrying dishes to the sink. "I'll help clean up and then I'm out of here."

"No. Leave that stuff. Won't take me five minutes. You going to drive over to Lara's tomorrow? I have a few things to attend to, but I can join you Thursday or Friday."

"No need to," she said with a shrug. "Whatever's going to happen will be over here, stuff from Bailey or Shelley. Nothing's happening over in Bend or Salt Creek. Just wind. It's our move out there."

"Okay," he said. "Give me a call when you get back. Or if you need me for anything. You can hand the pertinent citations to Manny about the child psychologist; doesn't take two of us to do that."

He started to walk to his study, and she trailed after him, and arrived in time to see him hastily blank out the screen on his computer. She moved in closer as he turned several pages of typescript facedown, then rummaged without a word in a small pile of other papers to find the citations.

Barbara glanced curiously at the sheets of paper he had turned over; simply legal papers, like a thousand others that passed through his hands, like a thousand that had passed through her own hands. She shrugged, and they walked back to the hall; while she was pulling on her jacket, the phone rang, and they both heard a woman's voice when the answering machine took the call:

"Frank, it's Wanda. That sounds fine to me. Same place, one o'clock. See you then."

"Business," Frank said swiftly.

Barbara nodded. Right.

 **26**

On Friday Barbara and her team met with Shinizer and his assistant Gregory Melchior in a conference room in the courthouse, with Judge Henkel presiding. Shinizer looked as tanned and lean and healthy as she remembered, and Gregory Melchior looked to be near death. He was a pale, cadaverous type so gray and bloodless, it seemed a miracle that he was up and about instead of lying in a box clutching a lily. His voice, when he said, "Pleased to meet you," sounded as if he were standing in a vast cavern.

"Now, folks, let's get a few things settled," Judge Henkel said, adjusting himself with a grunt at the head of the conference table. "You'll get your testimony a week from Monday, and today we can settle some of the details. Like, for instance, is everything going to be videotaped?"

He looked genial and easygoing, and his slow speech reinforced that, but his eyes were cold and unblinking. He would turn the hose on her if she gave him half a chance, Barbara thought.

It took them nearly two hours to establish the ground rules, and by the end of that time, everyone was snapping at everyone else. Shinizer did not want any media allowed in, and wanted the videotapes sealed afterward. Barbara agreed that no media person should sit in, but the tapes had to be made available, the perpetuation of testimony was as public as any trial.

Henkel sided with Shinizer. "We can set our own rules to a certain extent," he said, "just as long as we all agree to them beforetimes. Lots of trials have certain matters under seal. I see nothing amiss with that. So be it."

Barbara wanted her objection on record. Henkel scowled at her for a long time before he nodded. "All right. It's on record. Are you planning to be difficult through this meeting?"

She shrugged. "I voiced my objection, a valid one. I don't believe anyone here wants a mistrial, or even a simple misunderstanding. To that end, I suggest—no, I formally request—that this entire procedure be on record."

His look was pure venom when he nodded. "So be it."

"It didn't get any better," she reported to Frank on Saturday. "Henkel and Shinizer are blood brothers who share a world-view."

Frank nodded. "Didn't we sort of know that beforehand? Anything in particular bring you home today instead of tomorrow?"

Most weeks she had stayed at Lara's house through Saturday night. "I think Lara and Nathan are ready to have a talk," she said slowly, "and I might have been in the way. They're both really frightened."

Lara had looked ghastly, in fact, and Nathan only slightly less so. He had been getting a lot of static in school from the other kids, Lara had said, and there was a lot of talk around town, much of it intended for her ears, or his, or both. "A small town can be a snake pit," she had added tiredly.

At that moment Lara and Nathan were at the table in her dining room silently eating spaghetti.

Most of the time, she was thinking, the silence wasn't so noticeable, or they even filled it with small talk: how was school, anything new with so-and-so, did you return those library books. . . . But that kind of talk seldom lasted through dinner, and then the silence was there, thick and heavy. It reminded her of the silence of the intensive care unit when everyone knew the patient was dying and there was nothing that could be done about it. They tended to bustle a little more then, to try to keep their chats with family and friends even more cheerful than usual, but when the chatting ended, and there were only the hums, beeps, and buzzes of machinery, then the silence was heavy, like a physical presence.

She wished Barbara had not left early, wished that Frank had come over this time. Especially Frank with his funny stories, his reminiscences, his pseudostern warnings about things like butterflies that lured cats and people to leap off cliffs, always fluttering just out of reach of the net or claws. They were *X-Files* aliens that got together and plotted the downfall of the human race, he had said once, his expression gloomy and concerned. He had even managed to look hurt when Nathan laughed. How long, she wondered, since she had been able to get a laugh out of her son?

She stopped pushing food around on her plate; he was nearly finished eating by then, his plate nearly empty, her dinner hardly touched.

"Nathan," she said finally, instantly forgetting the words she had rehearsed most of the day, the speech she had tried to put together gone, and only his look of fear and a new stillness between them. "Nathan, I have to tell you this. I didn't hurt Vinny; I didn't kill him. I never would have hurt him any more than I would hurt you. I don't know what happened to him, but I didn't do anything to him. I swear it to you."

She never had dreamed she would have to declare her innocence to her child, she thought suddenly, and averted her gaze, stared out the broad windows at a reflected sunset in the eastern sky. Her eyes were hot with tears that threatened to form and fall, but remained instead as burning hot embers just behind her eyelids.

"You went out," he said hoarsely, the words hardly audible.

She ducked her head, then lifted it and faced him again. "I can't talk about that night," she said. "Barbara and Frank, Manny, they all say I can't talk about it. I can only tell you I didn't do anything to Vinny."

"They're afraid if you tell me anything, I'll tell the police, aren't they?" His voice had gone shaky; he had changed from a mature adolescent to a frightened child in a flash. "Mom, I told them. I already told them. They know!"

She pushed her chair back and jumped up and ran to him, to hold him, stroking his hair, hushing him, just holding him. "It's all right, Nathan. Shh, shh. It's all right." He was shaking as if with a terrible fever chill. "It's all right. Really." She had her eyes shut hard. No tears, not now, no tears! "Honey, no matter what you said, they can't use it. Not like that. It's all right."

After a minute or two, she drew him away from the table, into the living room, where she had made a fire earlier. Now she moved the fire screen away and added a log to the blaze. They sat on the floor near the grate. The fire felt good.

"They said, Dad said, I had to tell them what I saw that night, what I heard," Nathan said in a low voice. She did not look at him; he would not like for her to see that he had been crying, she knew. "I told them I heard Vinny close the garage door and leave, and then a little later I heard the door open again, and I looked out and saw you driving away. Then I went to sleep. After a while I heard the door close, but I didn't look out, and I didn't look at the clock or anything. I just thought you were both home again."

"You had to tell the truth," she said in a near whisper. It felt as if the heat of the fire no longer could reach her. "You know that Vinny and I were happy here. I loved him very much. Nathan, I never saw him again after he went out that night." She still didn't look at him. "Remember when we went to Crater Lake the first time, how we all said it was more like the postcards than like a real lake? So blue! Remember the hawk that nearly flew into the windshield that day?"

He nodded. "We nearly got lost in the snow when we couldn't find the trail," he said.

"And Vinny thought it was funny since the road was only a hundred or two hundred feet ahead, and we could even hear the cars. We were pretty ignorant, you and I."

"He knew all about the woods and trails. . . ."

"Yes, he did."

"Remember that time we were looking for the petroglyphs? I thought they'd be like billboards or something. He showed us how to look for them."

"And find them."

They talked about other days until the fire burned low and he went out to bring in more logs and she made popcorn and hot chocolate and they talked longer. When Nathan yawned finally and said he guessed he'd go to bed, she hugged him and he hugged back. She had left the table, dirty dishes and all, and after he went upstairs, she straightened up, put dishes in the dishwasher, then returned to the living room to sit gazing at the fire. It had burned low again.

"I won't let them hurt him again," she whispered to the quiet flames. Juniper wood burned very quietly, with little smoke and hot blue-and-white flames, for the most part. "They can't hurt him," she said under her breath. She knew she would do whatever it took to protect him, to keep him from the disaster of betraying her, of testifying against her. Whatever it took.

In Frank's living room another fire was burning, not for heat, since the weather was continuing warm and pleasant west of the mountains, but because Frank liked a fire and had one unless it would have been madness to add to the heat of the day. Frank and Barbara were waiting for Shelley to arrive with her tape of Lolita Juarez's statement.

During the past few months, Frank had bought a new Chinese rug; it had a pale blue and rose pattern with a lot of intricate little geometric shapes in the border done in gold. He had changed the subject when Barbara asked how much it had set him back. He had a new glove-leather, soft-as-a-cloud beige sofa of no particular period, and indecently comfortable. The two Things loved it; they had claimed it the day it was delivered, and any person who wanted to sit on it had to move a cat first. Barbara had moved a cat and taken its place and was stroking the sofa and the other cat alternately. Thing One crept back up and tried to nudge her out of his way; she resisted.

Neither she nor her father had ever referred again to the Arno case, the New Year's Eve incident, the shooting that had necessitated the new purchases. In so many ways, she mused, they were alike, she and her dad. Although he gave the impression of being a real talker, there were more areas that he steered conversation away from than most people suspected. And she knew very well that she had secret places where she kept bits and pieces of her life that were off-limits.

Keeping your private life private was well and good, she thought then, but one of these days she would bring up the subject of her father's lady friend, Wanda. She had not been able to think of a good and yet subtle way to let him know she was onto him. *Hey, Dad, who's the doll?* Nope. *How's the new squeeze? Is she someone I know?* Closer, but no cigar, not that way . . . The doorbell rang and he went out to admit Shelley.

Shelley was in a pink phase that night—pink sweater, pink sweatpants and socks, pink raincoat. She was the golden-haired pink fairy princess, according to Frank, and that night she looked the part.

"I think I got everything she had to offer," she said to Barbara in the living room. Frank handed her a cup of coffee, and she continued. "I talked to her three different times, and she added a little more each time, but at the end she said that was it, she had recalled things she never knew she knew." She smiled, dimpling, then said, "She's pretty and smart. She and her husband run a trading post, gift shop sort of thing. The main story is the same one you already have, about Babe trying to hit Roger with the Jeep. Lolita remembers that all right."

She retold the story, but added details that Beatriz Miranda had not known. Babe had had a wall of photographs, snapshots, newspaper clippings, many of them pictures or articles about Roger. She had loved him and expected to marry him, but Lolita had never seen anything on his part to indicate that he was aware of it.

"She would have noticed," Shelley said. "She went to work for the Lynches when she was fourteen, and Mrs. Lynch and Babe were the most glamorous women she had ever seen; she hung on every word, copied every gesture, tried to make herself over to be like them. She would have known if Roger returned

Babe's love. Okay. So much for Roger. It's on the tapes. As for
Harris McReady, Babe mocked him unmercifully when he tried
to hang out at the ranch to be with her. Lolita said he had other
girlfriends at first, but he dropped them all and concentrated on
Babe after he was in the area a few months. He knew where the
bread was buttered—Lolita's expression. And Babe couldn't
bear him. She called him boring, suffocating, dim, and useless.
He couldn't ride, hunt, shoot, rope cattle, do any of the things
that she was interested in and that Roger was an expert at. Useless."

Shelley grinned. "You said you wanted particulars, and I tried
to get some. Babe had a newspaper photograph of McReady, a
big one taken at a rally of some sort, and she used it as a dart-
board. She taped it up over a corkboard and threw darts at it
after his visits." Shelley's smile broadened and she said, "Here's
another one. Lolita was wonderful, I must say. One day Mc-
Ready showed up when Babe was planning to go riding with a
couple of friends, just a little ride up the mountain or something,
eat sandwiches, and ride back. He insisted on going with them,
and she had another horse saddled, but she changed their plans,
and it became an all-day ride. They got back at dark, and he
could hardly walk." They all laughed.

"When did Lolita leave the ranch?" Barbara asked.

"In January, a few weeks after Babe shot Lewis. When Mrs.
Lynch took Babe away in the summer, everything got really
quiet, of course, and there wasn't a lot of work, but she stayed
on as housemaid. Then Babe and her mother returned in December, and Lolita said it was a very busy time, a lot of company,
entertaining, Christmas shopping going on, visitors staying for
days at a time. McReady was hanging around, and Babe was
ignoring him or insulting him, humiliating him in little ways all
the time. There are a few incidents she talked about on the tapes.
Then that last day Babe went out riding late in the afternoon.

Lolita said Babe never cared what kind of weather it was—hot, cold, snowing, raining, it made no difference to her. So she went out, and when she came back, she was as pale as a ghost, and she told her father that she had shot Roger. Lolita heard her say it. He made her go back out with him to show him where it happened, and when they both got back the next time, Mr. Lynch carried her back in. He said she had fainted—from not eating enough or the cold, or something. Mr. Lynch told Lolita to put her to bed, that Roger was not hurt, no one was hurt, and like that. Lolita stayed with Babe, and the Lynches both left in the car. In a short while they both came back, and this time when Mr. Lynch walked in, he found Babe on the telephone to McReady, confessing. Lolita heard what she said, and was terrified because she had not been able to stop Babe, to keep her in her room."

Shelley drank some of her coffee, then said, "It's all on the tape, so I'll skip to the next morning. Just at daybreak, McReady showed up. He and Lynch talked in the study for a while, then he left again. He returned a day or two after Christmas, and this time the whole family talked with him in the study one whole afternoon. When they came out, Babe looked as if she had been sick for a month, pale and shaking, and she threw up that evening and went to bed. Lolita thought she had the flu or something. There was a New Year's Eve party, and her engagement to McReady was announced."

"The girl didn't tell anyone that Babe had shot and killed a man?" Frank asked incredulously.

"No. She said the day after all that, Mr. Jessup and Roger came around looking for Lewis, so she knew Roger was all right, and she thought that Babe had been out of her head, and maybe was even crazy. It didn't occur to her that Babe had shot Lewis, not Roger."

Shelley drew in a breath. "It's so ugly," she said almost apologetically. "Babe and her parents were fighting a lot. At one point Babe screamed that she'd rather die in prison, and her father slapped her hard and yelled that his daughter would not stand trial for murder. Lolita said he acted crazier than Babe. Babe pulled all of Roger's pictures off her wall and burned them in the middle of her bedroom in a wastebasket, and it was a miracle that she didn't burn the house down. Lolita was only sixteen, but she began to put the pieces together and came up with blackmail. And if McReady was blackmailing them, there had to be a reason, and she put that together with the disappearance of Lewis, and that's when she became so frightened that she ran away."

"And she still didn't tell anyone what she knew," Frank muttered in disgust.

"She was too afraid. She realized that if Babe had shot Lewis, and if they could cover up murder that easily, Lynch's threat was real, she and her family were in danger, and no one would believe her, but Lynch would kill them all anyway. She didn't tell anyone until a year and a half ago, after her mother died."

Barbara nodded in satisfaction. "Good work. It's the same story Beatriz Miranda gave me, but it's no longer hearsay. Lolita was there; she knows what she saw, what she heard."

"I promised her that we wouldn't call her without her permission," Shelley said. "You said I should reassure her, remember."

Barbara nodded. "I know. The promise is good. This is just ammunition." She shrugged. "I don't have a clue at this moment as to how I'll use it, but ammunition is okay to stockpile, just in case."

Silently Frank agreed. In another week, when they gathered to take testimony, she would need as much ammunition as she could muster.

✧ 27

"The system works like this," Barbara explained to Lara on Saturday. She and Frank had driven over the day before and were in Lara's living room with Lara and Manny. "We all gather in the conference room at the courthouse on Monday at nine. We'll have a professional video-camera operator, a court reporter, Shinizer and anyone else from his office he chooses to have attend, the various witnesses, and our team." She was aware that her father was grinning slightly and ignored it. "The idea," she continued, "is that we can find out what they all would testify to if they were called as witnesses. Since they're all just witnesses, not accused of anything, we can't force them to return if they're out of state. And they all say they'll be out of state during the trial. So we get their testimony this way. On the court order it's called evidence *de bene esse*, and that just means that it's all conditional and won't be used if they are available for the trial. Or it's called perpetuation of testimony. Shinizer will get them to testify to where they were and what they know about the night of Vinny's death, and I'll cross-examine them. That simple."

Frank laughed out loud, and she frowned at him. "I'm talking theory, Dad."

"Do I have to do anything?" Lara asked. It was very clear that she didn't want the answer to be yes.

"Not a thing except be there. You don't even have to do that, but I think it would be a good idea if you tough it out with the rest of us. You're the one they're trying to frame; let them face you for hours at a time in a fairly small room." She added, "If you catch anyone making a mistake of fact, make a note about it, and if anything occurs to you to ask, note that. It will go on for about six hours every day until we're finished. The various attorneys might work later than that, but you won't have to stay longer. Is Nathan taken care of, where he'll be, who will be with him? Things like that."

Lara smiled briefly. "Now that he's thirteen, he thinks he's old enough to take care of himself. He'll come home from school and do his homework, and just hang out."

Manny and Barbara exchanged a look. They had argued about whether to tell Lara about Babe, and in the end had agreed not to, not yet, not until they found a way to bring it into the trial.

Manny said, "Lara, there's something else we have to discuss. Up until now and maybe through next week, they don't know what we've found out, what our plans are. But if they see that we're still fighting, they might conclude that we really have those missing papers. To put it bluntly, you might not be safe."

She stared at him in disbelief. "They wouldn't try anything, not now, not with everyone so suspicious!"

"We don't know that," Manny said. "We've come up with a few guidelines for next week, and we'll add more when the time comes." He sounded and looked very stern, like a man used to being obeyed. "First, no going out alone, day or night. We're all going to be around, and if you need a jug of milk, anything like that, someone goes to the store with you. And not after dark. No visitors. You'll be too tired for company, I expect, but there it is. Check and double-check your doors and windows, and keep your car locked, even in the garage. Lock it."

There were a few more things, and with each one she became

more disbelieving, more incredulous. Then he said, "And Lara, we don't think it's a good idea to leave Nathan alone at this time."

The color washed from her face in a rush, and she jumped to her feet, her hands clenched in hard fists. "You're serious, aren't you?"

Manny nodded. "I'm serious." He looked at her steadily, stating facts, not asking for opinions or ideas. "For the coming week, Wynona is going to bring me to town every day while my Rover is in the garage being worked on. She'll leave her office in Bend and wait for me at your house each afternoon and be here when the school bus drops off Nathan, and Barbara or Frank or someone will drive me up when we finish at the court-house."

Lara looked as if she wanted to argue but could not find an argument with any validity. After a moment she drew in a breath, then blurted, "I have to tell you I don't think I can go through with all this, put Nathan through it. I just..." She looked very frightened.

"What do you mean?" Barbara asked. "Exactly what do you mean?"

Lara twisted her hands and sat down; she kept her head low-ered, her gaze on her hands. "You say he might be in danger. And even if no one hurts him physically, there's the psychologist coming. I can't let them interrogate him, make him testify. I'll take the plea you told me about first. I just can't let them do that to him! It would kill him," she whispered.

For a moment no one spoke. Then Barbara said, "Lara, we won't let them get to him. He's safe enough all this week while we're taking testimony, and we'll see what happens next, what their next move will be, but I promise we won't let them hurt him."

Frank took Lara's hand; it was like an ice carving. "I give you my word," he said. "We won't let them destroy your son. I'll treat him like my own child, protect him like my own child." She did not respond, and he touched her cheek. "Look at me, Lara. Believe me. I won't let them hurt your son."

She looked at him and slowly nodded. "For now. But if the judge . . . You won't be able to stop them if . . ."

"Lara, I'm an old man, been around a long time. I know more tricks than they ever dreamed of. If the worst comes to pass, with your permission, I'll take him on a long trip. But we won't do anything without talking it over first; they can't get to him without going through us, our team."

"All right," she said softly. No one in the room doubted that in her mind she added, *For now.*

"Good," Frank said, as if completely satisfied.

"While we're wrapped up in trial business," Frank said, "I aim to do the cooking here, and Nathan will assist me. By the time this is all over, you just might have a junior gourmet chef on your hands," he added. "You just might."

Barbara felt a fleeting twinge of jealousy. He had tried to teach her to cook a few times, and it simply had not taken. And she had tried on her own many times, concentrated hard on learning to cook, in fact, and that had not taken, either. She would rather eat frozen dinners the rest of her life than tackle a cookbook again.

"Well, back to work," she said then, and got up to return to Vinny's study and the desk piled high with papers.

Promptly at nine on Monday they entered the conference room that had been set aside for their use. Already present were the video technician and the court reporter; Shinizer and his assistant Gregory Melchior were standing at a window, their heads close together in a hushed conversation. Barbara's group entered, and almost instantly the Lynch party arrived. Introductions were

made, and they all settled themselves at the big table, as if for a
meeting of the board.

The conference table was big enough to seat eighteen people;
the video camera was set up at one end, and several chairs arranged at the other end so that the witness would be at the head
of the table, the prosecutor on one side, the defense attorney on
the other of the person being examined. The only observers
would be the cameraman, Lara, the witnesses themselves, and
the various attorneys. As soon as the court reporter administered
the oath, he would leave, since the sessions were being taped,
and the videotapes would be the official record. Nothing said
off the record would be taped, and both sides would keep track
of the number of interruptions for any purpose at all, their du-
ration, and also who called for them to go off record. Only the
people at the end of the table would be taped; everyone else was
free to move about, to change chairs, leave the room, and return
at will. They had also agreed that while the examiner and the
cross-examiner could stand and move about, the camera would
not track anyone; it would remain fixed on the end of the table
and the head and shoulders of the witness, and only incidentally
tape one or both attorneys if they were within range, although
their voices would be recorded.

Shinizer began by stating the date, who was present, and the
purpose of the proceedings; then he called for Mrs. Hetty
Dorchester.

The court reporter swore her in, then left, and Mrs. Dorchester seated herself at the head of the table. A plain woman in
her forties, with hair dyed the color of ripe wheat, too light for
her dark complexion, she wore glasses, and her teeth were very
crooked. Her hands were large and bony, with heavy veins, like
the hands of a farmer. She kept looking at the video camera
nervously and chose her words with care, obviously very self-
conscious about being taped.

Shinizer asked about her background in a leisurely way, and she began to relax as she talked; she had been the cook for Mr. and Mrs. Lynch for nearly four years. She and her husband had a small apartment in the Lynch house, and they spent their winters with a daughter in Arizona.

He asked her to tell in her own words what happened on the night of May tenth.

"Yes, sir," she said. The family had an early dinner, and at about eight Jessup called. They went to the game room to wait for his visit; she served their coffee in there and at about ten o'clock she removed the coffee things, and they were all still there.

"Did the security system go off?"

"No, not all night."

"Did you hear the doorbell?"

"No, sir."

"And Mr. and Mrs. Lynch and Judge and Mrs. McReady stayed in the game room until about eleven waiting for Mr. Jessup. Is that correct?"

"Yes, sir."

"Who else was in the house that night?"

"Well, me and my husband, and Mr. Cardona. He's Mr. Lynch's secretary. He has an apartment in the house, too. That's all."

"Tell us about the security system," Shinizer said in a friendly way.

She described it in vague terms—they all had a plastic card key and a password they had to punch in after the system was turned on. They had two chances to get the password right, and if the attempts failed, the alarm would sound. She looked at the video camera helplessly and stopped talking.

He didn't press her for a more detailed account of anything, and clearly had what he wanted from her. He nodded to Barbara

soon after that and leaned back in his chair; they both understood that this was her fishing expedition, her search for relevancy, for something that could possibly help her client. He
would wait to see exactly what she was fishing for, how seriously
she was going to try to lessen the impact of the state's witnesses.

"Good morning, Mrs. Dorchester," Barbara said pleasantly.
"I have a few more questions for you. What time was it that you
last saw your employers and Judge and Mrs. McReady the night
of May tenth?"

"I said about ten. I don't know exactly. Harvey went up to
watch the ten o'clock news, and it was on when I got upstairs.
It must have been five or even ten minutes after ten."

"When you picked up the coffee things, what did you do with
them?"

"Do with them?"

"Yes. I mean, did you wash them, or put them in the sink or
in the dishwasher?"

"Oh. In the dishwasher. I already cleaned up everything, and
those few cups wouldn't make any difference in the morning. I
just put them in the dishwasher."

"You were eager to go to bed, get a good night's sleep, I
imagine, since you had to get up again so early the next morning.
Is that right?"

"Well, yes. It was going to be an early start, about five-thirty."

"Is this a fair copy of the house plans for the Lynch residence?" Barbara asked then, taking a folded paper from her
briefcase. She opened it to show Mrs. Dorchester the layout of
the house. "Can you identify the rooms in this layout?"

They were all labeled: TV room, game room, great room,
library . . . Mrs. Dorchester nodded. "Yes, that's the house."

"Point to your private rooms, will you, please?"

She put her finger on the plan. "Here, two rooms over the
kitchen, and a bathroom."

Barbara nodded and had the layout admitted as a defense exhibit. Then she put her own finger on it. "And this is the game room where the Lynches and the judge and his wife waited for Mr. Jessup. Is that right?"

"Yes, it is."

"The house is approximately ninety-four feet from end to end, Mrs. Dorchester; your apartment is on the second floor at one end, and the game room on the first floor at the other. How can you know if anyone went in or out from the game room that night?" Barbara leaned back in her chair and watched as the woman struggled with the house plans and the impossibility of her statement.

"Well, there's the security light," Mrs. Dorchester said finally. "It was on by the kitchen door to the terrace."

"All right. Let's talk about the security lights," Barbara said. "When the system is turned on, what happens?"

"A red light comes on at each outside door, and if anyone tries to get in without the key or password, then an alarm goes off, and one goes off in the sheriff's office."

"What if someone inside the house wants to go outside after the system is turned on? Then what happens?"

"You have to go to the master control and turn it off first, that's all."

"Where is that control? Can you indicate it on the house plan?"

Mrs. Dorchester studied the schematic again and pointed. "Here, near Eliot's door, in this hall to the terrace out back."

"Next to the game room," Barbara said. "Isn't that right?"

"Well, close to it."

"After you turn off the system here, you can go out or come in without any alarm?"

"Yes, but the red lights aren't on if that happens."

"Where are all the red lights?"

"At the side of or over the top of every outside door."

"Do you have an outside door in your upstairs apartment?"

"No."

"Did you leave your apartment once you went upstairs that night?"

"No."

Mrs. Dorchester looked miserable now. She was casting frequent glances at Anna Lynch, who had moved away from the table and was seated across the room at a window, leaving her face in shadows, impossible to see clearly. Thomas Lynch looked bored, and Harris McReady was making notes and following the questions and answers closely. Babe looked as bored as her father and had begun fidgeting a lot, moving from her chair to a window, back, examining her fingernails, worrying a cuticle. . . . Barbara did not indicate by a glance that she was keeping track of them all, aware of every motion they made.

"Mrs. Dorchester, actually, you don't know if anyone went out or came in after you went to your rooms, do you?"

"The security light was on when I went up," she said. "And Eliot, he was still in the office, he would have seen it if it went off, and he didn't. He said it stayed on. He told me so."

"You don't know, of your own knowledge, that no one went out or that no one entered the house that night, do you?" Barbara asked, sharper this time.

"No. But I would have known if it happened."

"Do you have ESP, Mrs. Dorchester?"

Shinizer made an objection, and she went on as if she had not noticed.

"Where is the typewriter kept?"

Mrs. Dorchester blinked at the change in subject, then she glanced at the house plan. "You want me to point to the room it's kept in?"

"Please," Barbara said.

Off the kitchen was a small lounge. Mrs. Dorchester pointed to it.

"All right. Who had access to that room?"

"Access? You mean who can go in there?"

Barbara nodded. "Exactly. Who can go in there?"

"Everyone that lives in the house, the family, me and Harvey, Eliot Cardona, Mildred Olsted—she comes in to clean every day—Pat Murillo, he's the gardener. Maybe a couple of others that don't come to mind now."

"All right. Counting Judge McReady and Mrs. McReady, that makes nine people so far. Is there usually paper handy at the typewriter?"

"Most of the time. I keep some good stationery in my room, but there's typewriter paper in the desk where the typewriter's at."

Barbara had her describe the day of the reception on the various terraces and gardens.

"So eighty more people had access to the typewriter; is that correct?"

"No!" Mrs. Dorchester said. "I mean, they were outside, not wandering through the halls. That room's not that easy to come across, over sort of behind the kitchen."

"Would you have seen people wandering back there?"

"Yes. I mean, if I was in the kitchen I would. We had caterers for the party, and I helped out, so I wasn't always in the kitchen. Sometimes I was out on the terrace helping with the drinks. We had a bar set up, and it got real busy at times."

"How would anyone reach that room where the typewriter is kept?"

"From the back terrace?"

"We can start there. There's an outside door to the kitchen, and from there it would be easy, wouldn't it?"

"Well, it usually is, but that day no one except the caterers and me and Harvey could use that door. They had the bar set up to block it off from the guests, so no one would be in the way in the kitchen. Handling that many guests isn't easy, you know."

"I suspect you're right. So how would a guest get to that room?"

"Well, this first outside door after the kitchen door? It goes to the hall here, past the breakfast room, and the lavatory, and turns and goes past the pantry, and to this little hall with the steps to upstairs, and then into the lounge."

"So what would be a pretty straight path to the lounge from the kitchen door turns into a maze from the other doors, isn't that right?"

"I guess so. There are several turns. I'm used to it and it doesn't look like a maze to me."

"Did you know Vinny Jessup?"

She said no, she never met him or his wife.

Barbara glanced at Lara, who was making notes, and asked, "If you had seen Mrs. Jessup at the reception, would you recall her now?"

"I don't know. Maybe. I was awfully busy that day, no time to pay a lot of attention to people, except to see if they had food or a drink, and now and then tell someone where the bathroom was."

"Do you recall seeing Mrs. Jessup that day?"

"No."

"Do you use the typewriter yourself?"

"Sometimes. I write a letter to my daughter in Arizona sometimes, or make a list for Mildred, things that need doing, things like that."

"So you know that when you come to the end of a line a bell rings?"

"I guess so."

"Do you know what kind of typewriter it is?"

"Underwood, I think. A portable machine, not electric."

"Is it noisy?"

"Not really, a little bit maybe."

"Well, can you hear it in the kitchen if someone is typing in the lounge?"

Mrs. Dorchester was looking more and more distressed. She shook her head, then said, "I don't know. Probably not if the radio or the television's on. I don't know."

"Have you ever heard anyone using it while you were in the kitchen?"

She shook her head harder. "I don't know. I don't remember."

"On the day of the reception, was anyone in the lounge with the radio or the television on?"

"No. We were all too busy."

"Did you see anyone go into the lounge?"

"No."

"Did you hear the bell ring at any time that day?"

"No."

"How were the various family members dressed the night of May tenth when you served dinner?"

"Dressed?"

"Did they dress formally? In casual clothes? How?"

Shinizer tapped his fingers on the table. "For heaven's sake, Counselor, what's the point of that question?"

Barbara didn't even glance at him. "Will you answer the question, please?"

"Just regular clothes. Unless there are other guests, they don't dress up for dinner."

"By regular, what do you mean? Mrs. McReady, for instance. Today she's wearing blue jeans, boots, a sweater. Is that what you mean by 'regular'?" She didn't add that Babe's designer jeans would cost as much as half a dozen pairs of jeans in Barbara's closet.

Mrs. Dorchester shook her head hopelessly. "I don't remember what they were wearing. Regular. Things I was used to seeing and didn't pay any attention to."

At eleven-fifteen Babe left the room; Anna Lynch followed, and after a moment Shinizer said, "Let's have a ten-minute recess. We can all use a break."

"Fine with me," Barbara said. She nodded to Robert Sheffield, who made a note of the time and the reason for the recess.

"See how it works?" Frank said to Lara in the hall, where Barbara paced the length and back, then again and again. Manny and Robert had stayed in the conference room, and all the others had gone into a room at the far end of the corridor. "She can ask leading questions all she wants in this kind of procedure. And Shinizer can make as many objections as he wants, and she doesn't have to answer to them. Shinizer knows she's fishing, and he knows she has something on her mind, and it can get pretty hard to tell the junk fish from the fish she's really after. I imagine she'll ask a lot of what will appear to be very random questions before she's done with this witness. Then it's up to the judge to pass on the relevancy of the questions and answers, and on the objections that will come along. The tape will be edited, the disallowed questions taken out, and the rest of it can be presented at the trial."

After the break Barbara questioned Mrs. Dorchester about the outside lights at the Lynch house, about the small parking area at the beginning of the driveway, about the stone steps leading to it, and how they were lighted; she questioned her about the sleeping arrangements at the house. Babe and McReady had separate rooms, as did Anna and Thomas Lynch. She asked about

Delia Kersh, who had trained Mrs. Dorchester, and asked pointed questions about her need for additional training as a cook. She asked about the ranch, how often the family stayed out there, if she was there with them on those occasions, if Babe was out there often without her husband. . . . She asked about the layout of the ranch house, where the servants slept, where the driveway was, who lived there year-round. They broke for lunch, and when they returned, she resumed with Mrs. Dorchester, and kept at it until Shinizer began to interrupt her frequently.

"Objection. Stop harassing this witness, Counselor."

She paid no more attention to him than she had done before. "Mrs. Dorchester, I asked you to describe the condition Mrs. McReady appeared to be in, the morning she and her husband left the Lynch residence. Will you please do so?"

"Objection. Off the record!" Shinizer jerked away from the table and glared at Barbara. "You are trying to intimidate this witness, to exhaust her with your endless questions that have absolutely no relevance to the matter we're here to deal with."

She said calmly, "I believe that's for a judge to decide, Mr. Shinizer."

"And you know damn well how he'll decide. Let's get on with this, for God's sake!"

"By all means, let us move on. Mrs. Dorchester can answer my questions any time now."

Shinizer flushed angrily, and down the room she could see that Babe had an equally red face; Anna Lynch was standing near the door as still as a statue, but Thomas Lynch was whispering something to McReady; his whisper sounded angry, almost understandable. McReady was watching Barbara through narrowed eyes, listening to his father-in-law; he, at least, knew that she could keep this up until someone petitioned the court to put an end to it. Which they might do, she thought with interest.

Shinizer motioned to the video cameraman and resumed his seat; they were back on record. Barbara kept her focus on Mrs. Dorchester and repeated her request for information, and now Babe jumped up again and stomped out of the room. Anna Lynch was tight-mouthed, so close behind her that she probably was pushing her along. Shinizer waved the cameraman to stop taping and called for a break, and Barbara said coolly, "Not with a question hanging, Counselor. You know that. Or would you like a cite or two to refresh your memory?"

He glared at her; she returned his gaze calmly, and he said in a grating voice, "Answer the damn question." He motioned once more to the video cameraman, and they were back on record.

Mrs. Dorchester's response to the question made it seem almost trivial. She said she didn't remember anything about how Mrs. McReady was that morning; it was too early, and she was too busy making coffee and a little breakfast for the judge and her to eat on the road to Portland.

"Now we take a break," Shinizer said, and hurried out with Lynch and McReady.

"Barbara, what are you doing?" Lara asked in a whisper in the hallway.

"Wearing them down. I want them to split up, not stay and listen to every question, every answer, and I want them to think about and maybe even start to worry about my cross-examination of each and every one of them in advance."

She really wanted them very angry, but she didn't add that. An angry witness was a good witness for the opposition, and she would use every trick she knew, every trick she had learned from watching her father, to make them all mad as hell. From the sound of angry voices coming from a room behind a closed door down the hall, she guessed she was succeeding.

28

That night, while Frank and Nathan were creating mouthwatering aromas in the kitchen, Lara and Barbara sat in the living room with Robert Sheffield, who was coaxing a fire to life.

"It seems awfully hard on Mr. and Mrs. Dorchester," Lara said quietly.

Barbara said, "Hah! It's their original statement that helped get you in the mess you're in. They were both more than willing to swear that no one went out or came in that night. And they were lying." She had kept Mrs. Dorchester all day, and tomorrow it would be Harvey Dorchester's turn.

From the kitchen Frank's voice sounded low and reassuring. He and Nathan both laughed, and then his voice rumbled again. Probably telling a story, Barbara thought. The words were inaudible; it was the tone, the sound of the voices, the ease of them that was comforting.

"I want to keep him," Lara said, her head tilted, listening to the voices.

Robert turned such a pitiful gaze toward Lara that catching a glimpse of it made Barbara feel almost like a voyeur. What he would give to have Lara say something like that about him.

"I'll keep Harvey Dorchester all morning," she said briskly then, "and after lunch start on the secretary, Eliot Cardona. What do you know about him, Robert? Personally, I mean."

She had the written reports, his dossier, and she knew very well how old he was, where he had gone to school, more or less what he did for Lynch, but all that could be beside the point sometimes. How he treated a waitress or if he kicked dogs— those were often the meaningful tidbits.

"Late forties," Robert said. He poked the fire and watched sparks for a few seconds, then said, "He plays pool okay, drinks a beer now and then at a bar in Bend, or more rarely here in Salt Creek. Divorced some years ago, I've been told—before my time here—and for a while after that he did some chasing. I don't know if that's true, but if so, he's stopped now. If he has a love life, he keeps it pretty quiet. I've never said more than a dozen words to him, or heard him say more than a dozen to anyone. He seems to get a lot of time off when he'll be gone for weeks, don't know where he goes or why."

In other words, Barbara thought, he didn't know zilch about Cardona.

"Dinner's ready," Nathan said at the door then, and Barbara was, too. Suddenly she felt ravenous.

The weather had changed; it was sunny and quite warm, not summery warm, but not what most people thought of as November, either. Barbara put on a heavy sweater the next morning, took it off again, and decided to carry a different one just in case there was a blizzard before dark, and they set off for the courthouse. That morning Babe and Anna Lynch were not present.

Shinizer called Harvey Dorchester in a no-nonsense way that suggested that he, at least, wanted to move things along.

Dorchester was a slightly built man with wiry muscles, sinewy hands, and a wiry and sinewy neck that unfortunately had skin that closely resembled the skin of a turkey ready for stuffing. He had sparse gray hair and pale gray watery eyes.

It took only half an hour for Shinizer to finish with Dorchester, who said little more than that McReady and the others had stayed home all night, and no one had come by, and that the typewriter was in an area accessible to the reception guests.

Barbara nodded pleasantly to him when it was her turn; she said good morning, and he responded to neither, merely sat there looking at her suspiciously.

"Mr. Dorchester, how do you know if anyone left the house that night?" she asked.

"I just know," he said. "The security system was on, and they was all in the game room drinking coffee."

"Did you go into the game room to see them drinking coffee?"

He gave her a look of contempt. "No, I didn't."

"Did you look at them through the windows?"

He turned his gaze to Shinizer, as if asking if he had to answer dumb questions. Shinizer did not move or make a sound.

"No, I didn't go looking in the windows."

"Well, you can see the problem," she said in a very reasonable tone. "You were in one part of the house, and they were as far from that part as space permits, so you couldn't see them or hear them, or really know where they were or what they were doing, could you? Or did you listen at the door?"

"No! I never listened at any door."

She smiled at him. "Let's take the evening minute by minute, and try to learn how you know where they all were," she said, perfectly willing to do just that. Although he looked outraged at the idea, she started.

"Let's begin with six o'clock on the evening of Sunday, May tenth. Where were you and what were you doing?"

"I don't know where I was at exactly six."

"All right. Where was Thomas Lynch?"

He didn't know.

"Where was Anna Lynch?"

He didn't know.

He didn't know where the judge was, or his wife.

"All right, let's move forward ten minutes. Where were you at ten minutes past six?"

His face was a dull red, and a vein was pulsing visibly in his temple, his hands clenched on the table. "I don't know. I can't account for every minute that way, no one can. I put the car away and ate supper in the kitchen, and at seven I was done for the day."

She nodded. "You put the car away at what time?"

He didn't know.

"Where was Thomas Lynch?"

He didn't know. Shinizer objected and she ignored him, and in a second or two he objected again. As before, she might not have heard him, but kept focusing on Harvey Dorchester. "Where was Mrs. McReady?"

He didn't know.

"I want a break," Shinizer said angrily.

She turned toward him, motioned to Robert to make a note, and said, "All right."

"You're being unreasonable, and you know it," Shinizer said furiously. "People can't account for every minute like that. This is harassment, pure and simple. You're browbeating this witness."

"Strange," she said calmly, "how he can account so precisely for the period from eight until eleven, more than an hour after he went up to the apartment, but not for any particular time before eight. Don't you think that's strange, Mr. Shinizer?"

Harris McReady was watching her with a face so devoid of expression, he might have been dead; only his eyes were alive, narrow and unblinking, but watchful.

Abruptly Shinizer motioned to the video cameraman and

leaned back in his chair, the fingers of one hand tapping furiously on the table.

"Mr. Dorchester," Barbara said, picking up where she had left off, "where was Mrs. Anna Lynch at ten minutes past seven?"

What if the man had a stroke? she wondered idly, and didn't particularly care, except it would look bad on the record, no doubt. She watched him and waited for him to respond.

"I don't know," he said meanly. "I didn't keep track of any of them all night. Hetty said they would have coffee in the game room and that's what they did, and they were still in there when she brought the coffee cups out."

"Were you in the kitchen when she brought the coffee cups out?"

"No. I went up to bed."

"Were you in the game room at any time that evening?"

"No! I never set foot in it."

"How do you know they were in there?"

"Hetty told me."

"Your wife told you, is that what you are testifying to?"

"Yes! That's what I said!"

She continued to harass and browbeat him until he admitted in a loud voice that he didn't know of his own knowledge where anyone was at any particular time that night, or if anyone left or arrived.

"I went upstairs to go to bed right after nine-thirty. I don't know what they all did after that!" he yelled.

She nodded. "All right. What time did you leave the next morning to drive Judge McReady and Mrs. McReady to Portland?"

"Ten minutes before six."

"How did they appear that morning?"

"Same as always."

"That was an early start for everyone, wasn't it? Were they both alert, friendly?"

"I don't know."

"Was there conversation in the car during the drive?"

"I don't remember. I was just driving."

"You were rested, weren't you? Didn't you go to bed before ten, get seven hours or more of sleep?"

He didn't know.

"Well, did they seem to be rested?"

He didn't know.

She kept at him, over many objections from Shinizer, until another break. Afterward she asked, "Mr. Dorchester, did either Judge McReady or Mrs. McReady say a single word directly to you on the drive to Portland that morning?"

"I don't remember. I think they dozed a lot."

"All right. You stated that you put a car away earlier on the evening of the tenth. When was that?"

"I don't know. Before supper. I eat about six."

"All right. You put it in the basement garage?"

"Yes."

"Did you close the big overhead door at that time?"

"Yes. I always close the door."

"How did you get back upstairs after that?"

He was snarling his answers, snapping them, glaring at her, all but foaming. "There's back stairs up to the hall by the kitchen."

"And you went up those back stairs?"

"I said yes."

"No, actually you just said they were there. Did you go up them?"

"Yes!"

She showed him the house plan and had him point out the lower-level garage, the back stairs, the basement utility and laundry rooms, and then she asked, "What room is this?"

"Eliot Cardona's apartment."

A hall separated that apartment from the garage; it led at one end to a short flight of stairs to the outside of the house, and to the interior stairs to the hall near the kitchen at the other end.

"Was Mr. Cardona's door closed?"

"Yes."

She left it there, and asked him about the day of the reception; he had not seen Lara Jessup, he said, and wouldn't have known her if he had seen her. He said he couldn't type and had never even heard the bell of the carriage return. He had not seen anyone enter the lounge where the typewriter was, or use the machine. Then it was time for lunch, and Barbara was finished with him.

That afternoon the Dorchesters were gone; Babe and her mother were still absent, and those who remained seated on the side opposite Barbara's group all were grim-faced and looked angry. She couldn't think of them as the prosecutor's team. They were the Lynch gang in her mind.

Eliot Cardona was sworn in. He was forty-seven, divorced, no children, with a master's degree in business from Northwestern University; he had worked for Thomas Lynch for sixteen years. He was well built with broad shoulders and a deep chest. His complexion was swarthy; he had straight coarse black hair that was cut short, and a shadow beard that looked ready to erupt into whiskers at any moment; his eyes were very dark, with thick lashes and eyebrows. Altogether a hairy man who probably had a thick pelt on his chest, his body, legs. He was dressed in a handsome gray suit, Brooks Brothers or a relative of theirs.

Shinizer asked about his duties as Lynch's secretary, and the responses were so vague and generalized that although he apparently had answered, Barbara felt that little information had been given.

Shinizer asked him to tell about the night of May tenth.

"I was in my office on the first floor," he said, speaking carefully, almost as if English was his second language. "When the telephone rang at eight, I answered. It was Mr. Jessup calling Judge McReady. I asked Hetty Dorchester if they were finished with dinner, and when she said they were, I went to the dining room to inform the judge that he had a call. I knew he would leave in the morning very early, and I thought he might want to take a call at the table rather than miss it altogether. I carried the cordless telephone to the dining room, and he took the call there. When it was concluded, I took the telephone back to my office. At about ten Mr. Lynch stepped into the office to say he wouldn't be needing me anymore that night. He continued down the hall to turn on the security system. I worked at the computer a little longer, and then I went to my room."

"Did anyone else go past your door that night?"

"No."

"Would anyone have had to pass your door to get to the security system?"

"Yes."

"You don't have dinner with the family?"

"Usually I do, but often if there's company, I excuse myself. And that was a family dinner, which I felt would be inappropriate for me to attend."

"Did you see the security light before you went to your room?"

"Yes. It was on. I always check, and if it's after ten and the system has not yet been turned on, I take care of it. That's one of my duties. That night I checked as usual, but there was really no need, since I had seen Mr. Lynch go down the hall on his way to turn it on."

"You kept the door open that evening?"

"Yes. I often do in the evening. My office is at the end of the hall; no one passes it at night except to turn on the security system."

"What time did you go to your room?"

"It was shortly after ten, ten-fifteen perhaps."

"And the light was on at that time, ten-fifteen?"

"Yes, it was."

Shinizer asked him to describe his living arrangement, and he said his room was the one behind the garage on the lower level of the house; it was a studio apartment with a tiny kitchen, bath, and sleeping/sitting room. He also had the first-floor office and use of the rest of the house, including the big kitchen. He had an outside door, he added.

"Was the security light at your outside door turned on when you went to your apartment?"

"Yes."

"Did it go off during the night at any time?"

"Not that I am aware of. It was on at ten-fifteen, and when I turned off my lights to go to bed at five after eleven. I have no knowledge of it going off at any time that night. It was on at five-thirty when I woke up."

Shinizer looked quite smug, almost gloating when he turned Cardona over to Barbara.

"Good afternoon, Mr. Cardona," she said.

He inclined his head fractionally and said good afternoon.

"Do you belong to a union?" she asked.

He frowned and looked puzzled. "No. What union?"

"I wondered, since you seem to work such extraordinary hours. Until ten on Sunday night, then starting again at five-thirty on Monday morning. Is that your routine?"

He smiled and shook his head. "No, of course not. I was up early in case Judge McReady or Mrs. McReady had last-minute problems that I could help with, or if Mr. Lynch had any last-minute tasks for me before they departed. My day generally starts at about nine."

"Ah. I see. Thank you. What about Sunday nights?"

"I wasn't really working. I check the e-mail every day, including Sundays if I'm home, but the rest of the day is mine, and I was on the Internet for my own personal reasons." He shrugged slightly. "I no longer even remember what I was pursuing at that time, perhaps nothing more exciting than a new computer game. I simply don't know."

"But you do remember when you went to your room, what time it was then?"

"Yes. A few years ago, when we first got onto the Internet, I realized what a time sink it could become, and I bought a clock I keep in the office, permanently set to alarm at ten at night unless I turn it off before then. That's my deadline for surfing the Net. So I know I was there at ten because the clock alarm sounded; I turned off the computer as soon as I exited the programs after ten. I straightened up my desk, made certain the outgoing mail was sealed and stamped, turned off lights, and went to my apartment. Ten minutes past ten, or perhaps fifteen minutes past."

Barbara nodded, then picked up the house-plan exhibit. "Will you point out your office for the record, please?"

He pointed to the last room off a hall that led to the back terrace. Opposite his office was the game room, although the door was at the start of the hall, apparently about fifteen feet from his door.

"That room is about fourteen by sixteen feet, I believe," Barbara said. "Is that correct?"

"I think so. I don't know exactly."

"I'd like you to place furnishings, indicate where your desk is, where the computer is, the printer, things of that sort. Just sketch them in freehand. I have a pencil here." She took a pencil from her briefcase and handed it to him.

"I'm not a draftsman, or an artist," he said with a rueful expression. "I'm afraid this will be a childish end product."

"That's fine," she said. "I'd just like to get a better idea of the space and how it's used."

He drew in a rectangle and said, "That's the computer desk."

"Where is the chair?"

He sketched a chair.

Barbara looked at it, puzzled. "Mr. Cardona, do you keep the computer with the back that close to the door? Most people try to put them against a wall, I believe. You know, all those wires and cable connections . . . Yours are all exposed to anyone entering the office. Are you sure it's like that?"

He looked at her, then at the drawing, and raised his eyebrows. "I think it might be more to the side." He started to erase the desk.

Barbara said, "I have another copy." She slid the old one away, and replaced it with a fresh copy, then smiled at him. For a moment there was a suggestion of a smile on his face; it vanished, and he frowned at the paper.

"You're right," he said after studying the room. "Windows here, door, closet door. The computer desk is here." He sketched it in lightly this time, against a wall, with the chair facing the wall.

"Ah," Barbara said. "So you were actually facing the wall, turned ninety degrees away from the door. What's in this space?" She pointed to the wall on the side of the door.

"A bookcase," he said.

"So the door couldn't have been all the way open, not all the way back against the wall. It had to stop at the bookcase, didn't it?"

She waited for him to say yes, and then asked, "Mr. Cardona, when my father, Mr. Holloway, walked past you a few minutes ago, what did he do?"

He blinked and turned to look at Frank, whose chair was pushed back from the table as if to give him plenty of room. Frank had been up and down several times; now he smiled at Cardona, and they all waited.

"I believe he went out the door, into the hall. I wasn't paying any attention."

"Of course not. You were concentrating on answering my questions. He walked to the window and looked out, and then returned to his chair," she added.

Shinizer made an objection, which she ignored.

"When Mr. Lynch stopped by your office that night, did he actually enter the room?"

"Yes, a few steps."

"According to the layout of your office, your door is a standard door, two feet eight inches wide, and it was standing open that night. If your desk is here against the wall, and your chair here," she said, pointing to the layout as she spoke, "then he had to enter the room before you could even see him. Isn't that correct?"

He looked at the layout, then at Lynch, and finally said, "Yes."

"Who turned on the security system that night, Mr. Cardona?"

He hesitated only a moment, then said, "Mr. Lynch."

"At what time did he do that?"

"I don't know for sure. Before ten."

"You were facing the computer screen, interested in whatever you were doing, and paying little or no attention to others in the house. Is that right?"

"I guess it is. I assumed it was Mr. Lynch because he generally was the one who did it, and he was on his way to do it that night when he came by."

"Did you leave your computer and follow him to the hall when he left you?"

He flushed slightly and said no.

"So you didn't see him turn on the system that night? Is that your testimony?"

"I believe it was Mr. Lynch since no one else ever touches the system, just he or I."

Shinizer objected, louder this time.

Barbara nodded. "I see," she said. "What you really mean is that someone turned on the system. Isn't that right?"

He hesitated, then said, "Yes. It was turned on before ten."

"Did you see anyone turn it on?"

"No."

"So you finished up in your office and then went into the hall. Is a hall light kept on all night?"

"Yes."

"So it was still on when you left your office?"

"Yes."

"How far from the terrace door is your office door?"

He shrugged and said he didn't know. She took a ruler from her briefcase and measured the house-plan schematic, then murmured, "Twelve feet. How big is the red light that indicates the system is on?"

"Small, just a little red light."

"Smaller than a dime?"

"Yes. About the size of a . . . a ladybug."

"And you walked down the hall to check and make certain it was activated. Is that right?"

"Yes."

"Why, Mr. Cardona? Couldn't you see the red light from your office door?"

He hesitated. Very stiffly he said, "It's a habit. I walk down the hall to check it, and if it's not on yet, I turn it on."

"Mr. Cardona," she said softly, "can you see that red light from your office door if the overhead hall light is on?"

"Yes. I just always go down all the way to double-check."

"Is the light on the side wall, or the end wall of the hall? Put an X on the wall where it's located, will you, just to help us visualize it."

His X was on the side wall.

"Is it recessed?"

It was.

"So you probably have to get close to it in order to see if it's lit. Don't you, Mr. Cardona?"

He drew in a breath, then said yes.

Shinizer asked for a break; actually, he demanded a break, and he and the Lynch gang all walked out together.

Barbara walked to the end of the corridor outside the conference room. The beveled-glass windows sparkled, and through this one she could see the desert reaching to the horizon. The light changed on this side of the mountains, she mused; in November Eugene air, burdened with wood smoke, exhaust fumes, and mist, softened hard edges, but day after day here on the high desert, everything was sharply delineated. The brightness of the sun was eye-hurting, even from indoors. After work, she would take a long walk, she decided, maybe up Salt Creek Road. . . . Somewhere.

Then they were back in the conference room, and she resumed.

"Mr. Cardona, will you place an X on this drawing of the

lower level of the house where you said your outside door is located."

He drew in the X.

"It's not actually in your room at all, is it?" she said. It was in the long hall behind the three-car garage; the hall had steps at one end, going up a half a flight to an outside door at the side of the house.

"I think of that hall as part of my room," he said.

"I see. Anyone coming down the house stairs to do laundry has access to your room?"

"No. I . . . It's a private apartment."

"Then you keep your door closed down there? Not like the office door?"

"I keep it closed," he said stiffly.

She took out her ruler and measured from the inside stairs to the outside door at the far end of the hall, and up the other flight of stairs. "That's a large garage, isn't it?" she murmured. "Fifty-two feet wide." She looked at Cardona and asked, "Is that light recessed like the one at the upper terrace door?"

He said yes.

"Can you really see that security light from your door?" His door was at least twenty-five feet from the outside steps.

"I can see it," he said.

"It's on the side wall, up the stairs, recessed, and the overhead hall light is on, and you say you can see it," she said in disbelief. "You understand that we may have to demonstrate that feat to a jury."

"Objection!" Shinizer yelled. "You're trying to intimidate this witness!"

She smiled at him. "He doesn't look terribly intimidated." Cardona looked angry or disgusted or just tired, and he continued to regard her with interest and apparent concentration.

"So, you left your office, walked through the maze of halls

to the interior stairs, and went down them. Your door is here; it looks like about five feet from the stairs. Did you walk past your own door, down to the end of the hall, and go up that flight of stairs to check the security light, to make certain it was still on, although you had seen one on only a minute earlier on the first floor? Is that what you did, Mr. Cardona?"

"I walked down partway, far enough to see the light," he said evenly.

"Was the overhead hall light on?"

"Yes."

"And an overhead light at the top of the stairs at the outside door?"

"Yes."

"But you could still see the red security light the size of a ladybug? Is that what you're telling us?"

"Yes."

Harris McReady cleared his throat, nudged Shinizer, and whispered something. Shinizer asked for a break. Everyone except Robert left the conference room.

"McReady's going to explain to Cardona the problem of impeaching his own testimony," Barbara murmured, watching the Lynch gang vanish into the office off the corridor.

"Yep," Frank said. "It's sort of between a rock and hard place he's put himself in."

She grinned at him, and walked down to her favorite window to gaze out at the desert. To her surprise, the desert had been growing on her; she felt almost as if it had been concealing things that only gradually would be revealed. Today, and yesterday, too, she had seen colors she had not noticed in the heat of the summer; delicate rose tints on the ground that had appeared to be a monotonous dun color, a green tinge on sage that had been gray and dusty brown all summer, and the sky was farther away all the time, she felt certain, as if it were receding all of a piece, the entire sky being lifted, higher and higher, farther and farther away.

And then she was wondering what it was that Harris Mc-Ready did not want Cardona to reveal. What did the man know to reveal? She swung around and walked back through the corridor to where Frank and Lara were standing, talking in low voices.

"Dad, do something for me?"

He was at her side instantly.

"Get hold of Bailey. Everything he has and can find out about Cardona, where he goes when he leaves here for weeks at a time, about his divorce, where the ex is, everything. By tomorrow."

Frank shook his head. "He'll flip."

"I know. But I bet he has most of that stuff or he knows how to get it with a phone call or two. Here they come back."

The Lynch gang was approaching to resume the session. Frank nodded and walked out, and everyone else returned to the conference room. It was nearly four. Barbara had intended to finish with Cardona that afternoon, but now she knew she had to stretch it out, and she proceeded to do so.

That night she explained to Lara, "See, in cross-examination of a hostile witness, you have a chance to uncover evidence, discover what people are hiding, if they are, what they're sidestepping, if they are. Cardona hasn't been willing to talk with any of us, but he has to answer questions now, and I have several more for him."

She had been on the phone with Bailey twice since leaving the courthouse, and he was planning to drive over later, be there by one in the morning, he had said morosely. She had said, "That's pretty late," and he had said, "Jeez, Barbara, give me a break. It's a long drive. One, maybe two. I'll want coffee or something."

After the rest of the household had gone to bed, she sat in Lara's living room, moving the pieces of jigsaw puzzle back and forth. There was a pattern, an outline forming, and for the first time she thought maybe not too many pieces were missing after all.

 ## 29

Too exhausted to pace, too restless to sit still, Barbara sat on the couch watching a tiny fire burn, waiting for Bailey. She suddenly thought of John, his outburst when she had put his children at risk. And she had done that, or would have done it if he hadn't seen to it that they avoided the state a year ago. Was she doing it now to Lara's child? To Lara?

She hugged her arms around her body, chilled in spite of her sweater, in spite of the hot little fire, the central heating that was really very good.

Then she realized that she could think of him now without a hard physical reaction, a yearning, a desperate need. The tsunami did not happen. She even said his name under her breath, "John. John."

Nothing.

She wanted to cry. Monster, she thought then, she was truly a monster. Was she substituting the adrenaline rush, the excitement of a case nearing its climax for the excitement of love, of sex? Sublimation of desire for a higher cause? She was like a nun, she thought almost hysterically, except instead of marrying Jesus, she was marrying the chase, the danger, the thrill of a case at hand. . . . She wanted to cry.

Just then—*thank you, God*—she heard the car in the driveway, and she hurried to open the door for Bailey. It was fifteen minutes after one; she knew it would be a long time before she went to bed.

The entire Lynch gang was in the conference room the next morning. Babe looked unhappy and fretful, her mother looked disgusted and bored as they took chairs, as far apart as they could get, Barbara noted.

Eliot Cardona seated himself at the head of the table in front of the video camera, and they began.

"Mr. Cardona, I understand that you keep Mr. Lynch's ranch records for him, stock sales, purchase accounts, things of that sort. Is that correct?"

"Yes."

"And you handle his correspondence, and do various other tasks for him—summarize speeches by politicians, make travel arrangements, all the usual secretarial duties as well. Is that correct?"

He said yes, looking as bored as Anna Lynch.

"Do those various duties occupy you full-time?"

He hesitated, then said, "I only work an average of nine or ten months a year. I have time off, spaced throughout the year."

Barbara nodded. "I see. Where do you reside during those times when you are not part of Mr. Lynch's household?"

His hesitation lasted longer, and he glanced at Shinizer, as if seeking advice. Shinizer objected, but he sounded weary, as if it was pointless, since the judge would strike it later.

"In San Francisco usually," Cardona said.

"Do you have your own apartment in San Francisco?"

Now he was looking at Thomas Lynch frequently, as if turning to his employer for advice.

Thomas Lynch's mouth was a tight, hard line.

Cardona said no.

"Do you share an apartment with anyone?"

Shinizer objected furiously this time and motioned the video operator to take time out. "Counselor, that's all beside the point here. Mr. Cardona's private life has nothing to do with this case, as you well know. Why don't you get on with it?"

"Oh, I think we may be getting at something that has a lot to do with things, Mr. Shinizer," she said coldly. "I'm trying to get on with it. Why don't you give me some space!"

"This is a waste of time; you're trying to manipulate facts to suit some far-fetched, convoluted twist of your mind and to no end. Stop wasting our time!"

"Are you finished, Mr. Shinizer?"

He flushed a deeper red and motioned to the cameraman to start again; then he leaned back in his chair and watched her with a venomous expression.

"Will you answer, Mr. Cardona? Do you share an apartment with someone?"

"No, I don't."

"All right. That didn't hurt, did it? So you pay rent for an apartment full-time and use it a few weeks of the year. Is that correct?"

"No, it isn't. I stay in an apartment that is a privately owned condominium unit, not mine. I simply have permission to use it from time to time."

"Why did you and your former wife separate and get a divorce?" She asked the outrageous question in a conversational tone, as if they were old friends.

Shinizer's objection was so loud, even Cardona appeared shaken by it. He looked as furious as Shinizer, and he said deliberately, "I don't believe that's any of your business, or that it has anything to do with the matter at hand."

Shinizer demanded a break. Lynch whispered something to him, and he nodded.

"Not with a question pending, Mr. Shinizer," Barbara said coolly. "Will you answer the question, Mr. Cardona?"

"I will not."

She nodded. Across the room, near the window, Babe was standing rigidly, staring at Barbara, her face frozen in an expression of hatred.

Barbara motioned to Robert to note the break, and she stood up. "Ten minutes? Will that be sufficient, Mr. Shinizer?"

"An hour," he snapped, and shoved his chair back, getting up.

"We'll be in Manny's office," Barbara said. "Send us a message when you're ready to resume." She watched the Lynch gang depart without a glance in her direction. Anna Lynch, no longer bored, looked infuriated now, she noted. And Judge Harris McReady had no expression whatever.

"What's happening?" Lara asked, bewildered, in Manny's office a few minutes later.

Manny and Robert looked no less puzzled, and although she had had a few minutes to bring Frank up to date, it had been a hurried, abbreviated report.

"There's a condo in the name B. A. Lynch down in San Francisco," Barbara said. "That's where he stays down there. Bailey's sure it's Babe's, or her father's in her name. She uses it most of the time when she and McReady are in California. They also have a house in Marin County, but chances are pretty good that she wouldn't be able to find her way from the top floor to the basement without a map."

"They don't live together?" Lara asked, surprised.

"Nope. Haven't for years. They get together for show-and-tell, public appearances, official business trips, things like that."

Lara was regarding Barbara as if she were seeing her for the first time. "How did you guess?"

"Not really just a guess. I saw them together, acting like barely polite acquaintances, and Manny said they don't pay much attention to each other. I told Bailey to dig a little about San Francisco. And he delivers, like Domino Pizza. It *was* a guess about Cardona, I'll admit. He had to go somewhere and light when he's not in Lynch's house. Bailey checked it out." She glanced at Robert and shrugged. "You said Cardona used to be a chaser after his wife left, and then he stopped, and I made a wild guess."

"Not so wild," Robert said. "Okay, so they'll confab and probably ask for a continuance or something, long enough for him to get a lawyer at least."

"Not McReady," Barbara murmured. Both Robert and Manny grinned, and Frank snorted. "I'll refuse it, of course, and Dad will cite whatever he has to cite to make it look good."

"They'll slow things down until lunch," Manny said then. "And Lynch will be absent for a time, I expect, lining up someone to make an appearance later on."

And by then Bailey would have reported back in, Barbara was thinking, and the afternoon might become a little more exciting than what had gone before. Barbara could see that Lara was still completely confused, and she said, "That gang has shown a united front, really solid, unbreachable, and I intend to drive some wedges into it. I'll explain tonight. Okay?"

Frank, Manny, and Robert spent the rest of the time-out collecting what they called ammunition, and Barbara paced, thought, paced some more. At eleven the messenger came; the Lynch gang was ready to do battle again. They returned to the conference room.

"Mr. Cardona," Barbara began, "when you listed your various duties for Mr. Lynch, you mentioned assisting with the stock-improvement program at the ranch. Is that correct?"

"Yes." He was surprised, apparently, at her change of subject.

Thomas Lynch was not present, as Manny had predicted, but Anna Lynch and Babe were now seated close together at the long table, and McReady was at the far end, without expression, watching closely. Cardona kept his gaze on the video camera.

"Have you had training in animal husbandry, cattle breeding?"

Cardona's eyes narrowed, and a muscle in his jaw tightened visibly. Before he could respond, Shinizer slammed his hand down on the table and yelled, "I object to this whole line of questioning!" He leaned in closer and said furiously, "You know damn well that none of this will be allowed in; no judge would permit this line of questioning. You are wasting time, harassing this witness, going off on one tangent after another. We ask for a continuance in order to prepare a petition for Judge Henkel to rein you in. Here and now I am placing in effect a blanket objection to any question of this witness concerning his private life, his work for Mr. Lynch, and his travel." He glanced at McReady, who didn't nod, but it was apparent that he was the one who had supplied this new tactic. Thomas Lynch returned and took a chair close to Shinizer.

Calmly Barbara said, "I believe there is a question pending, Mr. Shinizer. Have you had training in animal husbandry, Mr. Cardona?"

"No, not really. I help with the business end of the transactions."

Shinizer started to rise, to demand his break probably, Barbara thought, but Lynch gestured to him, and he slumped back in his chair.

"I see," Barbara said. "Does this work entail much travel, to inspect other herds, for instance?"

"Some. I don't actually inspect the livestock, only the paper-work."

"Who does the actual selection of breeding stock?"

"There's a ranch manager," he said. "That's his job."

"That's Charlie Childress, isn't it?"

"Yes."

"Does he oversee the day-to-day operations of the ranch?"

"Yes."

"When you travel to handle the paperwork, does Mr. Childress go with you?"

He hesitated, then said, "Not usually. There are different operations, one's my department, the paperwork, the other's his, the animals themselves, selecting for insemination of stock, things of that sort."

"So, if, for example, the ranch was interested in a bull in Brazil or in France or just in Georgia, you would both make separate trips to take care of the matter?"

"Break!" Shinizer yelled, this time not looking at either McReady or Lynch for approval.

"Not with a question pending," she said calmly. "Do you need a refresher in the rules of perpetuation of testimony, Mr. Shinizer? Dad, will you read the proper rule so that we can get on with this."

Frank opened a very thick book to a marked page and began to read. Shinizer turned redder.

When Frank finished, Barbara said again to Cardona, "Will you answer the question?"

"We take separate trips," he said.

"Thank you. How long has this stock-improvement program been going on?"

"I believe it's a continuing process," he said.

"How long have you been involved in working on this program?"

"I've handled the paperwork for years."

"Five years? Ten? How many years?"

"About five."

Shinizer called for a break, and when the cameraman turned off his video camera, Shinizer said in a tight, cold voice, "I demand that you stop this insane line of questioning and get on with the business at hand. What in God's name does the cattle-breeding business have to do with the murder of Vinny Jessup?"

"That's what we're trying to find out," Barbara said patiently. "Do you mind if I continue?"

"I do mind. There's no connection between any of this ranch business and the murder we're here to inquire into, and you know it. I don't know what you're trying to do, except delay the proceedings, and I intend to inform the judge to that effect."

"If I can continue now," she said equably, "I'll make a connection."

With a curt nod, Shinizer told the video cameraman to go back on record.

"Mr. Cardona, I have a statement from Mr. Childress that he has never taken a trip with you or separately for the purpose of acquiring new breeding stock or disposing of stock or arranging for artificial insemination of stock. Are you certain he is involved in the program?"

Shinizer objected, and she ignored his objection.

"He's the manager. I assumed he was in charge," Cardona said carefully.

"Well, let me put it this way. If he denies that he has anything to do with the livestock program, then who is actually in charge of that aspect of the ranch business?"

"Mr. Lynch ultimately is in charge of it all."

"Do you report directly to him about the paperwork you do?"

"Yes, I do."

"And does he make the trips to select the cattle to be bred? Did he make the trip to Brazil in 1994 to acquire a certain breed of cattle? Did he go to France in 1996 for the purpose of inspecting a herd there? Did he spend a week off the coast of Georgia a year ago to inspect another herd?"

Cardona's face became totally expressionless, and Shinizer, evidently forgetful of the earlier blanket objection he had made, was yelling one objection after another. Barbara gazed at Babe, who had turned pale, and next to her Thomas Lynch, who was as red-faced as Shinizer. Near the end of the table McReady had become even more like a statue. He appeared not to be breathing. Only his eyes were alive, staring at Barbara with fury. He looked like an insurance broker who had just learned that someone he had recently insured for a million dollars had gone into a hospice.

"I don't know," Cardona said deliberately.

"You arrange his travel, don't you? Don't you employ the World International Travel Agency and make travel plans for your employer? Isn't that what you stated earlier?"

"I arrange some of his travel," he said.

"Break," Shinizer said then and stood up. "This is enough. More than enough."

"Since it is nearly lunchtime," Barbara said agreeably, "I accept that. Break it is. Until two."

Before today, they had gone to Dorothy's Bar and Grill in Salt Creek for lunch, but today they went back to Lara's house. Frank had bought enough food for an army, he said cheerfully, leading the way into the kitchen. He started to hum almost inaudibly as he washed his hands at the sink, and then went to the refrigerator and brought out ham and roast beef, tomatoes, pick-les, lettuce. He eyed the lettuce suspiciously, but washed it and put it on a plate. Lara made coffee.

"Okay," Barbara said. "It can go several different ways. We can be called to the judge's chambers, if Shinizer rustles up his petition. A new attorney probably will make an appearance to advise Cardona, who could suffer a terrible loss of memory or will stick to the simple I-don't-know expedient. But they don't know what all we have; we have to remember that. They don't know if Vinny had something, and if he did, if we have it now. McReady may want to toss Cardona overboard." She picked up the platter of cold cuts and took it to the dining room.

"Or," Manny said thoughtfully, "Cardona might say he and Babe actually have business meetings in San Francisco and made those trips together, business trips, and they wanted to avoid even the appearance of impropriety and kept it quiet. They can't deny that the whole stock-improvement program is Babe's, after all. It's pretty common knowledge that Lynch has little if any-thing to do with the ranch business anymore. It's Babe's."

What he had told Barbara very early was that Anna Lynch had insisted on that; she was tired of ranch life, isolation, and she had grown fond of the big cities, fond of travel, winters in Maui.

"Their best bet is to make that claim," Barbara said, "and count on Judge Henkel to make it all come out shining clean in the end."

"Can the judge do that? Just edit things out like that?"

"Yes," Barbara said.

"To a certain extent," Frank added. "You see, Lara, the judge in a case is like a little god up there on the bench. He decides what's relevant and what isn't, what will be admitted and what won't be. But once it's on tape, it's part of the official record, and there's always the appeal process, and a different judge quite often allows what has been disallowed." He did not add that he was tape-recording every word. It was illegal as hell, but he always did that.

Barbara would have said *sometimes*, not *quite often*, allows what had been stricken, but she did not. Lara looked too dismayed at the idea of an appeal. Instead, Barbara said, "Now, what I don't think will happen is that they will try to stop at this point. See, an interrogation like this is a two-way street. We find out things and hint that we know more, and they try to determine exactly what we have found out, and the direction we intend to pursue. They'll want to learn more than they have yet and where I'm heading with this whole line of questioning. So far, two of their witnesses have been discredited, their testimony shown to be worthless. They won't use it. Cardona may be the third witness they have to discard; they'll want to know."

"What I want to know," Frank said then, "is why is the table groaning with food that no one's doing a thing about? This is a do-it-yourself spread. I suggest we start." He began to build himself a sandwich.

They had just finished eating when Bailey showed up, looking as if he had been dragged behind a horse from Eugene. He glowered at Barbara. "Something to eat first," he said darkly.

"You look like hell," she said.

"Some people get to sleep at night."

"I didn't get any more sleep than you did," she pointed out.

"You're young, made of steel and plastic. Some people are pitiful human beings. You know, blood and flesh that gets tired."

"Bailey, that's the nicest thing you have ever said to me. Just give us the reports and go eat. I don't think anything's been put away yet."

"It's all on the counter in the kitchen," Lara said. "This way."

Bailey tossed his old denim bag onto a chair. He was carrying a grocery bag, which he kept. "Help yourself. It's in there, and rough. I haven't had time to sort through anything or write up anything." He followed Lara to the kitchen.

"I think we should clear off the table and use it," Frank said as Barbara began to pull papers and folders from the bag.

Presently the four attorneys were seated at the table scanning the reports Bailey had delivered. And they didn't make any sense at all, Barbara decided after a few minutes.

She got up and went to the kitchen, where Bailey was eating a sandwich as if he had not seen food for months.

"Are you sure about that condo?" she demanded. "Is that raw data or verified?"

"Verified," he said shortly, and took another bite. He had brought his own beer, she noticed. He had been disbelieving that no one in this bunch drank, and had grumbled that everyone knew cowboys were notorious drinkers. As far as he was concerned, everyone east of the Cascades had to be a cowboy.

Bailey swallowed, drank beer from the can, and then said, "Barbara, I just find out stuff. I don't pretend to know nothing about what it means. That's your department."

"Just tell me."

He sighed melodramatically. "Right. The whole condo belongs to Lynch. Babe has the seventh floor and stays there most of the time when she's not out here on the ranch, or else visiting her folks in Hawaii. When Cardona goes to San Fran, he goes to the same condo, different floor, the sixth, where a woman lives with her kid. And he stays there when he's not on the ranch or traveling." He eyed her judiciously. "Maybe you don't look so hot after all. A little sleep will put you right." He moved the sandwich to his mouth, but before he took a bite, he added, "All

I could find about the other woman is in there. Now if you don't mind." He took a big bite of the sandwich.

She walked back through the dining room, where there was a grim silence as the others skimmed through Bailey's information. She kept going.

"Barbara," Robert said anxiously, "we have to talk about this."

"Later," she said, and kept moving, up the stairs to the next level, Vinny's study. She paused at the door but didn't enter, continued down the hall, up the next flight of stairs, and walked through the hall to her room, back, again and again.

She was startled when Frank appeared at the top of the stairs.

"Time," he said quietly.

"Just give me a quick summary. The woman he stays with, who is she?"

"Secretive, has enough money to live in that condo. The boy goes to a private preschool every day. She doesn't have a social life, goes away every winter, takes the boy with her. Doesn't talk to the neighbors. Rumor is that she's hiding the child from her ex. Not much more there. He's still digging."

Barbara drew in a deep breath. "Time," she said dully.

They all got into the several cars and drove back to the courthouse. When he parked, Frank patted her arm, "Honey, we've seen things go wrong before. We've seen worse."

"Maybe. Hard to see how it could be much worse."

Inside the courthouse, nearing the conference room in a group, they saw a man approaching. He stopped in front of them and said, "Mrs. Jessup?"

Lara nodded. "Yes."

"For you," he said and handed her a paper. She glanced at it, and swayed, turned so pale, she looked translucent.

Frank snatched the paper from her hand and read it. "A sum-

mons to surrender Nathan at nine tomorrow morning for questioning in the presence of Dr. Jeremy Abrams."

Robert had a firm grip on Lara's arm; otherwise, it appeared
that she might fall down. And, Barbara thought bleakly, things
could always get worse. They just had proved that.

 # 30

"I'll take care of this," Frank said. He patted Lara's
shoulder and marched down the corridor toward Judge Henkel's
chambers, a soldier going into battle.

Shinizer was standing in the doorway of the conference room,
not smiling but looking pleased. He was watching Lara. Behind
him McReady was watching also, and he had a tiny smile on his
face. When Barbara's gaze met his, his expression became sober,
even sad; he turned and reentered the conference room.

"Ms. Holloway," Shinizer said, drawing near, "I'd like to
have a word before we start the afternoon proceedings."

"Fine," she said. She started to walk toward the conference
room, then turned and said to Manny, "Oh, Wynona called right
after you left the house. She wants you to call her when you
have a minute."

He nodded. "Lara, Robert, let's go down to the lobby for
some air. I'll use the lobby phone."

Barbara entered the conference room and followed Shinizer
to the far end, away from the Lynch gang, out of hearing.

"Ms. Holloway, the offer's still good," Shinizer said. "If she doesn't produce the boy at nine in the morning, the sheriff has orders to pick him up and bring him in. If we all meet in the judge's chambers and hash this out, you plead her case for her, he'll no doubt reduce the probationary period. Three years, maybe just eighteen months. Be done with this farce."

Everyone else around here, she thought, was losing their deep summer tan, but his glowed as smooth and even as ever. Magic lamp. She regarded him thoughtfully. "You'd be willing to miss important testimony in order to grill a child?"

"It's my duty," he said solemnly. "Melchior will fill in for me here. And, no doubt, one of your many associates will fill in for you, if you prefer to be present when we ask the boy some questions. It's unfortunate, this timing, I admit, but Dr. Abrams has assured us that tomorrow is his only available date. And the boy is a material witness. He saw her leave that night, which she has denied in a sworn statement, and he knows she returned home and began to do laundry. Bloodstains, I'm afraid. His testimony is important to the state's case."

"I have to confer with my client," she murmured. "Ten minutes."

"Take as long as you need," he said generously. "We won't start without you."

She took her time walking down the corridor, down the stairs, and out to the sidewalk where Lara, Robert, and Manny were talking.

"Did you reach Wynona?" she asked Manny.

"Yes. It seems that she has a bunch of books to deliver up at the reservation, and she's drafting a couple of kids to help carry them. She said she might be late today, and I said I would stay in town tonight. Lara kindly offered me a bed." He was absolutely straight-faced as he spoke, as if they had not planned this well in advance.

"It's a stopgap only, getting Nathan out of town," Lara said miserably. "They'll issue an arrest warrant or something." Her lovely face was pinched and drawn with fear.

"No, they won't," Barbara said sharply. "Pull yourself together, Lara. Dad's giving Judge Henkel an earful of constitutional law right now. He said he'd take care of it. Trust him. He knows exactly what to do."

She turned to Robert. "There's something I'd like you to do when we go back in. Call Bailey's beeper and wait for him to call back. You'll have to use Manny's number and wait in his office, that's the number Bailey will recognize. I want to know exactly when and where that child in the San Francisco condominium was born. And who was named as the father. ASAP. Like this morning, tell him."

"He can find out that fast?" Robert asked doubtfully.

"I can't and you can't, but Bailey can. Tell him I said that, too, when he bitches about it." She glanced at her watch. "I want to give Dad a couple more minutes explaining the universe to Henkel, then back to work. Meanwhile, let's get inside. I'm freezing."

That's the kind of weather they had out here on the desert. In the shade, where they were standing, it was freezing cold; in the sunshine it was almost shirtsleeve warm. And everywhere it was sauna-dry. They returned to the lobby and, after a few more minutes, went back upstairs.

Shinizer met them at the door of the conference room.

"Well, I think we have a quorum," Barbara said pleasantly. "Can we begin now? My client, our side, is more than ready to get on with it."

Shinizer's eyes narrowed and his mouth tightened in a disapproving grimace. Wordlessly he turned and went into the room. The others were standing in a huddle by the window. Slowly they all took their seats, and the afternoon session began.

At that moment Frank was sitting back comfortably in a deep, leather-covered chair watching Henkel read a court order for the second, or possibly the third, time. He didn't move his lips as he read, Frank noted, but he was not a quick student, either. Or, he thought, being fair about it, perhaps he was using the court order as a cover while he pondered what Frank had already told him.

Henkel put the paper down and glowered at Frank. "Dr. Abrams is a highly qualified psychologist, well trained in child psychology. This court has used his services on many occasions."

"You know that, and I have no reason to doubt your opinion," Frank said soothingly, not quite condescendingly, but close enough to deepen the florid complexion of the judge. "But since the child was questioned without proper care taken in the past, Judge Wyandot issued his own orders concerning future procedures."

"I have jurisdiction over this court and this trial," Henkel said harshly.

Frank spread his hands in a placating way. "Judge, no one is disputing your authority in this case. No one. However, your order puts our client in a very difficult position. Judge Wyandot presided over a terrific custodial battle concerning the child, and he assumed jurisdiction over him; he specifically ordered that the boy not be questioned again unless there is present a psychologist approved in writing by the custodial parent, and with his own written permission." He sighed. "You can appreciate our dilemma, Your Honor. If she obeys one court order, she necessarily must disobey the other. Contempt of either court is out of the question, of course. Absolutely no officer of the court could legally or ethically subject her to such a decision."

"There's no legal or professional reason for her not to approve of Dr. Abrams, who is a disinterested party."

"Well, I've observed in a very long practice, over fifty years, that clients can be capricious, not to say difficult."

Judge Henkel picked up the court order once more, and Frank thought he was going to read it again, maybe hoping the letters had crawled around to mean something different as it lay on his desk. He didn't read it, however; he let it fall as if it had burned his fingers. His jowls were quivering, Frank noted, and he did not even begin to smile. The judge stabbed a button on his phone and yelled, "Get Shinizer in here."

Cardona was going on at some length about being trained in ranch affairs. "I was happy, of course, to add that kind of training to my business education. I was more than willing to learn about ranching."

"And when did all that start?" Barbara asked.

"It was a gradual process, six or seven years ago, probably."

"Mr. Cardona, did you believe that Mr. Lynch was preparing you to take over the management of the ranch?"

He hesitated, then said, "I didn't speculate about his reasons for training me."

Just then the court clerk entered and approached Shinizer, whispered something, and left again hurriedly.

"Break," Shinizer said. He stood up and walked out stiffly without a glance at Barbara, without waiting for her assent to the break.

Everyone stood up then, stretched, the cameraman left the room; those remaining moved to the windows or just stood at the table, two hostile groups who tended to ignore one another admirably. Then Barbara thought how so many people were making what had to be a deliberate effort to avoid looking at certain other people. Babe never once looked at Cardona, and he looked at Lynch or at the camera only. She thought she was the only one there who ever glanced at McReady. Lynch and

Anna alternately kept their eyes on Babe, who was now standing
by her mother, gazing out a window, not talking. Lynch stood
at another window with his hands in his pockets, and McReady
looked like a man planning a sales pitch, withdrawn, concentrating on his own strategy. Manny was as unreadable as ever.
He stretched, poured water and sipped it, then sat down again.
Lara looked lost, undecided what to do, and Barbara went to
her.

"Take a walk down the hall?"

"Yes. Anything," Lara said.

"You're doing great, by the way," Barbara said as they left
the conference room. The video man was at the far end of the
corridor lounging against the wall. Barbara steered Lara in the
other direction.

"I don't feel so great," Lara said in a low voice.

"Well, you're putting up a wonderful front," Barbara said.
Lara was in better shape than Babe McReady. Babe was pale and
nervous, never still for more than a few minutes at a time, up
and down, up and down. It was telling, she thought then, how
Anna or Thomas Lynch, often both, were so aware of her every
minute, and her husband was simply looking inward. "Lara,"
she said softly, "I want to say this, or I might forget later when
I get too busy again: I think you have reservoirs of inner strength
that not even you knew existed. I'm very proud of you."

Lara faced her, startled. "I'm scared to death," she whispered.

"I know you are. That's what real courage and strength test
to the limit, and you're passing the test with flying colors."

"Thanks, Barbara. You know, you're just like your father.
You know exactly what to say and when to say it. I needed that.
I've been watching you a lot, how cool you stay, unflustered no
matter what they do. I couldn't do what you do."

"Dad's training," Barbara said, grinning. "He always said get
hot and fight cool. Honey, I'm as hot as a working grill in hell.

Speaking of the dragon, here he comes, and I do believe he's cleaned out the cage, eaten every single canary." Frank wasn't smiling, but she could tell. She could always tell.

Shinizer, right behind him, looked mad as hell. "Let's get on with it," he snapped. When he turned to reenter the room, Frank gave Barbara a thumbs-up sign. Barbara gave Lara's arm a reassuring little squeeze, and they followed Frank back in.

Inside the conference room, Cardona and Lynch were now together talking in low voices. Shinizer joined them, and Cardona left, to take his chair at the head of the table. No one else seemed in a hurry to resume. The video cameraman took his place, and just then Robert hurried in. Barbara went to the door to meet him.

"Bailey bitched. And he said Callagher's two prize asses are in town. He said you'd know what he means."

Callagher's men were the two detectives who had followed Lara to Eugene when she first consulted with Frank. Barbara nodded and returned to the table and her chair, thinking furiously. Shinizer and Lynch were still in a hushed conversation. After another minute or two, Shinizer crossed over to take his chair.

"Before we start, off the record, Ms. Holloway, are you prepared to finish with Mr. Cardona this afternoon?"

It was four o'clock.

"No way," she said.

"In that case, I propose that we adjourn for the day. It's getting late."

"Fine with me," Barbara said, motioning to Robert to make a note of the new interruption. Nothing suited her better than to break it off right now.

"Until tomorrow morning at nine," Shinizer said, and the second day of testimony ended.

⬧

Barbara and her group walked to Manny's office, where Frank told them what had happened in the judge's chambers. "So that's fixed for quite a spell. He'll get in touch with Judge Wyandot, who will contact you eventually, Lara, and you'll say you want Janey Lipscomb from Eugene. He'll have to go through her boss, an ogre, according to Janey, who will schedule a meeting in due time. The ogre won't be pushed into anything fast, she believes quite strongly in regular procedures, which means, with her full calendar, you'll have to get in line. So forget that for the next month or so." He grinned. "Told you," he said. "Now, what I propose is that you sub for Nathan today, take me shopping and such. Game?"

"Where's Nathan now?" Lara asked Manny.

He shrugged. "I couldn't say. With Wynona and the Corning boy, Tod. Delivering books throughout the reservation." He waved his hand generally toward the north. "It's a lot of territory to cover. No doubt they'll bed down with one of Wynona's friends somewhere. She'll call in at the house eventually." Lara continued to look troubled, and he added gently, "That's *our* country up there. No one's going to get to him."

At last she nodded, and she and Frank left together to shop.

As soon as they were gone, Barbara told Manny that Callagher's two detectives were in the area. "What are they after now?"

Manny said thoughtfully, "Probably to keep an eye on Nathan, make sure no one squirrels him away somewhere. No one trusts Silly Gooey to find his own car in a lot with two other cars parked in it."

"Will Wynona be onto them, lose them?"

Manny smiled. "Yes."

Barbara glanced at her watch. She had calls to make, things to do, but she felt her exasperation rising. "Manny, real quick, a little history lesson. What gives? You have a corrupt judge and an incompetent sheriff, plus a D.A. who seems to take his orders from Lynch. I guess I just don't understand the system over here after all."

Robert crossed over to the desk and began keying in his notes of the day.

"Real quick," Manny said. "Capsule history. It was like this: first the fur barons moved through taking what they wanted, and they moved on. Then the railroad barons ruled, but they moved on, too. The lumber barons followed, Paul Bunyan–style, and they mostly moved on. And you got the land barons, and they stayed, and they're still here. There are two Wests, Barbara, yours and ours, and they have nothing to do with each other. We don't even consider folks on the other side of the mountains as westerners; you're urban, your ties are to the cities, to the eastern cities, the cities of the whole world. Our ties are to the land. In the beginning the land barons seized what they could, and fought to hold it and increase their holdings. They put judges in office, put sheriffs in the jails, put their people wherever they needed them. They weren't politicians and didn't want to be; they wanted to be ranchers and own the politicians. And they still do. For a long time it was enough to own them regionally; then territories became states, and the states began passing silly laws, and they had to go beyond their little regions, go to the state legislators and own enough of them to make a difference. Then the feds began to pass silly laws, and they had to move up, a senator here, a congressman there, a federal judge or two, enough to make a difference."

He was talking faster and faster, and for the first time since she had met him, she saw the passion behind his mask.

"The problem is that cracks are starting to show," he said. "The system is showing signs of breaking down. A federal judge has power, understand, but a Supreme Court justice has more. They want to own enough of them to make a difference. Mc-

Ready is made to order for their purposes. He is theirs exactly the same way that Silly Gooey is, and Henkel is, and Shinizer. It isn't just here, it's from the Canadian border to the Mexican border, all the Old West good old boys are joined in a common cause: to maintain the status quo, to maintain their power over the land they seized and still hold. Most of them are indifferent about what goes on, or even benign, unless their own interests are threatened. Lynch for the most part has been indifferent, but, Barbara, he's quite willing to stamp on anyone who threatens his interests."

His gaze was so intense that she felt pinned by it, immobilized by it. Abruptly he turned away and went to the window.

"You said cracks are showing. What cracks?" she asked.

He faced her again, but she no longer could see his features; he was a short, bulky silhouette against the bright light. "Now and then, here and there a rancher has come awake, has seen the land, what's been done to it, what's being done to it. There aren't a lot of them, but every year another one moves over into that group. Roger Jessup was a new idea starting to happen. I believe that when Babe finally gets the whole ranch as her own, she'll move over. Roger was a good influence on her. She's already implementing some of his ideas, land and water reclamation, improving the herd, taking care. Just taking care."

Another side of Babe, Barbara realized, one she had not anticipated, that took her by surprise. She remembered the look that had crossed Babe's face when she talked about riding at dawn. At the time she had dismissed it as dreamy, distant, even a little removed from reality, the way a heavily tranquilized patient was removed, but she thought now that Babe had been seeing the desert at dawn, that in her mind she had been there, seeing it, riding. "Her Ancestors were from the desert," she said softly.

Manny nodded. "They were."

"Well," she said briskly then, "I have to make a call, and then let's put our heads together and talk about tomorrow and the next day or two. I have some ideas I want to run by you both."

Since Robert was still at the desk, using the computer, she crossed the hall and used her own office, her own telephone to dial Shelley's number. Shelley sounded almost pathetically happy to hear her voice. "You tied up with anything you can't leave for a couple of days?" Barbara asked.

"No! If anything comes up, Maria can say I'm at my grandmother's wedding."

Barbara laughed. In Shelley's family it might even be true. "Okay. What I want you to do is check on the cats, leave them tons of dry food and plenty of water, and make sure the cat door is fastened with them on the inside, and then drive over to Bend. I don't care what time you get in, just tonight. Bring all the mail that's been accumulating in a big manila envelope, Dad's and mine. Add a couple of snapshots. I don't care whose, just so they're identifiable as snapshots from a distance. Promptly at nine-thirty in the morning I want you to come to the courthouse in Salt Creek and say you have an urgent message for me. Tell whoever is in charge that you're my associate. They'll let you in. Hand me the envelope and we'll have a little chat, and I'll call for a break. Further instructions to follow. Got all that?"

"Yes! I'll be there!"

"Good. You might be over here a couple of days, and tomorrow you'll have to do a lot of driving, so be prepared. Get a motel in Bend when you arrive. Don't come to Lara's house."

She continued to sit at the desk thinking a little longer, then returned to Manny's office, where Robert was still at the computer keying in his notes. He was a meticulous note-taker.

"Manny, before we get into anything else, fill me in on the

living arrangements at the Lynch ranch, will you? What did they do with the Jessup house, for instance?"

She listened carefully as he described the situation. For several years they had not used the house, but then the manager, Childress, had moved into it with his family, and soon after that the hands who had lived at Lynch's place had been moved over there. There were a couple of small cabins, and several house trailers for the hands. By the county roads the distance between the two houses was about four or five miles; on horseback it was a mile.

"No one walks," Manny said with a slight smile. "You want to go somewhere, you get in the Jeep or the truck or get on your horse. So gradually they added a one-lane road connecting the houses. Nowadays at the Lynch house there are a few live-in people, housekeeper, a cook, a servant girl or two, and the family. All the rest of them live over on the other ranch." Rucfully he added, "I always think of it as the other ranch, but it's just one great big spread."

"Do the live-ins stay year-round, even when the family is gone?"

"The cook comes over here, but she goes to Arizona when the Lynches leave for a few months in Hawaii. The girls come to Salt Creek with the Lynches, but they don't work when the Lynches go to Hawaii. The housekeeper stays. She's been there since Lincoln was president. Babe's there for months at a time, often with a friend or two, and Cardona is in and out."

"What about Babe's friends? Women? Men?"

"As far as anyone knows, just lady friends. Barbara, they don't come calling in Salt Creek. They go to the ranch, stay a week, a month—who knows how long?—and they go away again."

"Strange setup," she said. "Do any of the servants talk?"

Manny smiled and Robert laughed. "The rumor is that Lynch

pays well, half for the work they do, half to keep their mouths shut," Manny said. "Lynch has the money; he can buy a lot of privacy."

"Okay," she said. "Let's talk. Manny, have you been observing Babe?"

"Yes. She's falling apart."

"I think so, too. And I think Thomas Lynch is running this show, running Shinizer, the judge, maybe even the psychologist they so conveniently found today. I think he's determined not to let Babe sit in that chair and be cross-examined. He sees that I can and will ask anything I damn well please, and Shinizer can't stop me. I think both he and Anna Lynch are terrified for her. The summons to produce Nathan didn't work, so he'll look for another way to stop it. Manny, you know these people, you know Lynch. What else will he try?"

For the first time since she had met him, Barbara thought she could read the expression on his face. Robert was easy, he clearly was badly frightened for Lara and had been from the beginning, but Manny had remained alien, his expression written on his features in a language she could not comprehend. What she read now, she felt certain, was fear.

"Barbara," he said slowly, "I don't believe there's anything he wouldn't do to protect her. If he decides blowing up the courthouse is the only way, he'll make a bomb."

"We'd better sit down and talk about this," she said faintly.

That night Frank and Lara had made beef Stroganoff with chanterelles, and everyone groaned when they finished eating.

"He makes it look so easy," Lara said. "All I did was get in the way and wash things."

Barbara laughed. "He won't even let me in the kitchen when he's cooking. You're one of the chosen people."

"I made plenty," Frank said. "If Bailey comes in as hungry as usual, it can be heated and no harm done."

"He'll be in by ten or eleven," Barbara said. "I'll point him toward the fridge."

She had hours of work to do. Robert had finished his notes, and she wanted to read them all thoroughly, and her own as well, and she had to organize her questions for Cardona. . . . And depending on what Bailey brought her, possibly add more questions to her growing list.

It was after eleven when he arrived, looking disgruntled and sleepy. "It's a wash, Barbara," he said. "Got any chow?"

They went to the kitchen together, and he eyed the beef Stroganoff suspiciously and opted for a sandwich instead. "Too heavy for beddybytime."

"Why a wash?" she demanded, watching him make a mammoth sandwich that would sink a normal person at bedtime.

"Okay. Okay. The kid in San Francisco was born in Honolulu, February tenth, 1993. A boy. Anthony Thomas Neal. Mother, Holly Neal. Daddy, Eliot Cardona."

She stared at him in dismay. "Shit."

"Yep. No trace of Babe ever being in a hospital anywhere that I can get at. Not me. Alan. He's the hacker, and he tried every trick he knows. Just didn't happen. Got any beer?"

"I don't know. Look. What about him, Cardona?"

"His wife took off back around 1990, divorced a year later. When he goes to San Fran, he goes to Neal's place. When he got two tickets for Brazil, one was in the name of Neal, ditto France, ditto Georgia. When he travels, she goes with him, and so does the kid, at least to Georgia and Hawaii." He closed the refrigerator. "God, what a house! Not a drop to drink."

"There's wine."

"So I settle for wine."

She scowled at him as he started to eat. He paused and said, "Hey, Barbara, I don't make the news. I just report it."

"What about Neal? Where did she come from? Who is she?"

"Barbara, give me a break. This stuff takes a little time, which I notice has been in short supply. As far as I've found out, she was born the same day she had the kid. Before that, zilch. Few months later she moved into the condo in San Fran."

She was thinking: Babe tried to run over Roger with a Jeep; she had become hysterical and suicidal, and the next day her mother whisked her away. But damn it, she thought savagely, she was certain they hadn't gone to Paris to do a little shopping. She had been suicidal. And the way she was now—twitchy, nervous, ready to crack wide open, from all appearances. Barbara had been sure that Babe had been under psychiatric care off and on for years, and that meant a hospital sooner or later. She had counted on that. And where in hell did Holly Neal fit in? She didn't know when she had started to pace, but she found herself walking faster and faster.

"Bailey, did Alan check for Holly Neal and hospitals back through the years?"

"No. What for? You said you wanted the dope on the kid."

"Put that sandwich down and get Alan on the pipe. Tell him to check hospitals for Holly Neal going back eighteen years."

"You know what time it is?"

"I'm still awake, and you are. Call him. Tell him to call back at this number. I'll take the call, and you go on to bed."

Resignedly Bailey took one more bite and went to the kitchen phone to place the call. Alan was as wide awake as Barbara, he said in disgust when he hung up. Alan loved this kind of thing, he added morosely. Permission to break the law, hack his way into hospital computers, medical databases, dig out confidential information. He finished his sandwich, drank a second glass of wine, and went to bed.

At two A.M. when Alan Macagno called, he still sounded wide awake and as cheerful as if it were two in the afternoon. "Jackpot, Barbara," he said.

She listened, sitting at Vinny's desk, without making a sound until he finished his report. Then she let out a long breath. "Okay, Alan. Back up and do the dates again, will you." This time she made notes, and when she finished, she said softly, "I owe you big, Alan. Thanks."

After hanging up, she sat for several minutes putting puzzle pieces together. Then she whispered, "Dear God." She pulled her notebook closer and started to write.

31

"Barbara, it's almost time to leave," Frank called up the stairs the next morning.

"I know. I'll be down in a sec." She looked like hell, she knew, and there was nothing she could do about it. She had stayed under the shower a long time, hoping the spray would do more to revive her than food. But neither water nor food would undo the effects of a sleepless night. She snatched up her briefcase and went down.

"Bailey, I have something for you," she said, hurrying to the kitchen, where Frank placed a cup of coffee in her hands. She drew Bailey aside and said in a rush, "Shelley will come to court at nine-thirty, and we'll talk a few minutes—ten, fifteen minutes.

If Callagher's guys are around, they should recognize her and send a message. I want to know to whom. When she leaves, I want you to drive her down to the Klamath Falls area. I'll give her the address and directions. If the other guys follow, don't try to lose them or let on that you see them, but don't let them get near her, either. She'll talk to someone for about an hour maybe; then bring her back to Lara's house. Got it?"

He was eyeing her with disbelief. "Klamath Falls."

"I know. I know. I've been there. Believe me, I know. I've got to run."

They arrived at court a few minutes after nine and found Robert waiting outside. He looked at Barbara with the same startled and worried gaze that everyone else was wearing that morning. She ignored it.

Upstairs in the conference room, she could feel the scrutiny she was getting from the entire Lynch gang and shrugged that off, too, but with growing irritation. She didn't look all that awful, she thought. Cardona was already seated, waiting.

"Shall we start?" she asked.

"By all means," Shinizer said silkily.

Assume what you want, buster, she thought at him, then addressed Cardona in a crisp manner. "Mr. Cardona, just to clear up a few little mysteries, will you tell us when and where you met Holly Neal, and what your relationship with her is?"

Shinizer objected, and she kept her gaze on Cardona, waiting for his response.

His face tightened, and he drew himself straighter upright in his chair. "I have no objection personally," he said. "I'm quite sure Judge Henkel will rule that my private life is entirely irrelevant to this matter and accordingly will strike everything I have to say about my personal affairs." He was gazing straight into the video camera as he spoke. "I met Ms. Neal at the ranch many years ago when she was visiting there. We developed a friendship, and in the course of time as our friendship deepened, our relationship shifted to that of lovers. My wife had left me and we were divorced by then; there was no reason for me not to develop a relationship with Ms. Neal. But because we both had had unfortunate marriages, we were not ready to take that step again. When I go to San Francisco, I live with Ms. Neal in her condominium, and on occasion she comes to the ranch to be with me."

"Thank you," Barbara said. "When you go to Hawaii with Mr. and Mrs. Lynch, does Ms. Neal accompany you?"

"Yes."

No one was moving in the room; even Babe was still. In fact, Barbara realized, Babe looked as if she had taken a lot of tran- quilizers, her stillness had such an unnatural look. She continued to ask Cardona about Neal, about their child, when and where he had been born, whether Cardona was in attendance, all of which he answered without hesitation. And then promptly at nine-thirty the court reporter came in with Shelley in tow.

"Excuse me," Barbara said. "Break. This is my associate Ms. McGinnis." The reporter left, and Barbara rose to speak to Shel- ley away from the table. Shelley handed her the big manila en- velope; Barbara glanced inside it, handled a few pieces of mail as if examining them, took a snapshot partway out as if to get a better look at it, then grinned at Shelley. "Thanks," she said, loud enough to be heard. She returned to the table but did not sit down now. "I would like a break at this time," she said. "Half an hour."

"Haven't we had enough interruptions?" Shinizer said meanly. "I object to further delays."

"Mr. Shinizer, the record will show that I have requested ex- actly one break, this one, and as you well know, I am entitled to it. I need to consult with my associates. Now." She turned to Frank and Manny and motioned to them to come, and she said to Robert, "Do you mind keeping Lara company for a few minutes, hold down the fort, so to speak?" And he, she knew, would keep an eye on the assembled group and tell her later exactly what every one of them did, what they said, if he could overhear a single word. So far, during the breaks all the conversations had been in whispers.

Carrying the big envelope, she left the room with Shelley; Frank and Manny followed. They went to the window at the far end of the corridor and huddled.

"There isn't enough time to fill you in on details," she said. "I'm sorry. I don't like playing the Lone Ranger, but we'll catch up as soon as one of them calls for an extended break, which will happen pretty soon, I believe. But for now. Callagher's guys are hanging around. They probably recognized Shelley as the person Lara met when she went to Eugene the first time to consult Dad. They lost her there, but no doubt they suspect she was carrying the papers Vinny was supposed to have had. And they may suspect that Shelley has delivered them to me now. I want her to go down to Klamath Falls and ask Delia Kersh about Holly Neal and Cardona, everything she can find out. And I think the Callagher men will tail along. Bailey will go with her, and they'll both come back to Lara's house afterward."

She drew in a breath and then told Shelley about Delia Kersh, and how to find her house. "Don't let on that you're interested in the Lynch group, just Holly Neal and Cardona, and their child. She'll feed you cookies and give you excellent coffee, and I think she'll talk until you decide it's time to get on your horse. Okay?"

Shelley had a few questions, and Barbara answered them until she ran out of answers. She rubbed her eyes and shook her head. "I haven't had time to come up with a good reason for you to be asking her questions. Between you and Bailey, you'll think of something. It's a long drive. Now, listen, this gets a little tricky. I want to know who those guys report to. They won't be allowed to enter the conference room, but I suspect that either Lynch or McReady will go out to speak with them. Bailey will recognize which one it is. If it's McReady, just ask Kersh some questions about Neal and Cardona and hightail it home. If it's Lynch, try to get a snapshot of Neal and the child, and one of Babe when she was four or five. Don't push it too hard, but ask if she has one or two." She glanced over her shoulder. Down the corridor Shinizer was watching her little group. She rummaged in the manila envelope, brought out the snapshots, and passed them to Shelley, who slipped them into a pocket without a glance. "Your stage props," Barbara said. "When you leave Kersh's house, if she's given you a snapshot, wave it at Bailey and put on a happy face. If she doesn't give you one, wave one of those. If those guys follow you down there, let them see that you have pictures, that's all. Then you and Bailey examine them in the car before you take off. Got all that?"

Shelley was almost breathless with excitement. She nodded, and Barbara knew she had every word of it. Shelley looked like a schoolgirl, but she was like Bailey; she delivered.

"After that, just get yourselves back to Lara's house. Oh, one more thing. Tell Bailey I said for him to wait at the car, and if those guys follow you, it would be nice if they didn't get a chance to interrupt your conversation with Delia Kersh. Short of bloodshed, tell him. And tell him to park in the sun to keep warm while he waits. Be sure to tell him I said that. He'll be grateful."

Shelley laughed. Not only did she look like a schoolgirl, today she was dressed like one. Sherpa boots, a fleece jacket, wool tights. What she didn't look like was an attorney. Delia Kersh would love her.

Frank was pissed as hell, she knew, and Manny was so still that next to him Al Gore would have looked frenzied. Couldn't be helped right now, though. When Shelley left in a dash, Barbara said, "Hey, you two, relax. First real break I'll tell all. Promise." It was time to go back to the conference room.

As they passed an open office door on the way back, she caught a glimpse of the Lynch gang, having their own conference. They all returned more or less together; Cardona took his seat at the head of the table, the cameraman took up his station, and they were ready.

"Mr. Cardona," she said slowly, "do you have any knowledge about what papers Vinny Jessup said he would deliver to Judge McReady on the night of his death?"

Well, she thought in satisfaction, that one took him by surprise. He looked at her and then quickly away, back to the camera. But he was startled enough that he didn't have an instant answer.

"I have no idea," he said after the brief pause.

"Do you understand that in a perpetuation of testimony such as this, the witness is free to speculate if asked to do so?"

He shook his head. "I didn't know that."

"It's true. I ask you now to speculate, based on what you might have heard or observed or simply guessed. What do you think such papers might have contained?"

Shinizer objected loudly.

"It's a fair question," she responded. "I'm asking for speculation, not factual information. Mr. Cardona?"

"I don't have any idea what such papers might have been," he said.

"Was Judge McReady visibly upset when he took the call from Vinny Jessup that night?"

"I don't know. I don't know him well enough to know how he is if he's upset. He didn't seem so."

"Could you overhear any of his conversation with Vinny Jessup?"

This time he was very prompt. "No. I handed him the phone and walked across the room to wait for him to finish talking. I couldn't hear a word."

"Did he appear surprised that Vinny Jessup wanted a meeting at that hour, that he said he had papers or documents to deliver?"

"I don't know," he said slowly. "I really wasn't watching him, or paying any attention to the conversation."

"Does Judge McReady have a computer-card key to the house on Lookout Mountain?"

"Yes."

"And a password?"

"Yes."

"Did he have the key and password on the night of Vinny Jessup's death?"

"Yes."

"I'm going to ask you another speculative question, Mr. Cardona. Please look at Lara Jessup. Do you believe she murdered her husband?"

He was shaken by the question. He had not looked directly at Lara a single time, and appeared reluctant to do so now. Then he gazed at her for just a moment; his face changed subtly as a frown creased his forehead, and his mouth tightened. A small muscle in his jaw jerked, then again. He shook his head, and looked back at the camera. "No," he said quietly.

"I have no further questions," Barbara said.

Babe had jumped up from her chair at the question and was now at the window facing out, as rigid as a board.

No one else moved until Shinizer snapped, "Break." He went to Lynch's side, and they had a whispered consultation. Then he said, "Since this is an unexpected development, we'd like to adjourn until two this afternoon, at which time Mr. Lynch will be sworn in."

Barbara nodded. "Two o'clock it is."

❧

They trooped back to Manny's office. Barbara's feet were made of lead, her legs ached, and a driving headache had started behind her eye. Tonight, she promised her protesting body. Tonight you sleep.

Inside the office she asked Robert what had happened when she left with Shelley.

"They milled about, you know, the way they do. Then a clerk came in and said something to Lynch, who went out with him. Five minutes later he came back and said something to McReady, and they all left."

"Ah, so Lynch hired the detectives. That's what I wanted to know." She poured coffee and drank some; it was heavenly. Then she said to Lara, "Why don't you go on home and get some rest. Robert, would you mind keeping her company?"

"I really don't think I need a sitter," Lara protested.

"We think you do," Frank said. "For now. If anything happens around here, we'll fill you in. Just get a little rest. Something to eat. We'll order sandwiches here."

Robert, it was evident, was torn between wanting to be at the office when Barbara explained what she was up to and wanting to spend every minute possible with Lara. Wanting to be her protector, Barbara thought. He was so transparent where Lara was concerned, to everyone but her, apparently.

"Orders," Robert said lightly. "Let's go."

Lara hesitated, then shrugged, and they left together.

"Now," Frank said.

"Now," Barbara agreed. She poured more coffee and sat down. "I know what McReady holds over them, why they march to his band. Of course, we know that Babe shot Lewis, and McReady must have proof tucked away somewhere. She's been in and out of hospitals many times over the years, suicidal, clinical depression, but not for the last seven years. In the past six years she's been taking charge of the ranch more and more, staying there months at a time; usually Cardona, the other woman, and the child are there at the same time as she is."

There was a knock on the door, and Nadia looked in and said softly, "Mr. Lynch wants to see you, Barbara."

"To be continued," Barbara said. She refilled her cup and walked out to see Lynch. Behind her she could hear Frank cursing in a low, savage tone.

Thomas Lynch was in the corridor; a few feet away Cardona stood with his hands in his pockets. "I want to talk to you in private," Lynch said curtly.

"My office is across the hall," she said.

He nodded and she walked in front of him to open her door. He made a gesture toward Cardona. "He'll see that we're not interrupted." Inside the office, he glanced about quickly, then pointed to the uncomfortable chairs around the low table. "Over there, if you don't mind."

She would have preferred her desk chair, which was comfortable, but she went to one of the wooden chairs and sat down and sipped her coffee. He did not sit down.

"I assume that this office is not bugged," he said. "Is that a good assumption?"

"Of course."

"Good. Ms. Holloway, I want to tell you something. My great-grandfather homesteaded in the Oregon Territory. He had to fight to hold his land—marauding Indians, outlaws, other ranchers, whoever came along and challenged his claim, and he held onto it and prospered. My grandfather fought to continue to hold it, as did my father. I am no less willing to fight to protect what is mine. The weapons change with the times, but the fight doesn't change, and we don't lose. I want to end this mess now."

He was a fighter, that was clear in his stance, the way his heavy face had hardened with deep lines cut into his cheeks, bracketing his mouth, his eyes narrowed to slits. In her mind's eye she could see him on a dusty little street, his hands twitching and his gaze as unwavering as a snake's, waiting for his enemy to blink, to move, to draw.

She took another sip of coffee; it was cooling off enough now that she could actually drink some, and she needed it. She wished she had brought the carafe.

"I said the weapons change," he went on, "but take my word, they are still weapons. I will propose two possible courses of action. I feel sorry for Mrs. Jessup. She behaved in an impetuous, reflexive way when she found Vinny dead. I understand that the law can be harsh, or it can be forgiving. This is not true of the insurance industry. She would have to give up her claim for insurance. She would have to sign a statement affirming that hysteria overcame her good sense, and the matter will end there. No probation. No penalty. But she will have to leave the area. Living here with her child would be impossible with the shadow over her. I'm sure you grasp that. I will personally guarantee full financial restitution for the expenses she has incurred for her defense. And I will finance her relocation."

"And Harris McReady will continue his march toward the Supreme Court, unimpeded."

"That is no concern of yours." He had not moved as he spoke; now he walked to the window and stood gazing out at the desert stretching out to infinity.

"You said two courses," she said. She drained her cup and set it down.

"I will destroy her, her child, and you, Ms. Holloway. She will be convicted of premeditated murder; her son will testify against her, as will many others." He turned to regard her, his own face hidden by shadows. "And it will become known that the young woman had a way out, an honorable way out, but that you chose to grandstand instead and let her face a possible death penalty. I believe that alone is enough to bring about your own destruction, Ms. Holloway. If that assumption is wrong, I am prepared to do whatever it takes."

He started to walk toward the door. "I'll expect an answer before the afternoon session resumes, no later."

"Mr. Lynch," she said, "you've been forthright and succinct. I appreciate that. Before you leave, however, let me have a say. I'll try to be as clear and brief as you have been, not take up too much of your time." He stopped midway to the door. "It's a little unorthodox, but I'd like to preview a few of the questions I intend to ask you and your family in the days to come. I haven't brought my notebook in with me, so I'm afraid I can't read them; I'll have to paraphrase, and there's a good chance that I'll leave out some, but you'll get the drift, I'm sure."

"You know damn well that nothing you ask beyond the night of Vinny's death will ever see the light of day."

"Perhaps. But it would be useful to try them out on you. You see, I'm quite concerned about the health of your daughter. I'll ask her where she spent six weeks the summer of 1981, beginning a day or two after she tried to kill Roger Jessup. Not with her mother, apparently, since Mrs. Lynch was in daily attendance on a young woman named Holly Neal, who had been admitted to a hospital in Massachusetts, and in fact Mrs. Lynch even paid Holly Neal's bills. I'll ask your daughter where she was the evening Lewis Jessup was shot. I'll ask her about a number of hospital admissions from 1982 until about seven years ago. And why Mrs. Lynch paid hospital bills for a Holly Neal for each stay."

Lynch had taken several more steps toward the door when she began, but he had stopped with his back to her and was immobile, both hands clenched hard at his sides.

"I'll ask where you and Mrs. Lynch and your daughter were the night of February tenth, 1993."

He turned very slowly, as if moving was agony; his face had

become completely gray. "Not a single question that you're posing will ever be heard at the trial, or anywhere else."

"Perhaps you're right," she said. "But they will be heard in
the conference room by everyone in there. Including Harris
McReady. There's a credo drilled into doctors, Mr. Lynch: Do
no harm. For attorneys there's another one: Ask no questions
you don't already have answers for. Most secrets are perfectly
safe just as long as no one suspects there are secrets. And there's
a spectrum of suspicion that ranges from the totally paranoid to
the arrogance of never harboring an idea that anyone in your
control would dare cross you. McReady read you perfectly years
ago; he understood completely that you would sell your soul to
protect your daughter, keep her out of prison, keep her from
her suicidal course. Was a time limit put on the deal? The day
he was sworn in at the Court, she would be freed? Something
like that? Something you could all live with, you thought? Now
you all must fear that if he learns about the child, he will be
forced to claim him as his own son, have Babe declared incompetent on the basis of her medical history, bringing no discredit
to him, but making him appear rather as a long-suffering husband who has bravely borne more than his share of grief."

She stood up, stiff and sore, and said softly, "Mr. Lynch, I
want no harm to come to your daughter or your grandson.
There's a saying among some women: If I had killed him when
I left him, I'd be out now. She's served her time, Mr. Lynch. It's
time to free her. Look at McReady, at his arrogance; consider if
he would throw away his federal judgeship by exposing her.
That's the problem for blackmailers; often in order to use the
threat they hold, they have to reveal themselves also. You said
that back through history your ancestors fought for what was
theirs, but you've forced Babe to accept, to yield. Let her fight
for her son, if it comes to that. She can prove whose child that
is. It may be a very nasty fight, a brutal fight, but one she won't

lose. She's her father's child, Mr. Lynch; she will fight for her son as hard as Lara Jessup is fighting to save hers, as hard as I'm fighting to save Lara."

Barbara went to the door and held the knob. "You know my answer to your two proposals, Mr. Lynch. I can promise this much: if Lara is exonerated completely, I will not ask a single question that goes beyond the night Vinny Jessup died." She opened the door and stepped aside.

He walked out like a man heading for the death chamber.

◈ PART FOUR

JUDGMENT

✦ 32

She stood at her closed door listening to receding foot-steps echo through the bare-wood floor of the hall and down the stairs until there was nothing more to hear. Then she retrieved her coffee cup and went over to Manny's office, where she stopped in surprise just inside the doorway. When she walked out of the office, Frank had been cursing like a mule driver with a recalcitrant team; now he was holding a letter or something and laughing like an idiot. Hastily he stuffed the paper inside his briefcase on the floor by his chair and stood up, sobering instantly.

"What happened over there?"

"What happened in here?" she asked in return.

"Later. It's nothing. What did he want?"

"Coffee first. I may be dying." She headed for the carafe, but Frank took her arm and turned her toward a chair. She sank down into it and groaned.

Manny came in and pulled the door closed after him. "I ordered sandwiches. They'll be here in a few minutes."

Frank took her cup and filled it, then sat facing her.

She started at the top, with Lynch's offer of financial support, all of it. When she finished, Frank whistled softly.

"Christ on a mountain. King's law." He looked at Manny. "Can he pull it off?"

"Yes. And she'd be a fool not to accept. Robert certainly will urge her to accept."

"Wait," Barbara said, and repeated the threat.

Manny and Frank exchanged glances. Manny nodded. He could do that, too, bring in as many witnesses as it would take to put Lara on the mountain that night.

"Wait," Barbara said again, and told the rest of it.

No one said a word when she finished. Manny was eyeing her with what looked suspiciously like awe. She hoped it was awe; that would be nice, to elicit awe from Manny. Frank was frowning, his thinking frown, not his disapproval frown. There was a difference.

Nadia knocked on the door and called, "Chow."

"Leave it on the table and go get yourself some lunch," Manny called back. "Barbara," he said then very carefully, "can you prove a word of it?"

"A lot of it," she said. "Not all, not yet. But it's true that a secret's safe just as long as no one suspects there is a secret. Once you start looking, that's it. We have a hacker pal who could get into heaven and read Saint Peter's private roll call. He found out about Holly Neal's hospital admissions and the fact that Anna Lynch was always there to foot the bill at the same time that she and Babe were ostensibly on a pleasure trip together somewhere or other. All the other pieces were in hand; I just didn't know what to do with them, but that was the Rosetta stone, and everything began to fall into place. Never once did Cardona look at Babe in the conference room. She'd jump up and go to the window or something, and he'd keep his eyes on the camera. I think he's afraid to look at her in public. He might be as transparent as Robert is when he looks at Lara." She shrugged, remembering how torn Robert had been between wanting to take Lara home and wanting to stay with the group.

"Anyway, everyone kept handing us pieces, a bit here, another bit there. Lynch despised McReady and wanted him to lose the Lewis Jessup case, knew he would lose it. Then he married Babe off to him, although she had scorned him from the start. You told me, Manny, how Babe suddenly began to take an interest in the ranch after a lot of years at loose ends. Suddenly she was stable again. Managing things. I think she fell in love, and her folks helped her set up a secret life in the condo and at the ranch. Babe used the name Holly Neal over the years; the name of the mother on the child's birth certificate is Holly Neal. Cardona's the father.

"But McReady still has whatever it is he holds over Lynch, a signed confession probably, maybe her taped call when she said she had shot Roger, maybe something more tucked away in a safe-deposit box somewhere. And the fear is still there. No statute of limitations on murder. But I honestly don't think they ever considered that if McReady exposes her, he has to admit to being an accessory after the fact. And there goes his judgeship, maybe even his freedom. All they could think of was protecting their child."

Abruptly Frank said, "Let's go eat before you fall down. No sleep, not a bite to eat today. Running full-speed on nothing but caffeine. You'll make yourself sick."

She grinned at Manny and said, "See. Parent-kid thing."

They went to the next room and started on the sandwiches, and no one spoke as they ate.

"He might have covered his ass," Frank said when they were done. "McReady might have covered up his part in the Lewis Jessup affair completely."

"If Thomas Lynch turns on him," Manny said slowly, "his

name never will come up as a nominee for the Court. He knows that."

"I don't think he ever wanted Babe at all," Barbara said. "She was simply his route to Lynch. What I'm afraid of is that at this minute Lynch and crew are packing their bags to take off for Argentina or someplace."

Manny shook his head. "They can't do that. They can't leave this country any more than I could. You don't see the ties, Barbara, but they're strong. They're tied to their land."

"Anna Lynch, too?" Barbara asked skeptically.

"Anna, too," Manny said. Then he said, "We tried to figure it out, Wynona and I did, many times. Why the house on the mountain, why winters in Hawaii? Anna rides like a rodeo performer and she loves the ranch; why suddenly give it up so much of the time? How did she talk Thomas into it? We couldn't figure it out." Softly he said, "I think they must have been giving Babe her own space, hers and Cardona's. They moved all the hands over to the Jessup place. And they all go to Hawaii together. I think they've sacrificed a lot for Babe."

"And when McReady pops in for a visit?"

"They're in the mountain house. A call to Babe, and she's there, too. I don't think McReady's been to the ranch since they bought the mountain house. He hates horses," he added dryly.

"Will they risk it all now? Will Babe break?" Barbara asked.

"I don't know," Manny said.

Frank had been silent, deeply troubled. Now he said, "Another possibility. They may spirit the nanny and the child away and hide them. Lynch is a fighter. If he decides you're bluffing, that without the child nothing can be proved, he is as likely to call your bluff as not."

"Right," Barbara said tiredly. "Lynch could decide that, but would Babe? If it meant giving up her child for the next several years, however long it takes for McReady to move on into the

Court? Give up Cardona? She would have to, you know. If McReady finds out, he'll keep her on a short rein, have her watched day and night." She poured more coffee, although she knew she'd already had enough to satisfy her caffeine addiction for a week. Miserably she said, "If that happens, Babe will be back in the hospital within a week. Or dead."

She tasted the coffee and put the cup down again. Too much. "During this break," she said, "if Lynch's detectives followed Shelley and Bailey, they'll report back to Lynch that Shelley visited Kersh and that she came out with a photograph."

"A picture of a baby," Manny said. "Delia Kersh wouldn't have a more recent picture of the child; she left when he was still an infant. So what?"

"Not a baby—Babe. When she was four or five. They saw me looking at a snapshot, now there's a second one for them to think about. If I were Lynch, I would call Delia Kersh and ask what Shelley was after and if she got it. He would have to wonder if I'm comparing Neal's child at that age with Babe when she was very young. If her son looks as much like her as Nathan looks like Lara, they can't very well deny him. He'll know I'm not bluffing, but going after hard, physical evidence. At least I hope that's how it will play with him."

"Christ," Frank muttered. "Bobby, it isn't just Babe at risk, it's all of them. Anna, Thomas, McReady, they're all accessories. He might see it as bringing down the whole goddamn castle."

"It's a sand castle, Dad. And the tide has turned."

She could hear the lack of conviction in her own words, be-cause, she thought bleakly, money could buy a lot of privacy, a lot of protection, a lot of immunity from the consequences of actions, no matter how murderous they were. If the Lynch gang maintained their united front, if they got to Nathan eventually, and they would—she could delay that interrogation, not prevent it—then Lara was a goner unless she admitted to tampering with evidence, faking a murder, trying to defraud the insurance company. She would have to move away, and be suspected ever after of killing Vinny Jessup and getting away with it. Curtis Stroh might even get custody of her son.

And Harris McReady would likely be the next Supreme Court justice sworn in.

When they entered the conference room at two, Anna Lynch and Babe were at the window, their backs to the room. Anna's arm was around Babe's shoulders. Cardona was not there. McReady was already seated at the long table, imperturbable, as handsome as ever, as solitary as ever. Thomas Lynch did not glance at Barbara or anyone in her group; he seemed as isolated as McReady, his face wooden.

When everyone was seated and the video cameraman in place, Lynch was sworn in.

After the preliminaries, Shinizer invited Lynch to tell in his own words what happened the night Vinny died. Then he leaned back in his chair and regarded Barbara with what she decided must be a smirk. She never had been really sure before what a smirk was.

"Yes," Lynch said in a firm, steady voice, facing directly into the camera. "My family—Anna, my wife; my daughter, Bethany; and Judge McReady—were at dinner when Judge McReady received a telephone call. He told us the caller was Vinny Jessup, who proposed meeting him at ten o'clock to deliver some important papers. He agreed to the meeting. We finished with dinner and went to the game room for coffee. Shortly before ten the cook came in to remove the coffee service, and almost immediately after she left the room, my daughter remembered that she still had a little packing to do. She and the judge planned an early departure the next morning. Anna said she would help her finish, and they both went up together."

It might have been that everyone in the room was holding their breath, the silence was so intense when he paused.

Lynch continued as if unaware of the unnatural quiet. "I asked Judge McReady if he had his house key with him, and he said he did. I said that since he was to meet Vinny Jessup down at the parking area, he might as well go on down and wait for him, and I would turn on the security system and go to bed. He could let himself in later. He went out by the side terrace door. I went down the hall, spoke briefly with Mr. Cardona, and then turned on the system. After that I went up to my room, where I remained the rest of the night."

Something crashed, McReady's chair, as he jumped to his feet, his face livid. Shinizer looked like a man who had been hit between the eyes with a two-by-four. At the window Anna Lynch had drawn Babe in closer and was holding her firmly.

Finally Shinizer spoke in a strangled voice, "Break!"

The cameraman moved back, but Lynch didn't move. He said, "Carl, I prefer to finish this now."

Shinizer hesitated, then he motioned to the video cameraman to resume. "I've got no more questions," he said in a hoarse voice. He nodded to Barbara.

"I have no questions for Mr. Lynch," Barbara said.

Then they had the break.

The tableau held for seconds; Robert was as stunned as Shinizer, and Lara appeared too dazed to comprehend what had just happened. Frank was sitting back in his chair with a benign expression, watching everyone, and Manny was as unreadable as ever, as unflappable as ever. Barbara wanted to scream, to cry out something, anything; she could feel the adrenaline coursing through her like a flame, feel her heart racing. She fought to hold a neutral expression and felt she had long ago lost the fight. My God! she thought. My God! It's over!

Then McReady spun around and strode to Babe and Anna Lynch. He grasped Babe's arm and said, "Come with me. I want to talk to you."

She jerked free, looked directly at him and said, "No."

She and Anna were both standing very erect. When McReady reached again for Babe, she said distinctly, "Keep your hands off me."

Shinizer finally moved. He leaned in toward Lynch and said in a hoarse whisper, "We have to talk."

"I expect we do," Lynch said coolly. "Babe, Anna, you'll want to be in on this."

Both women walked past McReady without another glance at him. He stared at their backs as they left the room; then, his face set in grim lines, he hurried out after them. Casually Frank got up and moved to the door, where he stood watching.

"What does it mean?" Lara finally whispered.

"Well," Barbara said, "I think it means the case will be thrown out; the state's case has been blown out of the water." She couldn't believe how calm her voice was when inside she was screaming and jumping up and down.

Lara looked from her to Manny, to Robert, to Frank at the door. She was very pale and seemed unaware that tears had started coursing down her cheeks. "How can that be? Is it true? Is it really true?"

Robert put his hand over hers on the table; she was trembling as if with a fever chill. "It's true, Lara. Without Lynch there's no case left."

Then Lara buried her face in her arms on the table and her shoulders shook. Robert looked agonized and didn't touch her again. Manny took her in his arms and held her as she wept.

"I've been so scared," she said, sobbing. "I've been scared to death."

He made hushing noises and held her.

When Lara calmed down, Barbara said, "There will be formalities, and we'll have to wait for them, but it shouldn't take too long."

From the doorway Frank said, "Shinizer and Lynch were heading for the judge's chambers even as you spoke, Bobby. And it appears that Judge McReady has decided to go get some fresh air. He's leaving. He looks just a mite upset."

The next half hour was confused. Barbara took Lara to a restroom so she could wash her face, blotchy from crying, red-eyed and joyous. Barbara glimpsed Manny in a quiet conversation with Babe and Anna at the doorway to the private office the Lynch gang had used before. He entered the room and closed the door. Robert hovered, never more than a few feet from Lara, almost as if he hoped she would faint and he would be the one to catch her, and Frank was at the long table making notes in a notebook.

Then, finally, a clerk came to say Judge Henkel wanted the attorneys in chambers.

"I'll wait here with Lara," Frank said. "Don't reckon I'll be needed in there." He patted Lara's arm. "They'll call you in a few minutes; meanwhile, there's something we should talk about."

Barbara shot him a hard look. There were many things they were not telling Lara, she warned him with the glance, and he nodded, knowing exactly what she meant.

"I'm planning a little party," he said. "I need some guidance."

Right, she thought, exactly the way he needed guidance about planting peas. She, Manny, and Robert went down the corridor to the judge's chambers.

Judge Henkel was behind his desk, choleric and tight-lipped. Shinizer was standing before the desk, and in the back of the office, in a deep leather-covered chair, Lynch was apparently at ease, comfortable.

No one offered the new arrivals chairs.

"In light of certain new evidence that has surfaced," Henkel said in a grating, mean voice, "I am throwing out the case against Mrs. Jessup. The case will be closed as of today."

"No," Barbara said.

"What the hell do you mean, no!"

"I mean we want complete exoneration, a public apology from the district attorney's office, and the case is not closed. If the district attorney had evidence of murder, that evidence has not changed. It's still murder, by the hands of person or persons unknown. I want a public statement to that effect. I don't want even a shadow of suspicion to hover over my client, not a whisper that she got off because of a technicality."

"Not a chance!" Shinizer snapped. "We followed the evidence where it led us. No apology is called for."

"You want too much," the judge said harshly. "Be grateful that we're ending it now."

"I think her requests are entirely reasonable," Lynch said.

King's law, Barbara thought. Henkel's face turned a shade redder, more purple than red now, and Shinizer didn't move a muscle. Then Henkel stabbed a button on his phone and barked, "Bring Mrs. Jessup in here!"

Frank escorted Lara to chambers. She was red-eyed, composed, and beautiful. Henkel's statement to her was brief and mean-spirited, but it was thorough. She was freed from all restrictions; the case was dismissed. He added that Mr. Shinizer's office would issue a statement to the press and make an apology, and she was hereby released.

Lara inclined her head in a slight bow. "Thank you," she said in a low voice. Then she turned and looked at Lynch and said, "And thank you, Mr. Lynch. You are an honorable man. I am grateful."

She maintained her dignity until they were in the corridor

again, when she whirled and grabbed Barbara and hugged her. "There's no way I can ever repay you. I know that. But I'll try, somehow I'll try. Thank you, thank you." She hugged Frank and Manny and even Robert, who blushed. Then she looked at her watch and cried, "I have to go home and tell Nathan! Can I leave now?"

"You're in no shape to drive," Frank said.

She looked at her hands, both of them shaking hard. "I know. I feel like I might explode or something."

"Come on," Robert said. "I'll drive you."

"Go," Barbara said. "Tell Nathan everything."

Lara nodded, turned, and started to run. They watched her fly down the corridor with Robert, who, in spite of his stiltlike legs, had to run to keep up. They looked like two children racing.

Very slowly Barbara, Frank, and Manny started down the corridor also. How silly, she was thinking; she wanted to laugh and to cry, one as much as the other.

"I have a few things to pick up at the office," she said. "It won't take long."

"I'll wait for you and drop you at the house, and then I have a little shopping to do," Frank said. His voice was suspiciously husky.

"I can drive her up later," Manny said. "I believe my Land Rover is repaired. I'll pick it up on our way back to the office."

They separated at the door to the conference room, and as Frank headed toward the stairs at the end of the corridor, Barbara heard Thomas Lynch call her name.

"Ms. Holloway, may I have a word with you?"

Manny vanished inside the conference room, and she moved a few steps from the door and waited.

"You haven't told Lara Jessup about our past history, have you?" Lynch asked.

"No. I won't tell her."

He nodded. "I wanted to tell you, Ms. Holloway, this was Babe's decision. I told her the facts and the possible consequences, and she decided. You've restored our daughter to us, Ms. Holloway, and our grandson. I'm indebted to you for that. I told you that the Lynches are fighters; we are, all of us. And we pay our debts. I don't want your client to suffer financially. She has suffered enough, God knows. When you have your accounts in order, send me the bill." He bowed slightly, turned, and walked away, down the hall to the office he had used with his gang. At the door he said, "Babe, Anna, let's go home."

She cleaned out her desk, checked the closet for a stray sweater or jacket, and then stood at the door, giving the office one last look. Done. The files would remain in Manny's keeping; he would do whatever cleanup was necessary, and as far as she was concerned, she was finished here. She closed the door. Manny was waiting for her.

In the Land Rover, driving toward the highway, he said, "Want to take a little ride before we head for the house?"

"Sure."

He didn't drive very far. A few miles north of Salt Creek, he pulled off the highway onto a dirt road, stopped, and turned off the engine. They sat quietly for a moment, gazing at the desert ahead. In the distance a cloud was moving almost lazily at ground level, an unseen car on an invisible road betrayed by dust.

"Babe asked me to handle her divorce case," he said. "I'm a country lawyer; we handle all kinds of cases. I said yes."

"Ah."

He glanced at her, then turned back to the desert view. "She also asked if we, our team, would take her for a client if McReady brings up the past, if she's charged." He looked at her again, and this time he kept his gaze on her. "She meant you, of course. I said I would, but I couldn't speak for you."

"It won't come to that," Barbara said slowly. "Lynch will see to it. As long as the Jessup murder case is open, unsolved, no one's going to bring past charges against anyone else. Two guys facing off with drawn guns. Lynch won't blink."

Manny nodded. "You catch on to the system out here pretty fast. The point is, Barbara, she can't be sure. She went into this today knowing she can't be sure how McReady will react, what he'll do. He's destroyed. Whether he's charged or not with Jessup's murder, he'll be the suspect forever. And with the divorce following today's testimony, few people will have any doubts, charge or no charge. Without Lynch's support, his other backers will fade away; even if he keeps his judgeship, he'll be just another name on a list of judges. He knows that. She doesn't know how he'll take it." He stopped and became silent.

Damn Babe, she thought; she didn't want to make such a decision, not now, not ever. A herd of animals moved in the distance. Horses. Cows. She squinted. "Antelopes?"

"Mule deer," he said. "You want to be careful driving around dusk. They don't pay a lot of attention to cars and right-of-way."

She told him about Lynch's offer to pay for Lara's legal expenses. "Maybe he was trying to bribe me."

Manny shook his head. "I think what he said was true. He pays his debts. He admires courage, and Lara has shown courage enough to hold the Alamo all by herself." Suddenly he laughed. "I was going pro bono; Robert, too, as you know. But maybe I'll let Thomas Lynch buy me some carpeting and new furniture. Robert's coming in with me, a partnership. I'll let him buy his own office furniture. Custom stuff. Lynch can afford it."

She smiled. But he was still waiting, she knew, and she thought about Babe as a client. A guilty client, one who had paid and paid and then paid some more. And she didn't know any more than Babe did how McReady would react. He had climbed the mountain, the summit within reach, and an avalanche had swept him back to the base. She remembered the first time she had seen Babe and McReady, how he had taken her arm, marched her out, how docilely she had gone, and today when he touched her, how she had said no.

She said slowly, "Lynch asked me if Lara knows about the past. I told him no, that I wouldn't tell her. But if Lewis Jessup's murder is raised again, she'll have to know. Roger and Alene should know the truth about their brother, in any event. They deserve to know that much."

Manny turned to face her; his gaze was very steady. "Babe said something else. Lynch is turning the ranch over to her; they want it done all the way as soon as the divorce is finalized, and the day it's all hers, she intends to offer to let Roger buy back the Jessup ranch. She wants me to approach him about it when the time comes. Talk him into it. She and Cardona will be married the day the divorce is final. He's gone to meet their son and the nanny at the airport in Portland and take them to the ranch, home. Babe wants me to convince Roger that she loves Cardona deeply and isn't after Roger in any way except as a friend." He drew in a breath and turned to gaze at the desert once more. "He'll do it. There's nothing he wants more than to come home to his ranch, but if he knows she killed Lewis, he won't be able to come back here."

"Vinny knew and he forgave her, or at least let it drop," Barbara said.

"And Roger is his father's son. He might understand that Babe today isn't the same girl who tried to run him down with a Jeep. He might understand what drove her to shoot Lewis, and he would be able to forgive her. But he couldn't forgive himself, Barbara. He would never come back again."

She remembered what Roger had said, he had been so damn dumb, the incident with the Jeep was his fault because he had been blind and dumb. She knew that Manny was right; Roger would take full responsibility for the death of his brother.

"And so they'll just continue to live with two unsolved murders in their family, brother and father," she said in a low voice. Even as she said this, she knew it was false; in the minds of Alene, Roger, and Lara, there were no unsolved cases. She said, "Anyway, it probably won't happen, because he doesn't have that kind of money."

"She'll charge back taxes, that's all. And I'm to arrange whatever payment schedule he can manage. She wants her son to be friends with his children, for her and her husband to be friends with Roger and his wife. Between them, the Lynch ranch and the Jessup ranch, things will change out here, Barbara. The changes have already started. She could have asked Robert to handle her divorce, or a dozen others from around here. She asked me. And she asked me to finalize the transfer of the ranch from Lynch to her, and later to arrange things with Roger." He sounded a little dreamy, wistful. "It will make a difference." He reached for the key. "You did it, Barbara. I'm indebted, too. And damned if I know how to repay you. When you make up your mind about what I should tell her, let me know."

"It won't happen," she said grumpily. "He knows we'd get her off on her medical history alone. But there's no escape hatch for him. Tell her yes."

He reached for the key again, and she said, "Wait, don't start yet. While we're clearing the decks, there's one more thing. I didn't do it. Vinny Jessup did. He finally knew he couldn't pin Lewis's death on McReady, that Babe had done it, and he couldn't find anything else big enough to bring McReady down. He knew he was dying and he planned his own death down to the last detail, and framed McReady for his murder. Then Lara acted out of character and drove up the mountain."

Manny didn't move; he appeared to be hypnotized by the mule deer grazing the dry desert grasses.

"And I believe you've known from the beginning," Barbara added.

"What made you come to that conclusion?" Manny finally asked.

"The phone call to McReady. Why would he agree to meet Vinny unless they'd had a conversation beforehand, and he believed Vinny really had incriminating evidence of some sort. No, Vinny made a point to meet him several times that spring, and he must have hinted, or said outright, that he had something. And the reception for the Lynches. Why would Vinny go unless he had a real purpose? He did. To steal the napkin he used to hold the gun. And to use the typewriter. He knew about the typewriter Delia Kersh had used, and he knew where it was. He went to the reception in order to use that same typewriter for the phony suicide note, and then made sure he left a hint for us to look her up—the note on his calendar, and her letters in his files. He trusted Robert to find the letters, and track them back to that typewriter in case the sheriff somehow failed to make the connection."

"Why didn't you say anything?" Manny asked, still not looking at her, still fascinated by the mule deer.

"The same reason you didn't," she said. "I'm not a prosecutor and I don't work for the insurance company. They know damn well it was suicide, but they were willing to charge Lara with murder. If they had kept up a united front this week, I would have advised her to take Lynch's last offer. There wouldn't have been any choice."

"Me, too," Manny said. Now he turned to regard her. "Vinny was a proud man; he wouldn't have lingered on in the slow, agonizing death that he knew was coming. And he had unfinished business to attend to. No one who knows Lara would ever believe she would drive up that mountain road at night. He never would have dreamed she could overcome her terror and follow him. I think he went to the parking area, wiped prints off everything, held the gun in the napkin, and shot himself. And minutes later McReady came and found him. If he didn't know instantly that he'd been set up, he must have known when there were no papers in the briefcase. He'd been framed, and good. So he had to try to get out of it any way he could, because he couldn't afford to have a whiff of suspicion attached to him. So he pushed the van back down to the road, and off the side."

"They've all paid, even Lara; now it's his turn," Barbara said.

Manny reached once more for the key; she put her hand on his. "You knew Vinny. What was his point with the box of files, all that material on McReady? What was it for?"

He was silent so long, she thought he would not respond. Finally he said, "I think he wanted someone to know why he did what he did. Not vengeance. Maybe to reveal McReady, to bring him down. If he failed with his own death, then maybe someone else would pick up the fight where he left off and find a way."

Not vengeance, she agreed. Or he would have gone after Babe. And not just someone else, she understood. He had wanted Manny to know, his friend, his blood brother. Lara had told her that when she got the files back, she would hand them over to Manny, and the burden would have fallen on him.

"But he didn't fail," Manny said. "He did exactly what he set out to do, and here, on this insignificant speck on the universal map, the tide has turned."

She nodded. Finally that's what made a difference: one man, one idea, one small change.

The mule deer were gradually moving toward them, their ears

twitching nervously, keeping an eye on the intrusive Land Rover, but not afraid enough to turn and run.

"Let's go to the party," Barbara said.

Manny switched on the key, and the deer turned as one and fled when the motor started.

33

It was a grand party, everyone said so, some more than once. Barbara drifted in and out of conversations with a glass of wine in her hand, and somehow no matter how many times the glass was nearly empty, magically it was filled again. She couldn't explain how that happened. Manny was explaining to Lara how often, no one even knew how often, cases were settled, thrown out, dismissed as a result of the deposition process. Robert and Bailey seemed to get into a very involved discussion about basketball, and she squinted at them. To her knowledge, Bailey never had played basketball in his life, but then she looked at Robert and thought sagely, ah, that explained his long legs and arms. She caught snatches of the cooking lessons going on in the kitchen. "You want the butter to harden up, doesn't hurt a thing if it freezes before you wrap it in the chicken." His version of chicken Kiev, she thought knowingly, and if her life depended on it, she couldn't have said how it differed from the cookbook version, but it did, and it was better. Ah yes, she thought, he used sage, or was it mint, or something weird like chervil? She saw Lara and Shelley with their heads together, glancing her way often, smiling, and she wondered if she had forgotten her shoes, or if her zipper was undone, but she didn't have a zipper, she remembered, not in these pants anyway. She checked to make sure, and found that she was now wearing jeans, and there was a zipper, but it was exactly how it should be. She didn't remember changing clothes. They ate chicken-not-Kiev. Chicken Leningrad, she decided, or was Leningrad the one that was now Saint Petersburg? Or was it Stalingrad that had reverted? To hell with it, she decided, chicken Paris. She saw Lara and Nathan look at each other many times with broad smiles, or tears in their eyes, or both, and she saw Lara grab him and hug him hard and he didn't pull away or look embarrassed or anything. They both were radiant, she thought, and then worried: could a thirteen-year-old boy be described as radiant? Maybe she had invented something new, maybe she was really a writer posing as an attorney. Bailey was teaching Wynona how to open a lock with a plastic card, and Nathan came to watch until Lara said that probably wasn't a trick he should know. Bailey showed him anyway. She heard coyotes howling outside and someone said the wind was coming up, but she knew it was coyotes, knew they had circled the house and were performing a howling concert. Then she realized that everyone in the house was getting quite drunk, and that was clearly a miracle if there ever was one since most of them were teetotalers. Drunk on juice, on ginger ale, Cokes? But there they were, blurry and not making a bit of sense, and not any too steady on their feet. She could tell. Then Robert and Lara began to dance, but it was a strange Balinese kind of dance, she decided, one in which the dancers didn't actually move, and you had to watch their fingers, or even their eyes to see anything happen. She sat on the floor with her back against the couch to watch them dance, and to wait for the whole crew to sober up enough to start making sense. It was too hard to see Robert's eyes, they were so near the ceiling, and his hands were out of sight, so she watched their feet—hers small and dainty even, and his like canoes—until that got too hard, and she rested her eyes.

She came wide awake all at once and had no idea where she was or how she had gotten to wherever it was. Slowly she realized she was on the couch, a throw over her, and sitting in an easy chair nearby, Frank was watching her, smiling. She didn't try to move yet; she was afraid to.

"My God," she said miserably. "I passed out. Is it tomorrow?"

"Half past."

"Half past tomorrow?"

"Twelve-thirty."

She began to maneuver herself to a sitting position. "Well, they've seen the real me, drunk, passed out on the floor."

"Oh, you were snookered all right. I told them you were punch drunk. Maybe four hours of sleep night before last, none at all last night, dead on your feet. They tiptoed around you. Manny put you to bed and Lara covered you up. I believe everyone in the house kissed you when they said good night."

She groaned. "Did I disgrace myself, more than just by passing out, I mean?"

"Honey, you're one of the sweetest drunks I ever saw. You didn't say half a dozen words all night, and you smiled and smiled. Then you took a nap. That's all."

"I think I'd better get a cup of coffee and a few aspirin." She started to get up, and Frank laughed.

"I think you'd better stay exactly where you are. I'll fetch and carry."

He brought her coffee and aspirin, and a glass of water. The coffee was good and strong. "I guess you want to know what Lynch had to say, things like that," she said after swallowing the aspirin.

"Nope. Not tonight. You can fill in the blanks when I drive us home tomorrow."

"Good." She suspected that she couldn't have told him anyway, not just yet. She drank coffee, and they sat in silence for several minutes. Then she asked, "What was so funny in your mail?"

He began to chuckle. "Wait a minute, I'll get it and show you."

While he was gone, she tried out her legs, a mistake; she decided to sit down again and have more coffee instead.

"Remember when we celebrated my book sale at the Chanterelle?" he asked, returning with a couple of letters in his hand.

"Sure. You reverted to childhood, as I recall."

"Yep. My editor and I were just like that." He held up two fingers. "I was his pal Frank, and he was my pal Don and we were in it together, all the way. So he sent me a contract. . . ."

When he mentioned Wanda Doolittle, Barbara narrowed her eyes. His lady friend? "Who's she?"

"She teaches creative writing at the university, and she's published a few books, and knows a thing or two," he said. "So she's been acting as my expert witness, my private literary consultant. I did a little work for her some years back; she's grateful."

He was laughing again. "So the letters went back and forth. They'd give an inch here and take it back there. My good pal Don was ever so patient with me, a neophyte who knows nothing about publishing, and I was ever so patient with him, an editor who doesn't know shit about contracts. He finally confessed that he was out of his depth with all the legal terms, so he turned me over to someone in the contract department and we went a few more rounds."

"Oh, Dad," she said in dismay. "That must have been awful for you. Why didn't you say anything?"

"Hold on," he said. "See, when it started to stretch out like that, Wanda said she'd bet good money that they already had excerpted a section and had it written into a script for one of their television shows. Maybe it was already in production, or even in the can waiting to be aired. They would have kicked me out the door otherwise. Meanwhile, I had sent the book to a regular university press. And wrote another letter to my new pal in the contract department. In this one I suggested that if all they really wanted was a section of the book—one of the trial scenes, for example—maybe we should be negotiating for that instead of the entire work. I might have mentioned that one of my eager young associates was a fan of their various shows dealing with the law and would be overjoyed to see my work there." He was laughing too hard to continue.

Barbara laughed, too. "I wonder when your good pal Don realized he was in battle with a dragon."

"I suspect it got through to him," Frank said. "Anyway, last week, Thursday, I got this letter from the university press." He started to hand it to her, but she waved it away. "Just tell me."

"Okay. 'Dear Mr. Holloway: We were very pleased that you thought of us for your book, *The Art of Cross-Examination.* We feel it would fit very nicely with our line of books concerning legal matters. While we don't foresee a large popular audience for it, we would include it in our listing of supplemental reading that is recommended for law students throughout the country." He paused to scan the letter. "He goes on just a bit. Then he wrote, 'Since you tell us in your submission letter that you have not previously published, I would suggest that you avail yourself of the services of an experienced literary agent, and to this end I have enclosed a short list of agents we have worked with many times in the past to our mutual satisfaction.' There's a little more," Frank said. "But that's the gist."

"Good heavens!" she said, awed. "Two offers!"

"Well, remember, the first one's not quite what I thought it was at the start."

"But what was so funny?"

"I'm getting to it. Don't spoil a story by jumping to the last page. See, I showed the letter to Wanda, and she looked over the list of agents and said they're all reputable. I called the first one on the list, and I guess I have a literary agent now. It seems that if there's an offer already, you can have your pick of agents, more or less." When she started to say something, he held up his hand. "I'm getting there. In the mail Shelley delivered, there was a big fat envelope, and this letter. I'll skip to the part that made me burst out laughing. 'Accordingly, you would retain all other rights to the work. We offer five thousand dollars for the film rights to the material from pages 209 to 257 inclusive to be used in our television series *Bench Marks*. I have enclosed a standard contract that has the approval of the Screen Writers Guild, which will inform you of the scale of payments for reruns, et cetera. If you find the enclosed contracts to be in good order . . .' And so on. Wanda had the sons of bitches nailed. They never intended to publish a book; they wanted that section only."

They both laughed. "I do believe you've got them by the short hairs," Barbara said, wiping her eyes. "What's next?"

"Oh, I'll send it off to my new agent. First, I want to see what's in those pages. If the bastards are offering five grand, maybe we can get it up to ten. I'll send the agent all the correspondence and my phone notes while I'm at it."

He stood up and stretched, then he closed the firescreen. "Think you can manage the stairs yet?"

"One can but try," she said, and tried. She was steady enough, she decided, but the floor was definitely not completely level.

"Ah, Bobby," he said, taking her arm. "I'll walk you home. It's been quite a day. Quite a day."

He walked her up the stairs, all the way to her room, where he kissed her cheek. "Don't set a clock. I won't start without you. Good night, honey." He closed the door softly when he left.

Moving cautiously, she undressed, letting her clothes fall where they would; she pulled on a nightshirt and collapsed into the bed. Parents and their children, she thought, shifting her legs restlessly, almost too tired to relax, to sleep. Vinny and his son Lewis; Lynch and his daughter, Babe; Babe and her son; Lara and hers. Frank and his daughter, she added, and then John Mureau and his children. Something happened to them all, she thought, when they became parents, something happened, something important. She couldn't follow the thought further; instead, she began to hear the wind again. It sounded like wild things howling.

A pair of coyotes trot toward the sprawling Lookout Mountain house with one dim light in a downstairs window. There is nothing human to smell; the house is deserted. They run across a wide terrace and stop to sniff the wind. It smells of snow, and from farther away of rain. They run on.

Barbara is dreaming. She is racing through a forest of towering fir trees, all wearing emerald coats of furry moss that sparkle with diamonds. She runs like the wind, laughing.

ABOUT THE AUTHOR

Kate Wilhelm is the author of more than three dozen books, including such novels as *The Good Children, Justice for Some, Where Late the Sweet Birds Sang,* and *Margaret and I.* She is the author of four previous Barbara Holloway thrillers: *Death Qualified, The Best Defense, Malice Prepense,* and *Defense for the Devil.* Her fiction has been translated into many languages and received such honors as the Prix Apollo, the Nebula Award, and the Kurd Lasswitz Award. She and her husband, Damon Knight, helped found the Science Fiction Writers of America organization and the influential Clarion Writers Workshop, at which they taught for many years. They and their family live in Eugene, Oregon.

BALDWIN PUBLIC LIBRARY

3 1115 00446 3013

24.95

FIC
Wilhelm, Kate.
No defense.

NO LONGER THE PROPERTY OF
BALDWIN PUBLIC LIBRARY

BALDWIN PUBLIC LIBRARY
2385 GRAND AVENUE
BALDWIN, N.Y. 11510-3289
(516) 223-6228